COLLISION

*Book Three of
the Prophecy Series*

LEA KIRK

Collision
Lea Kirk

Copyright © 2018 Heather Jarecki
California, USA

This book is a work of fiction. Names, characters, places, and incidents are the product of the author's imagination or are used fictitiously. Any resemblance to actual events, locales, or persons, living or dead, is coincidental.

ALL RIGHT RESERVED, including the right to reproduce, distribute, or transmit in any form or by any means. For information regarding subsidiary rights, please contact the Author.

First Edition 2018
ISBN: 978-1720816713

Content Edits: Sue Brown-Moore
Copy Edits: Laurel C. Kriegler
Cover Design: Danielle Fine
Print Formatting: Nina Pierce of Seaside Publications

In memory of
Tommy
Wish you were here to see this

ONE

Near-future Earth.

This is stupid. Stupid, stupid, stupid.

Flora Grace MacDonald Bock ground her teeth together and bunched the skirt of her sundress in her fists. No one had asked *her* if she wanted to stand in the hot sun with her adoptive parents, brother, sister, and countless dignitaries from Terr and Matir—and practically the entire town of New Damon Beach. No one had asked *her* if she wanted to smile and be polite. And *no one* had asked *her* if she wanted to give a warm, New Damon Beach-style welcome to the first ever Anferthian ambassador to Earth—or Terr, as the planet was now called.

But since when did a ten-year-old's opinion on politics matter? It was her "duty" as the daughter of the *Profetae*—the peacemakers. Mama and Poppy had freed Terr from the Anferthian occupation, and they still worked to strengthen Terrian and Matiran relations with those killers. How were they going to keep the peace if they allowed the invaders back on Terr?

Mama slid her cool fingers over Flora's hand and gave it a reassuring squeeze. "Ambassador K'nil's party will disembark from their shuttle soon, sweetie."

Translation from Mom-ese: *Stop wrinkling your dress, Flora.*

She forced her hands to release the crumpled teal material. Who really cared how her dress looked, or if the Anferthians were impressed by the condition of her clothes? Why did they have to come anyway? *They'd* invaded Earth. *They'd* killed her biological parents, Mommy and Da. She hated them—all of them. Stinking oversized, green-skinned 'Ferths.

She glanced up at her adoptive parents. Mama's dark hair was pulled into a bun, her fair skin shaded by a white, wide-brimmed sun hat. On her other side, Poppy held Mama's hand, looking so handsome in his full-dress Unified Defense Fleet Admiral's uniform. The dark grey material complemented his blue Matiran skin tone. Three years ago, Flora didn't think she'd ever be happy again, but Mama and Poppy had changed that when they adopted her and two other orphans of the invasion, Juan and Maggie.

But they were more than just her parents, or the *Profetae*. They were also *emo amin*, soul mates, bound together in this life and the next, which was the most romantic thing ever. If she had a soul mate, he would be noble, and strong, and together they'd keep the Anferthians from invading anyone's planet ever again. Just like Mama and Poppy.

She loved them so much, and that was the *only* reason she was standing here on the hottest day of the year, waiting to greet Ambassador K'nil of Anferthia and his entourage. No matter how she felt about that, she never wanted to disappoint them.

She blew her breath through her teeth with a soft hiss. If only the ambassador didn't have to bring his eleven-year-old grandson. But he was, and that meant she'd probably be part of the entertainment committee for the little green monster. Ugh.

Okay, maybe he wouldn't be so little. Adult Anferthians were nine to twelve feet tall, so he'd be a lot taller than her for sure. Although, she was pretty tall for a ten-year-old Terrian—five feet-five *and three quarters* inches. At least a foot taller than most of the girls her age in New Damon Beach. And when she grew up, she'd be taller than Poppy's six foot one. At least, that's what Uncle Dante said, and he was a healer, so he would know.

The Unified Defense Fleet honor guard snapped to attention, and Flora jerked her head up.

They're coming.

She squinted at the ambassador's delegation, their figures all fuzzy through the waves of shimmering heat as they crossed the new-mowed tarmac. Time to paste a fake smile on her face and pretend she was happy to see them. Ha!

But as their forms emerged from the wavy mirage, her gaze

was drawn to the shortest member of their delegation. That must be the little monster. She drew her brows together. No way was he eleven. He should be at least a foot taller than her, not just a few inches.

She leaned down close to her brother's ear. "He's a shrimp."

Juan glared up at her. Oops. Height was a sore subject for him, especially since he was only four months younger, and only four and a half feet tall. Words like shrimp made him cranky.

She squinted her eyes at the height-challenged Anferthian kid. His thick reddish-brown hair was short, unlike that of adults flanking him. He was too young yet to grow his hair out in the ritual Anferthian braid. A *tirik*, they called it. And what was up with his walk? He was all stiff and formal, like he had a stick up his butt. A soft snort escaped her. Probably thought he was better than everybody else. If he was too stuck-up to talk to her, then she might be able to ditch entertainment duty.

The delegation arrived in front of Poppy, who began formal introductions of the other dignitaries. Flora rolled her shoulders back and raised her chin. As long as she didn't embarrass Mama and Poppy, then everything'd be fine. Her gaze darted back to the little monster. He looked up at his grandfather with an expression of hero-worship.

Cinnamon. That was the color of his hair. Not true red, like hers. And his skin tone was a light olive green. His eyes…well, they were just weird. A freaky reddish-purple color.

The weird eyes blinked, and in slow-motion they shifted to look directly into hers. An electric shock snapped through her. The little monster's eyes widened, and his face turned chalky grey-green. A flame of heat prickled up her neck and face, and a buzz became a roar like a waterfall in her ears.

Mama.

She reached her hand toward her mother as the ground lurched under her feet.

"Flora?" Mama's voice was distant, as if she was at the other end of a long tunnel.

What was happening? Was the little monster trying to kill her? Could an Anferthian do that just by looking at someone?

The flaming heat receded, and the roaring waterfall gave way to her rapid heartbeat thudding in her ears. Mama must be using her healing Gift to make her better. If the 'Ferth kid had tried to kill her, Mama would figure it out and say something. Then Poppy could order him to be arrested or sent back home.

Flora blinked as reality rushed back. Above her, Poppy's face reflected his worry. "*Puella?*"

"It's probably just the heat." Mama looked concerned too. "Drink some more water, sweetie."

Poppy pressed a bottle to her lips and the cool liquid slid down her throat. After several small sips, she pushed his hand away. "I'm okay now, Poppy."

As her father helped her to her feet, she dared to meet the killer's gaze. The Ambassador's grandson stared wide-eyed at her, like he knew her deepest secrets. Her insides squirmed like a pile of worms. No one had ever looked at her like that before. She narrowed her eyes at him.

I know you did something to me, you little creeper.

His grandfather bent and murmured something into his fan-shaped ear, and the boy blinked rapidly, like he was waking up from a spell. His cheeks and the edges of his ears darkened—the Anferthian equivalent of turning red. Guilty people *always* turned red.

A tug on her hand drew her attention away from the 'Ferth kid. "You 'kay, Flowa?"

Flora gave her little sister a smile. "Yeah, I'm fine, Maggie."

Juan made a scoffing noise. Great. That turd was going to tease her later about fainting in front of the Anferthians. What an immature little—

"Flora MacDonald Bock?" The deep voice above her head was low and rich. The perfect voice for telling bedtime stories.

Flora tipped her head back—way back—until she gazed into the friendly black eyes of the Anferthian ambassador. She swallowed hard. "Yes, sir."

An adult was always sir or ma'am, even if they were a 'Ferth.

The ambassador kneeled on one knee in front of her, putting him almost at eye level. He extended his left hand, palm up, in the traditional Anferthian manner of greeting. "I am Ambassador Fynn K'nil." He presented himself. "Great is my pleasure to finally meet you, Flora of Earth."

He said "Earth," not Terr. The name of her home-world before his people attacked. Why would he do that when everyone else called the planet by its new name, Terr?

Collision

It'd be so much easier if she could give him a Terr-style curtsy; that way she wouldn't have to touch him. But since he'd already presented his hand, it would be the height of rudeness to not reciprocate.

She placed her right hand atop the ambassador's huge palm and bowed her head in unison with him. "Mine is the pleasure, Ambassador K'nil of Anferthia."

Withdrawing her hand, she suppressed a sigh of relief. That wasn't so bad, and the formal welcome was almost over. Wait, why was the ambassador reaching out with his right hand now?

"Is there not an old Earth saying: when in Rome, do as the Romans? I don't know any Romans, Flora of Earth, but I do understand and appreciate this bit of wisdom."

He wanted to shake hands, too? Terr-style? She met his gaze again. Black eyes twinkled. The corners of her mouth pulled up into a smile. She couldn't help it. He was so not like the Anferthians who'd killed her parents. He seemed...nice.

But that didn't mean she *liked* the man. Nuh-uh. No way. She'd shake his hand, but she wouldn't forget that his grandson had just tried to kill her.

She stuck out her hand and it disappeared as the ambassador closed his fingers around it. For a guy with such an enormous hand, his grip was gentle. Firm, but gentle. He released her and she drew her hand to chest. There, she'd done it, and it wasn't *that* horrible.

Ambassador K'nil beckoned to his grandson. "Great is my pleasure to introduce my grandson, Fander K'nil."

So, the little monster had a name. Hmph.

Mama nudged her. Oh, yeah. She placed one foot behind her and bobbed a quick curtsey. "Welcome to Terr, Fander of Anferthia." *Now go home.*

"Thanks be to you, Flora of Terr." His English was as stiff as the way he walked.

And now he was, what? Bowing? She flinched back just enough so his thick wiry hair missed the front of her dress, then froze. Had anyone noticed? Mama wasn't giving her *the look*, so maybe not. And the K'nil's were moving down the line to greet Juan, Maggie, and the remaining dignitaries. She released a soft sigh. All clear. Another thirty minutes and she'd be back home in the tempur-cooled comfort of her parents' cube—away from the

'Ferths and everyone else.

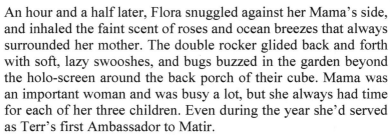

An hour and a half later, Flora snuggled against her Mama's side, and inhaled the faint scent of roses and ocean breezes that always surrounded her mother. The double rocker glided back and forth with soft, lazy swooshes, and bugs buzzed in the garden beyond the holo-screen around the back porch of their cube. Mama was an important woman and was busy a lot, but she always had time for each of her three children. Even during the year she'd served as Terr's first Ambassador to Matir.

What a great year that'd been. How many Terrian kids could say they'd lived aboard their father's space cruiser? Or that their dad was a blue-skinned Matiran with enough love in his heart to adopt three Terrian orphans? Yeah, living in space had been a fun adventure, but living on Terr was better. At least here they could all go out to play without worrying about accidentally entering a restricted area.

"Do you remember Adra Patrum?" Mama asked.

The mother of Vyn Kotas, the man who'd betrayed Poppy, nearly destroyed the Guardian Fleet, and helped the 'Ferths invade Terr? He'd tortured Mama too, the creeper. "Yeah, I remember her."

"Did you know that by Matiran law I could have requested her death?"

She could've? Flora lifted her chin and met Mama's gaze. "She gave birth to him, and he was so bad, Mama. He hurt so many people, and he tried to *kill* you and Poppy. Why'd you let her live?"

"There are people who earned death for what they did, sweetie; Adra wasn't one of them. Her death would not have brought peace. Not everyone on Matir or Terr agreed with me, so I made a point to publicly forgive her so we could all move forward and heal."

Mama picked up one of Flora's bright red curls and twirled it around her finger. "I know it's hard at your age to really understand why I did what I did. As you get older, experience will give you the wisdom to comprehend why others make certain decisions. It will help you to make thoughtful decisions, too. Once you can do that, you will find peace in your heart, and forgiveness."

Flora gave a slow nod. This probably had something to do with the Anferthians. "I'll try to be good tomorrow, Mama."

Her mother pressed a soft kiss on her forehead. "I know you will, sweetie."

Two

Why was being good so *hard*? Flora trudged behind her siblings and the 'Ferth kid along the hot road to the playground. As she'd suspected, he hadn't even been here twenty-four hours and she'd been made an official member of ABEC—the Anferthian Brat Entertainment Committee. She quirked her mouth in a satisfied smirk. She'd made that up all by herself just before falling asleep last night. And no one else knew about it yet, not even Maggie or Juan.

She narrowed her eyes at the backs of her traitorous siblings. The way they were acting, she wouldn't be sharing it with them either. Juan had already chummied up with the little monster, and Maggie skipped alongside him as though he was something special. Which he wasn't.

The 'Ferth kid glanced over his shoulder at her.

Lookin' for another chance to try to kill me, creeper?

He turned back and laughed at something Maggie had said. Flora stuck her tongue out at the trio's backs, then quickly retracted it and gave a surreptitious glance around. No guards jumped out from behind rocks and bushes to arrest her, but they were out there. Watching. No one in their right mind would allow the Anferthian ambassador's grandson to wander around on Terr alone. If she wasn't careful, she might get in trouble.

Juan pointed to the rows of long-neglected trees. "It's too hot to go to the playground. Wanna go sit in the old pear orchard instead?"

Collision

First good idea he'd had all year. The temperature had to be like *a thousand* degrees, and hiding out in the shady orchard made more sense than going to the sunny playground. One more day of this heat wave, then the fog would be back. At least, that's what the weather forecast had said this morning. Fog was one of the best parts of living on the edge of the Pacific Ocean. That and wading in tide pools on the beach.

She gave her purple tank top a few tugs to create a breath of air against her stomach, then trotted between the trees to catch up with the others.

Several rows in, everyone else flopped to the ground in a loose semi-circle at the base of one of the old trees. She chose a spot slightly away from them and plucked a couple of white clover flowers, tying them stem-to-stem to start a chain while the rest of them blabbered. Even if she *were* interested in being part of the conversation, Juan probably wouldn't shut up long enough for her to say anything.

Twenty minutes later and the two boys still dominated the conversation. Flora made a soft snort through her nose. Those two talked more than Maggie had spoken in her *entire* life, and that was a lot. Maggie hadn't started talking until she was three, and she'd been making up for those silent early years ever since.

At least their yakking gave Flora time to watch the 'Ferth kid without him noticing. Except for his eye color, he looked kinda normal. The curved slashes of his eyebrows matched his cinnamon-colored hair. His long, thin nose was as straight as an arrow shaft, and his full lips were a slightly darker shade of green than his skin. He did sorta have a nice smile. It made his face look friendly.

She pursed her lips together. What was she thinking? Especially after what happened yesterday. He was anything but friendly. And the four points of his fan-shaped ears looked ridiculous. Like a bad guy from an old movie before the invasion. The only way he'd look more bad was if he was bald, and taller. Bet that's why he came to Terr; because everyone on Anferthia teased him about being too short.

"Is your grandfather your mom's dad or your dad's?" Juan asked.

Oh, good question.

"My mother's." Fander spun a clover stem back and forth

between his thumb and forefinger.

How did that work? Everyone knew that 'Ferth kids used their father's name. "Then why's your last name K'nil?"

Crap. She hadn't meant to say anything. Now she'd done it; she'd *have* to talk to him.

Stupid, stupid, stupid.

Fander's weird colored eyes met hers, and fizzies tickled her stomach like the sodas she used to drink. "Because that is my family name, like Bock is yours."

She gave a snort. "Well, K'nil sounds like a place where dogs sleep."

Hurt flickered in his eyes. "It means sea cliffs. When my father died, K'nil became my family name." He said it as if the matter was closed, which is wasn't.

"Never heard of *that* happening before." He must be lying. "So, what was your father's name?"

Fander's gaze averted to the clover in his fingers, and he shrugged. "It does not matter."

"Sure it does."

"What are those?" He pointed to the chain of flowers in her hands.

Was he really trying to change the subject? She gave him a hard glare. "They're flowers. Don't you have flowers on Anferthia, or do you have to steal them from other planets?"

His eyes widened, and his mouth hung open as if her hostile tone shocked him, which it shouldn't. He must've known before coming here what his people had done to hers. "Of course, we have native flowers on Anferthia, but nothing this tiny. Most of them are big and smell good."

"Well, goody for you." She picked another clover flower.

"Do those have a scent?"

"Do you ever shut up?"

Maggie gaped at her, and Juan shifted uncomfortably, like he'd rather poke a stick in a hornet's nest than be in the middle of this conversation.

"You do not have to be rude," Fander said.

She threw down her flower chain. "*You* don't have to be on *our* planet." She'd just crossed an invisible line, but she couldn't help herself.

"If it were not for your brother and sister, I would think *all*

Terrians are as rude as you."

"At least we don't go to other planets and kill people's parents!" There. She'd said it, and now he knew.

Fander looked as though she'd just thrown a rock at his head.

"Stop it!" Maggie jumped up. "Just *stop* it." Covering her ears, she ran back toward the road, but not fast enough to hide her sobs. Juan couldn't seem to decide if he should stay with his new-found BFF or beat a hasty retreat with their younger sister.

Fander rose to his feet, bristling. Oh, no way was he going to stand over her. She pushed herself to her feet and scrunched her nose into a sneer. "Aren't you kinda short for an Anferthian?"

"Aren't you freakishly tall for a Terrian?"

Years of pent up anger exploded through her like a bomb. She pulled back her fist and swung. The punch connected with his eye and he stumbled and fell back on his skinny green butt. A victory whoop popped out of her and she danced on her toes, shaking her tingling hand.

Now who's crying, creeper?

His hand shot out in a blur. Green fingers closed around her ankle and he yanked, taking her down in an undignified sprawl. Holy cow, he was actually fighting back? Then he was on her. It was just like when she and Juan got into it, only this time the guy was bigger. She pushed up and they rolled in the dry, crumbly dirt, name calling in two languages—three, once she switched to Matiran—ending with her on top.

She gave him a gloat as she perched on his stomach and drew back her fist. Fander's eyes went round with surprise and a hint of fear. A laugh erupted from her. He was afraid of her!

A large blue hand clamped around her thin wrist like an iron band. Another hand grasped the back of her shirt and jerked her up and off the 'Ferth kid. As her feet hit the ground, her heart sank to the pit of her stomach. It was either Poppy, Uncle Dante, or.... The hands spun her around.

Uncle Graig.

A very angry Uncle Graig.

She should've known Fander hadn't been afraid of her. Narrowed eyes the color of the sea during a storm, and just as unforgiving, bore into hers. This was the glare that scared so many adults, and now she totally got why. Her uncle who loved her so unconditionally had never looked at her like this before. She tried to swallow, but her mouth was bone dry.

"What have you done, Flora?" Uncle Graig ground out.

What had *she* done? What about what the 'Ferth kid had done? She raised her chin a notch. "He made me mad, so I punched him in the eye."

A whole bunch of weird expressions crossed Uncle Graig's face. It almost looked like he was trying not to laugh. Weird.

"I see." He straightened and released her wrist. "Help Fander up and apologize."

"*What?*" How could he ask her to do that when he knew how she felt about Anferthians?

The iciness returned to Uncle Graig's eyes, and he folded his arms over his chest. "Do. It."

Only an idiot would keep arguing, and she wasn't an idiot. Just the tone of his voice told her he wouldn't relent. She turned around and gave Fander her fiercest frown. Then she offered him her hand, uttering a halfhearted apology she'd take back as soon as she could.

He swatted away her hand. "I do not need *your* help."

As the 'Ferth kid scrambled to his feet, she turned to Uncle Graig, spread her hands out and mouthed, *See?*

He was unmoved. "To your parents' cube, both of you."

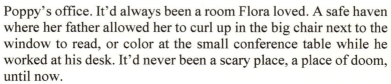

Poppy's office. It'd always been a room Flora loved. A safe haven where her father allowed her to curl up in the big chair next to the window to read, or color at the small conference table while he worked at his desk. It'd never been a scary place, a place of doom, until now.

"Alex, Gryf, a moment please?" Uncle Graig's muffled voice carried through the kitchen, down the hall and through the open office door.

She chewed on her bottom lip. Her parents were coming, and she was dead meat. Cradling her now throbbing hand, she shot a nasty glare at Fander standing silently next to her. No response. He didn't even look at her. This was all his stupid fault.

Mama stepped through the doorway first. "Oh." Her lips formed a perfect circle. From over each of her shoulders, Poppy and Uncle Graig frowned.

"The situation is self-evident," Uncle Graig said in a dry voice.

Collision

Mama's eyes went wide, and she clapped her hand over her mouth. The ticking of the lone Terr clock in the room was the only sound. Flora counted off twelve seconds before Mama finally lowered her hand and cleared her throat. "Flora, did you...punch Fander in the eye?"

She looked down at the floor. "Yes, Mama." Didn't anyone care that her hand hurt?

"Why?"

"Because he made fun of my height, and that made me mad." Which was true. Sort of. Fander shifted his weight from one foot to the other, and she caught her bottom lip between her teeth again. She should tell Mama what really happened before he ratted her out, but the words were stuck in her throat.

Poppy gave Uncle Graig one of those all-knowing grown-up looks. "Graig, would you please go back to the living room and ask Ambassador K'nil to join us?"

Oh, no. Her stomach dropped like a rock to her feet and she swallowed hard. Now she was in for it. An angry adult Anferthian could tear a person to bits in seconds. Her hands trembled, and she tucked them under her armpits. Mama and Poppy wouldn't be able to stop the ambassador from killing her.

She snuck a peek at Fander. He still faced straight ahead, as if he couldn't bear to look at her. Not that she could blame him.

Uncle Graig left and her parents came the rest of the way into the room. Poppy leaned back against his desk, the heels of his hands resting on the edge. Mama stood next to him, her back to Flora. Guess Mama couldn't bear to look at her either. But Poppy could. Look at her, that is. His vivid blue gaze bore into hers. She had to look away, look anywhere else, because she'd let them down.

Two sets of booted footsteps came from the hallway, closer and closer. Her parents looked at each other and Poppy nodded.

Uncle Graig led Fander's grandfather into the office. The ambassador was so tall he had to duck his head and hunch a little because the ceiling was too low for his great height.

"What happened to your eye, Fander?" The ambassador's voice was just as kind as it had been when she'd met him yesterday, not at all angry. But that would change once Fander told him what she'd done.

Fander looked down at the floor. "I am very sorry,

Grandfather. I teased Flora about her height, and she punched me in the eye."

Heat raced up her neck to her ears and cheeks. He was building on her half-truth rather than let her get in trouble for the lie?

The older man nodded. "Have you apologized?"

Fander turned to her, his gaze aimed somewhere around her chin. "I am sorry for teasing you, Flora."

She gave her head a nod. She should say something because Poppy was giving her the stink eye, but what? Oh, yeah. "I'm sorry, too, Fander."

"Flora." Mama looked more serious than she'd ever seen her. "Do you have anything you wish to tell us?"

Of course she did. She should come clean and tell them all what really happened, but the words still refused to come out. She lowered her gaze to the floor, which only made the silence feel heavier. She was such a big, fat chicken turd.

Poppy sighed. "You will walk Fander over to Uncle Dante's surgery to have his eye healed."

What? She couldn't walk him over. Everyone in town would see her walking with a stinking Anferthian. "But…but, can't Mama heal it?"

"I could, but I'm not," Mama leaned back against the edge of the desk next to Poppy. "Make sure he gets there and back safely."

All the adults were watching her; she really didn't have a choice. Uncle Graig opened the door and made a sweeping motion with his hand. It was time to go.

"Come on then." She stomped out of the room. Let the 'Ferth kid keep up with her if he could.

Fynn K'nil met his grandson's pleading gaze. The boy wanted to go home in the worst way, but that was not possible. Isel T'orr, the head of the Arruch Union and self-appointed "Devine Warden" of Anferthia, had made that impossible. For now, at least. Someday, if all went well, Fander would be free of Arruch control. Until that day, though, they must tread with care. To do otherwise could cost them dearly.

He gave Fander a minute headshake. The boy's lips compressed into a thin, rebellious line, but he followed in young Flora's wake without a word. Graig Roble had moved a step back to allow the youngsters to pass, but he was giving the Profeta a pointed look.

A faint pink color rose to her cheeks. "Everything turned out fine for me in the end," she murmured.

Her husband covered his smile with one hand, but did not comment.

The sound of the front door closing reached Fynn's ear. For better or for worse, a journey had begun, the first of many for the two youngsters.

"Excuse me." Graig Roble nodded once and stepped out of the room, pulling the office doors shut behind him leaving Fynn alone with Flora's parents.

"Our apologies for our daughter's behavior, Ambassador," Gryf said.

Fynn turned toward Gryf Helyg, son of his good friend Zale Marenys. What a fine man he had become. Watching the boy grow up, he had had no idea what the extent of Gryf's accomplishments would be, both military and personal. "First, this is a private matter between us, so please, call me Fynn. Second, would you mind terribly if I sat on your floor? Our conversation will not be short, and bending over like this will put a knot in my neck."

Alex's hands fluttered, an expression of dismay or confusion Terrians sometimes used. "Of course, Amb...sir...." Her voice trailed off. She took in a deep breath. "Fynn. We will be restructuring our cube to make certain areas of it more accommodating for you and your people."

"My thanks to you." He lowered himself to the floor. Not the ideal place at his age, yet preferable to standing.

He rested his arms over his raised knees as Gryf and Alex sat in chairs. "To the point, the meaning and tradition of *fyhen* I believe you comprehend already."

Alex nodded. "*Fyhen* means 'my own' in Anferthian. When a person is chosen as *fyhen* by an Anferthian, that Anferthian considers you family. We, Gryf and I, are *fyhen* with the dissenters, and they are ours."

"An honor well-earned." It was rare for a non-Anferthian to be *fyhen*, and even more rare for a group of Anferthians to take in outsiders. "*Fyhen* is a choice. Few or many can an Anferthian have. But of *tangol*, there is only one. And who that person is cannot be decided by any individual."

Gryf's piercing blue eyes regarded him, curiosity in their depths. "*Tangol* translates as 'heart fire.' But, what is it?"

"First, it is not as rare or unique as the soul mate relationship the two of you share. Eighty-five percent of the Anferthian population discovers their *tangol* at some point in their life. For them, there is nothing they will not do to protect each other. To support each other. Once the connection has been made, there is no reversing it."

Alexandra's eyes widened. "Cripes. Yesterday when Flora fainted. That wasn't from the heat, was it?"

"I fear not." He moved his gaze to Gryf. "Flora is Fander's *tangol*. Already, he feels the bond, although he is too young to understand its significance. His first reaction when I confronted him moments ago was to protect her—the one who he will need at his side once he is an adult."

The young mother all but jumped up from her chair and began pacing a ten-foot line between them. "We have a serious problem. Flora's birth-parents were brutally murdered, shredded by an Anferthian patrol while she watched from the bushes."

An invisible fist squeezed his heart. "She did not come out?"

His people had done this to the girl, and others like her. No, he must not think that. It was Isel T'orr and his tyrannical Arruch Union who had done this to the people of Terr. A horrendous wrong that could never be righted, but might be made less horrific if he and his stayed true to their values.

"Her parents had made her promise, and despite her lying to us today, Flora does keep her promises."

So, there was honor in young Flora. "Today's events were fueled by fear leading to her childish reaction. She must have convinced herself that I would do to her what was done to her birth-parents." How terrifying that must be for the poor child. "At her core, integrity is woven. As she ages, her reactions will be less drastic."

"I hope so." Alexandra did not appear convinced.

Gryf rubbed one hand over his chin. "We understand what Fander will feel and experience. How will this bond affect Flora, as a Terrian? Will she feel anything at all?"

"She will, though maybe not to the same degree. There have been so few *tangol* bonds outside our own race, and never one with a Terrian. Given the events of her life, she will likely resist the pull, which leaves us with the task of moderating the two of them.

"Something else you must understand. *Tangol* is not romantic predestination." There was doubt in their eyes, and he could not blame them. They did not understand how the *tangol* bond worked. "Anything other than a devoted and deep friendship is free choice, no matter the gender differences or similarities. My own wife was not my *tangol*, that honor belonged to Holt Huunu. Him you remember?"

The pain of loss jabbed at his heart. In many ways, Holt's death a year ago had been harder to accept than his wife's. Despite the nearly forty-year age difference, Holt had been his dearest friend and staunchest ally.

"The same Member Huunu, from the Anferthian Coalition when we negotiated for the Terrian prisoners of war three years ago?" Gryf exchanged a glance with his wife. "We remember."

"This one thing concerns me more than any other: that someone besides the three of us will discover the bond our children share. Such knowledge in the hands of my political enemies will make Flora a target, and quite possibly lead to Fander's destruction as well." And the end of hope for a free Anferthia.

The young couple exchanged a worried look. Gryf nodded. "We will do all we can to protect them until it's time."

Flora kicked a stone down the road. They were almost to Uncle Dante's surgery and Fander hadn't said a thing. Zero. Zip. Nada. Which was fine. It's exactly what she'd do if things were reversed. But, why hadn't he called her out in Poppy's office? Why had he kept up her lie?

She opened the door and led the way into the surgery. "Uncle Dante?"

"In my office, *puella*."

He probably wouldn't think she was so sweet once he saw Fander's eye. She led the way toward the open office door. Uncle Dante looked up from whatever was on his desk and smiled at her. "Good morning, niece. What brings you here?" His gaze flicked behind her and his smile turned into a puzzled frown. "What has happened to your eye, Fander?"

Fander gave her an accusatory look, his lips a thin, flat line. Great. He was making her tell Uncle Dante. "We got into a fight and I, um, punched him because he said something I didn't like." She raised her hand to show him her reddened knuckles. "They still hurt."

Both of Uncle Dante's eyebrows rose. "I am certain they do. Come with me."

He got up and headed toward the door, but not fast enough to hide the upward twitch of his mouth. As he walked out of his office it almost sounded like he muttered, "Like mother, like daughter," under his breath in Matiran.

Why were all the adults acting so weird? The heat must be getting to them. She had looked over her shoulder and seen the look Uncle Graig gave Mama, and she'd heard Mama tell him that things had worked out just fine for her in the end. Flora wrinkled her nose. Whatever *that* meant.

In the exam room, Uncle Dante healed Fander's eye first, then looked at her hand. "It's not broken, *puella*." He closed her hand, wrapping his around it. "Get a cold pack off the shelf in the supply room; it will be fine in couple of days."

"Aren't you going to heal it, Uncle?"

"This one will heal better on its own. From now on, you are to *talk* first. Fighting is always a last resort. By order of your healer."

Uncle Dante had never *not* made her better. So, why wouldn't he fix her hand today? She nodded then motioned to Fander to follow her. Poppy had told her to see him safely back, and she couldn't fail. She was on such thin ice already.

A few minutes later, they walked in the middle of the *lizo* paved road. The Matiran pavement compressed the dirt road, which had cut down on the amount of dust during the dry season, and mud when it rained. And, it didn't absorb heat the way blacktop used to. Still, it seemed silly to pave any of the streets in New Damon Beach with anything since there were hardly ever any road vehicles in town.

"Why did you not tell them what really happened?" Fander's question interrupted her thoughts.

She sniffed. "Why didn't *you*?"

"It is common knowledge that you do not throw anyone in front of a charging razor-horn hellion." He frowned at her as if she might be one exception to this rule.

Whatever a razor-horn hellion was, it sounded very large and very mean. "You mean you didn't say anything so I wouldn't get into more trouble?"

"Well, yes."

"Oh." Just when she thought she couldn't feel any worse. No matter what she thought of Anferthians, she had to own her mistake. "I'm sorry, Fander. I guess I'm a big chicken."

His frown deepened. "You do not look like an egg-laying farm bird that Terrians eat."

"It's just a saying. It means scaredy ca…um, that I was afraid." She wrinkled her nose. Now he'd tease her for being scared.

"Uhn," he grunted and gazed down the road. "I fear my tutors only taught me your basic language, and no colloquialisms or slang."

Colloqu-what? "Well, just forget whatever they did teach you."

He jerked his head around and stared at her, confusion lines across his forehead. "Why would I do such a thing?"

"Because, Fander, no kid our age *ever* uses the word colloquialism." She gave her head a shake and sighed. "Don't worry, you'll learn. It sounds like you're going to be here awhile."

THREE

Four years later

"I turn fifteen tomorrow."

Flora stopped digging her stick into the sand and gave Fander an impatient stare. "We already know that. Besides, fifteen's nothing special."

"Pfft. So you say." Fander didn't look up, not at her or her siblings. He just sat with his back up against a weathered log, whittling a stick with his short-handled blade called a *labu-ba*, his long legs bent at the knees and his heels dug into the sand.

The light breeze off the ocean blew several strands of hair across her face and she pushed them back and hooked them behind her ear. "Special is getting an ice-cream cone for no reason. Or not having the fog roll in during a meteor shower. Things like that."

Juan snorted. "Or ditching that Arruch toady, Mid-Warden Clut, after being dismissed from our lessons early."

Ugh, yeah. Creeper Clut seemed to have a control issue with Fander. Even Professor Singh knew it and had released them out the back of the education cube today while Clut stood out front, oblivious.

Flora raised her stick above her head. "All hail Professor Singh."

"*Hail*," the others said in unison.

Eventually, Clut would find them here on the beach, which would put him into a worse mood than normal; mostly because he hated walking on the sand. Sometimes he'd shout at them from the top of the bluff, but they'd ignore him until he was forced to come down or give up. Even Fander's new bodyguard, Factor Nor Danol, would pretend not to hear Clut's calls. She glanced over her shoulder at the Anferthian sitting on the ground at the bottom of the trail. He was pretty cool for someone her mother's age. Fander trusted him and that was good enough for her.

Maggie sat back on her heels, her dark curls bouncing with every move. "What did you ask for for your birthday?"

"Nothing, Mags." Fander winked at her little sister. "You know that Anferthians don't give gifts for birthdays."

It was amazing how good his English had become in four years. His accent was largely undetectable, except when he was angry—which was every time she poked at him. She furrowed her brow. Why did she do that? It wasn't very nice.

"I know, and that's so sad." Maggie's expression was sympathetic as she patted his arm.

Fander chuckled and set aside his stick. "Well, I do get something."

"What?"

"At fifteen, an Anferthian has their first dreaming and is considered an adult."

Flora raised her eyebrows. Okay, that was new. And weird too, because Juan had more fuzz growing on his face than Fander. Fander didn't have any at all, and never would, even as an adult. Anferthians didn't grow body hair—except the hair on their head, and their eyebrows. Did that mean having dreams was the only way they could be an adult?

"You mean you've never had a dream?" Juan wrinkled his nose.

"Nope." Fander wiped his blade on his shirt and put it away. "We usually have our first dreaming, called *rywoud*, in the days just before our fifteenth birthday. Since mine hasn't happened yet, it should be tonight."

Maggie leaned forward like an eager puppy, her green eyes bright. "What if you don't dream?"

He tapped the tip of her upturned nose with his finger. "We still don't get gifts."

"That's not fair." Maggie made a pouty face.

Fander chuckled. "I'm sure I'll survive."

"What does *rywoud* mean?" Juan's pronunciation of word sounded awkward, ry-wood. "I mean, what happens?"

"*Rywoud* is a foretelling of our future." Fander brushed the wood shavings off his khaki shorts. Flora let her gaze drift to his smooth legs. "It hints at events that may happen to us. Sometimes it gives us warnings, or tells us who will be most prominent or have the most influence on our lives."

Oh, prophetic dreams. She'd been having those all her life. "Kind of like the second sight, right?"

Fander shrugged. "Something like that, only they don't sneak up on us without warning. We know it's coming, every year."

She sat up straighter and raised her chin. "I have dreams almost every night."

"Yes, but you're not Anferthian." He grinned at her.

"You're right. I'm *Terrian*." That sounded smugger than she'd intended.

Fander shook his head. "Must everything be a competition for you, Flora?"

She opened her mouth, but no witty response came out.

"She can't help it." Maggie nodded wisely. "It's because she's a redhead."

Amusement lit Fander's eyes. "I have heard stories about Terrian redheads."

He was trying to bait her, but no way was she going to say anything. Even if it killed her.

"Yup, she's fighting it," Juan teased. "She really, *really* wants to say something."

Heat scorched her ears and cheeks. Her entire face must be flaming red. "Argh!"

She scrambled to her feet, threw her stick toward the waves, and stomped away as best she could in the sand. The laughter of her siblings rang in her ears.

Bunch of jerks.

Half-way down the beach she slowed, and drew her brows together. Maggie and Juan had laughed, but Fander hadn't.

"Flora, wait up."

She glared over her shoulder at Fander. "Why? So you can tease me some more?"

He stopped next to her. "No. So I can apologize for teasing you."

He was up to something.

"And," he continued, "so I can walk with you."

"Do you know how stupid that is, blaming someone's personality on their hair color?" From Maggie, she could understand that sort of thing. She was only eleven. But Fander should know better.

"It is stupid. Especially since your hair color is every bit as pretty as you."

She stared at him. This was the second time in the last two minutes he'd left her speechless. She reached up and pinched the ends of her elbow-length hair between her fingers. "You...you think so?"

His expression softened. "Yeah. I do."

He thought she was pretty? It sounded like it, and there was a gentle inflection in his tone like he really meant it. Patches of warmth burned her cheeks and she gazed down at her feet. "Um, thank you."

"If you come back, I'll make sure no one teases you for the rest of the day." Fander extended his right hand. "Truce?"

She met his gaze again. Why had she ever thought his eye color was weird? Mama called it amaranthine. Whatever it was, it went well with his skin-tone.

"Flora?"

Oh, right. She placed her hand in his. "Truce."

His fingers were warm as they wrapped around her hand and the deal was sealed with a handshake. Then he released her, and a small stab of disappointment pricked her heart. But she fell into step with him as they headed back to where her siblings waited.

Something had changed between them just now, and whatever it was felt like a good thing.

The next morning Flora jerked awake, the dream disintegrated into wisps too fine to recapture. The sun wasn't even up, but the way her eyelids had just snapped open, she was so not going to be able to go back to sleep. An odd sense of restlessness stirred inside her. She let her gaze wander through her bedroom full of familiar objects—dresser, sewing table, chair, framed images of her family—all cast in blurred pre-dawn greys.

Fander. That was who she'd been dreaming about. Now it was

coming back. She frowned. It was sorta like a prophetic dream—sharper, more vivid and colorful than the cottony haze of regular dreams. Something was off about it, though. Not in a bad way, but still not right. The swing—yes, he was walking in the darkness to the playground to sit on a swing.

Alone.

If she went there now, he'd be there. And today was his birthday, so he shouldn't be alone.

She slid out from under her blankets and pulled on her pants, a sweater, and shoes. The quietest way out of the house was through her window. But first…she picked up McRawr, her kilt-wearing stuffed lion toy. She'd been hugging it to her chest when cousin Ora found her after the invasion. Her Da had given it to her, that much she remembered. It had something to do with him being Scottish, and her being brave. Something like that.

Now, it was more than a link to the parents she'd lost, but also a secret signal to Mama whenever she snuck out of her room to "walk off" a dream. Sometimes her dreams were that intense. By leaving McRawr on her pillow, Mama would know she hadn't been kidnapped or something.

Flora set the toy on her pillow, slid her window open and inhaled the cool, damp, autumn air. She swung first one leg, then the other, over the sill and scooted down until her feet touched the dirt of the flower bed. Then she reached up and gave the sash a tug, sliding it down until it was closed.

The peace of the early morning surrounded her. This was the best time of day, when no one else was around and only her thoughts kept her company. She strode down the road until the playground came into sight.

As she'd expected, the yard was empty, except for a lone, shorter-than-average fifteen-year-old Anferthian sitting on a swing. Although, being over seven feet tall on Terr wasn't exactly short. He was *well* over a foot taller than her now. Ribbing him about his height, or lack thereof, today would be mean. Especially since his downcast expression matched the mood of the overcast November morning.

The rope and board swing would've been too small for him if his hips weren't so narrow. His long, booted foot methodically rocked him back and forth, while his other foot was planted firmly on the ground as a counter balance. Exactly how she'd seen him in her dream. This was just too weird.

What if he wanted to be left alone? Now that she'd seen he was okay, she could just go home and let him have his quiet time.

If you looked that lost, Fander would never ditch.

He was kind of noble like that. Besides, wherever Fander was, Factor Danol wasn't far behind. And sometimes that Creeper Clut. She gazed around the area. There, leaning against the California oak down the road a short way, was Nor Danol, but no sign of Clut. She raised her hands in a shrug and gave the factor a questioning look. He made a downward slash with one hand, the signal that Clut wasn't around. Thank God. But, now he was pointing at her, then to Fander. Did that mean Fander needed someone to talk to?

All right then, she'd give it a try. She wet her lips with her tongue. "Hey."

Fander looked up and studied her with a look she couldn't decipher. Fine. She motioned to the empty swing next to him. "Is that seat taken?"

His gaze dropped back to the general vicinity of his knees, as if she wasn't there. Huh. Looked like she'd have to take matters into her own hands. "No, Flora, go ahead and sit down." She stepped forward. "Thanks, Fander, don't mind if I do." She slid onto the plank, but didn't kick the swing into motion. "Ah. That's comfy."

Absolutely no response from him. What the heck was up? "Um, so, any plans on how you're going to spend your birthday?"

No response again. Fine. Guess he didn't want company—or maybe he didn't want *her* company. She huffed out a breath and drew her feet under her to stand up.

"They say that in *rywoud*, the people who will be most vital in your life will be prominent during the first dreaming."

She'd never heard him speak so softly. Nothing more than a murmur. Something must've happened that upset him. On the bright side, he hadn't asked her to leave. Comfortable warmth flooded her chest. "So, you *did* dream?"

"I did." His answer was monotone.

This was confusing. *Rywoud* was supposed to be a good thing, right? So why did he act as if someone had died? Wait, what if someone *did* die? "Fander, is something bad going to happen to you?"

He shrugged. "I don't know. Maybe."

"Why are you blowing me off? A simple yes or no will work. Are you going to tell me what happened or not?"

Fander gave her a sharp look. His mouth was compressed in a flat line and his eyes were narrowed. "Okay, yes, I think something *is* wrong. But here's what I don't understand, Flora...why were *you* in my dream from the beginning to the end?"

"Me?" Oh crap, her voice had squeaked. How embarrassing was that? And what did that mean, in his dream?

"Yes, you." He wasn't swinging anymore. Instead, he rubbed his hands over his face in an agitated motion. "It makes no sense, because I don't think you especially like me."

Oh, that hurt.

Fander's shoulders slumped. "You don't have much reason to, I suppose."

Shame consumed her; shame for every mean thing she'd ever said or done to him—as if he'd personally led the invasion wiping out most of Terr's human population. As if it was his fault Mommy and Da had died. He'd only been eight years old when it'd happened, yet she'd treated him like some sort of plague all these years. Yes, he had stood his ground with her on occasion, which had led to some pretty epic battles of wills between them, but he'd always treated her with respect. More respect than she'd ever given him, and more respect than she deserved.

Tell him the truth. Tell him what you really feel.

"I don't hate you, Fander. You're a good person. If you ever went away, I'd miss you, a lot. You're my friend." There it was...the truth spoken from her heart. Every word of it. Almost. "No, not my friend. My best friend."

It was like she'd set a trapped bird free to soar in the sky. He *was* her best friend. How...when had that happened?

Fander blinked at her, and a slow smile softened his handsome face. "Didn't I tell you, Flora? You're not supposed to give me birthday gifts."

Pleasant warmth rose in her chest, much like the feeling she got when she drank hot cocoa in front of the fire place on a stormy day. Only better. She gave her shoulders a shrug. "You're on Terr, Fander, and we're the biggest gift-givers in the universe."

His smile radiated from him like the summer sun. Wow. No

doubt about it, she'd put that smile on his face. And if she had her way, she'd make sure it never faded.

Four

Flora kicked a fist-sized stone, and watched it roll in front of her along the zig-zagging path to the beach. The past week since Fander's birthday had been so much fun, even with Juan around. And today Mother Nature had decided to gasp out one final day of unseasonably warm weather, which sometimes happened in mid-November. It wouldn't last, though. There was a storm brewing up north that was predicted to hit in two days. Already the surf had kicked up. Not bad enough to keep them from enjoying what was probably their last beach picnic until next spring.

She snuck a glance at Fander walking next to her. His long, easy stride was shorter than normal, keeping him at her side. It was cool how he seemed to pay more attention to her since their talk on the playground. Although, Juan did get cranky when she monopolized Fander's attention. Somehow, Fander always managed to smooth things over with her brother. Yesterday she'd told Fander he should become a diplomat like his grandfather, and he'd smiled. It was one of those bitter-sweet smiles, as if she'd made him happy and sad at the same time. Why he'd be sad about what she'd said was beyond her. Being part of something bigger than yourself, and helping people find common ground, could be rewarding.

"Guess what Mama let me pack for our picnic, Fander," Maggie said, swinging the basket as she negotiated the incline while skipping.

Fander tilted his head and inhaled through his nose. A huge grin lit his face. "Her homemade fried chicken."

Maggie puckered her lips and squinted up at him. "How'd you know?"

"Trade secret." He glanced at Flora and winked. Her heart beat a little faster. God, he was cute. Most of the roundness of childhood had melted away, replaced by more angular features. The best of these were his high cheekbones and full lips. What did he see when he looked at her?

Probably a mess of freckles.

Maggie harrumphed. "Well, I bet you don't know what's for dessert."

"Brownies."

Maggie stopped dead where the packed trail ended and the loose, soft sand of the beach began and glared at him. "You're guessing."

"Isn't that what you asked me to do?"

A giggle bubbled up and escaped Flora, and Juan laughed along with her. They found a place next to a low rock formation that wasn't covered by sand. Maggie set up the blanket while Fander and Juan went to find driftwood for a fire. Flora dug out a bowl in the sand to use as a fire pit.

It was too early to start the fire, so she doled out a glass of lemonade to Fander, her siblings, and Factor Danol, who'd taken up watch at the base of the trail. Even though she really liked him, it was nice of him to not try to integrate himself into their group. It would've been weird to have an adult trying to hang out with them, and the factor seemed to get that. Unlike Mid-Warden Clut. A shudder of distaste trickled down her spine. Thank God he'd been called back to Anferthia for a few weeks.

Juan idly sipped, a faraway look in his eyes. "Remember the day after you arrived here, Fander?"

"I do."

Maggie leaned forward. "I remember Flora gave Fander a black eye."

Fander choked on his lemonade and Juan hooted with laughter.

Heat rushed to Flora's cheeks. She cast an apologetic glance at Fander, but he just coughed, grinned, and shook his head. "It was not the best first day, I admit. That night I tried to convince Grandfather to send me back to Anferthia." His gaze held hers and her heart sped up. "I'm glad he refused."

"I'm glad he did too," Juan said.

"Me too," Maggie chimed.

Flora fought to suppress her smile and failed. "I'm glad you stayed, too."

Pleasure lit his eyes. "I cannot imagine life without you." He glanced at Juan and Maggie. "All of you." He seemed to want to say more, but instead smiled down at his cup.

Maggie popped up and threw her arms around Fander's neck, gave him a quick hug, then tugged on his arm. "Can we go beach-combing now, please? The tide's already coming in."

Beach-combing was one of the best parts of hanging out here. If they were lucky, they'd find stuff dating from before the invasion. They called it "old Earth stuff" so Fander wouldn't feel badly. But, he always seemed to get as excited as they did when the sea washed these kinds of treasures onto the beach.

"Yeah." Juan stood, brushing the sand off the butt of his pants. "Maybe there's another message in a bottle for me."

That'd been a cool find. The note inside the old green wine bottle had been to someone named Juan and signed by "M", whoever that was. Juan had got to keep that one by default.

After an hour of wandering up the beach, it became obvious that the tide had changed, so they returned to their picnic spot.

Juan patted his pockets and groaned. "I left the fire-starting tools at the cube."

Well, that was about right. "Again? I swear, Juan, why do you even bother volunteering to bring it?"

"You could've asked me if I had it before we left."

"I'm not your mom."

Fander rolled his eyes. "You really don't need that stuff, you know."

Flora smothered a snicker. "Not everybody can light a fire with a nose hair and the stink-eye like you can, Fander."

Juan and Maggie guffawed loudly, and Fander really did give her the stink eye, which would've worked better if he wasn't trying so hard not to laugh. She mouthed an apology and he grinned. "Nor has an ignitor. I'll be right back."

She watched him walk away, her gaze drifting to his butt and long, muscular thighs encased in Terrian style linen pants. He always wore Terrian styles. The only time she'd ever seen him in an Anferthian *wysgog* was for official occasions. The two-piece pants and tunic garment looked comfortable, and the somewhat East Indian-style was attractive. At least to her. Making up a pattern for her next sewing project shouldn't be too difficult.

And *why* was she *staring* at him? She tore her gaze away as heat crept up her chest to her neck. That wasn't the way anyone should look at their best friend. Unless they thought.... No. No, no, no. Not *that*.

"You okay, Flora?"

She startled at her sister's question. "Um, yeah. I'm just going to go put my feet in the water for a few minutes."

Or her whole body. Her face must be glowing red now. She pushed to her feet and strode to the waterline. The cold tide bit as it rushed over her calves. So much nicer than the burning embarrassment. A light breeze lifted the ends of her hair and tugged at her shirt. This was peace.

She let her thoughts drift back to Fander. Again. It was safe to do that here, away from the others. He was her friend, her *best* friend; that was it. And, he was real smart. Not a show-off kind of smart, like some of the other Terrian boys in town, but the kind of smart that didn't make others feel inferior. He was funny and sweet, and seemed interested in what she had to say on any topic.

And he'd said she was pretty. He must need glasses. She'd spent hours studying her face in her bathroom mirror and couldn't see pretty anywhere under all the stupid freckles.

Maggie's cheer drew her attention back to where the others sat. The first flame had caught, and the fire's glow was growing slowly. Even in the daylight, it flickered over Fander's forehead, nose, and chin while shadowing the hollows beneath his cheekbones.

She turned back to face the sea. Had he always been so cute? She peeked over her shoulder again and her heart fluttered. He was walking toward her, his long, narrow feet sinking and twisting in the sand. She faced him fully and he smiled. Weakness infiltrated her legs. Tingles throbbed along her lips and she raised her hand to brush them with her fingertips. Maybe he would kiss her right here on the beach.

The expression on his face changed to one of horror, as if he had heard her thought. The burn raced to her cheeks, again. Great.

"Flora, watch out!" Fander broke into a run, panic in his eyes.

Something large and wet crashed against her back, first knocking her forward then dragging her back. Sand and water rushed passed her ears and stung her face. Sneaker wave. How had she been so stupid to turn her back on the sea? Now she was being sucked into the ocean.

The force of the currents pushed and pulled her body like a helpless ragdoll. Then her head broke the surface. She blinked the stinging saltwater from her eyes. Where was the beach? Land? All she saw were waves upon rolling waves. Panic welled in her chest, which wasn't a good thing. If she gave in to it, didn't control it, she would die.

She shoved the rising hysteria down. First things first. Find the beach. She waved her arms under the water to turn herself around. A rolling wave raised her up and her gaze found the dark line of the distant bluffs. So far away. Too far. She sank into a valley between waves. There was no way she could swim back, but she had to at least try.

Another wave lifted her. This was bad. The land looked even farther away. If she didn't move now, she'd be lost at sea. She began a steady side stroke. Thank God for that day cousin Ora decided to teach her to swim. Throwing a shrieking eight-year-old into a snow-fed Alpine lake took nerve, but her Matiran cousin never expected anyone to do anything she wasn't willing to do herself. Being a fleet captain had not stopped her from shrieking like a little kid when she'd jumped into the freezing lake barely two seconds later. Poppy said that was one of the things that made her a great captain.

Of course, Alpine lakes didn't have sharks.

Flora stopped swimming and pumped her legs to tread water as she peered down into the grey-blue ocean. The distorted pale flashes in the murkiness must be her legs and feet. It was disturbing that she could barely make them out. A shiver shook her from head to toe. What was the Pacific hiding from her in its shadowy depths?

The weight of fatigue dragged at her, and an aching burn settled into her arms and legs. "Keep going. Just keep going."

She lay into the water, stroking and kicking. Part of a childhood litany…or was it a prayer…droned in her head. *Lord, in Your mercy, hear our prayer.* Tears seeped from her eyes into the ocean and the inside of her nose burned.

Collision

I don't want to die.

A few minutes later she stopped to tread water again. This was not working. There was no chance she'd make it to the barely visible white line that marked the beach. Even floating seemed too strenuous now. If she just didn't move at all for a moment, maybe she could summon up enough energy to go a little farther. She leaned her head back, closing her eyes against the sun's glare.

An odd calm seeped into her. The water closed over her head. It was so quiet and peaceful under the waves.

Something clamped down on her middle from below and forced her upward in a rush of bubbles. A shark had her! She broke the surface, and her heartbeat pounded against her chest as she fought to escape. The creature tightened its hold. This was happening so fast, her body hadn't even registered the pain of the rows of razor sharp teeth as they sank into her flesh. A raw, terrified scream tore from her throat.

"Flora, stop!" Fander's voice sliced through the haze of horror in her brain.

Fander? He was in danger too. "*Shark.*" She pushed her palms against him to move him away.

"Don't fight me. I have you."

He would die with her if he didn't get away.

"Stop fighting, Flora." His big voice froze her in place.

"Fander?" She blinked, her gaze meeting his. Wide reddish-purple eyes full of concern, not black, beady orbs of death. It was him…Fander…not a shark. There was no shark.

"Yes, me. And Nor's here too. You're safe." He stroked his large hand over her hair. "I won't let go. Ever. Just tip your head back on my shoulder and relax for a moment before we swim back."

"Too far." Her voice sounded hoarse and flat. There was no way they'd make it back. A hard lump stuck in her throat. They'd all die because of her stupidity.

"We'll make it." He seemed so certain. "I swim out here two to three times a week."

"You … you do?" How come she hadn't known that? "How far out?"

"Normally we do a three-mile round trip."

"Oh." Her heart rate still bounced like a Super Ball, but at least it wasn't trying to jump through her chest anymore. A tremor shuddered through her, followed by another. "But, what about the sharks?"

"In the four years I've been swimming in this ocean, I have never encountered a creature known as a shark. But, Nor is watching for them just in case. Don't worry."

"He is? Where?"

"I am here." The factor moved around Fander, to where she could see him.

"Okay, then…we might make it." Hopefully.

"We will, no problem." Fander turned her until her back pressed against his chest. "Ready?"

She gave him a nod. Fander's muscles rippled as he kicked, and they sliced through the water in the direction of the shore, a small wake forming a V around them. Factor Danol disappeared under the waves, and a greenish blur flashed by her. He really was watching for sharks.

Fander's body was warm against her back, and his arm around her shoulders pressed her against him like she was precious cargo. It was the way Mama or Poppy held her after a bad dream, only better. Secure. Cared for. Fander had her, and nothing could get at her now. Not even a shark.

Especially not a shark.

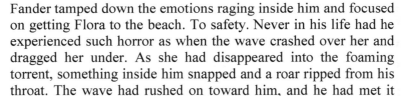

Fander tamped down the emotions raging inside him and focused on getting Flora to the beach. To safety. Never in his life had he experienced such horror as when the wave crashed over her and dragged her under. As she had disappeared into the foaming torrent, something inside him snapped and a roar ripped from his throat. The wave had rushed on toward him, and he had met it without so much as trepidation for his own well-being.

All that had mattered was saving Flora.

He tightened his arm around her shoulders and gave his legs another kick, cutting a path through the chilly water. Nor bobbed up in their wake, then dove back under the waves. If it had not been for his friend and body guard, he might not have found Flora. It had been incredibly foolish of him to dive headlong into the wave. But, his thoughts had been anything but rational as he had frantically searched for her, shouting her name as the undertow dragged him into deeper waters.

Then, Nor was there, talking to him, challenging him to school his thoughts until rationality returned. He nearly lost it all again when Flora had allowed herself to sink under the waves. How could she give up like that?

"The breakers are ahead." Nor's voice brought him back to the moment.

Fander brought them through the breakers until he found the sand with his feet. He moved his mouth next to her ear. "Feet down, Flora."

"We're here, already?" She rolled away from him and crawled through the surf toward the beach.

An odd mix of emotion—part relief, part bereavement—surged through him at her absence. As Juan splashed toward her and helped her to the sand, Fander bent and placed his hands on his knees, his chest heaving as the enormity of what had just happened hit him. The weight of a large, warm hand came to rest in the middle of his back.

"Are you well, my lord?" Nor murmured the words so low that there was no chance Flora or Juan had heard.

A tremor went through him and chill-bumps rose on his skin, but he managed to nod his head. "I am well."

"I commed for aid before going in after you. The ambassador is sending help, and a healer."

"It is well. Thank you." Fander straightened and gave the middle of his shirt a tug, separating the soaked, clinging material from his skin.

Flora was settled on the dry sand above the wave line, wrapped in the picnic blanket Juan had brought. The old thing was made from wool and dated to before the invasion. His nose twitched. It was unfortunate wool put off a rank odor when damp, but at least it would keep her warm.

She gave up.

A bead of anger gnawed at him. Why had she done that? He ran his fingers down the front of his shirt. The seal parted, and the flaps fell open to each side. The air touched his newly-exposed damp skin as he sloshed through the surf and tromped over the shifting sand toward Flora, his reliquary bumping against his chest. Her gaze moved from Juan to him. Or, to his chest, actually. Then a faint pink shade dusted her cheeks and she looked down.

Fander stopped in front of her. "Juan, would you ask Mags to feed the fire? Flora is chilled. I'll bring her back."

"Sure." Juan sprinted back up the beach, sand flying behind him with each step.

Nor gave Fander a nod before heading toward the trail up the cliffside, probably to meet whoever was coming. The time alone to speak with her would be a fleeting gift.

He dropped to his knees in front of her, his open shirt fluttered as he clasped her head between his hands. "Don't you *ever* give up like that again."

Her eyes widened as though surprised. "I *didn't* give up."

"You stopped treading, you stopped floating, and you let yourself sink." He ground his teeth together so hard a tinge of pain shot through his jaw. "That's giving up, Flora. Think about what that would mean to your parents, to your family, to your friends, to…." *Me.*

A dizzying array of color and emotion swamped his senses. Suddenly, he was eleven again. Meeting her clear blue gaze for the first time. The universe had spiraled down to a narrow point that day, and she was all he had been able to see. Then, she had crumpled against her mother. Fainted. And everything had changed. But he had not realized the significance of that moment, until now.

Tangol.

That is why they had both been affected that day. That is why she had been in his first *rywoud.* That is why he had lost his mind today when the wave dragged her toward certain death. And, that is why he was angered by her flagrant disregard for her own life.

Tangol lived for each other as well as themselves. Why had she not honored that by fighting to stay alive? Was it because she was not Anferthian? Did she even feel their connection? He gave himself a mental shake. She must feel it, otherwise she would not have passed out the day they had met. And all the gods knew, if she did not feel it, she would still hate him with unimaginable bitterness for what the Arruch had done to her birth-parents.

But, she did not. Hate him, that is. She had claimed him as her best friend and was pretty close to *fyhen*, for a Terrian.

What would she think if she knew the premise of his being on Terr? The way he was being used by the Arruch Union?

He let his gaze drift to her pink lips. The desire to tell her, to explain the bond that held them together, rose up. But, the rules were clear. Friendship was all right, but nothing more. Not even *tango1*. He must control himself or the future would die with him.

The muscles in his jaw clenched and he dragged his gaze up to meet hers again. "Don't *ever* give up, Flora." His voice was tight and strained, as the words had come straight from his heart. He released his grip, hauled her to her feet, and pulled her against him in a bear hug. "I am glad you're safe."

His reliquary dug into his chest between them, directly between where her soft breasts pressed against him. Warmth radiated from that point of contact. He turned his head into her briny, damp hair and inhaled her scent through his nose. Waves of contentment washed over him, carrying away the anger. She was his center, his peace. Eventually, a time would come when he could reveal the truth to her.

Right now, though, he risked revealing another truth to her— to everybody—if he did not let her go. A quickly hardening truth.

He moved, and she swayed forward before stopping herself. "Did you hit your head?"

She reached up and probed the side of her head with her fingertips, then drew them down and stared at them. "Yeah, there's a small bump but it's not bleeding."

He raised one hand. "How many fingers am I holding up?"

"Um, four."

"Wrong." He gave her the wickedest grin he could.

She frowned. "No, you...."

"Flora, everyone knows aliens have tentacles, not fingers."

Her lips parted, confusion in her eyes. Then she laughed clear and sweet. "You're such a turd."

"I know. And now I'm pretty sure that you don't have a concussion. C'mon, let's get back to the fire and warm up. Your mom or uncle should be here soon and I want them to know that we know what we're doing."

FIVE

Four months later

Flora jerked awake, a shriek lodged in her throat as dream-induced terror shuddered through her body. That was no prophetic dream. It had been way too…realistic. Each scene had emerged from a mist, played out with a clarity she'd never experienced before in any dream. Then it was swallowed back into the mist as a new one emerged. All of them had been different scenarios of the same event, with the same two key players. Herself and Fander.

And something dark, menacing…always just beyond her senses…lurked, waiting for them.

She pushed herself upright to sit in the middle of her bed and wrapped her trembling arms around her raised knees.

Breathe, in and out, slowly.

That's what Mama would tell her to do to calm her racing heartbeat. She cast a glance out her window. Dark. The sun wasn't even up yet. Not that the sun would be shining on New Damon Beach today. The edge of the first of three consecutive spring storms had silently slipped over them during the night. By mid-afternoon, it'd be raining.

Two soft thumps rapped against her bedroom door. "Flora?"

"Come in, Poppy."

The door opened, and her father stepped into her room. He always looked so dashing in his graphite grey uniform, the touch of barely visible silver at the temples of his snow-white hair only made him look more distinguished.

Poppy's loving smile turned to a perplexed frown. "Bad dream, *puella*?"

She nodded. "Mm-hm."

He sat on the edge of her bed facing her. "Do you wish to talk about it?"

"Not yet, Poppy, thank you." Maybe not at all, which was a first...like the dream. She hugged her knees closer to her chest.

His cool hand closed over hers. "All right, when you're ready. By the way, happy fifteenth birthday, *cori*." Daughter. He pressed a kiss to her forehead and stood to leave.

"Poppy?" Her father glanced over his shoulder at her. "Thank you."

"For what, *puella*?"

"For adopting me—all of us, but mostly me." She swallowed, the sound loud in the pre-dawn silence of their family cube. "I love being a family with you and Mama."

A smile lit his entire face. "Not a day goes by that I don't thank the Mother for the gift of my children. I love you more than you could know, Flora." His brilliant blue gaze held hers for a beat. "I look forward to celebrating with you tonight."

The door closed without a sound as warmth flooded her heart, chasing away the vestiges of fear the dream had brought. If only she had said those words sooner, and more often. They were a gift every parent deserved to receive from their child.

Tap. Tap. Tap.

She jerked her head around in time to see a green hand poised at her window. "Fander? What...?" She swung her legs over the edge of her bed.

Tap. Tap. Tap.

"I'm coming, I'm coming." As soft as his tapping was, Poppy had just left and might still close enough to hear. She hurried over and slid the window open. "What are you *doing*?"

He grinned up at her and leaned his arms against the window pane. The steel-grey light of the overcast dawn gave shadows to the hollows below his high cheek-bones. "I was trying to be the first to tell you happy birthday, but I think your father beat me."

She stifled a giggle and crossed her arms across her chest. Her pajamas weren't particularly revealing, but they also did nothing to keep her warm against the damp, misty air flowing around her.

"Yeah, he kind of did."

"Bummer." His sigh was full of dejection. Then he brightened again. "I guess I'll have to be the first to take you for a birthday ride."

"What are you talking about?"

His grin got wider, and he glanced over his shoulder. She followed the direction of his gaze and…wow! A Terrain Blazer Anti-Grav Hovercycle…the alien version of a motorcycle without wheels. And it looked brand new. "Where'd you get *that*?"

He was looking up at her again, as if taking in her reactions and storing them away in his memory. "Grandfather gave it to me."

"But, why?"

"I think he got tired of me using the surface skimmer all the time." He shrugged his shoulders. "The important part is that I got out of the cube this morning without waking up Nor."

"You mean your guard isn't following you?" That was almost as impressive as the bike. "What about Clut?"

"He had a little too much Terrian tequila last night." He flashed her the Devil's grin. "So, do you want to go for a ride? It'll be raining later. This may be your last chance for at least a week."

Excitement filled her. "Hold on. Let me get dressed."

The afternoon wind whipped Flora's hair back and stung her ears as the landscape rushed past them in a blur of pale wild grasses, dark bare shrubs, and deep green California oak trees. A whoop rose in her chest, and unlike when they'd slipped away from her parents' cube this morning, she let this one out. Fander's laugh reached her ears, then he whooped too, but his was amplified by his secondary, louder, voice box. The vibration of his joyful shout reverberated through her like electricity, zapping her right between the legs. She sucked in a short, sharp breath. God almighty, what was that?

It was nice, that's what it was. She shifted slightly, and the seam of her pants and the warmth of the seat pressed against her center, keeping the echo of pleasure alive. Nothing like that had ever happened to her before when an Anferthian used their big voice. It must be because it was Fander. He would never hurt her. She wouldn't have come out here with him if she thought otherwise.

And, what a day it had been so far. Fander had taken them south first, and inland. They'd eaten a picnic lunch not too far from Aunt Simone and Uncle Graig's place. It was obvious he'd been planning this for a while, as he seemed to have packed everything they might possibly need. Including the blanket Juan had wrapped her in that day on the beach last fall.

They sped across the wide-open field. In the distance, maybe a mile or two away, the low, unassuming cubes of New Damon Beach broke the flat monotony of the grassland. Ahead, the one place that brought her the most peace. The beach.

Fander brought the hover-bike to a stop at the edge of the bluff and set his feet down, but didn't get off. She sat up straighter to peek over his shoulder. The ocean was always so amazing just before a storm. Just the sheer power of the foaming grey waves crashing over the rocks and onto the shore filled her with awe. Even more so now than before her little adventure last November.

There was power in the knowledge that she'd escaped certain death in its dark, frigid depths. Somehow, the experience made her not invincible, but...worthy. If she could survive that, she could survive anything.

She lifted her gaze to the horizon. Not too far beyond the shore, a band of dark clouds marked the incoming rain. It couldn't be more than twenty minutes from landfall.

"Are you sure you want to go down there?" Fander gave her a dubious look.

"Of course. You're not going to chicken out on me, are you?"

He grinned. "Not a chance."

Moments later, they were crunching down the switchback trail. Her booted foot slipped and Fander grabbed her arm. "Are you okay?"

She looked up at him. Not so much as a blemish marked his smooth green skin, lucky guy. The light mist dotting her face probably pointed out every last one of her despicable freckles. "I'm fine."

Fander nodded, but he didn't release her arm. It was sweet of him to look out for her, and she kind of liked it. Okay, more than kind of. She *did* like it and wasn't about to pull away.

Once they reached the beach, they clambered up onto a flat waterworn rock, well back from the surf. Thank goodness the tide was out. Even with the storm pushing the water farther up the beach than normal, it still wouldn't reach them at the base of the bluff.

"At home, on Anferthia, my family home sits between the seashore and a forest." Fander toed off his shoes and sat back with his long legs stretched out straight, bracing himself with his hands.

She gave him a startled look. In all these years, he'd never told her anything about his home. "Do you miss it?"

He stared out at the white capped waves. "Sometimes." He lowered his gaze to his toes. "Yes."

"Do you want to go back?" God, she sure hoped not. Just the thought of him leaving filled her with a weird ache.

"Eventually I will have to." He met her gaze, a mischievous twinkle in his eyes. "But, not for a long time. I would miss this beach too much."

She gave him the stink-eye. "Just the beach, huh?"

A grin lifted the corners of his mouth. "The beach, and my friends." The grin faded a bit. "But mostly you."

Her lips twitched, and a mist seemed to rise in her eyes. She swallowed and gave her head a slow nod. "I'd miss you too, Fander."

"Maybe when I do have to go, you can come with me."

Her heart filled to bursting. "Maybe."

Seeing Anferthia would be fun, although not if the Arruch Union was still around. But, they were talking about the future, several years from now. Who knew what things would be like then? Besides, Fander's smile was all she needed to see to know she'd made him happy right now. Nothing else mattered.

She ran her tongue over her lips. "Actually, there is something I wanted to ask you about."

"Sure. What?"

"Well, remember the time I mentioned you should be a diplomat?" There was that bitter-sweet smile of his again.

"Did you change your mind?"

"No. No, I was thinking about…well…." How could she say this so he wouldn't laugh? "Do you think I'd make a good diplomat?"

Fander's lips parted and his eyes widened just enough to notice.

She waved him off. "I knew it. Just…never mind. I'd suck at

it."

"No." He sat up. "No, you wouldn't, actually."
"You're just saying that."
"Pfft. Hardly."
"Whatever."
"Flora, what kind of person lies to their best friend?"
Oh. Good point.
He turned to face her, crisscrossing his legs. "You have all the characteristics of being a great leader. You're smart, fair. You listen. You form well-thought-out opinions. You're not afraid to speak your mind...which is probably the one area you might want to work on."

A small snort got out before she thought about it. "Are you saying I'm a big mouth?"

"Nah. Your mouth is perfect."

Um, oh. She ducked her head and resisted the impulse to touch her fingers to her lips.

"I have something for you." He reached inside his jacket. "I know how you Terrians love gift-giving on birthdays, so I thought I'd stick with the local custom." He brought out a small circle of clover flowers. "I made it myself. Sorry they are a little crushed, but happy birthday, Flora."

That silly eye-mist got thicker, and she blinked to clear it. "Fander, that's so sweet. Thank you."

He leaned forward and set the flowers on top of her head, like a crown. "They remind me of you."

Was he serious, or was he teasing her about that day in the orchard? And, he was so close, his mouth only a few inches away. Her heart pounded in her chest and she couldn't look away. Should she make the first move? It'd be so much more romantic if he did, though, but he seemed frozen in place, so maybe she should.

A fat raindrop plunked her in the forehead and she jerked her head back. Fander moved away as if time hadn't stopped just then. The moment was ruined.

"So." He cleared his throat. "Do you always wake up so early, like you did this morning?"

The memory of her dream—nightmare—rushed back. Her wonderful lunch churned in her stomach.

"Flora?" He reached his hand toward her, covered her clenched fist. "Is something wrong?"

She looked down then around, anywhere but at him. "Nothing."

"Don't tell me 'nothing'. Something happened, I can tell." He didn't sound angry, but he clearly wasn't going to be blown off easily. "You had a dream, didn't you?"

Oh, no. Anferthians believed unapologetically in their dreams. And, he knew she'd had prophetic dreams before. There was no way he'd let this go.

He slipped his fingers under her chin and tilted her head back. Now there was nowhere to look except into his eyes. Judging by the deepening frown on his face, whatever he saw did not make him happy. He breathed out a soft sigh, almost one of wonder. "You received *rywoud*."

She'd expected almost anything but that. "I can't have *rywoud*. I'm not Anferthian. It was just a weird dream."

"Your eyes say otherwise." He released his hold and she rubbed her chin. "We need to talk."

No, they really didn't. But, then again, maybe he knew something that would help her understand.

"Don't worry, Flora, it's no big deal to have the dreaming. I'm just going to ask you some questions about it and see if we can figure out what it means. You don't have to answer anything you aren't comfortable with, okay?"

She swallowed her nerves down and nodded.

"Can you describe the overall feeling of the dream? Happy, sad...?"

"Um, well, sinister." How could she explain? "Remember the really bad lightning storm a couple of months ago, and how the air felt all dark and ominous a few hours before it finally hit? That's sort of what my dream felt like. I couldn't see *what* it was, but I felt like something scary was about to happen."

"Do you remember any specific events?"

Furrowing her brow, she concentrated on the images that rose in her mind. They were as clear now as when she'd dreamed them, which was weird. Normally her dreams faded within a couple of hours. "We were running because something was chasing us."

"We? You mean us?"

"Yes, you and me. Whatever it was wanted to stop us from doing...something. I don't know what, though. And then you were lost, or I couldn't find you at least, which scared me because I think you were in danger."

He gave her a wary look and shifted. "Who else do you remember being in your dream?"

"Well, my family, your grandfather, and you; you were always there, except when I couldn't find you. There were other people I don't know, mostly Anferthians. The only one I recognized was my parents' friend K'rona. Oh, and Factor Danol too, he was there." If Fander's eyes got any wider, his eyeballs were going to pop out. She turned to face him fully. "That means something to you, doesn't it? What? Tell me."

He stood up abruptly and began to pace, his bare feet sinking into the pale sand.

There was no help for it, her eyes rolled skyward on their own accord. "Guess we're gonna be here a while."

Fander either didn't hear her or was actively ignoring her. He continued his relentless pacing for several minutes. Finally, she let out a long sigh. Maybe she should just walk home and leave him here with his own thoughts.

He stopped and stared at her. Hard. Like she'd handed him an inverse trigonometry problem. He dropped to his knees at her feet, his head level with hers and his hands covering her knees. Well, maybe she'd stay here after all.

"Your first dreaming shouldn't be identical to mine. Even though you're...." He stopped and snapped his lips together.

"Even though I'm what?" A second raindrop pinged her on top of her head, then another hit the rock next to her hand. The rain was about to start for real.

He shook his head. "It just shouldn't happen. It *never* happens that way."

A snort escaped her before she could stop it. "Since you just said it did, then apparently it *does* happen, Fander."

"Apparently. But, why?" He glanced up at the darkening sky as more drops fell. "If you're all right with it, I would like to speak with Grandfather about this. He may be able to help."

"You don't think we can figure it out between us?" If she really did have *rywoud*, there'd be a bajillion questions. After all, she wasn't Anferthian, so how could that possibly have happened to her?

"Grandfather won't tell anyone else, and he may even have

some answers." The pleading look in his eyes reached her heart.

"All right, fine." She gave her hand a wave toward the trail. The random drops were now a steady patter on the sand. "Let's go to my parents' cube first, though. It's closest. And Mama'll probably have some hot chocolate."

It wasn't difficult to miss the light of victory in Fander's eyes. Well, whatever. At least his grandfather could explain that her dream was just that, a dream. Then Fander would have to listen to him when he said she hadn't had *rywoud* at all.

She followed Fander to the base of the bluff and up the narrow winding trail. Mama was probably getting worried by now, since the rain was pelting down pretty steadily. It'd already soaked through her clothing enough for the material to stick it to her skin. *Gross.*

Fander stopped, and she nearly rammed her nose into his back. What was he doing? They were almost to the top of the trail. A few more steps and they'd be able to see the hover-bike, and maybe even New Damon Beach if the rain wasn't too heavy. He turned to face her, a strange look on his face. Somewhere between apprehension and determination.

He threaded his cool fingers into her hair just behind her ears, his palms holding her head steady as he took her face tenderly between his hands. "May I?"

There was no misunderstanding what he was asking, his mouth was so close to hers. All he needed was her permission to kiss her. Like she'd ever say no. Her lips parted slightly as she looked into his eyes of amaranthine. "Yes." It was a breathless whisper, but that was all she could get out at that moment.

Fander bent his head; the first gentle brush of his lips against hers was warm and soft, and sent tiny shivers through her body. He tasted like rain and the ocean. The sound of the waves crashing on the shore faded to a dull roar and she exhaled a small sigh. The second touch was firmer, and she closed her eyes as little balls of electricity coursed through her with no semblance of order. Her bare toes curled into the sandy dirt of the trail and her arms moved around his waist of their own accord. She was being kissed for the very first time ever by Fander on the bluffs overlooking the beach and ocean she so loved. In the rain. On her birthday. It didn't get any more perfect than this.

Fander ended the sweet kiss, his face flushed as they pulled slowly apart. And he smiled. Heck, she was smiling too. There was just no way to hide it, even if she'd wanted to. And she didn't want to. Hopefully he'd enjoyed it just as much so he'd be more inclined to kiss her again in the future.

"I've wanted to do that for a long time." He ran his thumb pads along her cheek bones.

"And I want to push you off the side of this cliff," growled a voice from behind him. "Doesn't make it right."

Flaming heat burned her neck, face, ears. Her perfect first kiss had been witnessed by, of all people, Uncle Graig.

Oh, god.

Fander stiffened and then turned to face the fearsome Matiran. She stepped far enough out to peek around him. "Uh, hi, Uncle Graig."

Her Matiran uncle gave a curt nod but didn't stop glaring up at Fander. Poor Fander looked mortified, which was probably a good thing. Playing to her uncle's good side was the best strategy. After all, this was the same man who had told her he'd BBQ any boy who kissed her before she was thirty.

Something nudged her hand. Fander's fingers laced between hers and she gave his hand a light squeeze. They would face this storm together; it was the right thing to do.

Fander licked his lips. "Sir, I'm sorry to have disappointed you. My intentions are honorable, and I did ask her permission—"

"And I said yes." Best to get that out there too.

"—and she said yes." He looked down at her, a hint of a smile hovered at the corners of his mouth.

"And I'd say yes again." Which was also the truth. And if Uncle Graig didn't like it, tough.

Her heart beat a little harder as Fander's mouth crept up into a full smile.

Uncle Graig tapped his commlink. "Alex. The dreamer has been located, and the loose cannon as well."

"Uncle Graig!"

He gave her a look of infinite sadness. "I'm bringing them home."

"Thank you, Graig." Mama's voice came back. Why did they both sound so sad?

Her uncle's gaze moved to Fander. "We'll take Flora home first, then you." He turned away and strode up the path to where his mount waited.

"What do you think *that's* all about?" She gave Fander a mystified look. His jaw was tight and his eyes troubled. "Oh, god. Something's going on, isn't it?" Something she wasn't going to like.

Fander shook his head and cupped his hand over her elbow. "It's okay, Flora. Let's go."

SIX

Fander slammed the door to his bedroom, the bang doing nothing to satisfy the boiling self-loathing in his soul. In the space of a heartbeat, he had ruined everything. *Everything.*

He peeled off his soaked clothing one piece at a time and cast them into a corner. How could he have been so stupid, so careless?

Maybe Grandfather would not make him go back. Rain water dripped from his short stump of a *tirik* and rolled between his shoulder blades. A shiver ran down his arms. If only Flora's uncle had not shown up at that exact moment, their day of freedom would not have ended so…tragically.

He grabbed his robe from the closet and punched his arms into the sleeves. It was best not to use words like tragic when making his case. Appearing like an over-dramatic teenager never worked. He had tried that in other situations. So had Flora and Juan. The results of their efforts were always zero.

But, how could he argue his case and win? He cinched the robe closed, flopped into his reading chair, and closed his eyes. Flora's face rose in his mind's eye, just as she had looked the moment before he kissed her. Her face damp, droplets of rain shimmering on her pale lashes framing her clear blue eyes, and her pink lips slightly parted.

What was a kiss supposed to feel like? He had never kissed another, never desired to. Only Flora brought that need to the surface. But Mother and Grandfather were clear about the rules, and rule number one was not to get involved with anyone in a way that would bring them to the attention of Isel T'orr.

Tap, tap.

Grandfather had arrived. Fander blew out a gust of air and opened his eyes. "Enter."

The door opened inward and Grandfather stepped into the room, two steaming mugs in his hands. He pushed it shut it behind him with his foot. "How do you feel, Grandson?"

Something shifted around Fander's heart. Grandfather was concerned about his well-being above all the other issues? "I will not leave."

The sweet scent of hot cocoa wafted through the room. Grandfather nodded and set one mug on the table next to the reading chair, then moved across the room to sit on the edge of the bed. "You know the point is moot, Fander. We have discussed this before."

"I know." Fander curled his fingers until the nails bit into the soft flesh of his palms. "Nobody saw what happened…except her uncle. And he will not tell."

Except, he had. He had told Grandfather, and he had probably told Flora's parents, too. But, none of them would be jumping on the comm to the Divine Warden to let him know, that was for certain. He picked up the mug and sipped. The hot drink slipped down his throat and into his belly, warming his body but not touching his ice-encased heart.

"No, your secret is safe with those who love you." Grandfather clasped his gnarled hands together in his lap. "It is the little adventure you and Flora went on today that is widely known. Already there are those in New Damon Beach who believe the two of you are romantically linked."

"But, I was discrete." He had snuck out unseen and under the cover of darkness. Had avoided places where people might see them alone together. He took another healthy sip and set the mug aside.

"You were seen on the hovercycle together, and you have always known there are those in my own household who report back to their Arruch contacts."

Mid-Warden Clut. That cowardly fecal-sniffer.

Fander swallowed hard against the dread rising in his chest. The word that he had snuck out to rendezvous with a Terrian girl would get back to Anferthian quickly because of Clut.

Grandfather's enemies would watch her with interest from now on. More than they had done when she was just daughter of the *Profetae*. He scrubbed his hands over face. What had he done?

"Do you begin to grasp the enormity of your actions?"

He suppressed a snort. Yes, he grasped it all right. He pushed himself upright in the chair. "She is my *tangol*. I will not leave her unprotected."

Grandfather nodded. "So, you know."

"Of course I know."

"When did you reach this conclusion?"

He pressed his lips together. It was tempting to refuse to tell him, but that would be immature when what he most needed to do was to convince his grandfather that he was mature enough to handle the situation so he could stay. "The day she was swept away by the sneaker wave."

"That long? I am impressed." He raised his mug to his lips and took a few swallows. "You know she will be well protected in your absence."

"It should be me." He picked up his mug again and finished off its contents.

Grandfather shook his grizzled head. "You are the greatest hope for Anferthia's future, and for reasons yet unknown to us, Flora is the key to that future. That is why there is nothing I will not do for you, including protecting your *tangol* with my very life, if necessary. This I vow."

Nothing, except allow him to stay on Terr. "But, what if we are not seen together alone again? If we take Juan and Maggie with us everywhere—"

"You know the damage is done, you know this deep down."

He did know, but he had to try. "How do you plan to get T'orr to agree to sending his prized intelligence collector home?"

Odd how his father's murderer was now his ace-in-the-hole, as the Terrians said. There was no way the Divine Warden would give up his gullible little trophy. In *theory*, child-Fander had cultivated the trust of the Terrians and was able to report information overheard in various locales such as in town, social gatherings, official functions, and from inside the Bock household. In *fact*, Isel T'orr did not have an inkling that Senior Admiral Helyg and the Terrian Council controlled that flow of information. Grandfather had done his part to make sure the

Arruch believed it was worthwhile to keep him here instead of on Anferthia. It was probably one of the reasons he had not met an abrupt end, like his father.

"This has already been handled. I vid-commed Isel's second in command, Supreme Warden Tusayn, and led him to believe you had been revealed as a spy by an unknown source, and you must return to Anferthia immediately before the Terrians take action."

Very neat and tidy. Now, there were no arguments left to use, and the ones he *had* used were flimsy at best. Still, he had to try one more thing. "May I at least say good bye?"

Grandfather raised his eyebrows and gave him a look that said, I know you're not so great a fool.

"This will hurt her, Grandfather. Please...?"

Grandfather sighed and rose from the bed, his keen black eyes conveying that he understood. "You know that is not possible. Pack, now. I shall send Kapit Tymo when the transport is ready. Factor Danol will return with you and continue in your service."

Of course he would. Nor was a trusted friend and loyal to the cause.

At the door, Grandfather paused and met Fander's gaze. "If you write her a note, I shall deliver it. Just be judicious of what you tell her."

He departed then, quietly closing the door.

Fander reached behind his head, closing his fingers over the metal *kadura* holding back the short stump of hair that had grown out since his birthday. It was still too short to braid but it was just enough for the hair binding. He gave the clasp a yank and it slid off, freeing his hair to fall loose and damp over his neck. The band was all he had left of his father, that and the vague memories of a two-year-old boy. It was in his possession only because his mother had not been caught removing it from her beloved husband's *tirik* after he had been murdered.

For years, the *kadura* had served as a reminder that Divine Warden Isel T'orr had much to answer for. Now the blood-colored hair piece also represented what Fander couldn't have.

Flora.

He heaved himself out of the chair and stood in the middle of the room, curling and uncurling his fingers. A carefully worded note, that was all he was allowed to leave for her. It seemed a poor gift in light of the kiss they'd shared, but he would make every word count.

He ran his tongue over his lips, the faint honeyed taste of her was still there, but for how much longer? Would he ever taste her again, and if so, when?

Part Two

SEVEN

Nine years later.

Flora panted as she flopped down on one of the benches lining Uncle Graig's training cube and wiped the soft nano-fibrous towel over her face. "I think…you're getting…better, Uncle."

"I think you're a smart ass." Uncle Graig scrubbed a similar towel over the back of his neck as he took a seat a few feet from her. "You have come far in nine years, *puella*."

She forced herself not to cringe at the reminder. It'd been nine years since that horrible day Mama had handed her the note from Fander. Nine years since Fander had been sent back to Anferthia because of her. Yet, the all-too-familiar pang of loss that burned in her heart was still as raw now as it had been then. Like a wound that refused to heal. She still missed her best friend, even though she hadn't heard from him the entire time.

"Thanks."

Despite the ever-present sadness, she had managed not to die like she swore she would when she was fifteen. God, she'd been so dramatic, even going as far as taking a pair of scissors to her hair as a visible protest of her defiance against the adults in her life.

She hadn't cut her hair since.

Once it was long enough, she'd taken to wearing it in a single braid, similar to the Anferthian *tirik*. What would Fander think of that? And why the hell couldn't she get him out of her mind? It was like her most secret desire was to get back to him, but why? Grandfather K'nil had promised to tell her once the time was right, but God only knew when that would be.

"You'll get your next assignment tomorrow." Uncle Graig's gaze was as penetrating as ever. Like he could see her pain.

She gave him a crooked smile. Best decision she'd ever made was deciding to pursue a diplomatic career. "Yep. It'll be nice to know where I'll be going in a year."

Spending the last four years working as a liaison between the Terrian Council and Ambassador K'nil had been educational, but there was more that she aspired to in the long run. A junior ambassador position on Anferthia would place her in a position to help Fander's grandfather, the dissenters, and others wishing to see the Arruch Union ousted. Recent reports indicated the Anferthian government was more unstable than ever. And no one had seen or heard from the Divine Warden, Isel T'orr in months. Speculation ran from him being in hiding, to having taken his latest lover to an isolated manor, to even his death. No one knew. Or, *someone* knew. Someone always knew, they just weren't saying. Politics were a crazy-scary thing sometimes.

And, it was very likely she'd also cross paths with Fander. It would be nice to talk to him about her decision to become a diplomat, especially after the conversation they'd had just before he'd left. Did he already know? Or would it be a surprise?

"I'm sure the Terrian Council's decision will be well thought out." Her uncle's normally stoic features softened with his smile. "No matter where you go, at least I know you will be able to defend yourself."

No doubt about that. "Uncle, why did Mama insist I train with you?" Insist was putting it mildly. Ultimatum was a better word.

"Your mother has never told me her reasoning, and I have never asked." He wadded his towel and shot it into a laundry bin. "If it's important enough for her to make the request of me, that's all I need."

Of course, it would be. Mama was like a sister to him.

She reached up and gave the hair cap on her head a tug. Her braid unrolled and swung down with a heavy bump between her shoulder blades.

"I will say this," Uncle Graig continued in a lower voice. "Because she asked, I know you will need this training at some point in your life."

She huffed out her breath and tossed her towel in the direction of the linen basket...and missed. That was about right.

"Do you question your mother's motives?"

She startled and met Uncle Graig's sharp gaze. "No." Why would he ask that?

"Good." He nodded, apparently satisfied with her answer. "Never forget that there are monsters in this universe, Flora. Your mother has faced her share of them and come away stronger. She may be a healer now, but under that mantel a warrior exists. She would fight, kill, and die for those she loves, and her capacity to love is infinite."

It was true. Mama was the strongest woman she knew. "I will not forget, Uncle. I will be a warrior like Mama."

He reached out and clasped her shoulder. "I believe you will be that, and more."

That evening Flora rubbed a bit of puke-green material between her thumb and forefinger. Juan's birthday wasn't for another four months, but it was never too early to design some completely obnoxious piece of clothing for him.

At the sound of light footfalls, she glanced up and smiled as Maggie sauntered into the workroom of their shared cube. Moving out of Mama and Poppy's had been a huge step, one that wouldn't have been half as fun without her little sister to share the experience.

"Ew." Maggie nodded at the material, her riot of dark curls bounced around her petite face. A silly grin matched the mischief lighting her green eyes. "Is that going to be Juan's birthday gift?"

A laugh bubbled out. "You know it is...and, I bought extra material to make you something to match."

"Oh, ha, ha." Maggie flopped onto a cushy pillow-chair, nearly disappearing in its fluffy comfort. "When he's advanced to Lieutenant next year, you should make him some pajamas that look like his fleet uniform...but in hot pink."

"Ooh, now there's an idea." She released the material and sank into the other pillow-chair. Of course, she could never hope all six feet and five inches of her would come anywhere close to disappearing into it the way her sister did. But still, the casual design of the Matiran lounging chair was the closest thing to floating on a cloud. "I'll stitch little black ants on it too." Would serve him right for all the times he'd told her to go piss on an ant when they were kids.

"That'd be perfect." Maggie's eyes twinkled, and she leaned forward as much as the chair allowed. "I heard Poppy tell Mama that Juan's super-secret project is on schedule to be transferred to Terr Base One next year."

"Really?" That was news to her. "I wonder why?"

"I dunno." Maggie shrugged. "So, plans for your birthday tomorrow...I'll leave early to check on the stable horses. Then I'll ride out to check on Aunt Simone's goats. Two of them are close to delivery—hopefully *that* won't happen tomorrow. I'll be back by the time you get home from your meeting with Ambassador K'nil, then we can celebrate your birthday *and* new assignment before going to Mama and Poppy's for dinner."

Leave it to Maggie to have everything planned down to the millisecond. It was one of the reasons her sister was such an outstanding veterinarian. She never missed an appointment, and she even made house calls. "Sounds good to me."

"I'm going to miss you." Maggie looked down at her hands gripped together in her lap.

Dang, her knuckles were white.

"You said that four years ago, and I ended up staying here, remember?"

"True." Her sister shrugged her slim shoulders. "But, it wouldn't be fair for the Council to keep you on Terr again. They're going to send you somewhere else this time, I just know it. I bet they'll even send you to your first-choice assignment. They'd be stupid not to."

Mag-pie had thought this one out, for sure.

"Hardly anyone gets their first choice, you know that. I'll probably be shipped off to the Terrian embassy on Agbahd X." Which was about the farthest planet from Anferthia in the known galaxy. "Besides, no matter where I'm assigned, I won't be leaving for at least a year. I have that long to learn about my new host planet." The people, the culture, the political system. Hopefully a year would be long enough.

"I know, but still...." Maggie stopped, nibbled her bottom lip, then met her gaze. "I'm getting ahead of things again, aren't I?"

Collision

"Just a little."

Her little sister's eyes brightened. "Okay, after you're done spending half your birthday with your boss, we're going out to have some fun."

"Grandfather K'nil is not my *boss*." She used her fingers to air quote the last word.

"Well, *Ambassador* K'nil sure is, and they're one in the same."

True, he was, but their relationship had well-defined boundaries. With the ambassador she'd learned so much about intergalactic diplomacy. It was equal parts fascinating and exciting. But, Grandfather was exactly that: a grandfather. A friend who listened and shared pearls of wisdom on a personal level.

"Do you think you'll dream Anferthian-style tonight?" Maggie asked.

Rywoud. The dreaming. It'd happened the night of her birthday every year since Fander had left, so why would tonight be any different? "Probably."

"Are you going to ask when Fander will be coming back again tomorrow?"

"Maybe. I'm getting tired of hearing, 'Today is not that day, Flora.'"

"Sorry. I know it's difficult to talk about, but I miss him, too. It'd be great if we could jump on a shuttle and go visit, but...." Maggie punctuated her sentence with another shrug.

"I know what you mean." At this rate, she'd be old and grey the next time she saw him.

A jaw-cracking yawn overtook her and she raised her hand to cover it. Obviously, her workout with Uncle Graig had wiped her out. She pushed up and out of the chair. "I think it's time to call it a night. Don't wake me up when you leave in the morning, 'kay?"

Maggie gave her a lazy wave. "You'll never know I left. Sweet dreams, sis."

A few minutes later, her pre-bedtime ablutions complete, Flora slid between her pre-warmed sheets and drifted into oblivion.

Blood. Blood was everywhere. On her hands, her clothes. Hot tears ran down her cheeks and her heart twisted with the pain of loss. Someone she loved was dead, but who? Frustration gripped her. *If the ever-present fog of rywoud would just clear she'd have her answer.*

But the fog didn't clear. Instead it thickened, cutting off the scene before it revealed the next. All she could do was wait, let the dreaming take its course. Darkness enveloped her, and she closed her eyes against it. This was different.

A heavy weight landed on top of her and air rushed out of her lungs. Her startled yelp was cut off as a hand clamped over her mouth and something cold pressed against her neck. Good God, this was more real than anything she'd experienced before.

She snapped her eyelids opened and bucked upward to dislodge her assailant. Only it wasn't an assailant. It was Fander...*gazing down at her. Surprise, confusion, and even a little bit of anger flashed across his face. He'd grown up, but his large, beautiful eyes hadn't changed a bit.*

Wait a minute. How had he gotten here? In her bed? And in her birthday dreaming? Her heart lurched in her chest. *If she'd known* that *was possible, she would've pulled him into all her* rywoud, *every stinking year since he'd left.*

His lips moved, soundlessly forming her name. Then he sat up and the cold pressure against her throat disappeared. The weapon in his hand changed drawing her gaze as it shrunk from his labuba, *short knife,* into a small, lethal-looking aquamarine-handled blade that looked ridiculous in his large hand.

Fander dropped the knife to the mattress and his fingertips grazed across her cheek. His lips moved. I miss you.

Tears flooded her eyes. *Was he really here? Really touching her? Really wearing nothing but a garnet-red sheet tangled around his waist...hiding all his good parts?*

The dream-fog closed in on her again. *Not now, please, not now.* Fander grasped her wrist, his frustration evident. A grey ghost-hand reached out of the fog, its fingers closing around her throat. There was nothing unsubstantial about the pressure it applied, or the way its grip slowly denied her oxygen.

She clawed the disembodied arm at the same moment Fander did. Only his hands passed right through the arm. The ghost-fingers tightened more, and the thing seemed to be getting larger. Dark spots danced at the edges of her vision. Fander's panicked gaze met hers as the fog closed around him, taking him from her. She clawed at the arm, thrashing. Pain beat at the inside of her

Collision

skull, keeping perfect time with her heartbeat. Had anyone ever died in rywoud *before? Blackness crashed over her....*

"Nnnggghhh." Flora rolled over in her bed, sucking in air with deep, greedy breaths.

Alive. She was alive, thank god. And awake. But, what a bitch of a dreaming. Nausea surged up her esophagus and she bolted out of the tangle of sky blue sheets toward the bathroom. The first wave of vomit just barely made it into the toilet.

Five minutes later, her stomach seemed to be finished rebelling. She groped her way hand-over-hand along the counter to the sink and scooped water from the faucet into her mouth. Some of the refreshing liquid splashed over the sides as post-barf tremors shook her hand. Her legs trembled too, but that could be more from the dreaming. She swirled the cool water around her mouth and spat, then raised her head to peek at her reflection in the mirror. Damn. That bloodless-faced woman couldn't be her, could it?

"My, Flora, what black eyes you have." She touched the fragile darkened skin under her eyes, then allowed herself a soft sigh. "Happy birthday to me, huh?"

Nope. The self-pity thing stopped now. Sure, the dreaming this time had been bad…horrendous, actually…but *she'd seen Fander*. In her bed. She swallowed hard. He'd seemed so warm and real, the weight of his body and the touch of his skin against hers. Did he sleep naked in real life? If he did, she wouldn't complain. But, seriously, who slept naked with a knife in their hand?

Why was she thinking like this? They'd shared one little kiss nine years ago, and here she was ready to roll all over her sheets with him.

Wait, something was off here. She inhaled a sharp breath. The dream sheets, they were *deep red*. She spun around and rushed to the doorway. Gripping the door frame to her room, she stared at her mussed bedding. Her sheets were very definitely as blue as a summer sky, not any shade of red. Where the hell had they been in that dream?

So many questions and no answers to go with them. If anyone could help her figure this out, it'd be Grandfather K'nil. The trick was getting him to tell her. He'd evaded all her Fander-related probes for so long. She loved the man as much as she loved

Grandpa Zale, but she was twenty-four now, for God's sake. Enough was enough. She'd already waited nine stinking years for an answer. There had to be a statute of limitations on this situation. If there wasn't, well, she'd create one.

She straightened her spine and set her jaw. With the morning she was having, something needed to go her way.

One thing was for sure, things couldn't get any worse.

EIGHT

Fander came out of the dreaming with a jerk and rolled to his left. The mattress abruptly ended, and he slid over the edge with a curse. The impact of his butt on the thick pile Alusian rug jarred him hard enough for his teeth to clack together. Alusian rugs were supposed to be the softest in the galaxy, a point he could debate. He scrambled into a defensive crouch and listened in the darkness. No noise other than his heartbeat thudding in his ears. No one seemed concerned enough to check on him, assuming they'd even heard him fall off the bed.

Flora.

Finding her in his bed, gods. Had he really put his *labu-ba* to her throat, thinking she was an assassin? May mercy fill her for his rash behavior.

But, by the holy ones, she had become every bit the stunning woman he had expected. Soft as silk she had lain beneath him, yet her muscles were firm and toned. She had been so real that his body had yet to realize *rywoud* had come to an end. It had to be *rywoud*, hers to be exact. Today was her birthday. How had he been drawn into her dreaming, anyway?

He scrubbed his hands over his face. If he did not exert some control over himself, he would not be able to help her. Dream or not, the hand at her throat was a figurative symbol that someone wanted—or would want—her dead. An Anferthian, obviously. Most likely an Arruch. They stood to lose the most once he made his move. Just her past friendship with him made her their liability.

Even now she could be in danger as he crouched on his floor in indecision. But, any action on his part could draw more attention to her, and inaction could cost her life.

It's too soon, too soon.

Yet, the time was almost upon them, only a breath away. Not knowing if she was safe at this moment was like a blade in his gut. His gaze was drawn to the comm unit on his desk. Grandfather could send someone to check on her.

No, too risky. If the Arruch intercepted his comm, they might figure out what her status really was and all the progress he had made during the past nine years would be for naught. How much longer would he have to put on the show of being the biddable and naïve young puppet-heir? How much longer before he lost patience with Supreme Warden Tusayn and the rest of the coalition members loyal to Divine Warden Isel T'orr?

One poorly thought out, emotion-driven mistake this close to his goal could throw it all away. But, there were moments when he had been sorely tempted to see how T'orr and his minions would react.

Time was wasting. There must be some way he could find out if she was safe. He pushed to his feet and something bumped against his bare chest. His reliquary. He closed his fingers around the slim burgundy pendant. The color of the blood of the people he was born to serve. He and Grandfather had worked out a schedule of times when they could communicate via their reliquaries, and now was not one of those times. The sun had risen in New Damon Beach, and with it an increased risk that Grandfather would not be alone and able to talk. But, Flora's life could depend on it.

Steel determination gripped him as surely as he gripped the sacred relic hanging on the cord around his neck. The situation outweighed the risk. He climbed atop the bed and lay on his back. Deep breath in, out, again. Calm flowed over him. Keeping his hand around the reliquary, he allowed his eyelids to drift down.

"Grandfather...."

Flora adjusted the strap of her document case on her shoulder just as one half of the great double front door of the Anferthian ambassador's cube opened to reveal a tiny grey-haired Terrian woman with a kind smile.

"Good morning, Mrs. Beck." Flora grinned back. The shower she took must have helped because Mrs. Beck didn't scream and slam the door in her face.

"Ah, Flora, dear. Happy birthday." Mrs. Beck reached up and patted her cheek. "The ambassador is in his study and your birthday muffins are in the oven. I will bring refreshments in an hour."

"Thank you." Flora stepped through the doorway and walked down the hall to her right, a little bit of spring in her step.

At the last door on the left she stopped and knocked.

"Enter." Grandfather K'nil's voice rumbled from the other side of the door.

She pushed it opened. Fander's grandfather sat on the long couch in front of the humongous picture window at the far end of the room. How many times had she, Fander, and her siblings stood in the garden outside that window, trying to spy on the adults in this room? But the window had remained frustratingly one-way, and the adults had probably had a good laugh out of their antics.

"Birthday greetings, Flora." Grandfather K'nil beckoned her forward with one hand. His other hand was closed around something in front of his chest. Judging by the chain of tiny silver links extending out of his fist and up around his neck, it had to be his reliquary. "Is it possible that you are twenty-four solar cycles already?"

She grinned and moved toward him as the door closed behind her with a muted thunk. "It is, sir."

"You are early. I had not expected you until fourth hour. You must be eager to learn your assignment."

Eager wasn't a big enough word. "I am, but, I have to talk to you about my dreaming first." She plopped down on the chair across from him and waved her hand in the direction of his chest. "Is that my birthday present you're holding?"

That was a totally lame thing to say, even as a joke. Anferthians didn't give birthday gifts, but she needed to butter him up a bit before she launched into an all-out interrogation.

Grandfather glanced down at his closed hand with a look of mild surprise, as if he'd forgotten he held anything. After a brief hesitation he met her gaze. "Would you humor an old man for a moment, dear one? I wish to speak to you privately."

That was not the answer she'd expected. "Sure."

She followed him toward the wall between two floor-to-ceiling bookcases on her left. The wall opened like an old-style Earth camera shutter, and he passed through. Now why would he be taking her into the shielded room? He only used the sound-proofed room for classified meetings.

No sooner did she step through the doorway, than the wall reformed behind her. "Um. Will Mrs. Beck be able to find us?"

Of all the idiotic things to ask. Here Grandfather K'nil trusted her enough to bring her to this secret room and all she could think about was missing out on Mrs. Beck's made-from-scratch muffins.

A warm chuckle rolled from him. "No fear, granddaughter, we will be finished here before the muffins are out of the oven. Have a seat."

It was like the man knew her. He waited for her to sit before lowering his eleven feet-plus frame into the chair opposite her own. "As I am certain you know, Fander is my heir. What I wonder is the extent of your knowledge of Anferthian reliquaries?"

"I know that they are sacred to your people, and they are family specific, and may even hold power."

He nodded. "Yes, they are sacred and family specific. There is also a certain amount of power within them; however, that's not relevant today. As I said, Fander is my heir and will inherit the contents of my reliquary when I die. Have you ever seen one?"

"A couple of times." The first one she'd seen was when she visited Uncle Nick and Aunt Sakura at the Anferthian dissenters' sanctuary on Matir. One of the dissenters, Storo, had taken a bullet in the shoulder and had removed his shirt so Uncle Nick could heal him. Fander's had been the second, the day he'd rescued her from the ocean. In both cases she hadn't realized the importance of the pendants. Even now, she still knew very little.

"Is that so?" Grandfather K'nil's keen black eyes sparkled with interest. His hand opened to reveal the pendant hidden in his fist.

It wasn't exactly like Fander's or Storo's, but it was similar. A long tubular crystal capped at each end with filigree metal work. The liquid inside, if that's what the swirling contents could be called, was seafoam green and silver. "Why's yours green and Fander's red and gold?"

Collision

Hopefully Fander wouldn't get in trouble for letting her see his. She met his grandfather's gaze and saw amusement. A good sign.

"Fander's reliquary came from his father."

The man who had died when Fander was barely old enough to walk. "Oh."

Grandfather lifted the chain over his head and handed it to her. "Go on," he encouraged when she hesitated. "It is quite all right for you to touch it. It will not hurt you, I promise."

There was no resisting the lure of the relic. It was as if it called to her. She pinched the pewter-color chain between her thumb and finger and lifted it from his wide palm. The soft green liquid swirled and eddied within the tubular vial.

"It contains my family's history," Grandfather murmured. "Generations of history. I need you to promise me something, Flora. Now do not look so wary, it is nothing terrible I will ask of you."

He leaned forward and covered her hands between his own, his reliquary pressed between her palms. It was warm, and the warmth seeped into her hands and up her wrists. He said something, but she couldn't understand his words. His kind eyes were deep black and compelling, impossible to look away from. So different from Fander's, yet they carried that same spark of light that she associated with Fander.

Unintelligible words washed over her, and the warmth crept through her body, comforting and strengthening her.

"Do you think you could do that for me, *fyhen*?"

"Um." She blinked and shook her head. "I'm sorry, do what?"

"Here, allow me to take this back." He lifted his reliquary from her fingers and the fog in her brain faded and whisked away.

"What...what just happened?"

He chuckled as he looped the chain back over his head and tucked the pendant away under his shirt. "I believe my ancestors took a liking to you. It happens, not to worry. What I asked was if something should happen to me—specifically, should I die and Fander is not here—would you be my custodian and make sure my reliquary is delivered safely into his hands?"

"I can do that? But, I'm not Anferthian."

Grandfather K'nil raised his brows. "One does not need to be Anferthian to help an Anferthian."

"Oh, well. That's not what I meant."

"No, it was not." He sat up straighter. "To answer your question, I may choose whoever I want as the custodian of my reliquary, so long as they agree. I choose you. Will you do this for me?"

This was something she'd never heard of before, and his expression alone implied that it was a great honor. How could she say no? "Of course, I will, Grandfather K'nil. Not that you'll ever need me to."

"I am not getting any younger, Flora, and because of this I find myself becoming more pragmatic." His expression turned wistful. "Where do the years go?" He shook his head. "Ah, but that is the lament of the elderly. You have become quite an exceptional young lady, and that is what we celebrate this day. Happy birthday, granddaughter."

"Thank you, grandfather."

"Now, tell me about your *rywoud*."

The vestiges of her dream rose to the surface, along with a fresh wave of nausea. She cast a quick glance around the room. Not a bathroom in sight.

"Do you not feel well, Flora?"

She gave him a bleak look.

Two vertical lines appeared between his grey brows. "It was upsetting, I can see."

"The beginning was. There was lots of blood and intense grief." Gut-wrenching, soul-crushing grief. She glanced down at her hands, then back at him. "I saw Fander, though, and he was alive, which was the best part. It was like he was right there with me…up until a giant, disembodied hand tried to strangle me. I woke up gasping for air, and then I threw up."

Grandfather's eyes widened. Had her dream alarmed him? Why did it feel like things were about to go haywire? There were few things in life she didn't like. Feeling out of control was one of them, and this dream had left her grasping at the side of a cliff for a toehold. But, years ago, this wonderful man had taught her that by sharing her fears she could minimize their power over her.

"When you say giant hand, am I correct in assuming it was Anferthian?"

"I don't know. It looked kind of grey, not green. And it started out small then grew to about the size of your hand."

He seemed to ponder this, a faint horizontal crease across his forehead. "I will share with you that you and Fander continue to share elements of your dreamings, which does not surprise me, given your unique friendship."

"After my first *rywoud*, Fander told me that he'd never heard of that happening even between Anferthians. So, how could a Terrian share the dreaming?"

"*Rywoud* serves as a guide to our lives." He kept his words careful and measured. "It is not common, yet it is possible for two people to be bound closely enough that they will share elements of each other's dreamings. I personally believe this applies even if one of them is not Anferthian."

So, it was possible, but rare.

He clapped his hands over his thighs. "I have your new assignment out in the office. Would you like to see it now?"

If anything could distract her from her current thoughts, that was it. Excitement bubbled through her. "*Yes.*"

Once they had returned to the study, Grandfather made straight for his huge keyhole desk, picked up the large envelope on top, and handed it to her. "Go on. Open it."

This was it. She took the envelope with both hands and stared at it as butterflies fluttered in her stomach. Her future was inside. She ran her fingers over the seal and it opened. If she didn't stop trembling she'd never get the paper out. She grasped the edge of the page inside and gave it a firm tug. It slid out.

She blinked at the words. The neatly printed words were Anferthian. Did that mean…? She scanned down.

"Your assignment as Terrian Junior Ambassador to Anferthia has been approved by the Terrian Council."

Anferthia. She was going to Anferthia, not Agbahd X, or anywhere else. She raised her gaze.

Grandfather was as close to literally beaming as any being could be. "This pleases you?"

A sense of joy blossomed in her chest, its fizzing jubilance racing down to her finger tips and toes. She hugged the paper to her chest. "I'm going to *Anferthia*." In a year, she'd see Fander again. "I had hoped, but really didn't expect it."

"My confidence in you is great, Flora. I would not have agreed if I did not believe you were ready for this challenge." He spread his hands out from his sides. "Besides, your Anferthian is beautifully fluent in speaking, reading, and writing. You have done well with your lessons with K'rona."

The praise for her hard work glowed in her heart. It wouldn't surprise her if she looked down and discovered she was floating six inches off the floor. This had to be the best birthday ever. "Thank you."

"But, now your Anferthian education begins in earnest. There is much you must understand, and some of it will surprise you." He turned away toward the floor-to-ceiling book case behind his desk and pulled a large, burgundy-bound tome out and handed it to her. "There are things we must discuss."

NINE

Flora set her assignment on top of the desk and moved around it to accept the book. It weighed less than she'd expected, but it was awkwardly sized. A little larger than the Scottish Highlands coffee table book her birth-mother used to have. How weird she'd think of that now.

She ran her fingertips over the inset gold Anferthian lettering. "The Anferthian Royal Family? I heard they were all killed when the Arruch Union seized control."

A timid knock sounded on the door and Grandfather chuckled. "I do believe Mrs. Beck has once again arrived with too many muffins and not enough hands to open the door. We will begin your first history lesson after she is finished fussing over us, if that is agreeable to you."

"Sure." She brought the book up to her nose and inhaled the scent of leather and paper. Why did real books always smell so good?

The sound of the door opening was followed by the soft whisper of a *telum* discharging. She jerked her head up. Six more shots hissed out and Grandfather tottered back a step, then crumpled to the floor. A scream of horror and denial welled up in her throat. She slapped her hand over her mouth. If she let it out, she'd give herself away to whoever had just shot Grandfather. She had to stay alive if for no other reason than to help him.

She lowered herself into a crouch behind the desk and creeped forward into the leg opening of the desk. It was almost five feet across and high enough for Grandfather to sit at comfortably. More than enough space for her to fit and get a clear view of at least half the office...including an unobstructed view of Grandfather's burgundy blood pumping from his wounds and staining the rug. At least his chest still moved in time with his labored breaths. Seven shots were a lot for an Anferthian to take, even from a weapon as small as a *telum*.

Long, black-clad feminine legs came into view, and judging by their slim size, they did not belong to an Anferthian. Whoever it was stepped stealthily around Grandfather, almost as if looking for someone.

The heavy sensation of a rock sinking into Flora's stomach hit her. The book she'd left on the desk wouldn't give away her presence, but the document with her new assignment would. If she survived this, Uncle Graig was going to ream her a new one for being so careless.

The shooter's booted feet turned toward the desk, followed by a throaty chuckle. Definitely female, and smaller than herself. But, armed and dangerous. Flora clamped down on the panic rising in her chest as the shapely legs carried the killer closer. She cast her gaze around the underside of the desk opening. There; a small, unassuming alarm button was attached to the left side.

In one fluid motion, the intruder crouched down and peered through the keyhole leg opening at her. Dammit. She had a hood over her head, one that was too deep to make out any facial features, even in the daylight. Who the hell was she?

"So, your assignment was to be Anferthia?" The softly accented words were spoken with a purr. Almost friendly, gentle, and in sharp contrast to violence she'd just wreaked. "It is a shame you will never make it there. Someone wants you dead pretty badly, did you know?"

That was news to her. She ran her tongue over her lips. "Who?"

Another chuckle. "A Nightshade never reveals their hires. You must know that."

Whoa. Someone had hired a Nightshade assassin to kill *her*? And Nightshades never gave up until their mark was dead. That was common knowledge. Well, this mark wasn't going down without a fight. Today was her *birth*day, not her death day.

The assassin raised the *telum* in her black-gloved hand. Flora slammed her hand against the button and a shrill screech filled the air like a raptor scream only fifty times louder. Then she launched herself from under the desk, shoulder-slamming into the smaller woman and carrying her backward into a fragile tea table. The spindly legs shattered, and the crystal vase of pink cabbage roses slid over the edge, dumping its contents on the white velvet upholstered chair next to it.

The advantage of size and the element of surprise had worked. Flora rolled away, gaining her feet. The Nightshade was already up, but her hood had been knocked askew, revealing her face. A Matiran! About Mama's age, with blue hair and mesmerizing eyes the color of the Caribbean Sea. Flora flicked her gaze down at the woman's hand. How in God's name had she managed to hold onto her *telum*? The assassin raised the weapon for what could be the killing shot. But, not today. Flora lashed out a foot, connecting hard with the elegant wrist. The deadly weapon spun from the woman's grip.

Their gazes locked. The assassin cradled her injured wrist. There was no room for mercy now. Flora snatched the book on Anferthian royalty off the desk and swung it like a baseball bat at the woman's face.

Crack!

Amazing how incredibly satisfying the sound of cartilage crunching in an assassin's nose could be. The woman staggered back a step, a stunned expression on her not-quite-as-gorgeous-anymore face. A bloodied and shattered nose did tend to detract from physical beauty. But, honest-to-God, she must have exceptional will-power, and a high tolerance for pain, to still be standing.

Air hissed through the assassin's clenched teeth, and her gaze darted to where her weapon lay fifteen feet away.

Flora brandished the book at her. "Don't even think about it. I'll break your back before you can reach it."

Seething hatred filled the aqua-marine eyes. "Well played, ***princess***."

The woman flicked her good wrist, and something flashed in the air between them.

Bang!

Blackness filled the room. A shock grenade. Instinctively, Flora hit the floor as something zinged passed her ear, slicing the air with a deadly whisper.

It seemed like endless minutes for the sensory-deadening effect of the grenade to clear. When it did, the woman was gone.

Where the hell were the ambassador's personal guards?

"Grandfather!" She crawled to the ambassador's side.

His eyes were open, and he was still breathing shallowly. But, the blood...*his* blood. It was all over, and more flowed from the gaping holes over his heart. A single *kagi*, the projectile a *telum* shot, was normally more of a nuisance to Anferthians unless they hit a vital organ. But, multiple shots to the heart....

"I'll get a healer—" She started to rise.

"No," Grandfather whispered. "Granddaughter."

He was beyond the help of a healer; the rattle in his breathing confirmed her suspicion. Not even Mama or Uncle Dante could do anything to stop the inevitable.

"I don't want to lose you." Her voice broke with a sob.

"Reliquary...."

What was the tradition when an Anferthian was dying? Did they need to see it? That didn't sound like anything she'd read, but if it was important enough for him to ask, she'd make that happen for him. Her hands trembled as she reached under his collar of his *wysgog* and tugged on the silver chain until his reliquary came free.

"Hold...in your hand," he told her between breaths. "Good. Now...call Fander."

"Call him?" The reliquary warmed at her touch. "You mean just say his name?"

"Yes."

She took a steadying breath in and blew it out. Here went nothing. "Fander."

Her vision abruptly narrowed, and she was speeding through a narrow tube toward a distant pinpoint of light. Blackness, stars, and planets swept passed her, even though she still sat next to Fander's grandfather in his study on Terr. The pinpoint expanded...a planet, night shadows of trees and buildings, hallway, door....

All forward motion came to a disconcerting stop, and the echo of her voice called out again. A completely different room superimposed itself over the study. A dark room with no lights on. Shadows separated themselves out in the dimness. What the hell was she looking at? Dressers? Bed posts? Someone's bedroom?

Collision

A wave of dizziness washed over her, and her stomach threatened to rebel. She closed her eyes to shut out the study. It *was* a bedroom, and she seemed to be sitting up in the middle of a huge bed, her unusually long legs tenting a sheet. That couldn't be right. Her legs were really tucked under her as she knelt next to Grandfather. So, whose legs were they?

"Flora?" The deep, rich voice had a slight echo. A voice she hadn't heard in nearly a decade.

"Fander?" She breathed his name out in a sigh. How was this possible?

"Yes, it is me, but, how did you—"

A sob escaped her. "It's Grandfather, Fander, he's been shot. I don't...I think.... Oh, God."

He's dying, and you aren't here.

"Flora, listen to me." Fander's voice wrapped around her, comforting and compelling at the same time. "Open your eyes so I can see what's happening there."

You don't want to see.

She forced her lids up anyway. It was worse than before she'd closed them. Grandfather's breathing had slowed, and his face was a pale, chalky-grey. Her gaze moved to the gaping wounds in his chest.

"*A nat!*" Fander swore, threw off the covers, and swung his bare legs out of his bed. Both rooms spun around her like an out of control merry-go-round.

"Fander, *stop moving*."

"There's blood all over you, Flora!" She'd never heard him sound this close to panic. "Were you shot, too?"

"No. I'm okay." Except for her stomach, which was ready to upchuck what little breakfast she'd eaten before she'd left her cube.

A large hand appeared and closed around a bedpost at eye-level, and then only the study filled her vision. "I closed my eyes. Is this better?"

"Yes." So much easier to have one stationary room to deal with.

"Where is the killer?"

"She escaped." Two spots of heat burned her cheeks. If only she'd been able to detain the woman.

"Are you *sure* she's gone?" His voice sounded strained.

"I'm sure. But, I broke her nose before she got away, and I have her *telum*."

There was a soft rustle of cloth behind her and she whirled, pointing the *telum* at the three Anferthians hovering in the doorway. How long had the ambassador's guards been standing there?

Kapit Tymo held up one hand at the three soldiers behind her. "Move not; she is in trance."

In trance? Was that what she was doing?

Kapit Tymo kneeled on the other side of Grandfather, subtly taking his vitals even though she must know he was dying. "Who do you converse with, Flora of Terr?"

"Fander." Her voice cracked with grief and she gripped Grandfather's cold hand. "Help him, please."

Tymo's eyes widened. She pressed her left palm over her heart and bowed her head. "My prince."

"Flora." Fander's no-nonsense tone snapped her out of her conversation with the captain of the guard. "Look at Grandfather, now. That's it. What I'm going to do next will be weird for you, but I am going to use your voice to talk to him, okay?"

"Okay." How the hell was he going to accomplish that trick?

She met Grandfather's gaze and a lump the size of a tennis ball rose in her throat, threatening to cut off her air supply. His skin was a mottled green-grey and his normally lively eyes were sunken and dull.

"I am here, Grandfather." Fander's words came out of her mouth, in Anferthian. That answered her question, and he was right, it was weird.

Grandfather's gaze met hers…or Fander's…and his mouth moved. "The path is set, Grandson. It is…well."

"I understand and accept." Fander's strained words came from her mouth again. "May your journey be one of peace. Until we meet again, Grandfather."

A tear fell free of her eyelashes and splashed on Grandfather's shoulder as his gaze moved toward the ceiling. His chest deflated with an expelled breath and the light left his eyes.

Another sob caught in her throat. "He's gone."

A low vibration came from Fander across the vastness of space between them. He roared his grief in the traditional Anferthian manner. The same urge rose within her. Kapit Tymo's hands clamped around hers, securing her grip around the reliquary. Flora tipped her head back and joined her voice with Fander's. Then she was surrounded by Anferthian mourning cries from the ambassador's guards. Death to them was a sacred moment, and to bear witness to the passing of another was an honor.

Fander's howl tapered off. "Be strong, Flora," he whispered. "I will be with you soon, *tangol*."

"Fander." Her voice sounded like a pathetic whimper, but she was drained of every emotion other than a sense of finality.

Fander's presence faded, along with his darkened bedroom. She covered her face with her hands, leaned forward, and let her anguish flow with her tears.

Ten

Fander bowed his head and pushed back against the black emptiness at his core. If he did not, the hollowness would consume him. He rested his forehead against the hand still gripping the bedpost and touched his other hand to his aching chest. This must be similar to what his mother had felt when his father was murdered by Isel T'orr. In some ways, it was good he had no memory of that time. His mother was a remarkable woman, having survived the loss of her *tangol*, yet still finding the strength to save the life of her son.

Now, Grandfather was dead, and Flora…if only they could stay connected through the reliquaries until he arrived on Terr. But it was not safe, most especially for her. Had she been the assassin's ultimate target and Grandfather just a victim of circumstance? Or was Grandfather the intended target?

Either way, this tragedy marked the end of waiting. Up until this point, Flora's safety had been the duty of others. Now more than ever, everything he said, every action he took, would hang their lives on a greater balance.

A faint swoosh of air being displaced came as the door between his chambers and those of his guard reached his ears.

"My prince?"

Fander opened his eyes. "Nor, please do not call me such unless you wish me dead."

"Never would I wish this upon you, Fander." Nor Danol's voice was a low murmur in the darkness. "You are the hope of our people, even if they do not realize it yet."

No, Nor's loyalty was never in doubt. Despite their age difference of nearly a decade, his personal guard, friend, and confidant would lay down his own life first.

A shadowy bulk detached from the doorway and moved into the room. "Did I imagine you called out to raise the soul of another? Has something happened?"

The icy hand of fear clamped around his heart. "How loud was I?" If anyone of the Arruch spies in the household had heard him, it was possible they'd figure out he had been in contact with someone on Terr.

"Loud enough to wake me."

He suppressed a curse and tipped his head to one side to listen. No sound of commotion from the passageway outside. No footsteps sneaking away on the other side of the heavy door.

"What has happened, Fander?"

A lump of lead rose into his throat and he swallowed hard. "Grandfather has been assassinated."

Nor gasped. "The Arruch would not stoop so low, would they?"

"They did kill my father." But that was not evidence that they were behind Grandfather's murder. There was no way to be sure. He would have pressed Flora for details had he been thinking clearly. No, that was not so. Keeping the connection open increased the chances the Arruch would discover him in the midst of an unauthorized communication and realize how much she really meant to him.

But what if they had already figured it out? He pushed away from the bedpost to pace the floor at his bedside. "I cannot even go to Mother to let her know and grieve with her." Not until "official" word came. Curse them all, it was *her* father whose link had fallen from the golden chain of life this day. She deserved to know.

The weight of a strong hand clamped onto his shoulder, stopping him mid-pace. He looked up at Nor's shadowed face. No colors could be seen in the darkness, yet he could imagine the compassion in the older man's pale blue eyes. "Fander, the time of your majority is near. Do not lose your vision now."

"*She* was with him."

"Who?"

"Flora."

Nor's grip tightened. "Is she…?"

"She lives. And somehow she was able to use Grandfather's reliquary to reach me." Which made no sense at all. "She was deeply shaken."

"She used his reliquary? I have never heard of such happening before." There was wonder in the guard's voice, then Nor shook him by the shoulder hard enough for his teeth to clack together. "She is your equal, your *tangol* is. Anferthia will be blessed to have her at your side through what is to come."

If she accepted her role. Many Terrians did not believe in pre-destiny and were not known to be reasonable when it was thrust upon them. Sometimes even those who did believe could be equally stubborn. It was unfortunate that his *tangol* was the most stubborn soul he knew.

If only Grandfather and Flora's parents had changed their minds and told her the truth, about *tangol and* about him, but they had refused, despite his urging. They believed in their hearts that withholding the information until the right time was the safest course of action. While he had understood their intentions, he had never agreed.

But, there was another facet to their relationship. He lifted his fingers to his lips. Unfinished business between them. He would never deny his soul-deep certainty that the two of them were meant to be together as more than *tangol*. Flora would be spitting mad once all was revealed. Possibly angry enough to turn her back on her destiny, and on him.

The abrupt lack of weight on his shoulder pulled his attention away from his musings. Nor stepped back a pace. "Will you accept my fealty now, my pri…my lord?"

Fander gave his head a shake. "Still too soon, my friend. If it all goes awry, and you are asked if you swore an oath to me, you must be able to say no truthfully. You must stay alive to carry on our work."

"As you command." There was a definite disgruntled edge to Nor's words, but he would not waiver in his duty.

"Thank you." Fander blew out a gusty sigh. "There is nothing to do now but wait for my keepers to see fit to inform me of the tragedy on Terr. Sleep well, Nor."

The other man touched his palm to his chest. "You too, my

lord."

That would not be possible. At this time, sleep held little appeal. No, the rest of this night would be spent praying for Grandfather's soul and Flora's safety.

The dirty rat-fink Supreme Warden Tusayn was trying to pin Grandfather's death on *her*. Flora shuddered and dug her fingernails into the edge of the satin-upholstered chair facing the ambassador's desk.

The hologram image of Supreme Warden Tusayn stood in front of the desk, feet braced apart and hands behind his back as he glared down his oh-so-arrogant nose at her. "Answer the question. Why did the guards not see anyone leave the ambassador's cube?"

"I. Don't. Know." God, she needed to get out of here, go home to where she would be safe with her family. And cry a great big, gulping breaths, ugly kind of cry. "She had a hood on—"

"You *claimed* she was Matiran."

"She *was*."

Kapit Tymo cleared her throat. "If I may—"

"You may *not*." The supreme warden didn't even bother to look over his shoulder to where Tymo stood at attention behind the desk.

A soft gasp from the doorway drew Flora's attention away from her interrogator.

"Oh, my God, Flora." Maggie's gaze went from the blood-soaked rug to her and back. Thank God the guards had already removed Grandfather's body.

"Who is this...*person*?" Tusayn waved his hand in Maggie's direction.

"This is my daughter, Supreme Warden." Poppy stepped into the room. Everything about him from his tone to his stance appeared ready for a battle. Yet, for some odd reason, a wave of calm clarity rolled over her.

"She does not belong here."

"Yes, I do." Maggie didn't even spare a glance for the supreme warden as she tromped across the room toward her. "Are you hurt?"

"A little bruised. Nothing Mama can't fix." She leaned into her sister's one-armed hug of support. Her family was here. She wasn't alone anymore.

Tusayn lifted his chin and wrinkled his nose as if he'd just caught whiff of a foul order. "The people of Anferthia demand an investigation, by our *own* representatives."

"Of course." Poppy inclined his head. "The ambassador's body is being attended to by his guards. I will personally oversee the sealing of his cube so nothing is disturbed prior to your investigation. We will also provide a venue for your delegation to question the witness."

"She will be brought to Anferthia for questioning."

"She. Will. Not." Poppy's tone was so frigid the air in the room seemed cooler.

Tusayn's mouth tightened. "Very well, Admiral—"

"Senior Admiral."

"*Senior* Admiral." The man's rust color gaze met hers. "Minister of Justice S'gow's delegation will be there within seven galactic standard days."

The hologram image blinked out of existence. Finally, she could release the rigid control and allow her emotions to surface. A shiver shook her body to its core and a chill crawled into the marrow of her bones.

"It's going to be okay, sis." Maggie wrapped both arms around her.

It didn't feel okay, but she gave her head a nod anyway as her teeth clattered together.

Poppy drew up a chair on the other side of her. "The shock is settling in now, *cori*. Do you think you can walk to our cube? Mama is there waiting for you."

"I th-think s-so." Her gaze was drawn to where Grandfather K'nil's body had been, just inside the doorway. He was gone. Really gone. Tears stung her eyes.

"I beg your forgiveness, Lady Flora." Kapit Tymo still stood in front of the bookcase behind the giant desk. "This blade, is it familiar to you?"

Flora stared at the aquamarine knife handle protruding from the spine of a book. That must have been what flew passed her ear after the assassin deployed the shock grenade. It was a good thing she'd ducked. "It l-looks like the knife in m-my dream." But this wasn't a dream anymore, it was all too real. Death, blood, soul wrenching loss.

Crease lines formed between Tymo's brows. "Your dream? Please explain."

"I've r-received *rywoud* s-since my f-fifteenth birthday." It would be nice if she could stop shivering long enough to answer the kapit's questions without stuttering.

Tymo's expression turned thoughtful. "How long is the blade, to your thinking?" Her English wasn't perfect, but it was a sign of respect that she used it instead of a translator.

"Probably as long as m-my hand, from wr-rist to my longest finger." She held up her hand. It of course chose that moment to shake uncontrollably. "L-like eight inches, or t-twenty *timits*." Which was about the equivalent of Terr's centimeters.

Poppy's hand tightened slightly on her shoulder. "Flora, I know this has been difficult, but can you give me more of a description of the assassin? I promise not to cut you off the way the supreme warden did."

Tusayn had cut her off, but he'd seemed more focused on hanging her than getting any real information about anything. "Sure. Sh-she looked like she was-s somewhere b-between your age and M-mama's. Tall—Mama's height—with b-blue hair, and eyes the exact c-color of that knife handle. And she was really p-pretty too. Before I broke her nose."

The corners of Poppy's mouth pulled downward. "Kapit Tymo, I believe a person of interest in your investigation is Haesi Velo, originally of Matir."

Why did that name seem familiar?

The kapit nodded. "Thank you, Senior Admiral."

"Flora?"

She met Poppy's deep blue gaze and the desire to be a little girl and crawl into his lap for comfort engulfed her. Her vision blurred.

"Shh, *cori*." Poppy dabbed her cheeks with a cloth and another wave of calm washed over her. "While I'm very proud of you for defending yourself today, you will be staying with your mother and me for the time being. Maggie, too."

"But—"

Tymo stepped around the desk. "I agree, Senior Admiral. My lady, Flora, this day no is good for you. A moment and I will arrange an escort."

"But—" This really wasn't necessary.

"Thank you, Kapit." Poppy straightened.

Tymo stopped in the doorway and met her gaze. "Regret is mine that my mentor, Ambassador K'nil, lost his life today. You are his *fyhen* and important therefore to my people. To protect you until his family arrives is my honor. My patrols I place in your service until your safety we feel is no longer at risk."

Flora shook her head. "Th-that's okay. You d-don't have to."

Tymo placed her palm to her chest and made a slight bow. "This we have discussed. It will be done for Anferthia."

Poppy leaned close to her ear. "Accept their protection, *cori*. You will need them."

"Um." Well, it couldn't hurt to have extra protection. "Thank you, Kapit Tymo. Your offer is generous, and I accept."

Flora sank to her chin in the steaming tub, the heat of the water seeped into her muscles. Leaving the ambassador's residence had been a miserable experience. Poppy and Maggie had guided her to the front door where another, redder, pool of blood was being cleaned by two guards. Mrs. Beck's blood, as it'd turned out. The assassin had killed the sweet lady before making her way to Grandfather's office.

Crossing that threshold had been like crossing out of the life she'd known into a bleak, uncertain future. Of course, her body's immediate response to this change had been to bend over and puke in the flower bed. Within full view of her escort, who waited in the yard. But, there had been no censured looks from the three Anferthian soldiers, only sympathy and understanding.

Mama had met them at the front door of their cube, led her to the bathroom, and helped peel her out of her blood-splattered clothes. Maggie had taken the Anferthian guards back to the cube they shared to grab some things, but Mama stayed and helped her bathe, all the while humming *Come Take a Trip in My Airship*. The childhood tune had soothed and calmed her frayed nerves, which was probably why Mama had hummed it.

Why did things seem so much simpler when she was a kid? If only she could roll herself into those memories and forget all of today's horror and violence.

"Ready, sweetie?" Mama held up a huge bath towel.

"I can still smell the blood." Even after scrubbing her body and her hair twice, the metallic odor was still there. Like it was stuck in her nostrils.

"I can turn off your olfactory senses for a while if you'd like."

"God, that'd be great."

Mama touched the tip of her finger to Flora's nose. The blood odor disappeared, along with the scents of soap, shampoo, and bubble bath. It was like she'd turned off a switch.

"Thank you, Mama." She rose, and the warm water sluiced down her body and legs. "I'm ready for a nap now."

Her mother wrapped the towel and guided her to the guest room. "Maggie's back and brought your favorite jammies."

Flora couldn't help but smile at the sight of her sky-blue P.J.s laid out on the bed. She had the best kid sister ever.

A few minutes later, she was dressed and under the covers.

"*Dormio?*" Mama asked, her hand poised ready to put her into a healing sleep.

"Just a few hours, and no dreams, okay?"

Her mother smiled. "Exactly what your healer ordered."

"Mama?"

"Hm?"

"He's coming back." She allowed herself a sleepy smile.

"I know he is, sweetie." Mama brushed her fingers over her forehead. "Sleep."

Eleven

"What are you doing, Fander?"

None of your business, T'orr.

Even if he had not left Anferthia without T'orr's permission, he still would not say those words out loud. It was a wonder that it had taken two days for the tyrant to discover his absence.

Fander forced himself to stare complacently at the divine warden's image on the vid-comm desktop screen. "Accompanying my mother to Terr."

Isel quirked an eyebrow. "Manners, son."

I am not your *son.*

"Accompanying my mother to Terr, my lord." Gods, he despised this sham.

"I do not recall authorizing you to do so."

He ducked his head as though contrite. "Forgive me, Divine One. Grandfather is *fyhen*. I did not think to ask your permission to travel to Terr to retrieve his body."

T'orr tapped one finger against his desk, holding Fander's gaze with his own. This stare-down was the divine warden's usual way of weakening his opponent's confidence. Good thing he did not realize his ploy had not affected Fander in years.

Finally, T'orr nodded. "I suppose your mother is distraught, as usual."

"Very." A movement at the edge of his vision nearly drew a laugh from him. His mother clutched her hands over her heart and sank back against the couch with a dramatic flourish. If T'orr only knew.

"Fani was ever so weak. How she became *ymere* I have yet to comprehend."

There were many things the son-of-a-dung-eel would never comprehend. Like the fact that his parents were *tangol* and a love match. And that Fani K'nil was far more brilliant than he gave her credit for.

The brilliant former *ymere* slid sideways on the couch in a mock faint.

Fander swallowed hard against the laugh lodged in his chest. "As you say, my lord."

T'orr sighed. "I do understand why you left without consulting me, Fander. Grief can lead to rash decisions, but I will not order you to return, even though you are only two days into your journey. Ambassador K'nil was your grandfather, and it is your right to escort his body home. Anferthia waits to receive him into our embrace."

You are not Anferthia, T'orr.

That was the honor and responsibility of the ruling B'aq *ymero* or *ymere*. Killing *Ymero* Zular B'aq twenty-three years ago did not automatically grant the honor to Isel T'orr. As the only child of the murdered *ymero*, it fell to him. He was Fander K'nil B'aq.

He was Anferthia.

Flora stretched, the friction of her cool sheets against her too taut skin sending a shudder through her. It'd been this way since she'd spoken to Fander through Grandfather's reliquary. Sleeping naked was less irritating than wearing her pajamas.

She slipped her hand under her pillow until her fingers bumped against the mysterious pendant. Still there and safe, waiting to be turned over to its "heir" once he arrived. She squinted at the hour displayed on her data device. "Fifth hour *already*?"

That was like ten in the morning by Terr standard time. Way past time to get her lazy butt out of bed. For someone under house arrest for the last four days, she sure had been sleeping a lot. Damn Supreme Warden Tusayn for demanding the Terrian Council take her into custody. It wasn't any surprise they'd denied the request, but they did ask her to stay put in her parents' home until the Anferthian delegation arrived. And in a further attempt to keep the peace, the Matiran government had requested Poppy take a leave of absence until the situation was settled, which he did. But now he was home all the time and ready to tear down the walls from sheer frustration. Poppy was a doer, not a sideline observer. He was also the calm parent. Usually Mama was the first to explode. It was as if they'd swapped roles.

Well, there were only three days left before the Anferthians…correction, the *Arruch* delegation arrived. They had to make it work.

And Fander. He'd be with the Panel of Justice. Maybe he'd be *on* the panel and able to keep them from doing something crazy, like executing her. Okay, execution might be a little dramatic, but what *could* she expect from them?

That was always the first question that sucked her into a whirlpool of dread every morning. She kicked off the covers and rolled to sit on the edge of her bed. This morning would be different. There *had* to be a distraction to keep her from wallowing in the unknown future ahead. Sewing, maybe? No. Her creative muse wasn't feeling it. Maggie was probably still out making her rounds, so talking to her sister would have to wait.

What to do? What to do? Her gaze fell on the newest addition to her bookshelf. The book Grandfather gave her just before he'd died. Her heart hadn't really been into reading it since then, but it *was* a distraction. And, he wouldn't have given it to her as a shelf decoration.

She blew out a sigh. "Fine."

A few minutes later, she sat cross-legged in the middle of her bed and flipped open the cover. Page after page of writing and images of Anferthians she'd never seen before. *Ymere* H'feli B'aq, *Ymero* Emyr B'aq. *Ymero* K'mar B'aq. All of them had the same last name, even the women. Weird, but it seemed like it wasn't necessarily the eldest child who inherited the royal title. Did they pick the next leader by a certain skill set? Or by a vote of the people?

She flipped through to the back of the book. "Ooh, a family tree."

Those were always fun to go through. Who married whom. How many children they had. It didn't look like any children were ever named after their ancestors. And this particular genealogy only followed those lines that inherited. For pages, and pages. She flipped to the last page. Ten, to be exact. She allowed her gaze to saunter down the lines of lineage to the last couple.

"Zular B'aq and Fani K'nil." A relative of Grandfather's, maybe? "And their son, Fander B'aq." Huh. Another Fander. What were the odds?

Her gaze flicked up again. Fani K'nil. Fander B'aq. K'nil. Fander B'aq....

Fander K'nil?

"*What the ever-loving fuck?*"

"You. Are. Fucking. Kidding. Me." Flora gaped at her parents.

Mama's lips flattened as if she was trying not to scold her for her language. But, god dammit, this was swear-worthy news. Fander was the fucking heir-apparent—the *crown prince* of fucking Anferthia!

The prince who was supposed to have been killed when the Arruch took over, but was apparently still very much alive. "You two are as good at keeping secrets as the Arruch."

Uncle Graig cleared his throat. "That's my cue to leave."

Poppy narrowed a glare at him. "Leave well-enough alone, Graig, and go home to Simone."

Uncle Graig set his jaw, the way he did whenever something happened that he didn't like or agree with. Obviously, she'd barged into the middle of a standoff between her father and her uncle. But she wasn't going to back down now and wait her turn. This was too important.

"I'll give Simone your regards." Uncle Graig stalked out the back door without saying good-bye.

Poppy frowned, then turned his attention back to her. "There are very few non-Anferthians who know that two members of the royal family are still alive, *cori*."

"But *you* knew. And so did Mama."

"Indeed."

"Why didn't you tell me?"

"We couldn't."

"Argh." She pushed her fingers into her hair. "I can't believe this. Why the hell is it such a big secret?"

"To protect you," Mama said.

"That's such bullshit."

Poppy slammed his palm on the table. "You will stop swearing at us immediately, Flora. We have done nothing to warrant such abuse."

A snort escaped her before she could think twice about it. Mama and Poppy didn't react. She looked at them, really *looked*, for the first time in what seemed like forever. There was only fifteen years difference between her and her mother, twenty-three between her and Poppy, yet it suddenly seemed like much more. Her father's hair had turned silver at the temples. In a few years it'd all be silver, just like Grandpa Zale's. Mama was only a couple of years away from forty and even she had strands of grey threading through her dark hair.

Those signs of aging weren't just because of the work they did to keep the peace between three worlds. Some of it was from raising three children. Three orphans. Three lost souls who'd needed someone to love them, care for them. Defend and protect them.

And here she was practically screaming at them for doing what they'd promised to do the day they'd become a family. God, she was a creep.

She sat down heavily on a chair. "I'm sorry. But, I'm really pissed about this."

Her parents exchanged a glance then Mama leaned forward across the table and slid her hands over Flora's. "We really do understand, Flora. And you can go right on being pissed, but you still need to understand why we made the choices we made."

"*Cori*, do you understand the Anferthian word *tangol*?"

One thing her parents always had been was a team. And right now, they were as together as they'd ever been. "It sounds like heart…burn? No, fire."

"Heart fire is correct. Most Anferthians have another in their lives that they share an irreversible bond with. The one person they are closer to than even their *fyhen*. They live and die for each other."

"Okay, so?"

"Fander met his *tangol* when he was eleven and she was ten."

She was ten when she'd met…. All the oxygen rushed from her lungs. "Fander? *Me?*"

Her parents nodded in unison.

"Ambassador K'nil met with us the next day, in my office, and explained it to us," Poppy added.

"Right after I took Fander to see Uncle Dante." The incident seemed like a lifetime ago now. "Does Fander know?"

"We don't know. Fynn never told us," Mama said. "He's a sharp young man, though, so it wouldn't surprise me if he figured it out on his own. But, here's the thing, Flora. We think someone else may have figured it out, and that's why Haesi Velo was hired to kill you."

Her jaw went slack, and she gaped at her parents. Well, that sure put things into perspective. "I'm going to my room, now. Just leave me alone. I...I need to think about this."

Twelve

An odd sense of déjà vu wrapped around Flora as she watched the transport carrying Fander and the members of the Anferthian Panel of Justice descend through the fog to the tarmac. This time, Mama and Poppy flanked her with Kapit Tymo and the loyal Anferthian ambassador's guard around them. Uncle Graig stood at the edge of the field with a handful of his students, including Gunner Reed and some United Defense Fleet personnel. And Aunt Simone, who'd apparently refused to stay home.

At least it wasn't unbearably hot this time.

The rush of air stirred up from the landing swirled and tugged at her *wysgog*. She hadn't had many opportunities to wear the Anferthian-style outfit and putting it on today was a calculated risk. But, it was her way of honoring Anferthian customs, and completely appropriate as a future junior ambassador to the planet. The minister of justice probably wouldn't agree, though.

An opening appeared in the side of the transport and a ramp extended until it rested on the tarmac. Figures moved down the ramp, Minister S'gow in front. Flora's heart thumped in her chest. What was she going to say to Fander? She searched for him, but the group all appeared to be the same height.

"I don't see him, Mama."

"I don't either." Mama frowned.

Flora caught her bottom lip between her teeth. Had they left him on board? "You don't think they made him stay inside, do you?"

"No." Poppy gazed upward. "Here he comes."

A hum thrummed in the air and a second ship-to-surface transport cut through the fog and settled to the ground next to the first. The minister's group had stopped to stare, then the minister began gyrating his arms in jerky movements. One of the guards saluted and jogged toward the new arrival.

Mama snorted softly. "Well, not too hard to figure out what happened there."

The scowl on the minister's face was visible even from this distance. He lurched forward with a determined stride. This was it. Flora ran her palms over her shirt to smooth any wrinkles.

Poppy nodded. "Welcome to Terr, Minister S'gow."

S'gow didn't acknowledge her father's greeting. Instead, his gaze raked Flora from head to foot. "What is," he waved one hand at her, "*this* that you wear?"

She'd called that one right. At least he spoke to her and not over her. His bulk was so massive she couldn't see around him. It was like he stood so close just to be intimidating.

Flora raised her chin. "It's a *wysgog*. I made it myself."

The minister sneered. "You mock Anferthian traditions. You insult us by wearing such garments and binding your hair in a manner of which you have no understanding."

She resisted the temptation to run her hand over her braided *tirik*.

Poppy took a half step forward. "Minister—"

"I got this, Poppy." Flora met S'gow's hard gaze. "The *tirik* is a ritual braid that is worn by adult Anferthians who have received *rywoud* for the first time, usually on their fifteenth birthday. It's held in place by a *kadura* that often is adorned with the colors of an individual's family. I received *rywoud* on my fifteenth birthday and for that reason I honor Anferthian traditions by wearing a *wysgog*, *tirik*, and the *kadura* Ambassador K'nil gifted me on my birthday a few years ago."

S'gow narrowed his eyes. "She lies." He flicked his hand in her direction. "Take her into custody."

For what? A braid? This was going south fast. Handing over Grandfather's reliquary to Poppy for safe keeping before leaving the cube this morning had been smart. Grandfather had trusted her to fulfill his dying request. It was a good bet that if the minister got his hands on the reliquary, Fander would never see it.

"*Hold.*"

Flora startled at the booming voice that came from behind the minister. Fander's voice, in real time finally, after so long.

S'gow turned partway. "There is no reason for you to sully yourself with such menial business, Fander. This is why I asked you to remain onboard your ship until the murderess had been detained. Your safety is my priority."

"I am able to see to my own safety, Minister S'gow," Fander replied. "I have been doing so for longer than you imagine."

Flora leaned to her left and her heart hammered in her chest. There he was, taller—but still the shortest Anferthian in the bunch—and impossibly handsome, wearing an austere brown *wysgog*. A white mourning sash cutting a diagonal line across his chest. His hair was swept back from his face, covering his ears. His *fusil* and *labu-ba* hung at his narrow hips from a belt decorated with red-gold studs.

Minister S'gow narrowed his glare at Fander. "Have you, now?"

Fander stepped forward, a vigilant and slightly-older-than-she-remembered Nor Danol on his heels. "I am as eager as you to find justice from my grandfather's murder, but not at the cost of plunging us into a war with Terr and Matir. As I'm sure you will agree."

S'gow curled his lip in a sneer that hinted he might not agree. Goosebumps ran down her arms. The creep was up to something.

"By taking the Terrian woman into custody, we can protect her from the mysterious Matiran murderess who she claims assassinated Ambassador K'nil."

Damn, there was nothing more grating than a person talking about her as if she wasn't standing right in front of them. "Well, good news on that front, Minister. I'm already in custody, so you don't have to sully yourself either."

The man turned his head just enough to gaze down his nose at her, again. If disdain was a visible thing, it would be oozing from his pores. Behind him, the corners of Fander's mouth twitched upward. His silent approval washed over her. No, no, *no*. No approval. No warm fuzzy feelings for him. He had kept too many things from her that she could not, would not, forget.

"I deem it too risky," S'gow said. "She could run."

"I'm not going to—"

"Senior Admiral Helyg." Fander cut her off. The rude jerk. "I request transfer of custody of the suspect, Flora Grace MacDonald Bock, be granted to me. She will be housed aboard my ship, under the watch of my personal guard, until the trial."

Poppy dipped his head. "This is agreeable, with the caveat that one of my own guards accompany her."

"I so agree. Minister S'gow." Fander turned to the minister, whose face had darkened so much an explosion seemed inevitable. "I request the ambassador's guard also be housed aboard my ship as an extra precaution in case the suspect attempts to run. This should provide you with the assurance you need, as they are under your command at this time. Agreed?"

S'gow's jaw worked. Fander had set him up so well there was no other choice unless the minister decided to be completely unreasonable. If that happened, whose side would Kapit Tymo and the rest of the ambassador's guard fall?

"Agreed." S'gow pushed his words through clenched teeth. "Kapit Tymo."

The Anferthian woman brought her fist to her chest in a salute. "Minister?"

"If the suspect attempts any violation of *our* laws, you are ordered to end her existence, immediately."

Poppy stiffened. "This is an intergalactic incident, Minister S'gow. Anferthian law only applies as far as they match intergalactic laws."

"Of course, Senior Admiral." S'gow spoke a little too smoothly. "Kapit Tymo?"

"As you command, Minister."

Flora nibble at her bottom lip. Obviously, she was going to have to be very careful. Sooner or later, though, she'd get her chance to kick Fander's ass for the whole crown prince thing.

Fander set his face to be devoid of emotion, even though elation flowed through his very veins. If Minister S'gow even suspected what he was up to, he would renege on the agreement. Manipulating the man into this had already cost Fander a steep price. The whole puppet-prince charade was over. By disobeying the direct order to remain aboard his ship, he had exposed his true nature, and word of this would get back to Isel T'orr quickly. Just like that, he officially had two backs to watch now: his own, and Flora's.

The sooner he had her aboard, the better. "Kapit Tymo, please bring the suspect."

The word left a bitter flavor in his mouth. Flora was anything but a suspect.

"As you command," Tymo replied. "Patrol, fall in. By your leave, my lady Flora."

The minister's eyes widened with disbelief at the title of respect, then narrowed like daggers with suspicion. By the gods, that wasn't good. The point of putting Tymo in charge of Flora's escort had been to allay the man's suspicions, not feed them. But he could not fault Tymo for what she did not know.

Flora broke away from the embrace she shared with her parents.

"We'll see you tomorrow, sweetie," her mother promised.

It was a shame there was no way to avoid separating Flora from her family. Not being able to say goodbye to Maggie would no doubt bother her, but there was no justifiable reason for Mags to be here today.

Fander locked gazes with Flora's father. Despite his stiff militaristic stance, there was understanding in the Matiran's blue eyes. And possibly a hint of relief. His beloved daughter would be safe. He gave the senior admiral a brusque nod, then turned away, allowing confidence he didn't really feel to show as he set a brisk pace back to his transport. Nor fell in a step behind and to his right.

As Fander stepped into the shuttle, warm air enveloped him.

Keep moving until the door closes.

A half a dozen steps later, the soft whoosh of the door and the interior adjustment of air pressure announced that they were safe, for the moment. He turned around and closed the short distance between him and Flora, wrapped her in his embrace, and rested his cheek on the top of her head. Her scent consumed him as her arms encircled his waist. Nine long years of separation were over, and he did not care who witnessed this reunion now.

"Isn't this what led to your problems?" A deep voice drawled.

A nat. The senior admiral had sent the one man Fander would rather not face. Graig Roble.

"You're right, Uncle, it is." Flora pushed back, and he released her. Her mouth was set, and her brows drawn together in the way that had always indicated she was about to unleash her fury. "What the hell, Fander? What the ever-loving hell?"

Fander spread his hands out in a universally recognized conciliatory gesture. "Which question would you like me to answer first?"

"You ass." She crossed her arms under her breasts. By the gods, the blue of her *wysgog* drew out the color of her eyes. "Let's start with the whole crown prince thing. Why didn't you tell me?"

He winced. "I could not."

"*No one* could, apparently."

"It was for your safety."

She snorted. "Tell me something I haven't heard and isn't utter bull. Maybe it'd be easier to start with: What is your plan to get the idiotic charges against me dropped?"

He took in the small crowd of expectant faces in the corridor. So, this was what the Terrian saying about rocks and hard places meant. "I would like to continue this conversation in private."

Graig shook his head. "That's disappointing."

Nor made a strangled sound as though struggling not to laugh. Great. Just great. "It will only take a moment. You deserve the opportunity to choose what you want others to know."

"She is not going anywhere with you." Roble had one look: angry glare.

"Oh, for God's sake." Flora raised her hands as though imploring the heavens. "I am sick to death of people talking about me in front of my face. For your information, I deserved that opportunity nine years ago. I'm not going anywhere with *anyone*—especially you, Fander. I'll find my own seat, *alone*, for the ride."

She pushed passed him and stalked down the corridor. The material of the *wysgog* shimmered and flowed over her hips with each step.

Of all the possible scenarios he had imagined for their reunion, that had not been one. They had ranged from shy awkward hugs to wild and passionate kisses. An extreme vision led to copulation, which had been pure fantasy on his part.

At least she was going in the direction of the passenger seating compartment. He turned back and met the level grey gaze of Graig Roble. The Matiran raised his eyebrows as though saying, Nice going, dumb ass. Then he moved past and followed Flora.

Fander pressed his lips together. How had things gone so awry so fast?

"You were wrong, my prince," Kapit Tymo said.

"It seems so."

"Not about that."

He turned toward her. "Excuse me?"

"And so was Minister S'gow. The ambassador's personal guard have given their allegiance to Lady Flora MacDonald Bock. We will protect her as we would our own. We owe it to Ambassador K'nil after we failed to protect him."

He gave her a deep frown. "What happened that day?"

"I was not in the room."

"So, why warn me of your allegiance and not give Minister S'gow the same courtesy?"

"To see what you will do with the information." She motioned to her patrol to fall out and led them toward the passenger compartment.

Wasn't this supposed to be the time when everything he had worked toward in his life should slip into place? If anything, the situation seemed to be spinning further out of control.

Nor moved to his side. "Most unexpected."

"My grandfather's personal guard have all but declared themselves dissenters without loyalties." To him, at least. They were more than loyal to Flora. Fander gave his head a shake. "Telling me so was a warning."

"She did address you as 'my prince'." Nor shrugged his shoulders. "We are on the cusp of change and you are yet untested, my prince. Once you and your *tangol* have reconciled, Tymo and the others will follow her and declare their allegiance to you."

If he and Flora reconciled. At the moment, that prospect looked bleak at best. "I hope you are right."

At least the exiled dissenters on Matir still appeared ready to back him.

The next morning, Flora paced the spacious sitting area of her quarters aboard Fander's ship. That little coward had barely acknowledged her as they had disembarked from the transport.

"'Kapit Danol will escort you to your quarters.'" She mimicked his words from yesterday. "'I hope you find them satisfactory. If you will excuse me.' What? Did he have to go take a royal dump, or something?"

"I wouldn't know." Uncle Graig appeared a little too relaxed as he stood with his back against the wall facing the door, one foot propped for balance and arms crossed over his chest.

She gave her head a shake. "He didn't come back to check in either. Some prince."

"You judge him too harshly, niece."

Did that just come out of *Uncle Graig's* mouth? "If he cared anything at all for me, he would've at least stopped by last night. But, he didn't."

Uncle Graig shrugged his shoulders. "You made it clear you didn't want him around. Aren't ambassadors trained to choose their words with more care?"

She opened her mouth, then closed it again. God, she hated it when he was right. Maybe she had left all her training in New Damon Beach. But, ooh, it'd be great to unload all over Fander's regal head right now.

Uncle Graig tilted his head to one side. "I'm not sure why—"

The soft ping of the door chime cut him off. Now what?

"Fander K'nil," the computer-generated voice announced.

"Oh, great." Her words were at odds with the sudden gallop of her heart.

"He could have news."

Uncle Graig had a point. She heaved a defeated sigh. "Come in."

Weird how that was still the phrase used to invite someone in, even in the technologically advanced universe Terr was now a part of.

The door slid open and there stood Fander, looking so...princely. The copper highlights of his *wysgog* complemented the matching strands in his hair. Her eyes misted. He really was a prince through and through. Why couldn't he just be Fander, the ambassador's grandson?

An older and taller woman stepped around him. Her long pale green dress flowed around her. The white trim at the end of her sleeves and the hem of her gown proclaimed her to be in mourning. Her brown hair was swept back, exposing her rounded ears. She must be someone important because the largest Anferthian Flora had ever laid eyes on stood directly behind her.

He had to be at least thirteen feet tall and half as wide.

She forced her gaze back to the meet the woman's black eyes, and a jolt of recognition snapped through her. "You're Grandfather K'nil's daughter." And Fander's mother, Fani K'nil. The same one from the book of royalty.

"And you are his Terrian granddaughter, at long last." The woman smiled and extended her hands, palm up. "Great is my pleasure, Flora of Terr."

All the years of protocol training finally caught up with her. She placed her palms over the woman's. "Great is my pleasure...." What was the proper address for the mother of the Anferthian heir apparent? "Your highness."

Fani K'nil inclined her head, withdrew her hands and turned her attention to Fander. "Rauc and I will await you in the corridor with Nor, and Flora's patrol."

Fander nodded, his full attention on Flora. He didn't say anything until the door closed. "The venue for the trial is set. We can travel together on one transport, or, if you wish, you and your guard may return to New Damon Beach aboard your own. Either way, your family insists they will escort you to the destination once you land."

It was so tempting to say separate transports, but that would be a selfish waste. "Fine. When are we leaving?"

"Now."

"*Now*?" She couldn't go now. She was still dressed in yesterday's outfit. "I can't go wearing a wrinkled *wysgog*. The minister is already looking for any excuse to discredit me to all Anferthia. This...this...." She waved her hands. There were no words. If she did not present well, then it was over. The minister would lie, cheat, and steal to get her convicted. And for what? Why did he have it in for her?

Fander grasped each of her flailing hands, locking them firmly in place simply by wrapping his fingers around them. Warmth radiated up her arms. His warmth. She stilled and met his gaze.

"Your mother will meet you at the landing site with a fresh *wysgog*. And Maggie said she will rebraid your hair."

Right. Mama will be landing and Maggie...no, that wasn't right. Dammit, she couldn't think with Fander so close.

"Fine." At least she could choke out that much. She tugged her hands back and Fander released them. "Then let's go."

THIRTEEN

Flora struggled to suppress a yawn. It was getting harder and harder to focus on the Minister of Justice's words. One thing was for certain, Anferthians could drone on endlessly when they put their minds to it. How much longer before all the translators in the room chose to self-destruct rather than decipher anymore of his ceaseless, one sided, let's-all-hate-on-Flora-Bock, speech?

She turned her head to sneak a glance around the impromptu court room. Half the spectators were staring with glazed eyes or looking down at their data devices. A few had even fallen asleep. Great.

At least her family remained alert. Mama and Poppy sat to her right and left, a privilege allowed to them because they were the *Profetae* and represented both Terr and Matir. Grandpa Zale and Grandma Charise sat together behind Poppy, holding hands; Cousin Ora sat with them—an unexpected surprise. Somehow Ora had wheedled a brief leave of absence so close to the departure of her science ship for a two-year deep space cruise. Being a captain had its perks.

Aunt Simone, Uncle Graig, and Uncle Dante sat behind Mama. Flora's heart twisted. If only Uncle Nick and Aunt Sakura had made it. And Juan, too. Despite their competitiveness, it would've been nice to have her brother here.

Fander, on the other hand, remained aboard the transport with his mother, which just proved that he couldn't care less which way things went today. And here she'd thought that he would stand up for her. That was what *tangol should* do, if she understood the bond right. Another thing to add to the list of hurts.

Grandfather K'nil's reliquary warmed near her heart, as if it sensed her mood and wanted to reassure her. Her hand twitched, but she suppressed the urge to touch it, to feel its reassuring pulse. If things didn't go well today, she'd somehow slip it back to Poppy, and he would return the reliquary to Fander.

Mama's sigh drew her attention back to the present. Her parents were looking at each other behind her back. Must be one of their ever-popular silent conversations. Telepathy, one of those soul mate things. It sure explained why she, Juan, and Maggie never got away with anything as kids.

Poppy shook his head and Mama pressed her lips together as though miffed. What the heck they were talking about?

Flora leaned her arms against the table. At least Mama seemed to be doing better than she was when they'd first arrived. Being aboard the converted Anferthian slaver had to have brought back some bad memories.

At the back of the room, the doors opened and the shuffle and clump of a large contingent entering almost drowned out the Minister S'gow's boring monologue. She tamped down the groan rising from deep inside. Dear God, please don't let them want to speak too.

"Minister!" Fander's deep, rich, voice boomed in English, and she jumped in her seat as a bolt of lightning seared a path from her heart to the juncture between her legs. Holy crap, what was *that*? "There are only a finite number of ways to say the same thing, yet it seems you have used all of them and still failed to get to the real point."

A murmur of laughter rippled through the observers. Flora swiveled in her seat. Fander was not alone. His mother stood just behind his right shoulder, with a grim-faced Rauc at her back. Kapit Nor Danol and his patrol stood behind Fander. A few hundred Anferthians rose in unison, blocking her view of the royal party.

"My Lady K'nil." The Minister addressed Fander's mother. "We had not expected you."

Flora frowned. Had Fander concealed himself in the transport for a reason?

"You will answer your *prince*, Minister." Fander's mother's words were clipped and Arctic frigid.

Maggie leaned forward in her seat and placed her small hand on Flora's thigh. "Prince? What's that all about?"

"Sit back, Maggie," Mama ordered. "Flora, now's a good time to remember your protocol."

Or maybe, since the court was already convened to charge her with murder anyway—

"Today is that day, Flora."

Her entire body jerked so hard she nearly fell off her chair. That was Grandfather K'nil's voice, which was impossible. She gave a quick glance around at her family, but all of them had their attention on Fander. Was it just her hearing dead people speaking? That couldn't be good. And, damn, she'd missed the minister's response to Fander's mother.

"My prince is only months from being of age to ascend the throne, Minister," Lady K'nil announced in a clear authoritative voice. "If not for the Arruch, he would by all rights be the voice of his people by now."

Another murmur, this one of uncertainty and excitement, buzzed through the room.

The Minister glared at her then at Fander, his expression calculating. "This is a hearing to formally charge your grandfather's murderess, *my lord*."

Could he really afford to be that condescending when there was an almost electric undercurrent of emotion charging the room?

One by one, then in groups, the Anferthians sat back down, the soft rustle of their *wysgogs* the only sound. Her gaze locked with Fander's over their heads and her breath caught in her throat. Still impossibly handsome. She blinked against the vision-blurring mist rising in her eyes. Dammit, why did that keep happening? How could she be so completely pissed off, yet ready to melt?

Fander turned his attention back to the minister and raised a brow. "I fear I must question your vision, Minister. This woman is neither Matiran, nor in her forties."

His dry observation elicited another murmur of laughter from the crowd.

"The fire-haired Terrian is—"

"Is *not* Haesi Velo." Fander's sharp, angry words silenced not only the minister, but also those murmuring together in the crowd.

No one in the room moved. It was as if they'd all been frozen in place. Flora ran her tongue over her lips. Fander had never cut her off when they'd argued as kids, no matter how angry he was or ridiculous her point may have been. But now—this new Fander, seemed determined to mow right over the minister. And the minister was too dense to see it coming. Wasn't that exactly what happened to Supreme Warden T'lik when Mama negotiated for the Terrian prisoners after the invasion?

"Please read the charges again, Minister." This time Fander's voice was as smooth as cream. "But, kindly dispense with your...*witty* personal commentary."

Minister S'gow's face darkened, then he cleared his throat and read the charges against her. Fander glided down the aisle. He even walked like royalty, fluid and unhurried. Whatever his plan was, he seemed confident as he turned toward the table where she sat. His gaze locked with hers again as he approached, and he caressed her face with his fingertips.

She blinked rapidly. Wait. How the hell did he do that without touching her? She narrowed her glare at him and frowned.

Focus on all the reasons you're angry with him.

He could've told her he was the heir apparent. He'd abandoned her, for years. Okay, not totally his fault, but he could've come back sooner. Then he'd all but ignored her after they'd arrived aboard his ship orbiting Terr yesterday. Well, except for that hug he'd given her. The one she'd almost caved in to before coming to her senses and pushing away. Then, this morning he'd left her thinking he'd abandoned her to face this trial without him. Of course, he must've reasons for all of this, but it still hurt.

Fander came to a stop in front of her and gave her a faint nod as he extended his hand to her. What? Did he expect her to just take it? Pressure from Mama's foot pressing down on hers under the table was another reminder to mind her manners. Did parents ever stop being parents?

Flora puckered her mouth and exhaled through her nose. Short of making a scene and undermining her own defense, she had to play along. She slowly placed her hand in his. A wave of rightness swamped her senses. Like she'd come home from a long journey. Awareness lit Fander's eyes, and his nostrils flared slightly. Good lord, he was scenting her. How could she possibly get out of her seat when her legs had turned to rubber?

Fander gave her hand a gentle squeeze. The heat lingered in

his eyes, along with an unspoken message: *you can do this.* She got her feet under her and he helped her rise with a gentle steady pull. Until this moment, eight feet had been just a number. He was the shortest Anferthian she knew, but he still towered over her. How come this hadn't occurred to her yesterday when he'd hugged her?

The Minister of Justice finished reading the charges, and silence blanketed the room again. Everyone seemed to be waiting to hear what Fander would say next. Including her.

Fander didn't break eye contact with her. "Minister S'gow, how is it possible that this young Terrian woman, who is dwarfed *even by me*, was somehow able to murder a fully grown Anferthian man and his Terrian housekeeper? Both of whom she adored."

"She is well trained in combat arts." The minister pointed out. "Former Matiran Commander Roble is her *magister*."

Flora's gaze was drawn down to their joined hands. Her skin was shockingly white against his darker green. Which of them would their children favor? She blinked and heat rose up her neck. Where had *that* thought come from?

"Magister Roble?" Fander's voice startled her out of her insane musing.

She squeezed her eyes closed then blinked rapidly. Time to focus on the here and now. Fander's gaze scanned the crowd over her head. A soft rustle came from behind her.

"Your highness." That was the same low growl Uncle Graig had used the day he had caught them kissing on the bluffs. *And*, he'd publicly acknowledged Fander as royalty.

Fander dipped his head in acknowledgment. "What type of students do you train out?"

"Students who can defend themselves and others with honor, your highness."

"Have you ever trained out an assassin, even accidently?"

"Once, your highness. Unintentionally."

"Who?"

"Haesi Velo."

"Is it possible your student Flora Bock also turned assassin?"

"Flora, like her mother, is a warrior, not an assassin," Uncle Graig replied. "I personally vouch for her character. Her code of honor does not allow her to exploit others. She is trained to defend her own, which is what she did the day your grandfather was murdered."

"My grandfather was one of her own?"

"He was as a grandfather to her, your highness."

Fander met her gaze again. The tears seeped into her eyes. Tears he would see. One escaped down her cheek, and his hand twitched like he wanted to wipe it away.

But, he didn't. Instead, his Adam's apple bobbed as he swallowed. "Minister, has anyone from the Panel of Justice asked the accused what happened?"

"She has made the usual duplicitous noises of a murderess attempting to blame someone else. Someone no one has seen in years, and who is not present to defend themselves. Overwhelming evidence against this *Terrian* says otherwise." It sounded like the minister really wanted everyone to believe that.

A small muscle ticked along Fander's jaw. He released her hand and turned to the Minister. "Is this not a court of justice, Minister S'gow? Or are we so far above justice that we can drag anyone before a panel with our minds already made up about their guilt?"

The minister leapt up from his chair and pounded his fist on the podium in front of him. "This is *Anferthian justice*."

"This is an Arruch diversionary tactic. *A lie*." Fander curled his fingers into fists at his side.

Poppy and Mama stood in unison, their shoulders brushing against her arms. Flora cast a quick glance over her shoulder. Kapit Tymo and her guard were already behind her, ready to defend her.

Fander's own guards stood in the aisleway behind his mother and bristled, but no one had pulled a weapon. Yet. It was as if they were waiting, holding their collective breath, for Fander.

"I will not stand for such justice in the name of my family, Minister."

The Minister looked beseechingly at Fander's mother. "Lady K'nil...."

"I have no desire to condemn anyone simply because it is convenient to do so, Minister," she replied. "If you're looking to me to gainsay my prince, you will be sorely disappointed. His highness and I are both interested in hearing what the only living witness present has to say."

"*Cymere!*" An Anferthian in the audience shouted his approval, and the room erupted with shouts echoing this idea.

As the commotion dwindled, the minister glared at Lady K'nil, then Fander, and finally at Flora. The deep-seated desire to choke the life out of her glowed in his eyes. She resisted the temptation to step fully behind Fander to escape the hostility.

Finally, the minister threw himself back into his chair and waved his hand. "Proceed."

The collective breath seemed to release. Her parents sat down again and Fander signaled both their guards to stand down. Then his gaze was on her once again. She raised her chin, defiance and determination sparking in her heart.

"Daughter of the *Profetae*." By addressing her with this title, he had neatly and clearly established her place in society. "Did you murder Ambassador K'nil's house attendant, Mrs. Beck?"

"No…sir," She just couldn't bring herself to address him as 'your highness', but 'sir' was completely acceptable in this situation.

"Did you murder Ambassador K'nil, my grandfather?"

"No, sir."

"Did you in fact attempt to kill anyone that day in the ambassador's receiving room?"

"Yes, sir."

Fander raised one eye brow. "Who?"

"A woman I had never seen nor met before—who I was later able to identify as Haesi Velo." Or, Haesi Vile, but no one knew that personal secret nickname.

"Why would you try to kill her?"

"Because." Images of the bloody room rose in her mind and her throat tightened. Now was not a good time for a break down. She pressed her clenched fists against her hips and focused on the sharp pressure of her nails digging into her palms. "Because she murdered Grandfather K'nil…right in front of me."

"Grandfather?" Fander tipped his head to one side, the same way his grandfather used to do. "He is no relation to you. Why would you call him that?"

Hadn't Uncle Graig established that already?

Minister S'gow jumped up, leaned over the podium, and pointed at her. "She stole the ambassador's reliquary!"

How the hell had he figured out she had it?

"Answer my question first, Flora." Fander's murmured words drew her attention back to him.

"He was one of my own, that's why." Her lips trembled and she couldn't stop her tears from flooding her eyes. "*Fyhen.*"

A whisper passed through the audience behind her.

"Did you steal the ambassador's reliquary?" Fander asked her.

"No, sir." Something soft brushed her right hand and she glanced down. Mama offered a hanky. Just in time to catch the snot tickling her nostrils. She gave her mother a grateful grimace.

"Do you have it in your possession?"

She dabbed her eyes and swiped the hanky under her nose. "Yes."

"Why?"

"Because." Another dab. Where was he going with this line of questioning? "Ambassador K'nil made me its custodian should anything happen to him. He entrusted me to deliver it safely to his heir."

"His heir?"

"To you. His heir is you."

"So I am." His lips curved into a small smile and held out his hand again. "My Lady Flora, I am prepared to receive my grandfather's reliquary."

So that's where he was going. And he still addressed her with a respectful title even though she'd refused to use his. She reached up and drew the reliquary from under the shirt of her *wysgog* and lifted the chain over her head. Then she presented it Fander. "My word is my honor, and my vow is fulfilled."

"Your vow is fulfilled, and your honor is above reproach." Fander let out the chain a little before he looped it over his head and tucked it away under his shirt. He took both her hands and bowed over them. "Thank you, My Lady Flora."

Turning to the minister and the Panel of Justice. "In light of the statement of the accused, Lady Flora Bock, along with the evidence withheld by the Minister and this Panel—including the positive identification of Haesi Velo's blood, and the recovery of the same Haesi Velo's knife stuck in the spine of a book in the ambassador's receiving room—the House of K'nil *and* the Crown of Anferthia will not pursue these charges against her. Members of the Panel, let us not further humiliate ourselves with falsified charges against innocents."

That was true. The panel hadn't presented that information, even though they'd known. Assholes.

Fander turned back to her, his expression like stone and she nearly took a step backward. Where was all the warmth from a moment ago? "Not all my people will be as convinced as I of your innocence. As the last heir of all Anferthians I represent them, and in their name, I challenge you, Flora of Terr, to the *ratig'a* combat."

The court room roared to life with voices. Her mouth dropped open. The *ratig'a* combat? Was he *crazy*?

The Minister rose from his chair, his face alight with hope. "To the death?"

Of course, that would be what the minister wanted, and it probably did not matter whose death either. Each would benefit the big blowhard.

Fander turned his head a fraction, his gaze still locked with Flora's. "To the satisfaction, Minister."

"But—"

"There has been more than enough death between our peoples, Minister. It is not a war with Terr that I'm looking for, merely the appeasement of honor."

"So, I don't get to kill you?" That was a stupid thing to say, but the words were out of her mouth before her brain could analyze the wisdom of saying them.

One of Fander's eyebrows winged upward. "Do you accept my challenge, Flora of Terr?"

She gave a very unladylike snort. "Bring it, Fander of Anferthia."

He regarded her then inclined his head. "Will fourth hour tomorrow give you enough time to prepare?"

"Make it third hour."

"Very well. We will meet at the New Damon Beach baseball field at that time." He turned and swept back up the aisle, his mother at his side and the royal guard following in their wake.

"Let's go. Now." Poppy took her elbow and propelled her toward the door, his sense of urgency palpable. Her mother, uncles, aunt, grandparents, sister, and cousin surrounded them forming a double circle of protection. Kapit Tymo's detail protected them all.

Fourteen

Fander suppressed a shiver as he waited by home base, surrounded by his guard. April mornings in New Damon Beach were exactly as he remembered; cool, and scented with the tang of the ocean and the promise of new life. Fitting, since today was the dawn of a new life—a new direction—for Anferthia. If he survived the next few months.

The town's baseball field was exactly as he remembered, too. The baselines, the short-clipped green grass, the handmade bleachers. This was a place where some of his best childhood memories centered. Here and the Bock's cube. And the beach. And a certain spot near the top of the switchback path to the beach.

He shoved that memory back down into a dark corner of his mind. It was time to focus on this moment, and how this was a perfect day, and the perfect place, to get his ass kicked. Which was exactly what would happen if he was not careful. He snuck a sidelong look at the brooding Matiran leaning against the post of the catcher's cage. To this day Flora's Uncle Graig intimidated him, which made no sense. The man was a good deal shorter than he. And older.

And more experienced.

Most importantly, the man had trained Flora. Fander pressed his lips into a flat line. She would not be an easy opponent and would test him as few had. The *ratig'a* was a competition of endurance and strategy, and she might not appreciate his strategy. But, she needed to earn the respect of as many of his people as possible today *before* they discovered she was his *tangol*. Earned respect was far preferable to begrudging or forced. The Anferthians filtering into the stands now might expect him to give them satisfaction, but if things went well they would leave with far more than that. They would leave with stories of her worthiness, and they would share those stories, because in truth, Anferthians loved to talk. About anything.

He turned his gaze toward the pitcher's mound. This must be one of the most unusual venues ever for a *ratig'a* challenge, but it was fitting for them. A smile tugged at the corners of his mouth as the childhood memories surfaced.

"What so amuses you, my son?" Nothing ever escaped the attention of his mother.

"Baseball." He allowed his smile to expand. "I learned to play the Terrian game during my time here. Flora did not like to lose."

And she rarely did lose, in the beginning. Once he had discovered his strength lay in running the bases things had changed.

Nor coughed and Fander glanced at his friend. "Something to say?"

"She was very competitive."

Fander's gaze was drawn to the cluster of Anferthian guards approaching. In their midst, Flora strode like an empress.

An *ymere*.

"Let us pray she still is." His plan hinged on it.

He stepped forward to greet his *tangol*. The form-fitting, ecru combat gear preferred by Anferthians for hand-to-hand combat gave her an air of maturity. As if the past twenty-four hours hadn't already proved she was no longer the girl he had left behind. "Good morning, Flora of Earth."

Her eyes widened slightly. Using a Terrian greeting and saying Earth over Terr was a tactic to unbalance the inner peace she had no doubt meditated to achieve before combat. Even though the *ratig'a* had not officially begun, he must lay the ground work for success, even in the subtlest ways.

"Good morning, Fander of Anferthia." She glanced over the field, apparently unfazed by his words. Outwardly, at least. "What are our parameters?"

He gave his shoulders a shrug. "Simple. We stay within the infield base lines."

"That's a lot of space." Her sky-blue gaze shifted back to his and something in his chest tightened. Life would be vastly easier if she would just accept his position and moved on. If she did, they could spend this evening ensconced aboard his ship getting reacquainted with their adult selves.

Gods have mercy, was she also employing pre-combat strategy? "Does that bother you?"

"Are you stalling for time, Anferthian?"

And there was the spitfire he knew. "Never. Kapit Tymo, as officiator you may begin the challenge at any time."

The kapit nodded. "Challenger and the challenged, enter the arena."

As Tymo moved toward the pitcher's mound, Fander fell in behind her, an action Flora quickly mimicked. All the way there, she kept a fraction of a step ahead of him. Yes, her competitive nature was alive and well.

Things were about to get interesting.

Flora came to a stop at the base of the pitcher's mound and turned to face Fander. Her opponent—she couldn't afford to forget that or she would lose focus. Exactly what Uncle Graig had warned her not to do. His exact words had been, "If you can best me, then you can take him." When she'd pointed out that she'd never bested him, her uncle, his grey eyes gleamed. "But, your mother has, and you are every bit the warrior she is."

That had been the highest praise he'd ever given to her. He believed in her. Mama and Poppy believed in her. Maggie believed in her. *She* believed in her.

"Combatants." Kapit Tymo's voice cut through her thoughts. "The rules of this match are determined by the unique dimensions for this arena. You are to remain within the borders defined by the...base lines. To step out is to award the win to your opponent. The challenge is not over until one opponent is pinned, too injured to continue, or signals forfeit. To signal a forfeit, the combatant raises their right fist, pinky finger extended. This is a challenge to the satisfaction. Do the combatants understand and accept the rules of the *ratig'a*?"

"I do." She and Fander spoke in unison.

"Is a healer prepared to attend as needed?"

"I am." Uncle Dante stood in front of the third baseline dugout.

The kapit nodded and raised her arms straight out from her sides. "Begin." She backed away, then headed toward the same dugout as Uncle Dante with a no-nonsense stride.

This was it. Flora moved left and Fander's eyes took on a steely glint as they circled each other.

Freaking crown prince....

Graig admired his niece's gumption. As she stalked Fander, she angled her body just enough for her womanly form to mess with the prince's concentration. She had learned to use every tactic at her disposal well, and there was an excellent chance this would work in her favor. However, Fander had been at least as well trained as she, and he should be able to desensitize himself from such a tactic in combat.

It was hard to say what the outcome of this challenge would be. But, he had his own game to play.

He reached into his jacket pocket and fished out a bag of Simone's dried apples. "She's damn good, you know, Danol."

"Surely not better than my prince?" The captain of Fander's guard gazed down his wide nose at him.

Graig gave his shoulders a casual shrug and opened the bag. The frothy scent of the sweet apples wafted into the air. "When she was nineteen, she surprised me by dropping out of the rafters of my training cube."

"*On* you?" Nor's nostrils flared and he eyed the bag of dried fruit. Bait detected.

"Of course. *And* she'd painted her face blue." Like a Pict. At least that's what Flora had told him. To this day, he still didn't know much about her strange ancestors, but there was nothing wrong with the whole blue thing.

Nor gaped at him, disbelief in his wide ice-blue eyes. Now for the hook. He tipped the bag of apples toward the speechless Anferthian. "Have you tried Simone's dried apples?"

Danol reached into the bag and almost daintily pinched a circle of fruit between his thumb and forefinger. A movement behind him drew Graig's gaze to the bleachers. Simone watched him with narrowed eyes. She knew what he was up to and had not argued against it, mostly because she understood him in a way no one did.

Gryf and Alex seemed too focused on the match to notice. As long as it stayed that way.

Nor took a cautious nibble and a smile of pleasure cracked his stern features. "For all the years I lived here, I had no idea this could be done to apples."

Gotcha.

Hook, line, and sinker, as his wife would say. Graig leaned back against the stair rail for the bleachers, folding his arms loosely across his chest. "How about a friendly wager?"

Flora dodged right, ducking and rolling away from Fander's reach. He was still fast, but then, so was she. A trickle of sweat ran down her temple and she swiped at it with the back of her hand. So far, they seemed pretty evenly matched. There'd been a couple of close calls when she'd almost stepped out of bounds. Almost. If she wasn't careful, though, it could still happen.

It'd been nearly an hour since they'd started, and the longest she'd ever sparred with Uncle Graig was forty-five minutes. Fander was showing signs of tiring as well. The loser would be the person who made the first stupid mistake, and it sure as hell wouldn't be her.

Fander came at her, and she used her legs and arms to flip him over her shoulder, scrambling to her feet to face him. He crashed into her, another full-frontal assault. How had he gotten up and turned himself around so quickly?

Crack!

Stars exploded in her vision and she staggered backward. The impact of her butt to the ground sent a jolt up her spine. "Oof." All the air whooshed from her lungs.

Damn.

What had hit her, a bus? She clapped her hand to her forehead and blinked several times until Fander came into focus. His ass was similarly planted on the grass. "Mother of God, Fander. You have a hard head."

He squeezed his eyes shut, opened them, and shook that hard head. "I would say the same to you, but since I'm not sure which of the three of you are real, I'll keep it to myself."

Her chest contracted as she fought against a laugh. The way his lips twitched and his eyes sparkled, it was hard to hold it in.

Oh, geez, now he was crawling over to her. "Is there only one of me now?"

"I'm aiming for the one in the middle, which means I'll be sitting on the one on your right. It's a calculated risk, but I hope that one isn't the real you." He patted the ground next to her as though testing to make sure she wasn't there. "I think we're good."

"You're kidding, right? Or should I call Uncle Dante over?"

He flashed a heart-melting grin and sat next to her with his hands dangling over his raised knees. "I'm okay. Are you?"

"I will be once my ears stop ringing." And her head stopped throbbing. She cast a furtive glance at the stands. "I think everyone is confused." Heck, she was confused. How had this changed from a battle to...whatever this was? Some sort of friendly chat?

"Probably." He scrunched his nose. "I have boxed myself into a corner, I'm afraid."

Uh oh. "How?"

"We need to end this, equitably. You're *tango*. I want you to be deemed worthy in the eyes of my people, but as their representative I can't forfeit."

Ah. "Or lose either." She gave her temples a fingertip massage.

"Yes." Conflict and misery showed in his eyes. His beautiful, beautiful eyes which had haunted her dreams for nine years. "So, we must get up and continue until...." He shrugged.

"Until one of us is a clear winner, or forfeits."

"Pretty much."

Poor guy really wanted this to be over. So did she, but.... "I'm not forfeiting either, Fander."

"I didn't expect you would." Was that a hint of pride in his tone? "So, our only choice is to continue."

"I'm ready. Unless you need more time to rest?" *Please say yes.*

"No."

Damn.

"Good." She pushed herself up and brushed off her hands.

Nausea roiled in her stomach. *Steady*. Oh, hell with that. It was time to end this thing so she could dunk her head in a bucket of ice. She took a step forward and her traitorous legs folded under her.

This was going to hurt.

Fifteen

One moment Flora had seemed fine. The next, her body caved to the force of gravity.

What in creation?

Fander reached for her as she went down. Not a good angle but at least he had slowed her rate of descent. He stumbled as her dead weight pulled him to his knees. Had the collision of their heads caused unseen trauma?

He rolled her in his arms until her cheek rested against his arm. "Flora?"

No response. Was she even breathing? He placed his fingers over her lips. There, the soft warmth of exhaled breath ghosted over his skin. "Flora?"

Still no response. This was not good at all. He cast a glance over his shoulder, the healer's name in his throat, but there was no need to call. Healer Dacian was full-on sprinting across the field toward them.

The lanky Matiran skidded to a stop on the other side of Flora like a player into home base. "What happened?"

"I don't know. We hit our heads together, but after the initial shock she seemed fine. Spoke in complete and coherent sentences." Dante Dacian bent over Flora, his fingers fluttering over her forehead. What if there was damage? "Is she bleeding internally? Should I signal Healer Bock?"

A shadow fell across him. "No, my prince. The *ratig'a* is still active. No one may enter the combat zone other than the contestants, the designated healer, and myself, unless the match is ended."

Tymo was right, and if he so much as looked in the general direction of Flora's parents, they might forget these rules out of concern for their daughter.

Flora's head lolled and her mouth went completely slack.

Healer Dacian straightened, shaking his head. "Call the match. Flora of Terr is not able to continue."

A claw of panic clutched Fander's gut. "What's wrong? Will she be all right?"

"Call it, Kapit Tymo."

The captain of Flora's guard nodded and strode to the pitcher's mound. "Flora of Terr is declared incapacitated and unable to return to combat. *Ratig'a* goes to the challenger, Fander of Anferthia. Satisfaction has been achieved and this match is concluded."

A raucous cheer went up from the Anferthians. The celebration was indecent and Fander shared none of their jubilation—and neither did Minister S'gow and his party, judging by the glowers. But that man was the least of his concerns. Flora's condition was all that mattered.

He pressed his lips together hard and hugged Flora to his chest as her parents rushed toward him. "Healer, you will tell me my *tangol's* condition, *now*."

Flora's mother half-fell to her knees next to him. "Tell us, Dante."

"Mild concussion. But, why not ask her?" He tapped one long blue finger against Flora's forehead.

Her eyes opened. They were glassy, but her attempt at a smile sent a beam of hope through him.

"Gonna puke."

A nat, that was not a good thing. And was it not amazing the reaction two little words could elicit? As everyone scrambled back, he rolled her away from him, then wrapped his arm protectively around her shoulders as she crouched and dry-heaved over the grass.

"It is well, Flora. Let it out. You'll feel better for it." What else could he say to her?

Finally, she stopped heaving and ran her tongue over her lips. "Good thing I didn't eat breakfast. That would've been messy."

"And smelly." He gave her shoulders a gentle squeeze. "Better now?"

"Mm-hm." She sat up. "Damn, my head hurts. Did you win?"

Was it quieter now? The spectators in the stands seemed to have settled down. Not silent, but most were watching with curious expressions.

He turned his attention back to Flora. "The terms of *ratig'a* are satisfied."

"Oh, thank God. Uncle Dante, can you take care of my head now?"

The Matiran healer grimaced. "I should not for the scare you gave me."

What did that mean?

"Sorry, but I couldn't let you heal me. My...um...*tangol* had a problem and I knew I could help him."

Fander frowned. "Please tell me you didn't fix the outcome."

"Not exactly. I'm legit hurt. Uncle Dante?"

The healer set his palm against her forehead and two breaths later the tension in her shoulders relaxed and she sighed with relief. "Better. Thanks." Her gaze met his and the glassiness in her eyes was gone. "Fander, don't be mad. I was just done, you know? On so many levels. And you seemed like you were too."

He had been, this was true. "But, it's not over, yet. There's more at stake here than you realize."

"What do you mean?"

She was not going to like this, but her life depended on what happened in the next few minutes. "Kapit Danol, this woman is one of my own. *Fyhen* and *tangol*. Keep her from all harm."

Nor snapped his fist to his chest. "As you command, my prince."

Fander extended his hands toward her and gave her what he hoped was a confident smile. "First, let's show everyone in the stands you're all right. They've been a little anxious about you, and Mags is going to revolt pretty soon because your aunt and scary uncle won't let her come onto the field."

Flora moved her gaze from Fander's face to his hands and back again. "All right."

She'd go with him for Maggie's sake, and for the rest of her family, but she couldn't care less about everyone else. She placed her hands in his, allowing him to pull her to her feet and guide her to the pitcher's mound.

The crowd quieted. They really did seem anxious, and curious. He faced them and raised his hands in a universally recognized gesture to draw attention. Not that he needed to, because every last one of them were already watching him. Several Anferthians even leaned forward as though in anticipation.

"Anferthia is satisfied and gives all honor to Flora of Terr as a worthy opponent. By that honor, the K'nil family willingly accepts responsibility for completing her junior ambassador training, which my grandfather began, and I am duty-bound to complete in his name."

He smiled down at her. This was great news. It sounded like Fander was going to stay on Terr for a year. Then maybe they could travel together to Anferthia once her training was finished.

"She will accompany me to my home on Anferthia to complete this training."

She opened her mouth with an audible pop. "Wait a minute—"

"Furthermore, powers beyond our understanding have made this woman my *tangol*. As such, she will be at my side as I prepare to fulfill my duty to my people as *ymero*."

"*What*?" How had this situation spun out of her control so fast? "If you think I'm going to agree—"

"*Cymere!*" The cheer rose from several Anferthians in the stands. Most of them seemed in favor of this insane idea, except Minister S'gow and the Panel of Justice. The minister shouted, but his words were lost in the greater commotion swirling around him. There was no mistaking his frantic expression, though. He was struggling for control as much as she was, but for different reasons.

Fander lowered his arms and the din tapered into a low rumble of expectation. Even the Terrians and Matirans seemed eager to hear what he had to say. And, Maggie…why was she bouncing up and down on her toes looking like she'd received a puppy for Christmas?

"Fander K'nil." The minister leaned his body over the rail so far, he was in danger of tumbling over it. "I declare you a traitor to your people."

Okay, *that* was bad.

"I was born the *servant* of my people, Minister." Fander seemed to stand straighter, taller. He took in a deep breath. "I. Am. Anferthia."

The three words spoken in his big voice silenced the crowd. The only sound was the morning birds singing in the trees on the backside of the stands. Three words that changed, well, *everything*. Her anger drained away, along with the blood in her face. A statement like that could push his people into a civil war.

She took a step closer to him and half-covered her mouth with her hand. "I hope you know what you're doing."

"I've had nine years to think about it." His reply was just as softly spoken.

Minister S'gow's smug expression was visible even from their place near the mound. "You have not reached majority, yet. *The Arruch* are Anferthia until your twenty-fifth birthday, but, I doubt you will survive that long after such a treasonous statement." He nodded to his guard. "Take Fander K'nil into custody...and his *tangol* too."

Fander punched his fist into the air. "Anferthia!"

Chaos erupted. The echo of Fander's cry went up from at least two-thirds of the Anferthians. Maggie ran the length of the stands shouting, "Fan-*der*. Fan-*der*. Fan-*der*." Soon every Terrian, Matiran, and most of the Anferthians took up the chant. The only ones not chanting were the Minister, the Justices, and their guards.

The minister made a wrist-flicking gesture in the direction of his guards. One soldier raised his *fusil* and aimed the gun in their direction. Fander grabbed her by the arm and shoved her to the ground, under him. More weight pressed her harder into the grass.

Phapt.

The discharge of the *fusil* seemed to echo, like the shot that could be heard around the world. Only this time it would be around the galaxy. A feminine grunt came from nearby.

"Mama? *Mama.*" Flora braced her hands but couldn't push up with the weight of Fander, and whoever else had landed on top of him, holding her in place.

"I'm okay."

Relief coursed through her at the sound of her mother's voice on her other side. She turned her head. Mama was on the ground, Poppy over her like a shield.

Poppy shifted to look over his shoulder. "Detain Minister S'gow and his party."

The sound of others rushing to obey orders was nearly lost in the din of shouting from the stands.

"Are you okay, sweetie?" Mama asked.

"Yeah." Squished, but not hurt. "You?"

"Fine." Mama grimaced as Poppy raised himself off her. "Cripes, I'm getting too old for this kind of stuff. Don't you dare tell your Uncle Graig I said that."

Yeah, Mama was fine.

"Tymo was hit." That was Uncle Dante. Mama scrambled in the direction of his voice.

Flora wiggled. "Let me up, Fander."

"Nor," Fander said next to her ear. "We are well."

The pressure lessened, then Fander moved off her and she rolled to her side and sat up. The stands were in chaos. Aunt Simone and Uncle Graig hustled Maggie away from the free-for-all brawl that had erupted. It appeared as though several spectators—mostly Anferthians—had pinned someone to the ground and were raining blows on the unfortunate soul. Too bad it wasn't the Minister. He was surrounded by most of his guards, and some Unified Defense Fleet troops as well. As she watched, other UDF personnel moved to break up the brawl.

All she could do was shake her head. "I can't believe you just started a civil war on a baseball field."

"I certainly fired the first shot." He gazed across the field at the minister, as if he wished the shot was real and was buried in the man's chest. "Not that T'orr will know the extent of it, yet."

"C'mon, stay with us." Mama's muttered words drew Flora's gaze to Kapit Tymo's prone body lying face down in the green grass.

Blood flowed through a gaping wound between her shoulder blades. The projectile of an Anferthian *fusil* was much larger than a *telum's*. It only took one to produce so much blood. A sharp pang stabbed at her heart. It was like Grandfather all over again. Uncle Dante and Mama's hands hovered over the entry point as they applied their combined healing Gifts. They were trying, but their faces already spoke the truth of the situation.

Uncle Dante's shoulders drooped. "We can only ease her pain now."

Mama blinked rapidly and nodded.

Fander scrambled forward and lay on his stomach, his head close to the fallen soldier. "Kapit Tymo?"

The officer opened her eyes and her mouth moved. "My *ymero*."

"My warrior." Fander reached out and cupped his hand over the crown of her head.

"Allegiance…is yours."

"I will fight for your own."

The corners of Tymo's mouth rose in a content smile and she closed her eyes.

Poppy leaned forward. "The situation is anything but stable, your highness. Go, while they're distracted. We will detain S'gow and the panel members."

Flora looked between the two men. "Go? You're *leaving* again?"

Fander pushed up into a crouched position and grabbed her hand. "Not without you, this time."

"I told—"

Mama rested her fingers against Flora's forearm. "After nine years, do you really want to turn your back on it all now?"

That brought her up short. No. The answer was no, she didn't. But, there were so many things that needed to be resolved first.

"*Cori*." Poppy cupped her cheek in his palm. "It's time to be the warrior you were meant to be. May the Mother bless your journey."

A sense of destiny settled over her. In the span of a few moments, everything had changed. Despite the unresolved issues between her and Fander, there was no going back now. And maybe that hadn't been an option since the moment she'd first met him. As much as she didn't want to leave her family, it was time to do exactly that.

Kapit Danol and the remainder of Grandfather's guards closed in around her and Fander.

Fander laced his fingers between hers. "Keep your head down and run."

Sixteen

Fander kept firm hold of Flora's hand as they closed the distance to the waiting surface skimmer. This reunion with his *tangol* had spiraled out of his control yet again. Once he got aboard the transport, she would probably finish the job Minister S'gow had begun. Things could not get much worse.

At least Flora's mother had faith.

"None of our solutions is perfect," she'd said via the private vid-comm last night, "but this one's the closest. She'll be as safe as we can make her, but the rest will be up to you."

Lady Bock had always found a way to calm him when he was agitated. She had been like a mother to him while he had lived on Terr.

He passed through the hatchway and into the passenger compartment of the multi-seat surface skimmer.

"Are you out of your ever-loving mind?" Flora wrenched her hand from his with so much force he almost stumbled.

She faced him, her hands clenched in fists at her side and wisps of loose red hair plastered to her sweaty neck. Somewhere along the way she must have lost her combat cap.

"Not yet." He gestured toward the empty seats. "We are taking off for the transport immediately, Flora. Please sit down."

"There aren't enough seats for everyone. I'll stand."

Why did she have to be so obstinate?

Nor cleared his throat. "My Lady Flora, as long as you stand my prince shall stand. None of us will sit if he risks his well-being in this manner. I would consider it a personal favor if you would secure yourself in a seat for the brief ride to the transport so at least some of us may do the same."

Flora's eyes widened and she appeared ready to argue. Then she pressed her lips together so hard they turned almost as pale as her skin. "Fine."

She glanced around and headed for the seat next to his mother. That was a blatant message. There would be no further discussion until she was ready to listen.

He shot a frown at the captain of his guard. "Thanks, Nor."

"Anytime, my prince." Nor grinned like an idiot, and nodded in the direction of the closest seat. "If you do not mind."

"Fine." Amazing how therapeutic it was to utter that word. No wonder Flora used it so often.

Thirty minutes later, the transport homed into the docking bay of the ship in orbit. Once again, Flora had chosen to sit away from him the moment they had boarded. It would have been nice if his *tangol* had a more amenable personality. Although, if she did, then he would miss out on watching her stomp out of the passenger compartment now as the remainder of Grandfather's guards hurried to keep up with her.

His mother gave him an amused smirk. "She has fire, I must admit. Like a razor-horned hellion. The universe has given you a worthy companion."

"Hopefully, she listens to reason."

"In that, I wish you luck, my son." His mother motioned to her own guard, and Rauc followed her out, ducking his head and turning his wide shoulders sideways to fit through the door.

"I wish you luck, too," Nor said.

"Thanks. I will need all the luck I can get." Fander gave his head a shake. "Come, now. It is time for me to confront my personal razor-horned hellion."

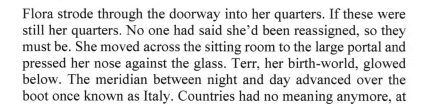

Flora strode through the doorway into her quarters. If these were still her quarters. No one had said she'd been reassigned, so they must be. She moved across the sitting room to the large portal and pressed her nose against the glass. Terr, her birth-world, glowed below. The meridian between night and day advanced over the boot once known as Italy. Countries had no meaning anymore, at least not to most people. There were still a few pockets of society who clung to the old ideals of segregation for various reasons, and the Terrian council had adopted a hands-off policy when dealing with these tiny tribes. In return, the tribes kept to themselves. They had no use for aliens or their technology.

"My lady?"

Flora took in a deep breath and expelled it, then turned to face Grandfather's guards, or what was left of them. Kapit Tymo's absence was almost a physical thing. "Yes, *Comtat* Cynto?"

The young commander glanced over her shoulder at the remainder of the double patrol, then back. "We know it is not part of your traditions to send off the dead with the death-lament. We appreciate that you did so when word of Kapit Tymo's death was announced en route."

Even though Tymo had still been alive when Fander had hustled her off the field, it'd cut deep when the news had come while they were aboard the transport. Yes, she had howled with the Anferthians. How could she not? "It's a beautiful way to honor a friend."

Cynto's eyes went wide, and then she kneeled on one knee and bowed her head. The others followed suit. "It is our wish to reaffirm our allegiance to you, Lady Flora of Terr. If you will have us."

The door chime pinged. It could only be one person. His exalted royalness. "Come in."

On cue, the door swooshed open and Fander stepped into the room. His gaze went from the kneeling guards to her and he raised one cinnamon colored eyebrow in silent question.

She raised her chin a notch. "*My* guards have chosen to reaffirm their allegiance to me, and I am all for it."

"As am I." Fander moved around the group until he faced them. His arm brushed her shoulder and she stiffened. "But, how does that affect your service to the crown, Comtat?"

Cynto didn't look down or away in deference. Instead, she made full eye contact. "Who does the crown serve, my prince?"

"The crown serves the people of Anferthia, as I stated to Minister S'gow."

"What about the Arruch?"

That was a great question. Flora gave him a pointed look. "Yeah, what about them? They're not going to just step aside, you know."

His gaze met hers. "I plan to convince them otherwise."

"You, and what army?"

The smack of palms striking uniform material filled the room. "We are that army." Cynto announced. "How may we serve you, my *ymero*?"

The corners of Fander's mouth twitched upward in a smirk. "There are others, as well."

"You're such a smug turd."

Great, now he was full-on grinning.

He turned his attention back to the guards. "Prince is fine for now, Comtat Cynto. I charge you with the protection of my *tangol*. I entrust her life to you."

"By your command, it shall be." Cynto's tongue darted out over her lips. "We will need a new captain assigned to us. I was Kapit Tymo's second, but I have two galactic years until I qualify for advancement."

"I happen to have someone in mind, Comtat. Will you remain in temporary command for now?"

"The honor is mine, my prince."

Damn, he was still good at turning potential setbacks into positive forward motion.

"Thank you, Comtat." Fander seemed inordinately pleased. "You are excused. I must speak to Lady Flora in private."

Cynto's gaze shifted to her. "My lady?"

"Don't worry. I held my own against him once already today. I can do it again."

"By your word."

The guards rose and left, the door closing behind them. She gave Fander a glare then turned back to the window. What the hell? Terr had dwindled to the size of a distant basketball. How had she missed the sensation of the ship moving out of orbit?

Hot tears blurred her vision. "I guess you weren't kidding. You really are taking me to Anferthia."

He stepped up next to her, facing the window. "Eventually, yes."

"Eventually?" She gave a skeptical snort. "What does *that* mean?"

He braced his forearm against the glass and leaned his forehead against it. "Before I bury myself in a hole of my own creation, I would first like to explain what has already happened."

"Oh, good. You're going to answer my questions from yesterday?" Terr was about the size of a tennis ball now.

"That is a good place to begin." He sighed, his breath visible on the glass for a split second. "As a child, I couldn't reveal my status to anyone on Terr. That was what Isel T'orr and those who call themselves my regents drummed into my head before I left Anferthia with Grandfather. I did not figure out you and I are *tangol* until the day that wave dragged you into the ocean. By then, I had already developed...feelings for you. Being forced to leave...." He shook his head.

The fight went out of her like a deflating balloon. She rubbed her hand over her forehead. "Why didn't you fight back? Why'd you let them send you away?" *You left me.*

He didn't respond for several heartbeats. Then, "Our lives were joined the moment we met, and there is no way to dissolve that bond. I lived for you then, and still do. And you for me, whether you realize it or not. What you did for me on the field today is a perfect example of how *tangol* affects us. But, I *did* fight back, Flora. I used every argument my teenage mind could conceive." He gave a little half laugh. "Nothing worked. It took me until I was eighteen to realize how important it was that you grow up unencumbered by a bond you could not possibly understand at that time. *I* barely understood it fully. But, I tried to leave you some sort of reassurance in my note. That the separation was only temporary."

Ah, yes, the note. She made a small huffing sound through her nose. *"Dear Flora, I'm sorry I could not stay to celebrate with you last night. I hope you had a memorable day anyway, as your fifteenth birthday should be. Unfortunately, I have been called back to Anferthia. Please do me the favor of visiting Grandfather. He will be lonely, and it would make me feel better to know you are keeping him company. Don't ever give up. Fander."*

Fander straightened and stared at her with a stunned expression.

"Yeah, I memorized it word for word in less than five minutes." And had recited it to herself like a daily mantra ever since.

She leaned her shoulder against the window and crossed her arms in front of her. "Grandfather and I had a standing date every year on my birthday. Even though we saw each other at other times, that was our special morning together. Mrs. Beck would bake muffins for us because she was afraid we'd talk so much we'd forget to eat."

A huge lump rose to her throat and she lowered her gaze to the matte black surface of the floor. Once again, she was on the verge of becoming a slobbering, sobbing mess.

Fander reached out and brushed his fingers along her upper arm. "Thank you. Not just for visiting him, but also for being with him—allowing me to be with him—as his life here came to an end. I don't know how you figured out how to work the reliquary, but I'm glad you did."

"He told me what to do." She sniffed and wiped the back of her hand under her nose. Anferthians were so lucky they didn't cry. Snot was gross.

Fander paused mid-stroke. It should bother her that he took the liberty of touching her, but it seemed to be the only thing keeping her from sinking all the way into the memory of Grandfather's murder. "It was my fault that he died."

"Why?"

"*I* killed him, Fander. I led her to his office. If I hadn't been there, he'd still be alive."

"No." He ran his hands up and down her upper arms, the light touch keeping her attention from disintegrating into remorse. "No, you're wrong. Haesi Velo would have killed anyone standing in her way. *Anyone*. Your parents, Juan, Mags. You cannot blame yourself because you couldn't control someone else's actions. Grandfather would never have wanted you to do so."

"Maggie." Her sister's name squeaked out. It could've been Maggie who died that day. The truth of the situation loomed over her like a giant black cloud. "I'm a target."

A walking, talking target who was a danger to the people she loved.

"Yes, you are." Fander pulled her into his embrace, her cheek resting against the stiff quilted roughness of his combat garment. "We both are. And it is not something either of us asked for. It was the lot given us through the chance of birth and the unpredictability of *tangol*. We have some powerful enemies, Flora. I've been hiding my true self from them all my life. Now, it is time to face them."

Enemies who had kept them apart, killed Grandfather K'nil, and— "They killed your father, didn't they?"

"Yes." The heat of his breath warmed the top of her head.

"They killed my parents, too." She curled her hand into a fist against his chest. "I want those motherfuckers to pay, Fander."

Seventeen

Fander let Flora's words wrap around him and inhaled her scent, drawing it into every cell of his being. Normally her swearing was of the damn, shit, hell variety. It was good to know her passion had not abated.

This was a breakthrough, a moment of hope that he would win her over and they could start planning their next move. Including the direction of their personal relationship. "I want that too, Flora. Ever since I learned the truth behind their power. Will you help me?"

She pushed away and gazed up at him. "You're asking? I thought I didn't have a choice."

"Our lives may be bonded, but I will never force you to do something you do not wish to do." The Arruch had forced him to do and say things he never would have on his own. Used him to reaffirm their power and spy for them. There was no way he would be like them. "I may not be perfect, but I am not another Isel T'orr."

Flora poked him in the chest with one finger. "You." Poke. "Dragged me." Poke, poke. "Off the field." Poke, poke, poke. "Forcefully." Hard poke.

He cupped his hand over hers in case she decided to poke him again. "It was more getting you out of the line of fire." She hmphed, but at least she did not interrupt. It was important she heard what he must say. "You are more to me than my *tangol*, you know. You're my childhood friend, my first kiss, and the memory that kept me going since I left. I'll do what I must to keep you safe."

"Including kidnapping me?"

"I was protecting you."

"Whatever."

He sighed and gave his head a shake. "*Rywoud* has shown us that we will be together throughout this life, for however long or short that is."

"Okay, that's another thing I need clarified. Does this mean we're supposed to get married, or something?"

"Some *tangol* are love matches, but many bonded pairs are not romantic partners. Grandfather and Holt Huunu were not."

"They were bonded...*tangol*? Like us?"

He gave her a grin. "Yes. But, here's the difference. I intend to convince you to marry me."

Gods, he loved seeing her cheeks turn pink. She took a half step back and raised her chin. "It'll never work."

"Pfft. So you say."

She pointed toward the portal. "You remember what you did back there on my planet, right? You laid the groundwork for a civil war. Your people might, *might*, accept me as *tangol* because that bond is part of your culture, but as your wife? I'm a Terrian. Lots of them will hate me for that reason."

"Once, you hated me for being Anferthian."

She lowered her arm and blinked, twice. Three times. Four, five. If she had to think about it that long, then he almost had her. He stepped into her personal space and cupped his palm along her jaw. "But, you changed your mind, didn't you?"

Her tongue darted over her lips. "You think we could change their minds?"

"I'd like to try." It was a good sign that she had not pulled away from his touch "That's why we are stopping at Matir to pick up the dissenters."

Her eyes widened and a shriek of joy was all the warning he got before she launched herself at him and wrapped her arms around his neck in the hug he had waited nine grueling years to receive.

He slipped his arms around her waist, lifted her small body as close to his own as possible, and buried his face in the warm curve between her neck and shoulder to inhale her scent again. "Nine years. I am so sorry, Flora. I have missed you for every moment of those years."

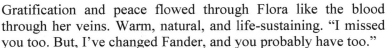

Gratification and peace flowed through Flora like the blood through her veins. Warm, natural, and life-sustaining. "I missed you too. But, I've changed Fander, and you probably have too."

His head moved from side to side and the hair covering his ear tickled her nose. "Not me. I just got taller."

A small bubble of laughter escaped her. "You're still short for an Anferthian, aren't you?"

"Smart ass." He loosened his hold and she slid down his body until her feet touched the floor. He leaned back far enough to make eye-contact but didn't let go. "Earth should never surrender to anyone, ever. Do you think that Earth and Anferthia have a strong enough foundation to build a relationship upon as equals?"

"We can try. But, I can't promise I won't challenge you, from time to time." Often.

"I need more challenges in my life." A teasing sparkle danced in his eyes.

Sure, he did. "And I'm still not sure about this whole marriage thing."

He grinned. "Are you okay with seeing what happens?"

"You mean, take it slow? I can do that."

"Start with dinner tonight?"

"Okay."

"I will return at twelfth hour." He stepped back, taking his warmth.

She suppressed a shiver. "Am I under house arrest still?"

That was genuine surprise in his wide eyes. "You never were. You are my *tangol*, and all aboard know it. Every area aboard this ship that I can go, is open to you. That means the whole ship, in case you're wondering."

She let out the breath she hadn't realized she'd been holding. "Thank you."

He smiled and held her gaze. "It is good to be together again, Flora."

"Yeah, it is, isn't it?"

Collision

Fander frowned down at the reliquary on his desk. He'd tried repeatedly to access the records kept within, yet was denied every time. As his grandfather's heir, he should be able to tap in and view the message left to him. But, even after an hour of trying every coding he could think of, the reliquary remained silent.

"What did you do, Grandfather?" Only the heir could access another's reliquary, unless....

He tapped his comm. "Mother?"

"I am here." As she always was.

"Do you have time for a conversation?"

"Indeed, I do. What matters occupy your mind?"

He allowed a small smile to creep up. There was no telling when someone loyal to the Arruch might be listening. Keeping comm discussions formal and bare of suspicious words was an engrained habit. Soon, none of this would be necessary. "Grandfather. May we speak in person?"

"Of course, my son." Her response was appropriately laced with motherly concern.

"I will come to you."

"I cannot access it." Fander held up Grandfather's reliquary between his thumb and forefinger.

Lady Fani K'nil's frown drew deep indentations at the corners of her mouth and the fine lines around her eyes multiplied as she squinted at the crystal. A pang of sorrow went through his heart. She had visibly aged in the days since Grandfather's passing. Even the slight touch of grey at her temples had spread.

She pursed her lips. "But, you are the K'nil heir. We decided it would be this way when you were only four summers."

"I know, but I have tried every possible avenue without success." His grandfather would have left him a message within the crystal, a final word, or parting advice. It was tradition. "Could you try? Maybe he changed it back to you."

"Unlikely, especially after he made Flora his custodian. If the heir had changed, he would have told her." His mother sighed. "However, I shall try."

He handed the reliquary to her and she retreated to the farthest end of the sitting room couch. There was nothing to do now but wait.

Ten minutes later, his mother let out a gasp.

He turned away from the view port, hope elevated his heartbeat. "Did you access it?"

"No." Then why was she smiling at him in such a triumphant manner? "But, I do know neither of us is his heir, which leaves only one person."

"Who?" There were no other descendants in Grandfather's line.

"Think about it, Fander. Who else calls him grandfather?"

That would be...Flora? He stared at his mother as his eyes widened. "No." He dragged out the whispered word.

His mother nodded. "Yes."

"Is that even possible with a Terrian?"

"You tell me. She is your Terrian *tangol*." She placed the reliquary in his palm.

True. He gazed down at the pendant. Seafoam green fluid speckled with silver swirled in a slow lazy pattern within the crystal, its contents and secrets protected until the heir accessed them.

The heir who wasn't him. "The last time I spoke to him through our reliquaries was the day of Flora's twenty-fourth birthday. I was...*in* Flora's *rywoud*, part of her dreaming. Something happened that indicated her life was in danger, and I thought he should know so he could take the proper precautions. At that time, my signature still resonated in his reliquary, yet he died a short time later."

"What about the time of his passing? You communicated with him then."

"Yes...no. Wait. *Flora* made the contact, not Grandfather."

"Ahh." A knowing smile curved the corners of her mouth upward.

He closed his fingers around the sacred crystal. "Flora thinks *I'm* the heir. If he did make the change, why didn't he tell her?" And how had he had the time to make the change? He had died less than an hour after their initial conversation.

Mother shrugged one shoulder. "I have no answers, my son. And we will not know if the change was made until you have her try."

EIGHTEEN

Flora shimmied the *wysgog* shirt over her head, the silky, forest-green material caressing her body as it slid down. There was something comforting and comfortable about the Anferthian style. And it was versatile. Amazing how one basic pattern could work for any occasion—formal, casual, utilitarian—depending on the type of material used.

She smoothed her palms over the fabric as she gazed at her image in the mirror. Mama and Maggie had packed every last one of her *wysgogs*, which totaled five completed outfits and three still in various stages of completion. She'd have to sew some more once she got to Anferthia. Even if things didn't work out with Fander, she would still be a Terrian junior ambassador to his planet. A wardrobe of *wysgogs* was necessary to honor Fander's people. That was a trick she'd learned from him as a kid. The only time she'd ever seen him dress in a *wysgog* was for official occasions. The rest of the time he'd worn Terrian styles.

Maybe he'd let her make him some more Terrian clothes to replace the ones he'd outgrown.

Ping.

"Fander K'nil," the computer announced.

Her heart fluttered in her chest.

He's here.

She gave her hair a final pat and tried not to rush out of her bedroom. How would an *ymere* behave? Calm. In control as she crossed her sitting room. Never hurrying for anyone, including her *ymero.*

Oh, God. Why was she even *thinking* like that? She pressed her hand against the reader and the door whooshed open.

Holy moly, Fander wore black...well. Really, really well. It made his slim body look taller, which was a good thing for a shorter-than-average Anferthian. Did short Anferthian males suffer from Napoleon complexes? How tall was Isel T'orr anyway? She gave her head a mental shake. If Fander was representative of that tiny segment of the population, then no, they didn't. And, in all seriousness, the others didn't matter. Only Fander.

"You are gorgeous, Flora."

Heat rose into her cheeks. She'd been so busy appreciating the way he'd dressed, she'd completely forgotten to pay attention to *him*. And his gentle smile, given only to her. "Thanks." Oh, well now, that sounded so freaking intelligent. "I...um."

"I can't believe it."

"W-what?"

"You." His grin widened. "Flora Grace MacDonald Bock, at a loss for words. That seldom happens."

Dammit. "You turd."

"I think it's adorable."

All these years she'd done so well being the staunch and strong woman who could stand on her own without him. Now, his words were the glue holding her together. Talk about doing a one-eighty. She was in such trouble.

"I have something for you."

Did the entire universe just get a little brighter? "You do?"

He brought his hands out from behind his back. A chain of wilted clover flowers hung from his long fingers. It was déjà vu, and her vision blurred with tears. "You remembered."

"I never forgot."

She looked back up into those amaranthine eyes. "Neither did I. How did you get these?"

"Mags." He looped the chain over her head. "She's still the best co-conspirator in the galaxy."

A small laugh escaped her. "Don't I know it."

"Are you hungry right now? Or would—"

"Hungry." Whatever else he had in mind could wait until her stomach was appeased. "Where are we going to eat?"

"Here is fine. May I come in?"

"Oh, right. Yes." Duh. She stepped to one side.

Fander glanced down the corridor and nodded once, then stepped into the sitting room area of her quarters. Several tray-carrying Anferthians filed in behind him, flowing into the room with practiced efficiency. The meal was set and the servants—if that's what they were—disappeared through the doorway again.

Savory scents filled the space and her stomach growled.

"Ready?" Fander's eyes twinkled with merriment as he made a sweeping gesture toward the table of covered dishes.

"This is the way you live, isn't it?"

He lowered his arm and looked at her as if trying to root out the underlying reason for her question. "Not normally. Things are a bit different aboard a ship than at home."

"Oh." This would take some getting used to, even though she'd attended her share of official dinners and stayed in political residences with full staffs. Even Grandfather K'nil had had servants.

She slid onto one of the chairs at the small table. Fander sat across from her and lifted the lids one by one. "*Gogi?*"

"Yes." The brined pork was one of her favorite Anferthian dishes. "With the *seuso* over it, and some *ardlyn* greens on the side. Oh, and a slice of the *bara* bread, please."

Fander looked pleased by her words. If he grinned any wider, his cheeks might pop off. She let him serve her since technically he was the host, even though they were in her quarters.

"This is like our first date, Fander." Which was mushy-romantic.

"It *is* our first date, Flora." He raised one eyebrow, and a laugh bubbled out of her.

Dinner went by in a blur of small talk, reminiscing, and laughter. It was comfortable, like things used to be between them. Better even, now that teen angst was out of the picture.

Once they'd finished eating, he reached for the decanter of Anferthian emerald wine and she turned her glass upright. After he'd poured, he sat back, his gaze now on the contents of the glass cradled between his hands. "May I ask you something?"

"Sure."

"How did you get the *kadura* holding your braid?"

She reached up and traced her fingers over the carved red-gold metal clasp set with tiny green stones, paler than peridots, at the back of her head. "Grandfather gave it to me on my seventeenth birthday. He said my hair was long enough to need one."

Fander frowned. "Your hair was always long enough."

She lowered her hand to her glass. "I keep forgetting that you have no idea what happened after you left." She raised the glass to her lips, and a light, slightly dry effervescence danced over her tongue. Delicious. "After I got your note, I had a fairly good-sized temper tantrum and took a pair of scissors to my hair. Hacked it real short. I thought by growing my hair out into a *tirik* in solidarity with you, it'd make me feel closer to you, somehow. It made perfect sense at the time. My mom cried—not in front of me, but I knew. It made Poppy sad too. Juan blamed me for you being sent away, and he teased me about how I looked like a boy, and that you'd never come back because of it. Things got pretty ugly.

"The only one who understood why I did it was Grandfather, but it took a year before I finally cooled down enough to go talk to him. It was my sixteenth birthday, and I marched into his office all sure of myself that I'd get him to tell me when you'd be back. Didn't work, of course. Instead, I found a friend who guessed the real reason behind my rebellion. It surprised me how supportive he was."

Fander stared at her, open-mouthed. "Flora, I am honored."

She gave her hand a wave.

"No, really, I am." He touched his fingertips to his heart.

"Really?"

"Really. And, I have my own little rebellion to confess." He set his glass on the table. "Nothing as drastic as yours, however I very intentionally left the *kadura* that's in your hair now on my nightstand where Grandfather would be sure to see it. My father had it made for my mother as a symbol of their joined families, the royal B'aq's and the K'nil's. Leaving it behind was my message to Grandfather that a part of my life—one as important to me as my heritage—remained on Terr, and I wouldn't have one without the other." He paused, then continued on a softer note. "By giving it to you, he sent his own message that the two parts weren't meant to remain separated."

Oh. *Ohh.* "The answer was in my hand all those years, and I didn't even know it."

She reached up, unfastened the *kadura*, and handed it to him.

Fander covered her hand with his, curling her fingers around the piece. "Thanks, but this is yours. It's my hope that you continue to wear it with honor, and in memory of Grandfather."

Her heart soared, and she reattached it to the top of her braid. "You know I will. He meant the world to me...to us." She tilted her head to one side. "How are you doing, Fander?"

"What do you mean?" He leaned back in his chair and lowered his gaze to his drink.

Poor guy. "With Grandfather's death. If it hurts me, I can only imagine how you're feeling."

He ran his finger from the rim to the stem of the glass. "I miss him, more than words can say."

Yeah, she understood that. She rose from her chair and moved around the table, then wrapped her arms around him from behind. "I'm sorry."

He leaned into her embrace, his head against hers. Almost cheek to cheek. "For what?"

"That I couldn't save him." She swallowed hard against the lump forming in her throat. "I miss him too."

"He loved you as his own. *Fyhen*...and his granddaughter." He placed his large hands over hers, their warmth feeding into her heart. "Would you like to visit him in state?"

A small flinch jerked her. "He's here? On the ship?" Of course he was. Where else would he be?

Fander turned in his chair and looked up at her. "He is. Only if you want to go...."

"Yes." A thousand times, yes.

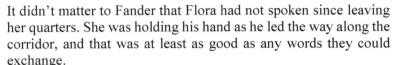

It didn't matter to Fander that Flora had not spoken since leaving her quarters. She was holding his hand as he led the way along the corridor, and that was at least as good as any words they could exchange.

The silence also gave him time to think. He still had no idea how to open the conversation about the reliquary? *"Hey, Flora. It looks like Grandfather made you the heir of his reliquary, and he probably left you a message in it. Oh, by the way, it can only be accessed through the transmission of a certain type of brainwave, which you might not be able to do because you aren't Anferthian."*

He pursed his lips together. Yes, *that* would go over very well with her. Would she even grasp the significance of being its heir? *If* she was the heir. That was pure speculation at the moment, even though everything pointed to that conclusion. But, if she was, and she could not access its contents, then all the histories of each family member who had worn this particular reliquary would be lost.

Including Grandfather's.

It had happened before; to other families, not his.

He slowed as he approached the door of the room in which his grandfather's body now rested.

A vertical worry line appeared between Flora's strawberry blonde eyebrows. "Is this it?"

There was a definite tremor in her soft-spoken words, and she stared at the door. He could not blame her, though. To the best of his knowledge, she had not seen Grandfather since the assassination. "It is. Do you still wish to go in?"

Her mouth was set in a tight flat line, but she nodded. This would never do. He moved to face her. "Something bothers you."

So many emotions crossed her beautiful face, but the only ones he could be certain of were indecision, uncertainty, and fear. She never did either of the last two well.

Her tongue swiped quickly between her lips. "It's just…well…."

"If you do not wish to go in, it is well. But, I can assure you that all traces of violence and death are gone. I swear to you, with the stasis blanket in place, he only appears to be asleep."

That got her attention enough for her to meet his gaze. Resignation, trust, and a touch of determination replaced the other emotions, and she nodded. "Okay. I'm ready."

He gave her the most reassuring smile he could. "I'm right with you." He pressed his free hand to the palm reader and the door telescoped open.

Flora entered first, which was the way it should be. She needed to do this herself, and he would be there to give her support if necessary. No one could ever mistake her as timid, but she did feel deeply and with great passion at times.

Often.

Much like an Anferthian.

Now, why had that not occurred to him before?

She leaned closer to him. "There are guards in there."

"Yes. It is an honor to stand watch over the body of those traveling to their final resting place." He released her hand.

"Aren't you coming with me?"

"I've seen and talked to him multiple times already." He gave her another smile. "Your turn."

"But, I can't talk to him. The guards will hear."

"Nothing anyone says leaves this room. For the guards to reveal the private words of another to the dead will bring them the greatest shame. It is a grievous dishonor."

"Won't they stop me from getting too close?"

"If you were a threat, yes. Since you're not, they will stand their duty for the requisite number of hours without moving or speaking."

Okay." She rolled her shoulders back and stepped farther into the room.

There was so much grace and determination in the curve of her back and the set of her shoulders as she crossed to where Grandfather lay in state near the back wall. A twinge of fear pricked at Fander's heart. Had he done the right thing by dragging her into the dangerous situation he had created? Just because she was his *tangol* did not guarantee she would survive. It had not kept his father safe, even though mother had been with him.

Unease roiled through him and he mentally shook it off. He could not think that way. Flora was safer with him than without; even her parents had agreed. The matter was resolved, for better or for worse.

NINETEEN

The platform Grandfather rested on was as high as Flora's chest, so she could gaze straight at his peaceful profile. Fander was right, he did look like he was asleep. Like all she had to do was whisper his name and his eyes would open and he'd smile at her.

But, he wouldn't. The black-eyed gentle giant of a man would never be there to help guide her again.

Her gaze was drawn to his massive, unmoving chest. The draping white death robe covered the holes created by the multiple *kagi* pumped into his body by Haesi's *telum*.

I'm so sorry.

If only she'd been able to stop Haesi Velo. If only *she'd* answered the door instead of Grandfather. If only, if only, if only. Wishing would never change the outcome. She could only move forward, help Fander. It seemed like he had a plan in mind, but he hadn't told her what it was yet. Aside from picking up the dissenters on Matir, that was. He couldn't be serious about taking them back to Anferthia, could he? The Arruch Union wouldn't like that at all and might use the dissenters for target practice. Good God, they really needed to talk before they arrived at Matir.

She gripped the edge of the high platform and leaned toward Grandfather. "Things are so crazy right now, and it'll probably get worse before it gets better. I wish you were still here to help us." Keep them from making any stupid mistakes.

Grandfather'd had a strong learn-from-your-mistakes philosophy, but in this situation, he might've set that aside.

Mistakes could kill a person, as Uncle Graig said, and right now they couldn't afford to make any.

She bowed her head. "I love you and miss you so much."

The sense of a presence hovering just behind her alerted her she wasn't alone anymore. She glanced over her shoulder.

Fander.

"I thought you might need a tissue." He extended a soft white cloth toward her. "It slipped my mind that we have nothing in here to use to wipe tears." He hesitated. "But, you don't seem to need it after all."

"I can't swear I won't cry again, but right now I feel like I'm all out of tears." How weird was that? "Besides, I'm done for now. We can go."

She stepped toward him, and an overwhelming sense that she had misplaced or lost something—some tangible item—crashed over her, and a gasp escaped through her lips.

The weight of Fander's hand rested on her shoulder. "Flora? Are you well?"

"I—where is Grandfather's reliquary?" That was it…right? It felt right.

Fander's eyes widened. In surprise? "I have it." His gaze shifted to the immobile sentries. "Let's talk about this in your quarters."

She nodded and slid her hand into the crook of his proffered arm.

The walk back seemed shorter than the walk to see Grandfather. Once there, Fander guided her to the couch and sat next to her, turned enough to almost be face to face. "There's an issue with Grandfather's reliquary."

There was?

"Were you at any time alone with my grandfather when he had his reliquary out?"

"Well, yeah. The day he died."

"Tell me everything that happened, as best you can remember."

"Well, he told me you were his heir, and asked if anything happened to him, would I be custodian of it until you could get here. He even allowed me to hold it."

An eager excitement lit his eyes. "Did anything…unusual happen?"

"Well...." She caught her bottom lip between her teeth. How could she explain? "I zoned out, I guess, while he was talking. It was weird, but once Grandfather took it back, my head cleared."

Now his whole face brightened. "That's what I thought." He reached under his shirt and lifted his grandfather's reliquary from around his neck and dangled it by its chain from his fingers. The shimmery green and silver contents swirled in the vial. "I believe Grandfather keyed his reliquary to you, Flora."

"What's that mean?" The swirls caught the light, reflecting it in silver flashes as the reliquary turned in mid-air.

"It means that I'm not his heir." He gave her a meaningful smile.

Was he serious? He looked serious. But, if *he* wasn't the heir, then who.... Oh, no *way*. That couldn't be right. "No. Just no. I can't be his heir, Fander. I'm not Anferthian."

"I have heard that about you." Amusement sparkled in his eyes. "Yet you still receive *rywoud*. Every night before your birthday, if I'm not mistaken. And, you're my *tangol*."

"But—"

"Could it maybe, just *maybe*, be that this has nothing at all to do with *being* Anferthian, and everything to do with being *tangol to* an Anferthian?"

She opened her mouth, but nothing seemed to be flowing between it and her brain. Again. She was so completely out of her element.

Fander raised one eyebrow. "Do you want to hear what I think?"

She moved her head up and down, and side to side. For all the good that would do. Trying to stop an Anferthian when they were on a roll was like trying to halt a glacier with a stop sign. But, he might have an idea she hadn't thought of.

"I think it's time we stop thinking about what we can't do individually and start discovering what we *can* do together." Fander took her right hand and lowered the reliquary into her palm, spiraling the chain around it. "There is no doubt, Flora; you are his heir."

Recognition and relief washed over her, and she curled her fingers around the pendant. She wet her lips with her tongue. "I...what do I do?"

He blew out a breath. "I've been trying to figure that all

afternoon and I still have no answer." That wasn't what she'd hoped he'd say. "So, I decided that the best first step would be to give it you and try to figure it out from there together."

That made sense...sort of. Okay, not really. "Well, you're the Anferthian. What would *you* do?"

"Immediately access it. But, you don't know how, so I'll have to try and teach you. Go ahead and put it on."

Sure, why not? She looped the chain over her head, as Fander dragged over a chair from the dining table and sat facing her, his knees bracketing hers. Intimate, even though it seemed like he was trying not to touch her.

"Let me preface this instruction with 'Do not ever try this without someone to monitor you.' Accessing a reliquary's contents is like entering another dimension. And it is easy to get lost. Always have someone with you to guide you back. Preferably me."

"Are you trying to scare me off?"

"Pfft. As if anything would ever scare you off." He winked at her, the turd. "Just warning you to take precautions."

"Okay, fine. I'm warned. Now what?"

He fished his own reliquary out from under his shirt and held it between them, the burgundy cord still round his neck. "Hold yours like this."

Okay. She mimicked him. "Why is yours red and gold and mine light green and silver?"

"Yours is from my mother's family. Mine belonged to my father, and every *ymero* or *ymere* before him for centuries. It is the only one that shares its color with the color of the blood of the Anferthian people."

"Oh. Ohh." Now she got it. "That's why your sheets are that color. It's like the royal color."

Surprise flashed in Fander's eyes. "You noticed that?"

"Not until after I woke up."

"That was a pretty intense experience. But, yes, just like that. Now, are you ready for the next step?"

"Yep."

"Good. Focus on the moving liquid within the vial, that's it. Let your mind drift with it, flow with it. Relax and imagine moving into the liquid, your thoughts riding its currents."

Twenty minutes later, Fander frowned. This was not working as he had hoped. The process was straight forward, should be easy, yet Flora could not seem to connect with her reliquary.

Flora blew out a frustrated breath. "I can't *do* it."

"You can. You just haven't figured out how, yet. It'll come to you." Even as the words left his mouth, doubt spiraled through him. What if she did not?

"I want to. It's just not working." She refocused on the vial.

He reached out and closed his hand over hers and she met his gaze. "No more, Flora. Not tonight. You will tire yourself unnecessarily."

"But, I want to."

"We will try again tomorrow."

"Fine." She tucked her reliquary away and leaned toward him, a coy smile curving her mouth. Very clearly, she was looking for something more intimate now. He drew back. Anger flashed in her eyes. "I don't get you, Fander. First you tell me you want to marry me, then you treat me like I carry a plague."

"I *do* wish to marry you."

"Funny way to show it."

She was right, of course. If he was careful not to let a romantic moment go beyond kissing, he should be able to restrain himself enough to satisfy both of them, for now.

She cupped her small, warm hand over his cheek. "In my mind, there is no future worse than one you aren't part of. I can't do that again, can you?"

"You know I can't."

"Then, kiss me, you fool."

Flora's crystal blue eyes were soft with the love and desire filling his own heart. He was more blessed than he deserved. He reached for her, cradling her head between his hands just as he had done the day of her fifteenth birthday.

"May I?" The whispered words hung between them, rebuilding a bridge.

"Yes." Her soft response catapulted him back to the rain-soaked beach trail as though no time had passed.

He touched his mouth to hers. Her lips were warm and soft against his, parting under his gentle pressure, allowing more access than she had nine years ago. More access then he had imagined back then as well. Gods, how many times had he dreamed of learning every inch of her body? Sliding his tongue along hers, then retreating to allow her to do the same. Touching her, everywhere. Inhaling her scent.

The hardened tips of her breasts brushed his chest and a rush of blood flooded his groin. The light touch of her fingers trailing over his back became more insistent, pulling him down with her as she reclined on the two-seater. Only a few layers of cloth stood between their most intimate parts. The scent of her desire underscored by something earthy filled his senses, enticing his very raw and wild Anferthian heritage to demand consummation.

This had to stop before it was too late. He drew deep for the strength and ended the kiss. Flora moaned, her lips parted, her eyes closed. Breathtaking. He rested his forehead against hers. "Flora."

"What?" She breathed out in a whisper.

"We can't do this." Although he craved nothing more than to jettison his words out an airlock and continue along this path of pleasurable discovery with her.

She opened her passion-glazed eyes and watched him for at least half a dozen heartbeats. "Oh, I think we can, but we're not going to, are we?"

"No." He gave his head a shake. "Not yet."

She made a small sound of disappointment in her throat. "Why not?"

He pulled his head back to see her better. "Because if we do, I will guarantee you that without contraception, our first-born will be created within the next few minutes."

That seemed to get her attention. "How do you know that?"

Now for the real reason. "You know how I scent you?" He paused until she nodded. "Well, when you're most fertile, your scent becomes slightly ... richer, I guess. It's subtle, but I can tell, and right now you're, well, you smell very fertile to me. That's how I know."

"Would having a child be so horrible?"

"Anferthia is less than stable. We need to fix that first before we bring children into a situation that could prove fatal to them."

Flora's eyes cleared. Now, it seemed she understood. "Don't Anferthians have some kind of contraception shot?"

"*Atolce*. But, it takes thirty days to be effective the first time, and I got my first shot seventeen days ago." It had been tricky trying to get hold of a dosage without his keepers finding out, but Nor had come through. "I'd planned to be fully protected by my twenty-fifth birthday, just in case things…worked out. For us, I mean."

"That's good planning ahead." Her shift under him was innocent enough, but it was enough to send another rush of blood straight to his crotch. He pushed up with his arms and rolled off her and onto the floor.

Breathe, in…out…in…out.

"Are you okay, Fander?" Flora stroked her fingertips over his hair, dangerously close to his ear. Not many off-worlders knew about that little secret. There would be no way to explain his reaction to her fast enough, either. Damn, there were so many things to tell her about.

"I'm okay, yes." Barely. It would be better if he put a little more distance between himself and her enticing scent. He moved out of her reach, grabbed the edge of the dining table, and pulled himself to his feet. "Just need to get myself under control."

He leaned his palms on top of the table and lowered his head as he drew in and exhaled measured breaths.

"Anything I can do to help?"

"Sure, pick your nose or something." For what that was worth. She'd probably look adorable with her finger up her nose.

Four small pops filled the silence. He raised his head and gave her an incredulous look. "Did you just …?"

Flora's grin was equal parts innocence and mischief. "Uncle Nick swears there's no better mood killer than ripping one. Please don't tell me farts are an Anferthian aphrodisiac."

He lowered his head again and let himself be taken by shoulder-shaking laughter. No matter how long or short his life would be, with Flora in it, it would always be entertaining.

Twenty

The next morning, Flora followed Comtat Cynto along a corridor, her thoughts full of Fander. And what'd almost happened last night. He could actually smell when she was fertile? Who'd have guessed that was possible? In a way, it was a handy skill to have, even though it'd effectively ended the most promising part of the evening.

She needed to get that shot. What did he call it? Atoonce? No, *atolce*. That was it. Uncle Nick and Aunt Sakura would probably have some in stock. They had to, since they were the only healers living with the banished dissenters.

The commander glanced over her shoulder. "My lady, is all well?"

"Yes. Fine. Just thinking."

Could Cynto also pick up on her fertility? Or any of the other Anferthians on board—like Fader's mother? God, wouldn't *that* be embarrassing? It might smell delicious to him, but what about to others? Why hadn't she asked Fander about that last night? If his quarters were close-by, maybe Cynto would take her there so she could ask before going to see Fani K'nil.

"We have arrived at Lady K'nil's quarters."

Too late.

Comtat Cynto placed the flat of her hand against the rectangular palm reader on the wall. An opening appeared in the wall and expanded into a doorway. And filling that doorway was Rauc, the humongous guard who was never far from Fander's mother. He scrutinized her, as though determining her worthiness to be standing outside his lady's quarters, let alone entering them.

Please don't let him smell my...condition.

Cynto nodded her head once. "It pleases me to present Lady Flora, by the request of Lady K'nil."

Rauc grunted, then placed his hand to his chest and bowed. "My lady awaits your company, Lady Flora."

"Thank you."

Cynto made an about face and took a wide-legged stance at the door. Guess the invitation had not included her. Flora follow Rauc as he led the way farther into the sitting room. The familiar, delicate scent of chamomile tea brewing permeated the air.

Fander's mother beamed at her from the couch. "Welcome, Flora of Terr."

Her voice was smooth and soft, unlike the authoritative voice she had projected at the hearing.

Flora bobbed a deep and respectful Terrian curtsey. "Lady K'nil."

"Fani, you may call me. Thank you for coming." Fani K'nil indicated that Flora make herself comfortable in any of the available chairs. "Long have I desired to speak with you, the one so important to my son. Would you care for tea? Your mother gave this to me...chamomile I believe. It is delicious."

There was that "D" word again. Flora reached across the space between them for the tea mug being offered. "It's one of her favorite blends. She was afraid she'd never have it again after the, um...." Oops. No, no, no. Bad form to discuss the invasion with this woman. Especially since having her as an ally was so important.

Understanding registered on Fani's face. "That she would never have it again after the invasion?"

Dammit. Heat burned up her neck. "I'm so sorry, Lady K'ni...Fani. I didn't mean to say anything that would make you uncomfortable."

"At the expense of your own comfort." Fander's mother smiled. "The day my father told me what happened between you and Fander at your first meeting, I was skeptical. A Terrian would be part of my son's life, forever? Learning of your loss and the deep hate you bore toward all Anferthians brought me to tears. I feared *of* you, and *for* you. Both. You were so young, and there were too many years before Fander's majority."

"What does that mean, exactly? His majority?"

Fani wrapped her hands around her tea mug in her lap. "To fully understand, you must know what happened, and why. The invasion of Terr, it was wrong, but I was helpless to stop it. Anferthia was under the control of a powerful and ruthless government. Two years before the invasion, my husband, the *ymero*, did not die of an illness. He was murdered in our bed by the self-proclaimed Divine Warden, Isel T'orr. My life was spared only because of Fander."

What a terrifying ordeal that must have been. Flora drew her brows together. "I don't understand why T'orr kept Fander alive."

"My son, Isel uses to legitimize his position with our people. As Fander's mother, my cooperation would solidify his power. I acquiesced to his demands, relinquishing my title as *ymere* and allowing Isel to believe he had control over us. It was a dangerous game, one my own father participated in by affecting his cooperation with the Arruch Union. While Isel T'orr used Fander as a political pawn, my father and I secretly taught him the truth. Gave him the knowledge he would need on the day of his twenty-fifth birthday—the day he reaches his majority. It is the day he can publicly claim the title of *ymero* and end the reign of the Arruch."

"But, wouldn't Isel T'orr suspect?"

"Only an utter fool would not contemplate the possibility, but until the day of your trial, Fander had played into T'orr's hands convincingly. It is the only reason my son still lives. Yet, I fear he has little time left. I have little doubt that T'orr plans to end Fander's life before his majority."

A spike of fear stabbed her heart.

Fani ran a finger around the rim of her mug. "The attempt on your life confirms this in my mind. T'orr is suspicious. Fander must make his move soon and expose T'orr for the tyrant he is. This is why we will stop to gather as many of the dissenters as we can from Matir. They swore their loyalty to him years ago, and they will be part of his army when he makes his move to establish himself as *ymero* soon, several months before his majority."

Good for him not waiting for his birthday. "That's good, isn't it?"

"Yes, and no. Taking back control too soon could destroy him. Many of our people have suffered under T'orr's regime, and therefore will not care that Fander is not of age. Others will see it as treason against his regents, and technically they would be right. Such a crime is punishable by death."

Flora's hand trembled and she set her mug on the side table of her chair.

"My choices cost you dearly, Flora, this I understand. My heart grieves that the children of others suffered, yet I believe those choices are what could save both our worlds."

If Fander didn't get himself killed first.

"Flora of Terr, I ask for your forgiveness."

Flora blinked, twice. "For what?"

"What my decisions cost you, and your parents. All four of them."

A tiny spark of anger flickered in her heart and faded. Fander's mother had made the best decisions she could in an impossible situation. Lady K'nil…Fander's mother…Grandpa K'nil's daughter…a woman. She was no better or worse than herself, and she'd suffered her own unimaginable losses. It even sounded as though her husband had been killed in front of her. There had been no way for her to win, not short term at least.

But long term, there had been hope. And that hope's name was Fander.

A chill ran down Flora's spine and she shuddered. "I wasn't anywhere near as strong as you when they died."

"You were a child."

"I know." That wasn't the point. "I was angry for so long, but I can't even be angry about this anymore. Especially now that I understand what and why things happened. I don't want to be, either. What I want is to be a part of fixing what's been broken for too long."

"Failure is a very real possibility."

"If I don't try, then my parents' lives mean nothing to me." And, everything Mama and Poppy had done to free Terr would be worthless, too. "*That's* what Poppy meant."

"I do not understand."

"Just before Fander hauled me off the baseball field, my father told me it was time to be the warrior I was meant to be." And years ago, Mama had told her that someday she'd find enough peace in her heart to forgive. Today was that day. "If not for your choices, my adoptive parents—my mama and poppy—might not have survived. *I* might not have survived. Or Fander." She extended her hand. "Fani of Anferthia, my forgiveness is yours."

Fander's mother placed her hand over Flora's. "You are gracious, kind, and wise, my son's *tangol*."

"I wish I had been all that a lot sooner. It might have saved Fander a black eye the day we met."

His mother chortled. "Yes, I did hear about that. It is good that you are not afraid of my son. Titles intimidate some people, but not you. You and he complement and challenge each other to be the best people possible. He needs you to do that...Anferthia needs you to do that, because they deserve a strong leader." Fani lifted her mug, her lips curving into a knowing smile, and raised her eyebrows. "Or possibly two strong leaders."

Twenty-One

Isel T'orr ground his teeth together. "He. Did. *What?*"

"Minister S'gow ordered a guard to—"

"I heard you." He made a lateral chopping motion with the blade of his hand. Supreme Warden Tusayn obviously did not know a rhetorical question when he heard one. "*Why* would he do this?"

Tusayn visibly swallowed. "The leader of the Terr Council did not elaborate."

Rotting slime worms. What had they said that had turned his second in command into a stuttering fool? "Start...from...the beginning, Tusayn."

"Yes, Divine One." Tusayn licked his thin lips and fidgeted with the metallic decorations on his shirt. "The heir arrived on Terr as scheduled, but he apparently made an unplanned appearance at the trial of Flora Bock."

That was unsurprising, if what Haesi had told him was true.

"S'gow said that the prince dismissed the charges against her."

"*What?*" Without consulting with him first? An inexcusable breach of trust.

"He then challenged her to the *ratig'a*."

Now, that sounded promising. "To the death. Excellent. And Fander won, of course."

"Not exactly, Divine One."

"What do you mean?"

"The Bock woman suffered an incapacitating injury that

granted Fander an automatic win."

Isel curled and uncurled his fingers. "So, she lives still?"

"Yes, my lord."

"And Fander?"

"Reports say that S'gow ordered his guard to shoot—"

"Shoot Fander. Yes, we covered that. Again, *why?*"

Tusayn's mouth opened as if he was going to speak, but no words came out. This was ridiculous. He raised his open hand and swung.

Crack!

The sound of skin smacking skin cut through the silence. "Spit it out, Tusayn, or I shall throw you in a cell at the lowest level."

Tusayn blinked and recovered his composure. "The reports are not clear if the target was Fander or the Bock woman, my lord."

"Are *either* of them dead?"

"They both live. Ambassador K'nil's captain of the guard took the shot."

Just one disappointment after the other.

"There is more, Divine One."

Of course there was. Isel braced his spine and raised his chin. "Go on."

"Fander announced that Flora Bock is his *tangol* and is bringing her to Anferthia."

"*WHAT?*" Isel drew back his arm and smashed his fist into Tusayn's jowl. The heavier man staggered back a few steps and toppled into a chair.

Of all the cursed things that could happen. The *Profetae's* daughter was *supposed* to be dead. Haesi had somehow failed to accomplish the deed and had disappeared like a coward. S'gow and his Panel of Justice were supposed to finish the job, but now they were detained indefinitely by the Terrian Council, pending investigation. Fander had over-stepped his bounds. First with the dismissal of charges, then with claiming Flora Bock as his *tangol*...if such a thing were even possible with a Terrian. And now, he was reportedly bringing her to Anferthia.

Isel turned back to the table and picked up the glass of liquid comfort he had poured moments before Tusayn had entered his private sanctuary. He raised the glass to his lips and the pungent acidity of the alcohol washed over his tongue and permeated his sinuses. Perhaps bringing the girl here might not be such a bad thing after all. Both of them would be in close proximity. Easy—*easier*—targets.

"Tusayn, get up."

His second scrambled out of the chair and stood at attention. "Divine One?"

"Fander will bring K'nil's body to his home. You will be there to officially greet him and give him my condolences. Tell them the Ambassador's Service of Internment into the Well of Rest will be moved to the official palace in *Sala D'eu* the evening after they arrive. State that I shall attend to give my respects."

"Divine One, his family will wish to have his service at the K'nil family estate. What if he refuses?"

"He will not dare." No one refused the Divine Warden, not even the displaced son of the last *ymero*. The soon-to-be-*dead* son. It was a shame he would have to accelerate the plan, but it had never been his intention for Fander to reach his twenty-fifth birthday. The young man had made his choices, and those choices now made him an extreme liability.

Flora gave Fander a nudge with her elbow and pointed at the snow-laden trees outside the shuttle window. "*Biete* trees, only found in Matir's southern hemisphere."

It'd been years since she'd visited Uncle Nick and Aunt Saku here at the dissenters' isolated sanctuary. This was the most desolate and beautiful place she'd ever seen. Harsh, yet stunning. Somehow, the Anferthian dissenters had managed to eke out a living here in a place where summer was only three months long. And her aunt and uncle lived and worked alongside them, attending their health issues. Her cousins William and Tamiko would be eight and five now. Tamiko probably wouldn't even remember her. What would Uncle Nick and Aunt Saku do after the dissenters left?

A barely perceptible bump under her boots indicated the shuttle had settled onto the landing pad.

"Your aunt and uncle are to be commended for staying here to care for my lost people." Fander turned toward her, his face partially obscured by the huge hood attached to his parka. "I can't imagine how difficult it has been for them to live and raise a family in such harsh conditions. It does not snow on Anferthia."

"What, never?"

"Only on the highest peaks, of which there are thirty-seven."

The clunk of the locking mechanism releasing sounded from within the hatch. Fander nudged her gloved hand and closed his fingers around hers. "Are you ready?"

She gave him a smile. "I'm ready."

The hatch opened and the frigid air of winter in the southern hemisphere of Matir blasted over her and creeped into her lungs with icy, questing fingers. She exhaled a long stream of white breath and squinted. The sparkling sunlight on the snow seemed brighter than she remembered. A lot of good her sunglasses were doing back in her quarters.

"*A nat*." Nor's muttered curse came from the other side of Fander. "It should be warmer as the sun is out and the sky is clear, but this is colder than the time we went to Lake Tahoe in the winter."

Flora leaned forward to peek around Fander. "You should see this place during a storm."

Nor shook his head vehemently and tugged a thermal cap from a pocket. A small paper-wrapped package came out with it and fell to the floor in front of his boots. The paper was stamped with tiny red hibiscus flowers.

"Hey." Flora drew her eyebrows together. "Are those my Aunt Simone's dried apples?"

"Yes, my princess." Nor shook out the cap and jammed it on his head.

"How'd you get those?"

He bent, scooped up the package and shoved it back into his pocket. "I would rather not say."

"Nor." Fander's tone was cajoling, yet firm.

The stalwart captain of the renegade Anferthian prince's guard shuffled his feet. "I may have made a wager."

"With who and about what?"

"Graig Roble." Nor stared down at his feet. "About the outcome of the *ratig'a*."

Fander frowned. "I do not understand how you profited from our combat when the unofficial outcome was a draw."

"We both so agreed and paid our prices."

Flora gave Fander a knowing grin. "That was gentlemanly. So, what did Uncle Graig get out of the deal?"

"I would rather not say."

The poor guy looked so uncomfortable her heart went out to him. "Fine. I'm willing to let it go. How about you, Fander?"

Fander nodded, but his attention was on something beyond the now-open hatch. "There they are." His half-whisper was part awe, part uncertainty.

The dissenters waited at the tree line. Not all of them, but at least everyone from the main village, Center. The other four villages had been creatively named North, South, East, and West.

"They have surrounded the transport, my prince."

"So they have, Nor. Do you see anyone you recognize, Flora?"

Flora searched the crowd for familiar faces. "Not yet." Not with so many of them bundled up in cold weather outerwear. One muffled Anferthian stepped forward, and a smaller figure followed. "The short one's got to be Uncle Nick. The other's probably K'rona, but it's hard to tell."

"Let's greet them, then." Fander stepped down onto the snowy landing pad, still holding her hand.

The hard-packed snow crunched under Flora's boots and the excitement of seeing her family and friends again expanded in her chest. The two groups met halfway, and the green-eyed Anferthian pulled down the mask. It was K'rona, and all her attention was focused on Fander. Neither of them spoke as the tension built in the frigid air between like a thunderstorm. It was all Anferthian posturing. The two of them had vid-commed before. But still, this face-to-face meeting had been nearly two decades in the making.

Fander released her hand, pulled off his gloves, and extended his hands, palms up, toward K'rona. "I am Fander, heir of *Ymero* Zular B'aq. You have sacrificed more than anyone should be expected to in the name of my father. I have come to bring you home, but the journey will not be without peril."

K'rona yanked off her own gloves and lowered herself to her knees in the snow, maintaining eye contact the whole time. She placed her bare palms to Fander's. "I am K'rona Zurkku, chosen voice of the dissenters. My prince," her voice wavered. "we are ready to follow you, to the death, if need be." She bowed her head until her forehead touched their joined hands.

The shoosh of cloth and the creak of boots filled the snow-dampened air of the clearing as all the dissenters kneeled around them, left hands pressed to their chests and heads bowed. Flora swiped her gloved fingertips under her eyes. The damn cold made her eyes water.

Uncle Nick pulled his scarf down and gave her a knowing wink. "Welcome to Hell frozen over, Red."

Fander sat at Flora's side on her aunt and uncle's couch, one arm draped over her shoulders. Sometimes being short paid off. The furniture was a bit small for him, but not impossible to sit upon, even though his knees nearly touched his chest. Nor and the three dissenters who had entered the healers' cube with them were not so fortunate and had made do with the floor—once he'd convinced them to sit. They had all been reluctant to do so in his presence, and the one named Storo still stood just inside the entry door.

Nick Bock sat in a stuffed chair rocking his five-year-old daughter, Tamiko. The little girl seemed unbothered by the crowd of mostly giants in the living room. As if their presence was an everyday occurrence, which it likely was.

"Are you really a prince?"

Fander turned his attention to the Terrian boy who had crept up on him. William, Nick and Sakura's son, stared up at him with wide dark eyes, a large mug between his small hands. His face was a perfect blend of his parents' ancestry. Jet black hair like his mother, but with the waves of his father, brushed the boy's shoulders. His wonder-filled eyes were rounder, with only a hint of an Asian slant, yet the deepest brown possible, just short of being black. Curls of steam wafted up from the mug, carrying the rich scent of hot chocolate to Fander's nose.

"Will." Sakura used a mother's warning tone as she handed a similar mug to Flora.

Fander lifted his arm off Flora's shoulders. "It is well, Healer Yamata." He braced his forearms against his knees and clasped his hands together, giving the eight-year-old boy his full attention. "I am a prince, but it would be a greater honor to be your friend."

Will nodded his head with a worshipful expression. "That's so cool."

The Terrian term would be star-struck. Somehow, he would have to help ease the boy past that awkward state.

"Here's your hot cocoa, your majesty." Will offered the mug.

"Thank you, Will. Please, call me Fander. That's what my

friends call me."

"Really? I can *do* that?" Will's gaze darted to his mother.

Sakura smiled. "Yes, but only in private, like now. There will be times when you must use his title, which is 'your highness' for now."

The boy's face lit with a smile powered by inner light, and he raised his hands in the traditional Anferthian greeting. "Great is my pleasure to meet you, Fander, Prince of Anferthia."

The words were spoken in flawless Anferthian, of course. Not surprising, given the influences in his life. He exchanged a glance with K'rona. The leader of the dissenters grinned back from her spot on the floor. Obviously, this Terrian family was closely bonded with his banished people. Something he would need to factor in when deciding who would come with him now, and who would stay.

Flora reached over and took his mug. "I got it."

"Thanks." He placed his hands over Will's and switched to Anferthian. "Mine is the pleasure, William. My friend."

It did not seem possible, but Will's smile brightened even more. Then the youngster crossed his arms in front of his skinny chest, and the smile turned to a glower. "Are you gonna marry my cousin?"

Flora made a strange noise somewhere between a choke and a laugh.

"*William*." Sakura frowned at her son.

Fander leaned in close to the child. "Can you keep a secret?"

Will swayed forward and nodded his dark head.

"That's my plan, but don't tell her."

The boy had the grin of a plotting imp. "You should kidnap her and show her your muscles like the guys in the books my mom reads."

Smack!

"Ow! K'-roh-*nah*." Will rubbed the back of his head.

"You disrespect both your cousin and your mother, youngster. Being nosy is rude, and abduction is a serious crime. Apologize."

"Sorry, Flora. Sorry, mama." Will met each of their gazes, then turned back to Fander. "Sorry, Fander."

"Why do you apologize to me?"

"Because I didn't mean to be rude, and I want you to still be my friend. Are you?"

"Of course, Will. Always."

The amount of relief in Will's expression was almost comical. "Good."

Nick rose from his chair and set his daughter on K'rona's lap. "Well, on that note; Flora, step into my office."

"What? Why?"

Nick waggled his eyebrows and strode in the direction of the closed door at the back of the large room.

Twenty-two

"What. Is. *That*?" Flora stared at the syringe Uncle Nick held up. No wonder he seemed gleeful. He always got like this when he gave shots. Sadist.

"Your ticket to a good time."

"Getting shots is not 'a good time'."

Uncle Nick rolled his eyes. "Seriously? Do I have to spell it out for you?"

"Maybe you should, because I'm not getting it."

"Obviously. And on so many levels."

"I'm not laughing."

"A-t-o-l-c-e."

"A-t-o—*oh*. That."

"Finally. Come sit down, you big faker."

He knew her too well. She slid her butt onto the metal stool. "Does it really take thirty days?"

"Uh-huh." The swipe of the cold antiseptic wipe sent a shiver down her spine. "Ready? Look away."

She turned her head and squeezed her eyes shut. "Has anyone ever tested that theory? I mean, maybe it doesn't take as long for Terrians." Or maybe it took longer. God, please not longer.

"Done."

Already? She glanced down at her arm. Nothing but a tiny red mark. "Wow. I didn't feel anything. You are the master, Uncle Nick."

"That's why they call me a *master* healer." He capped the

needle but didn't meet her gaze.

"Very funny. So, has anyone?"

"What?" He sure was making a show of cleaning up the microscopic mess on the lab table.

"You know. Tested the theory. Wait a sec, are you *blushing*?"

"Nope."

"You *are*." She pressed her hands to her cheeks. "You...oh, geez, Uncle Nick. *You and Aunt Saku*?" Heat burned up her neck into her face. Was that how William came to be? An accident? That was more than she ever wanted to know.

And *now* her uncle locked gazes with her. "Great detective work, Sherlock. Now, do you want the glorious details?"

"Ew, no!"

Flora pushed open the door to the conference room and slipped inside. Fander looked up and snared her gaze, wrapped himself around her without moving from his chair. Even if she was tired, there was no way she could look away. Not that she'd try.

"Did you hear me, your highness?" The voice of a woman speaking in Matiran came from the vid-comm speaker.

The spell fizzled, but the memory lingered.

Fander patted the chair next to him and turned back to the image of the Matiran woman on the screen. "I did, Administer Corvus. How many Anferthians can Ambassador Alexander's ship accommodate?"

"About one thousand, though comfort is questionable. The *Atlantis* was not built with Anferthian dimensions in mind."

The Atlantis? Poppy's command ship during the invasion, and Mama's official flag ship while she was ambassador to Matir. It was also her first home with them after being adopted. She lowered herself onto to the cushioned chair and mouthed "What?" at Fander. He shook his head and she gave him the stink eye.

"And," Corvus's prim voice cut in, "Ambassador Olivarius's ship will represent the Matiran delegation. Her ship can conceal another five hundred."

Fander nodded slowly. "That is more than I'd hoped for. Thanks be to you."

"Your grandfather was a man of honor, well respected on both Matir and Terr. We would be remiss not to give him an escort for his final trip home."

"Again, my deepest thanks, Administrator."

"How will you get the dissenters to the surface undetected?"

Fander's jaw tightened. "I wish to confer with my advisors about that first. I will get back to you with our plan."

"Very well." Corvus's tone didn't sound very well about it. "Comm me once you have done so."

The screen flickered off and Fander leaned back in his seat, his far-away gaze centered on the wall across the table even as he reached for her hand. Her instinctive response to clasp her hand around his seemed totally natural, and right. Help him stay grounded as he processed the conversation. She could wait. Not for long, but for at least a few minutes. Besides, the alone time together was probably a luxury they wouldn't get much of in the future, so she may as well enjoy it even though he wasn't completely with her.

After a few minutes, he turned his head toward her. "Are you well?"

"Of course. Are you?"

"Pfft." He waved his free hand in a dismissive gesture. "Never better."

"Administer Corvus isn't the easiest person to deal with, is she?"

"No, but she did figure out how to transport most of our lost ones home."

Our, not *my*. That inclusiveness should scare her, shouldn't it? Instead, joy at the subtle acknowledgment that they were a team gave her the sensation of floating in her seat.

"So, the *Atlantis*, huh? That brings back a lot of childhood memories." The year she and her new siblings had lived on board had been like a dream. They had been living in space, something impossible before the invasion. Mama's friend, Moises Alexander, had inherited the ship once he'd taken over her ambassador duties. "It's been a long time since I've seen Ambassador Alexander."

Fander gave her hand a slight squeeze. "Unfortunately, his wife is under a healer's care at the Collegium as of this morning. It will be Vice-ambassador Kahpoor who will represent Terr in the envoy."

That was a shame. "Hope it's nothing too serious." Carrie

Alexander must be in her mid-sixties by now, and the ambassador was almost seventy. "I've met the vice-ambassador a couple of times and he seems like a nice guy. Funny, likes to joke. At parties, at least."

"How does he feel about Anferthians?"

"He seemed to like Grandfather well enough."

"Good, because he will be hosting a third of the Anferthian dissenters aboard Atlantis."

"And Ambassador Kapoor will have about five hundred. I heard that part. But, what about the others?" There were a little less than three thousand who had survived hardship and tragedy in their Matiran sanctuary. It looked like half of them would be staying here.

"It will be a snug fit, but my ship should be able to accommodate another six hundred."

"Oh, that should be fun."

A teasing glint sparkled in Fander's eyes and he sat forward. "How did it go with your uncle?"

Oh, geez. "Fine. Thirty days and counting."

"Pfft."

"Really? That's all you have to say?"

He moved so fast she barely had time to register the sudden change in proximity and that now he cradled her head between his hands, his mouth centimeters from hers. "Thirty days for you. Only nine for me."

Nine? What? Her heart rate went from a gentle canter to a full-out gallop. "You mean…?"

"I mean." He slanted his warm lips over hers. Touching, caressing. Just enough to turn her mind to mush before he pulled back a few centimeters. "As long as one of us has reached full incubation, we're good."

Oh, hell, yeah.

Twenty-Three

Flora squinted at the steel-grey morning sky. What a difference a day made. It'd been bright and sunny for their arrival yesterday. Welcoming, in a way, despite the sub-freezing temperatures. Now today, as transport load after transport load of dissenters were being taken to the ambassadors' ships, it was like Matir was saddened by their departure. In the grand scheme of the universe, sixteen years was only the smallest fraction of a nanosecond, but still, it was like the end of a mini-era.

Flora gave her shoulder a shrug to rebalance Tamiko's beat up pink Hello Kitty duffle. Uncle Nick, Aunt Sakura, Will, and Tamiko were coming with the dissenters. Her aunt and uncle worked as a team, therefore the whole family was making the trip to Anferthia. Another healer would fill in until the final few hundred Anferthians could go home.

If they could go home. This might be a one-way trip for all of them. It could also be the beginning of a new life for all Anferthians. Remembering that was key to projecting a positive attitude to Fander's weary tribe of supporters.

Her boot sank ankle-deep into the snow, making a Styrofoam-like crunch. At least, that's how she remembered Styrofoam sounding. It'd been years since she'd even seen any of it, so maybe her memory had blurred since then.

A lot of things were different than she remembered. Her feelings about Anferthians was a perfect example of change for the better. She adjusted the pack on her other shoulder and cast a sidelong glance at the giantess striding next to her along the main street through Center. K'rona. Her friend, mentor, and as of last night, newly-appointed captain of her personal guard.

What a surprise it'd been when Fander announced K'rona's reinstatement, with a rank advancement. As nice as Comtat Cynto was, their relationship lacked the steel cord of friendship and trust. Having K'rona assigned to her also gave her someone to talk to, to share her confidences with, because there were some things she didn't want to discuss with Fander.

Actually, one particular thing weighed on her mind. And she needed feedback on it, soon.

Flora wet her lips. "K'rona?"

"Yes, my lady?"

"It's Flora."

"Yes, my lady, Flora."

"You know what I mean."

K'rona grinned. "I do, so I shall stop teasing now. What is it, Flora?"

Oh, boy. How to say it? Insecurities weren't an easy thing to discuss, especially for her. Thanks to her family, she'd spent most of her adult life confident in her choices, and in herself. But, this new and unexpected change of direction was bigger than anything she'd ever done. If Mama were here, that's who she'd turn to for guidance. But, Mama wasn't here.

"You are scared." K'rona spoke succinctly, as if she'd expected the topic to come up. "You fear what is ahead of you, and that your life is not going how you envisioned. You are afraid of being out of control, of messing up, of people hating you, and that the challenges you face may be beyond your capabilities. Did I miss anything?"

Flora gaped at her. "Um, no. You didn't. I was afraid you might not understand."

"Going to live on an alien planet with people you spent your life believing were your enemy? No, you are right; I would not understand that at all." The words were spoken gently. Kindness, understanding, and deep affection shone in K'rona's green eyes. "I still get scared."

"*You?*" That was a revelation.

"Often."

"That's hard to believe."

"Over sixteen years ago, I did what I believed was the right thing, and I lost everything. My family, my home—the man I loved."

Mendiko Gari. Mama and Poppy spoke of the Anferthian man who had given his life rather than betray K'rona and the dissenters.

K'rona drew a breath. "Is it so impossible to believe that I am not scared?"

"When you put it that way, no. It's not. But, how do you stop feeling scared?"

"That will never happen. Not for me, not for you." K'rona stopped and gazed down at her. "Trust in yourself, and trust those who stand by you and believe in you. My strongest supporters are your cousin Ora and your parents. Their faith in me kept a flame alight in my soul through some very dark periods of my life. All of them I had once believed to be my enemies."

"Little one," Her expression softened. "I have known you since you were tiny." Holding up her thumb and forefinger, she indicated how tiny. A complete exaggeration, of course. Flora snorted a laugh through her nose. "It is good to be scared, but when you are scared, remember that you have people who will always be there for you: Your parents, your family, and mostly your prince."

Recognition of the truth filled her heart and a smile tugged at the corners of her mouth. "Okay, but one more thing. You knew Fander was *tangol*, didn't you?"

"A few of us have known for years, *fyhen*." K'rona rested one gloved hand on her shoulder. "You are a warrior, Flora. This will serve you well on Anferthia, as you will be expected to earn your place. Being *Ymere* does not involve sitting on fancy cushions eating fine food."

"Assuming I ever marry Fander. Becoming *Ymere* isn't a done deal." Yet.

K'rona grinned mischievously. "My feelings about you two are strong. I have faith in your future together. Do not worry, little one. All will be well, and we shall celebrate your future en route."

"What does *that* mean?"

K'rona just grinned and turned away to continue toward the shuttle pad.

Fander peered around the corner of the ship's corridor. Not a dissenter to be seen, thank the creators. Two days into the ten-day trip home was not the best time to question his decision to bring so many more bodies aboard. The dissenters were not the problem; the problem was that he could not take more than six steps without—

"My prince."

A nat.

He turned to face the dissenter striding toward him. "Warrior." Who was blocking the corridor.

The man came to a dead stop, thumped his fist to his chest and bowed. "My prince."

The first time this had occurred, greetings were exchanged three times before he realized the encounter would not end unless he ended it.

Yes, the dissenters *were* the problem.

No. No, he could not blame them because he was not used to being practically worshiped in this way. He had done nothing to deserve such accolades. Even if he had, he wouldn't want it. Yet, the dissenters seemed persistent.

He gave the man a clumsy half bow. "You are dismissed to continue in your service, warrior."

"By your word, my prince." The man backed away as if stuck in a perpetual bow.

Gods have mercy, this was out of hand. He must locate Kapit Zurkku and request she speak with her *fyhen*.

"Fander."

At last. The sound of the only voice he wanted to hear. He turned.

Flora jogged up to him. "Whatcha up to?"

She still smelled damn intoxicating. Fertile, but near the end of her season. And there was nothing she could do to make herself less appealing to him. "I have to meet with K'rona and Storo to discuss the incessant bowing and scraping everywhere I go."

"Hum. Well, go easy on them, okay?"

"Why?" Must she cross her arms under her breasts like that? It was torture to be caught between wishing she would cease the action and praying she would never stop.

"Think about it from their point of view. They've given up everything on a hope that you'd live long enough to free Anferthia from Arruch tyranny. Now you're here and that hope has become a reality. A little bowing and scraping should be expected, don't you think?"

Clarity settled over him. "You're right." He spread his arms and she stepped into his embrace, which flattened her soft breasts against his belly. "I'm glad you're here to remind me of these things. I will 'go easy on them,' as you wish."

She pulled away far enough to look up at him. "I'm glad too."

"Shall we try your reliquary again this evening?"

"Actually." She reached up and fluttered her fingers along the chain. "Tonight's not so good. Your mom set up a little social for me in her quarters. I couldn't say no."

A social for Flora, but he was not invited?

"It's a girls' only thing, from what my aunt said."

"I see." He did not, really, but would accept her reasoning.

She leaned close. "Do I still smell, um, you know…fertile?"

The whispered word hung between them for several heartbeats. Why would she ask such a question? Was she still worried about pregnancy? "It will not be a problem in a few more days, love. I promise."

Red splotches flamed on her cheeks. "Not *that*…. I mean, yes, good, but I wondered if, well, can anyone else smell it on me?"

That was not what he had expected. He dampened the humor rising in him and pressed a kiss to her forehead. "Only if they're looking for it. No one has a reason to scent you, so it's unlikely. And it would be rude." He slid his hands along her arms until he reached for her hands and raised first one, then the other to brush his lips across her knuckles. "Enjoy your evening, love. We can resume our efforts with the reliquary tomorrow." And, more pleasurable activities after his *atolce* became fully effective.

She raised up on her toes and he met her, pressing his lips to hers. Her tongue ran along the seam and he opened to her. The touching of tongues was almost like a dance—an awkward dance sometimes, but that should smooth out with time. They were still getting to know each other and what the other liked and disliked.

He pulled back and she swayed with a silly grin. "I hope no one scents me now because they'll get a nose-full."

This time the laugh escaped. "Yes, your delicious factor has increased."

"Good." She stepped away slowly. "I'll see you in the

morning?"

"You know you will."

He watched as the one woman in the galaxy who could make him forget his troubles half-skipped down the corridor toward his mother's quarters. Because of her, his agitation with the dissenters' behavior had turned to understanding. Why? The answer was clear. The dissenters were not the problem. Flora was. Everything she did was an aphrodisiac to him, including farting and burping in his face, which she had done yesterday.

As some Terrians would say, he had it bad.

Twenty-Four

"*Ryma*?" Flora brought the heavy pottery cup to her nose and inhaled. Fruity, sort of like a pear, with an undercurrent of...nutmeg? Yummy combo. "Are you sure there's alcohol in this? I don't smell any."

"Oh, I'm *very* sure." Aunt Sakura kneeled on her chair, leaned forward across the table, and held her cup out. K'rona tipped the matching pottery carafe and poured a serving of thick golden liquid into it. "So, be careful."

Fander's mother shook her head. "The purpose of this social is to acclimate Flora to *ryma* before she must face the effects of it in public on Anferthia."

Dacey and Ita, two of K'rona's longtime friends, nodded their heads. Either they were all sincere, or they were suckering her about the alcohol content of *ryma*, or gold rum.

K'rona set the bottle in the center of the table. "Lady K'nil, will you grace us with the first toast?"

"The pleasure is mine." What a formal way to begin a party where the intent was for everyone to get drunk. "To Flora, *tangol* to my son, my daughter in spirit, and a path to peace for our people."

Whoa. Warmth rose in Flora's cheeks. Fani K'nil sure knew how to put someone in their place. At least it was in a good way this time, not like what happened with Minister S'gow during the trial.

"*Hyl*!" Cheers, or the closest Anferthian equivalent, filled

Fani's sitting room. The funny part was that it almost sounded like "hell" spoken with a Southern accent.

Flora brought her cup to her lips and tipped. A small amount of room-temperature liquid coated her tongue. Fruity, like a tropical smoothie. She swallowed. There was no way it was as potent as everyone was trying to convince her.

An hour later—or possibly two—Flora held up her hand and the other giggling women gave her their full attention. "We need...another toast. Who's got one?"

"I do." Dacey raised her cup. "To brilliant red-headed women." She patted her own dark ginger locks.

"There's only *one* of those in this room." Ita grinned and tipped her cup in Flora's direction.

Aw, that was sweet. "Thank you, Ita."

"*Hyl.*"

This was a great way to separate the lushes from the lightweights. Good thing she was somewhere in between the two extremes. One cup wouldn't be enough to put her under the table tonight. Two might, though. She pursed her lips and gazed into the half-filled cup. How many had she had anyway?

K'rona pounded her fist on the table top. "I have one. A very good one."

"Better than 'brilliant red-heads'?" 'Cause that was pretty good.

"Better. Definitely better." K'rona raised her cup and inhaled deeply, "Here's to Anferthian men who have kept their women well-satisfied since the dawn of time."

Flora pondered the table top with a furrowed brow. What did that mean, exactly? It sounded promising. She looked up. Uh-oh. Everyone was staring at her. Shit, did she forget to drink to K'rona's toast? She ran her tongue over her lips. Too hard to tell if the minute droplets were fresh or not. She set her cup on the table. The surface was expanding and contracting, as if the piece of furniture could breathe. Maybe she *had* been suckered about the alcohol content, but not in the way she had first thought.

She met the gaze of one of the three K'rona seated next to her. The one on the left. "How?"

"How what, little one?" All three K'rona's spoke in unison.

"How have the...men...kept you satisfied?"

"It is all in the ears." Ita's voice was heavy with innuendo.

That made no sense at all. "What is? Wait, this has something to do with the shape, right?" Fander's ears were fan-shape with at least four points. Fani, K'rona, and the other Anferthian women had rounded Terrian-like ears. Hadn't Grandfather mentioned something in passing about this being covered in her upcoming training? A small burp snuck out. "Ooh, excuse me."

Giggles erupted around the table. A lot of help that was. Even her future mother-in-law seemed to be enjoying the awkward turn of events, and Aunt Saku tittered behind her hand.

"Aunt Saku?"

"I wouldn't know." Her aunt waved her off. "I'm married to a Terrian."

Were the walls beginning to sway? "Maybe someone will explain before I pass out."

"An Anferthian male's ears are *sensitive* in certain places," Dacey told her.

"Sexually," Ita added. "Touch a man's receptors in the right spot in the right way and he will go into the frenzy."

"The frenzy?" That sounded hot, and completely made up. "You're pullin' my chair...chain." Whatever.

K'rona grinned. "There's not much that can stop the frenzy once initiated. A man will hit his stride three times before it's over."

Next to K'rona, Dacey held up three fingers on both of her right hands and mouthed the word "Three."

Hit his stride? What did that mea...ohh. *That*. "Well, that sounds like fuck...I mean, fun." She reached for her cup and she raised it. "To the ears!"

She threw back the remaining contents.

"That is most concerning." Fander's mother did sound worried.

"Looks like our first tragic victim is about to slide under the table."

Aunt Saku has the sweetest voice.

K'rona leaned forward and removed her cup from her hands. "The party is over, my lady."

"That's okay. I have to talk to Fander's ears."

"Not tonight, little one."

"I'll have Nick come get her." That was Aunt Saku again, "She's too dangerous for Fander at the moment."

Dangerous? She wasn't dane-jer-us. Was she?

"Hey, Red." Uncle Nick's voice came from somewhere above her. "A little too much of the gold, huh, kid?"

She opened her eyes and looked up. Yep, Uncle Nick and Fander kneeled on either side of her. How'd she get on the floor?

"Heeeyyyy." The word came out like a sigh and she tried to curve her mouth into a smile. "Fander, your fans look ear shape tonight. Wait. That sounded weird. What language am I speaking?"

Fander rolled his eyes. "You told her about the ear thing?"

"Of course we did." His mother sounded like...well, a mother, which was normal. "This could not be put off until later."

"Agreed," K'rona added. "Like her first experience with *ryma*, it is important she knows before we arrive on Anferthia."

What was that old song about ears? "Do your ears hang low, do they wobble to and fro..." That wasn't right. The words were supposed to rhyme. Why weren't they?

"I don't think that song translates well into Matiran, Red."

Oh, that's why. Maybe it'd work in Anferthian.

"I think that's worse," Fander mumbled.

"Fine. I'll sing it in English, then." She took a deep breath.

Uncle Nick clamped his hand over her mouth. "I'm going to put you to sleep now, and we'll get you to bed. Are you okay with this?"

"Mm-hm," A flutter of wings caught her attention. A Monarch butterfly floated passed Uncle Nick's nose and landed in Fander's hair, right over his ear. It shouldn't be trying to touch his ear. She reached up and waved her fingers at it. "Shoo." Funny. The word sounded legible to her even with Uncle Nick's hand over her mouth.

Fander grasped her wrist and lowered her hand until it rested on her stomach. What had K'rona told her about his ears? It was important.

"We'll see you in the morning." Uncle Nick smiled kindly. "Or the morning after. God knows you're going to be in a world of hurt. *Dormio*."

Flora tried to lift her right foot but it wouldn't budge. She gazed down. How had she ended up knee-deep in a wooden barrel of topaz honey? Stuck. On the pitcher's mound at the New Damon Beach baseball field. And no one was around to help her, except...S'gow. The smug Anferthian stood in the stands, arms crossed over his chest, gloating. Jackass.

S'gow's body rippled and flowed, his features changing into those of another man who looked an awful lot like an image she'd once seen of Divine Warden Isel T'orr. He was frowning, just like in that picture.

Crap, she had to get out of here. She gripped the sides of the barrel and leaned her weight from one side to the other. The barrel rocked as T'orr closed his hand over the butt of his fusil *and drew it from its holster. The ripples blurred him as he changed again, this time into the lithe form of Haesi Velo.*

No, no, no. This was beyond crazy. Flora threw her body from one side to the other. Haesi pointed the fusil *in her direction. The barrel balanced on its rim as though hanging on a precipice, then tipped over. The dirt of the pitcher's mound rushed toward her, then the thick gooey honey flowed over her body, head, face. Like a suffocating blanket. She tried to crawl away from the suffocating blanket but it held her in place. Air. Just one little breath would do. She opened her mouth and the honey filled it as Haesi's laughter filled the stadium.*

Flora jerked awake and inhaled a sharp, deep breath.

Alive. I'm alive.

A groan rolled out of her. *Ohh hellllll.* That dream had seemed way too real. But, at least it hadn't hurt like she did now. Achy stiffness throbbed in every muscle and joint, like a mule had kicked her down a gravel road then put her through a dryer cycle for good measure.

"How are you doing?" the kindest voice ever asked.

The voice had a name. What was it again? Fander? Yes, Fander. She forced her eyelids apart and squinted. Yep, he was here, looking all comfy and pain free leaning back against the wall in a chair, a real book in his lap. "I was hit by a bus, wasn't I?"

He shook his head. "I have no idea what a bus is, Flora."

"It's a big thing, has wheels." She tried to use her hands to mimic wheels going around, but they wouldn't cooperate. Why wouldn't they move right? She raised them and stared at the ugly light brown spots on the back of her hands. Tears misted her vision. "I hate freckles."

Fander dropped the legs of the chair to the floor, closed the book, and leaned forward to push a button on the nightstand. Then he set the leather-bound book down and shifted to sit on the edge of the bed. He gathered her hands in his and kissed her knuckles. "I love freckles. In fact, I have a particular weakness for your freckles."

His hands were so warm, like his words. "That's so sweet." A salty blurriness rose in her eyes and a small watery hiccup popped out of her mouth.

"Don't cry, Flora, all will be well."

"How do you know?" She sniffled as she pushed herself up to sit.

"Experience." He shrugged his shoulders. "Your uncle will be here shortly."

"Why?" There was only one reason to be under the care of a healer. Fresh hot tears seeped from her eyes. "Am I dying, Fander?"

He pressed his lips together, shook his head, and handed her a handkerchief. "I can understand why you might think so, but no, you're not dying."

"Oh, thank God." She unfolded the handkerchief and blew her nose.

"Do you feel like eating?"

Her stomach clenched and twisted, and an acid burn surged up her esophagus. Like magic, a basin materialized in front of her and she gagged and heaved into it. *Ryma*. The evil drink from hell. It tasted a lot better going down than it did coming back up. Smelled better too. Poor Fander. As nice as it was for her that he rubbed her back and spoke soft encouraging words, this was probably gross for him. She wiped the hanky over her mouth and straightened.

More tears spilled out and ran down her cheeks. "What's wrong with me? I'm crying about everything and throwing up. I feel miserable," She'd only seen symptoms like this once before, and that was when Aunt Saku…. "Oh, nooooo." She gave Fander a wide-eyed look. "*I'm pregnant!*"

A wail of misery rose from her chest and she flung herself to the other side of the bed. This was the worst news of all. There was a damn good reason why they'd decided not to have kids yet, if she could just remember what that was. It was important, though. The huge gulping breaths shook her body.

A moment later, the light touch of Fander's fingers stroked over her shoulder and down to her elbow and back up. The repetitive motion seemed oddly soothing and her sobs slowed.

"Flora, look at me."

She peeked up over her folded arms. Fander knelt at the bedside, patience radiating from him. "You are not pregnant, love."

"How do you know?"

"Because we haven't slept together."

She stopped crying and blinked at him. "Oh, right. That's good then. I want to remember it when we do."

Fander smiled at her and tenderly brushed her hair back from her face. "Me too."

There was that jolt in her lower region again. The Fander Affect, that's what she'd call it.

Swoosh.

The door opened and her aunt and uncle waltzed in. Or, more like walked with purpose. How come she felt like crap and Aunt Sakura looked like a fresh morning rose? And, where had that immature thought come from?

Uncle Nick stopped at the end of the bed and folded his arms over his chest. "How's the patient?"

Fander's expression turned to amusement. "She's been hit by a bus, hates her freckles, thought she was dying, projectile vomited, and we just established that she's not pregnant."

"Pregnant?" Uncle Nick snorted and placed his healer's bag on the table before he sat on her bed next to Fander's shoulder. "That could severely hamper Terrian-Anferthian relations."

"In my defense, I remember Aunt Sakura crying and throwing up a lot when she was pregnant, so I just thought...." She gave her shoulders a half-hearted shrug.

"Yeah, your aunt was a mess at that time."

"Watch it, buster," Aunt Saku growled, her back to them and her body blocking whatever it was she was working on at the table. It was like she was trying to hide something.

"And it was completely my fault." Uncle Nick sounded way too chipper for someone taking the blame. "So, what do you remember about last night, Red?"

"Why? Did I embarrass myself?" Please say no.

Collision

The memory of the gold-colored booze flooded back and her stomach did a massive flip followed by a flop. "Oh, no."

She slapped her hand over her mouth. Not again; not when the basin was on the other side of the bed. Fander swore under his breath and cupped his hands, ready to catch whatever spewed out, which would've just added to her humiliation. She swallowed hard. Breathe. Calm. No puking in her *tangol's* hands.

Uncle Nick pressed his fingers to the pulse in her wrist. "No more than any of us have when drinking the gold for the first time."

That was reassuring. Sort of. At least her stomach didn't seem to be on the brink of another explosion now. "If this is a hangover, shouldn't I have a massive throbbing headache?"

"Oh, it's coming, don't worry." Uncle Nick looked almost gleeful at this proclamation.

Fabulous. "That stuff should be outlawed."

"It is." Fander grinned, rather proudly. "Illegal on thirty-six planets."

And here she'd believed K'rona was her friend and Fander's mother liked her.

Aunt Saku placed something in her husband's hands and passed the now-clean vomit basin to Fander. "It won't be like this next time, Flora, I promise."

"You assume I'll be drinking that hallucinogenic swill again, *ever*."

Her aunt chuckled. "You will, at your binding ceremony."

Shit. She so did not want to do that. Drink *ryma*, not avoid the bonding. When had she started thinking of marriage to Fander as a done deal?

"It's not much." Fander stroked his fingers over her shoulder. "Certainly not enough to give you another hangover."

"Don't worry, Red. *Ryma* works like its own virus and vaccination. The first time you drink it is the worst. The beauty is that it leaves the equivalent of an antibody in you. When you drink it after that, your reaction will be nowhere near as severe."

"*Unless* you over-indulge." Her aunt gave her one of those raised-eyebrow-stern-mom looks. "The tiny bit you'll consume at your binding ceremony will have next to no effect, other than to maybe make you feel a little lightheaded, and that will make the *maitz'a*—the binding dance—less, um, constrained."

"Sounds fun." She peeked up at Uncle Nick. "What are you hiding in your hand, Uncle?"

Uncle Nick raised his hand from the other side of his leg. Oh, damn, that was one wicked-looking needle. Another shot. "Should've known."

"This is going to help alleviate your symptoms and relieve that raging headache you'll develop within the next six hours. You're also on bed rest for the next two days; I don't want you to be passing out in random places around the ship."

She gaped at him. "*Two* days?"

"Healer's orders." He uncapped the needle.

Fander looked up at the ceiling, a blissful smile curving his mouth upward. "This should almost make up for the banana slug incident."

Oh sure, he'd remember that now. She shot him a glare. "I was *twelve*, and I had no idea banana slug slime was toxic to Anferthians. Besides, you didn't *have* to take my dare and kiss it."

She straightened her arm for Uncle Nick.

"No, Red." Her uncle wore the Devil's shit-eating grin. "This one does not go in the arm. Roll over."

TWENTY-FIVE

Flora fought against her consciousness as it dragged her out of a dream. A really good dream this time, one with Fander in it. Fander's hands...Fander's lips...Fander's bare chest.... She reached for it but it dissipated like the fog under a warm summer sun. Her consciousness won the battle. There was no choice but to open her eyes to reality. If she was really lucky, "real" Fander would still be sitting at her bedside.

She forced her eyelids apart and her gaze was drawn to the chair at the end of her bed. An Anferthian was there all right, but not Fander. This time it was K'rona, one of the masterminds of her *ryma* downfall. So nice that she'd made herself at home with her feet perched on the corner of the mattress, ankles crossed. Not the least bit contrite.

"You are such a trouble maker." Dang, had someone force-fed her gravel while she was passed out?

K'rona grinned. "I will not deny it."

"Figures." She arched her back, stretched out her arms, and allowed a jaw-cracking yawn to take over. A little achy still, but at least she could move. And the hot-poker-induced headache seemed to be gone. Things were definitely looking up. "How long have I been asleep?"

"Fourteen hours." K'rona handed her the vomit container. "Do you wish to eat?"

She froze, but no revolt seemed imminent from her stomach. "I actually think so."

One comm message and five minutes later, the food arrived. A clear Anferthian broth, with all the magical properties of a bowl of chicken broth, plus it tasted amazing. After she finished, K'rona practically herded her into the steam unit to bathe. When she got out, fresh bed clothes were laid out for her and her pillows were fluffed.

The crisp airy material of the pajama pants slid over her bare legs. "Did you get into much trouble?"

K'rona raise both eyebrows. "For the *ryma*? No, not at all. My lady K'nil was adamant you experience it in a safe environment. My prince has come to see the wisdom of this action. Although, your condition for the last few days has pained him."

"But if I only drink a little bit at the ceremony, why worry? My entire first cup didn't affect me."

Her friend fixed her with a serious look. "You believe I do not know what I am talking about?"

"No." She gave her shoulders a shrug and pulled the P.J. top over her head. "I guess not."

"Do you remember what we discussed about Anferthian men?"

Flora tugged the material down to cover her hips. "If you're talking about ears, the frenzy and three times, then yes."

"It impresses me you remember so much." K'rona chuckled and sat down on the chair. "That was the fun stuff. Understanding you must now have about the not so fun stuff. It is your responsibility as a woman."

"This sounds serious."

"It is serious." K'rona gazed at her, the same way Uncle Graig did. "Anferthian men are as susceptible to rape as a woman."

"Because of the ear thing?"

"Because of the ear thing." K'rona nodded. "We must have care for them as they have care for us. It is not a perfect system, but it works most of the time."

"Do you know someone who the system failed?"

K'rona's green-eyed gaze slipped to study her hands in her lap. "After my mother died, my father was too busy grieving to pay much attention to what his own brother was doing. There was no one to look out for me."

Well, shit.

"My uncle was your mother's first kill, and I am still humbled by what she did for me."

It was hard to imagine someone as gentle as Mama actually killing a person, but she had done a lot of things to protect her loved ones. "I had no idea."

"There was no reason you should." A fleeting smile touched K'rona's lips. "It is the past and I am free of him, this is all that matters. Now, there are behaviors you must know to function in Anferthian society, things that your ambassador training has not covered yet. Time is too short for you to wait until it does. Anferthia is only six days journey from us.

"As *tangol* to my prince, there are expectations, knowledge of etiquette you should have before we arrive. To touch a male's ears in public is absolutely not acceptable and carries legal penalties. Our men wear their hair over their ears as a subtle reminder, which you may have noticed."

"I did, actually." And now she knew why.

K'rona looked thoroughly pleased by her observation. "Now, it is time for honesty between us. Your heart, it is with Fander even as we speak, is it not?"

Somehow the question wasn't rude or nosy, it was right on target. Flora gave her friend a secret smile.

"Ah, I see it is, as I had foretold." K'rona returned her smile. "It is well. Then this too you must know. To induce the frenzy is a very intimate act between a couple. There is only one place and time where it is acceptable for a female to touch a male's ears in public. The place is during *maitz'a*; the time...you will feel it as you dance."

Flora sat upright, her eyes wide. "Wait a minute, you mean I'll have to send him into a sexual frenzy *in public*? That's insane."

"It is part of the bonding dance." An amused smile hovered on K'rona's mouth.

"This isn't funny, K'rona."

"Do not worry, little one. Fander will get you back to your room before succumbing. Just do not touch more than once."

More than once? Hell, she didn't want to do it at all. Not in the way K'rona suggested. "I-I can't do that."

A horizontal crease appeared across K'rona's brow and she shook her head. "You do not wish to bind yourself to Fander?"

"Yes, I do, but...." Oops. Looked like her mind had decided her heart was right. "I just...can't do that to him." Not in public.

The look K'rona gave her was hard and the crease deepened.

Abruptly, she lowered her feet to the floor, stood up, and strode toward the door.

"Where are you going?"

At the door K'rona turned around, her hands clenched into fists and hurt flashed in her eyes. "Our culture, history, and traditions, you shunt aside for your convenience. *Wrong*. Choosing which elements you will be part of, and which you will not, is not for you to decide. The good and the not so good, the comfortable and the not so comfortable, you must accept as the rest of us do. The question you *should* ask is: do you believe you are truly ready to fully embrace Anferthia?"

K'rona slapped her hand against the ID reader on the wall. The door scoped open and she strode through without a backward glance.

Well, dang. The last thing she'd meant to do was piss off her friend. But, she was tired of being the last to know. The last to know Fander's true identity, the last to know she was his *tangol*, the last to know she'd been marked as a potential future queen, empress, whatever, of a world she'd never been to. The last to know she was expected to initiate a sex act in front of God knew how many complete strangers!

This was insane on so many levels. Maybe K'rona was right and she wasn't the right person for the job.

A sudden hollowness expanded in her chest. That was all wrong. *She* was all wrong. Fander was deeply entrenched in her life, right where he belonged. She never wanted to lose that...or him. The whole *tangol* thing was real. Everything that had happened to her since the day they'd met—*rywoud*, talking through the reliquary, the fact that she loved the man who would be the leader of the people she once thought were her most hated enemy—it was all meant to be. If she'd just embraced it. In concept, that had been easy to accept, but the reality of it had just slapped her in the face and she'd balked.

An odd vibration hummed in her brain and she gave her head a shake. Why couldn't she just accept and conform to the alien ways of Fander's people the way he had to hers?

A pinpoint of heat stung her chest. "What the...ow, ow *ow*."

She grasped the chain hanging around her neck and yanked the reliquary out from under her P.J. top, A warm blue-green light filled the room, like sunlight filtered through a clear tropical ocean. It'd never glowed like this before; not since it'd come into her keeping, at least.

"What's happening here?" She gave the crystal a gentle poke with her fingertip.

A flash, then a shower of blue-green sparkles exploded and she slammed her eyelids shut against the brightness. A moment later, the brightness faded to normal. Everything seemed unnaturally quiet…no, more like dead silent. Had the ship's ventilation system shut down? She blinked her eyes open. Everything still looked like she was underwater, but she definitely was not in her room anymore.

She turned slowly to get a lay of the land, or space, or whatever it was. Her roving gaze locked onto an endless sea of Anferthians standing behind her, their expressions frozen in peaceful expectation. As if they were waiting for something, or someone. One man stood in front of them all, his hands hanging relaxed at his sides. Eyes closed.

"Grandfather K'nil." Her voice sounded echo-y to her ears.

He opened his eyes and smiled.

TWENTY-SIX

Flora sat on the ground with her arms wrapped around her knees, the rhythmic beat of drums thudded against her eardrums as if they were real and not part of a memory encapsulated inside the crystal reliquary that now belonged to her. An Anferthian couple danced with unrestrained joy, their bare feet keeping perfect time with the drums. Fander's ancestors on his mother's side. They were nothing more than the memories of themselves, just like all the previous dancers.

Being inside her reliquary was exactly as Fander had described: another plane of existence. And it was a place of other people's memories and experiences, all stored like some sort of computer database. And she had access to everything. It hadn't taken long to figure out that all she had to do was visualize what she wanted to know, and the couples stepped forward, one by one, to share their *maitz'a* experience.

The female Anferthian pushed her husband's hair away to expose his ears—only three points this time—and their gazes locked. They looked blissfully happy, just like every other couple she'd observed. *Maitz'a* was a dance that told a story of the couple's life, before and after they'd met. More than once her cheeks had heated at the raw display of sexuality that had been a part of many of these dances. But not all of them were like that. Some were sweet, right up until the end when the wife touched her husband's ears. And, wow, who knew there were so many different ways to touch ears and induce the frenzy?

But, none of the couples had failed to reach their door. Not-a-single-one. So far, *maitz'a* seemed to be a loving thing, not porn performed in public. Very suggestive at times, but so far nothing explicit.

The woman dancing slipped her fingers along the curved shell of her husband's ear, heading for the trigger point.

"Stop."

Flora startled at the firm command spoken from behind her. The couple froze in place and the drums ceased.

Flora twisted around on her butt. "Fander?"

How had he found her?

"Intimidating, isn't it?" He inclined his head in the direction of the paused couple.

She caught her bottom lip between her teeth and gave him a nod. Fander sat down next to her and leaned back on his hands, his long legs stretched straight in front of him.

"Are you actually here? Or me, for that matter? Is this real?"

"Oh, this is real enough. Immersion into a reliquary is like entering a different plane of existence. But, you know that already." His gaze met hers and he frowned. "I told you to have someone with you—*me*—when you tried this. Why didn't you?"

"I *didn't* do it. It…I don't know…sucked me in and I haven't been able to figure out how to get back." She'd tried everything she could think of before giving up to watch dead people dance.

"Reliquaries don't just 'suck' people in. You triggered the correct brainwave somehow, possibly by accident, but it was you."

"Oh." That must have been what the weird hum in her head was. "Am I okay?"

Fander made a non-committal grunt. "You have been lost in your reliquary for two days."

"*Two days?*" It only seemed like a few hours had passed.

"When I couldn't find you in the first twelve hours, your aunt and uncle began intravenous fluids. Right now, you have tubes in places you don't want them, love."

"Oh, no!" She scrambled to her feet. "I gotta get back."

"We'll work on that in a minute. You came here to find answers and I can help you." He stood up next to her. "How many have you watched?"

"I don't know." He knew about what she'd said to K'rona.

They must have talked. She gave her shoulders a shrug. "A lot. I still don't see the point, other than to get everyone in the mood to procreate."

Fander chuffed a laugh and one corner of his mouth lifted in a crooked grin. "No, that is definitely not the point. Come closer." He led her toward the unmoving couple. "*Maitz'a* is not about sex. It's not even about love. It's a test."

"A *test*? Of what?"

"Trust. Just look in their eyes and think about what K'rona told you. Then ask yourself, would the man here allow his wife such power over him if he didn't implicitly trust her not to abuse that power?"

So, she guessed right. He had talked to K'rona. Flora turned her attention to the man's eyes and there it was. The answer she'd been looking for without knowing what the true question was. Implicit trust. Faith that this woman would treasure and protect his vulnerability.

That was all well and good, but what about the woman? She moved around to study the bride, whose eyes were the exact color of Fander's. Which made sense, since he was related to her. "So, what's her act of faith?"

"Watch." He moved his hand in an arc. "Resume."

The woman's fingers prodded gently into the fan-points covering the sensitive receptors on her husband's ears. Instantly his entire face changed and he sucked in his breath as a fierce wildness came upon him. In response the woman dropped to her knees and threw her arms wide with a shout. The man roared to the sky and scooped her up to carry her away.

"End memory." The couple faded back into the silent ranks of his ancestors. He gave her an expectant look. "Did you see it?"

She gave him a slow nod. "Her faith was that he wouldn't dishonor her in public."

Fander stepped close to her, filling her vision and blocking out everyone else. "I will not dishonor you, Flora. Please do not fear me, love."

A lump rose to her throat and she swallowed hard around it. "I know you won't. And, I'm not afraid of you, just of the unknown. Thank you for finding me and helping me understand."

Fander held open his arms and she stepped into his embrace. "I feared I had lost you. I will do better on teaching you how to use your reliquary."

"That'd be nice. At least I know what it feels like to make the connection now." Next time she came here, it'd be because she wanted to, not because she got sucked in unawares.

"What did Grandfather have to say to you?"

"Um, nothing." She pushed back slightly and met his gaze. "He opened his eyes and smiled, but hasn't said anything."

"I think I know why. Come with me."

She followed him back to where his grandfather stood, still silent.

"Now, stand in front of him and say, 'Your heir has come.'"

"That's *it*?"

"It is that easy."

Too easy. "Okay. Here goes nothing." She moved to face Grandfather K'nil and gazed up at his face. He seemed so real, but he wasn't. Nothing here was real, just memories. "Your heir has come."

Grandfather's smile brightened, and he spread his arms like Fander had done a few moments ago.

"What's this, Fander? What's he doing?"

"It appears he wishes to give you a hug."

"Is that possible? He's just a memory, right? So, how can he hug me?"

"It's true, the physical world has no place here. That being said, there is a sort of loophole to that rule. By all means hug him. That's part of what he did for you."

Ookaaay. She moved forward and Grandfather wrapped her in his warm, gentle embrace. The fabric of his *wysgog* pressed against her cheek. The same *wysgog* he'd been wearing the day he died. "Oh, my God. This feels so real."

Fander moved into her line of vision. His grin was full of joy and wonder. "He had a unique talent for inputting life-like memories. I hope you will let me walk with you through his memories in the future."

This had to be hard for Fander to watch. He was supposed to have been Grandfather's heir. "You know I will."

Grandfather released her from the hug and stepped back. "My dearest Flora, if you are seeing this then I suspect you will need that hug. Having never set one in a reliquary before, I hope it works." His eyes twinkled with humor. "Regardless, there are many important things you must know, not the least of which is my deep and abiding love and affection for you. You filled the great emptiness in my heart left by Fander's departure with unparalleled joy. It has been an honor for me to have been a part of your journey as you became a young woman.

"Speaking of Fander, he may or may not be with you as you receive this message. He certainly will figure out quickly that I made you the heir of my reliquary, a change I know he will understand and support. As of now, the memory of that moment is yours."

Something tingled inside her brain. An image rose up of her sitting with Grandfather in his secret room, her hands pressed between his. "To this soul I do bequeath you." This time she understood his words.

"Oh." She breathed out the word like a sigh. "So *that's* how it happened."

The vision cleared, and only Grandfather's memory-self remained. "You must be prepared for what lies ahead, and my reliquary will aid you on your journey. Fander will teach you how to use it, and yes, you can use it, Flora. As his *tangol*, you are bound to our family more deeply and more completely than any secular ceremony could bind us.

"Finally, I apologize to you for the grief you had to endure beginning on your fifteenth birthday. Your parents, my daughter, and I, along with many others, have labored for years to mend the rift caused by our invasion of Terr. To bring peace not only between our two worlds, but also with Matir. The discovery of the bond you and Fander share gave us great hope for the future, but in our efforts to protect our children and the future of our worlds, we brought both of you the great pain of *tangol* separated—a pain that grows with time rather than heals. I hope you can find it in your heart to forgive us, and that you will be part of the ongoing efforts being made on behalf of both our worlds.

"Be strong and build a future of happiness. Remember, even though I am gone, both you and Fander hold my love in your hearts."

The image stepped back to its original place and fell silent again. And just like that, he was gone again. She blinked to clear the watery mist rising in her eyes. It was almost like he'd died all over again.

"Come back now, Flora." Fander's voice surrounded her, drawing her away from the memory-Grandfather. The odd humming sensation in her skull returned. Something hot and wet rolled over her temple to her hairline. She forced her eyes open. It was so good to see the glow of her internally lit bedroom ceiling above her and the softness of her bed under her back again.

"She's back." Aunt Saku's face blocked her view of the ceiling. "Eyes are slightly dilated, but her blood pressure and heart rate are coming back to normal."

Where's Fander?

"I am here."

Had she spoken out loud? She turned toward his voice. He was stretched out on his side next to her, his arms cradling her body against him and one of his hands cupping hers. The reliquary still in her fist.

This was right where she belonged. "I'm going to marry you, Fander."

Oops. Hadn't meant to blurt that out. Or maybe she had.

"Healers, will you leave us?" Fander didn't break eye-contact with her.

"You're in bed with my niece," Uncle Nick growled.

"So I am." Humor danced in Fander's eyes. "Our conversation requires privacy. Please…Uncle Nick."

Aunt Sakura snickered. "Come on, Nick. Nothing is going to happen right now, anyway. She's in no condition for that, and it's Will and Tami's bedtime. They will want a story."

"Fine," Uncle Nick grumbled. "We'll be back to take care of the other stuff shortly."

Whatever that meant. The rustle of footsteps and the swoosh of the door opening and closing a moment later indicated her family was gone.

"Are you sure about this, Flora? About marrying me?" God, he looked…nervous?

"Isn't that what you wanted?"

"Yes. More than anything. But, is it what *you* want?"

Aww. Insecurity on an eight-foot-tall alien prince was adorable. "More than anything. I love you, Fander."

Relief flashed in his eyes. "I love you too, Flora." He kissed the tip of her nose and she scooted onto her side to face him.

Something tugged between her legs. What the heck? She

moved again and something hard and smooth rubbed against her leg. "Oh. Oh, my god. Fander, I have...I have a tube...in my.... *Ew*."

"Now you understand why your uncle left so easily?"

"I didn't even know healers used catheters in this day and age." That must be what Uncle Nick meant about coming back to take care of the "other stuff."

"Your predicament was dire."

Obviously. "I didn't mean to scare you." And the last thing Fander needed now was the disgusting tube bumping him.

She rolled away but he tightened his grip. "Don't."

"But...."

"It's okay, love. I don't mind it, and right now I need you close."

Being held close was nice. She allowed herself to relax against him. "I'm sorry I scared you. Thanks for helping me to find the answers I needed."

"All part of discovering what we can do together, right?"

She gave him a smile. "Absolutely."

TWENTY-SEVEN

Fander gazed down at Flora. For so long, having her lounging with her head resting against his thigh like this had been an impossible dream. Yet, here she was, smiling as the light of happiness danced in her eyes as she queried him about the *maitz'a*. The antithesis of her condition, and her opinion, just one day ago. Thank the creators he had been able to find her within the realm of her reliquary.

Flora poked her finger in his chest. "Fander?"

"What?"

"Are you going to explain why all of the dances I saw your relatives do were different?"

"No two are alike." He twirled a wayward strand of her hair around his forefinger. "Each dance is choreographed to reflect the personal experiences of the couple."

"Okay, so who's going to choreograph ours?"

He gave his shoulders what he hoped was a casual shrug. "Will you allow me?" Dancing was much more a part of his culture than hers, and he already had some ideas in mind to make their *maitz'a* special.

She grinned up at him. "You sure you can fit it in between staging revolts and defeating tyranny?"

"I can work it in."

"Fine. Go for it. Let me know if you need me to do anything else other than rehearsal."

He tapped his finger against her hair. "I do have one thing."

She groaned, right on cue. "Okay. What's that?"

"Would you sing during the *maitz'a*?"

Her eyes widened so far the whites showed all the way around her blue irises. So, it was possible to surprise her. "Seriously? What do you want me to sing?"

"Just one song. Anything you find appropriate. I trust your judgment."

She nodded. "It can be my gift to you and to your...our people. I like it."

And he liked the way she said *our*. "Thank you."

"Yep." She sat up on the lounger and turned on the seat to face him. "I, *we*, need to talk."

"I am talking. Have I ever mentioned that I love it when you roll your eyes at me like that?"

"No. And, I roll them at you because you're a turd."

"Yes, I am." Her turd. For life. That sounded nice.

She thumped her knuckle against his chest, then grinned like the fabled Terrian Cheshire Cat. Now she was definitely up to something. She rose to her knees and straddled his lap.

Holy gods. "Okay, now that you have my full attention," literally, "what do you wish to discuss?"

"The whole frenzy thing." Her tongue peeked out between her pink lips and his gaze locked onto it for the brief moment of exposure. "Fander, I don't want our first time to be like, you know. Like that."

Like that sounded pretty good to him.

"I want it to be slow, so we can get to know each other's bodies. Not three chaotic couplings in a row."

Ah, now that made sense. He reached up and brushed the little loose pieces of her hair back from her face. "It doesn't have to be that way. I will have some control over the...pace, even in the throes of the frenzy."

At least, in his inexperienced mind, he liked to believe he would.

She nibbled at her bottom lip. A groan of desire built in his chest. "I didn't know that. But, still...."

"You want the first time to be just us. Clearheaded and rational?" He waited for her to nod. "Good, so do I. You know, I have not...I mean..." Why did the words tangle on his tongue? It was not as though waiting to share his first experience with her was abnormal.

"I know. Me too." Her cheeks turned a subtle shade of rose. "I knew I had to wait right after I kissed Bobby Diaz. It just hit me that there wasn't any point in trying to fake a relationship with someone else."

"You kissed Bobby?" That should not bother him, but it did.

"And Gabe Carter." She shrugged as though it was nothing. Ouch.

"You kissed Gabe too?"

"They were the only tall boys in town, and I wanted to be sure." Bobby was not *that* tall, for a Terrian. "But, neither of them made my toes curl, not like you did. You ruined me for all other guys with just one kiss."

All right, that was better. It still stung that she had shared even a small part of herself with them. When had he become so possessive? And why was she giving him such a suspicious glare?

"You're not going to tell me that the extremely eligible and handsome crown prince of Anferthia *didn't* kiss any girls in the past nine years?"

He opened his mouth, then shut it. No good could come from redirecting this conversation. "There was one. The daughter of the brother of the woman who is bonded to my mother's brother."

"Huh?" The way Flora blinked her blue eyes at him would be funny in a different situation. She shook her head. "Never mind. Go on."

At least she hadn't climbed off his lap, yet. "After returning to Anferthia. I started reading about the nature of physical intimacy between males and females. Nor found the whole phase amusing, even though it was his reputation at risk."

"How?"

"He was the one who obtained the literature for me."

"*Hah.*" Her entire face lit with humor. "That was nice of him."

"So it was. The situation did become challenging when I asked for information about Terrian females. There was very little available, but somehow, he managed to obtain what I needed."

"Hmm. So, what about the girl?"

"Nebamu and I have been friends since childhood. She and her family often attend official functions. It was at one such function that she agreed to practice kissing with me."

Flora sat up straighter and raised her eyebrows. "Really?"

"It was nothing like *our* first kiss." Toe-curling did his memory of that moment a great honor. That would never happen again for him with anyone else. "It was awkward and uncomfortable, and once it was over we never discussed it again."

Thanks be to the gods that her expression softened with understanding. Hopefully it was a sign that this conversation was near its end and they could move on to *doing* some of the things he had read about.

"What about all the reading you did? Why'd you do that?"

"Because, I wanted to be everything to you. I wanted to make you happy. I did not want to let you down."

She leaned forward, her breasts flat against his chest and her lips a handspan from his. "Let's get one thing straight, here. You *do* make me happy, and you have never, ever let me down."

"Except for not telling you about being the heir."

"Why don't you see if you can make me forget that one little time?" She pressed her lips to his, molding them to a perfect fit, and the groan lodged in his chest broke free.

He stroked his fingers up and down her back, opening his mouth to take her in. Every deity of every world must have blessed him, because how else had he come to be with this woman? This strong, soft, stunning woman moving her hips to rub herself along his hardening length. And she was all *woman*, now, not the awkward girl she had been the first time he had kissed her. This time it seemed she knew what she wanted and was going after it. And there was no reason to stop her—or himself—this time, except for the two people outside the door.

He cradled her face between his palms and turned the one deep kiss into several short ones before pulling back. "The kapits of our guard details are standing beyond the door. They could check in at any moment."

"We can go into my room."

The invitation he had waited his lifetime to hear. "They'll still look for us there."

"I'll risk it." Flora slid off his lap and cool air rushed over his thighs and overheated groin. She grasped his hands and tugged. "C'mon, Fander. We can lock the door."

And pray Nor and K'rona did not smash it down in a panic.

Still, there was a tingle of excitement at risking discovery. He allowed her to pull him from the couch, across the sitting room, and into her bedroom. The door had barely shushed closed before she was wrapped around him, her teeth nipping along his chin. Her feminine scent filled every crevice of his world. He bent and captured her lips with his, and her response was a soft, muffled moan.

A half a moment later, he pulled back. "I need to see you, Flora. All of you. Please."

"I need to see you too." She set to work on loosening the seal of her shirt.

In less time than he imagined, he had shed his *wysgog*, and so had she. Her skin glowed, pale and covered with blessed freckles. Everywhere, as he had always hoped, including her pink-tipped breasts. At the juncture of her legs she had a nest of curls, just like the literature he had read reported to be common for Terrians. The exact shade of red as the hair on her head.

Flora breathed out a soft breath. "Anferthians really don't have pubic hair."

"I wish I did, now that I see yours."

Her hands twitched at her sides as though she contemplated covering herself. That was one thing he could not bear at this moment. He closed the distance between them in two steps. She swayed, but stopped short of taking a step back. He must be moving too fast. Slow and easy was the intent. As eager as he was to be joined with her, he must keep this in mind even though all his blood seemed to be redirecting to his groin. This time was as much about discovery as it was about their ultimate expression of love. And gods knew he loved her. Had loved her for years.

He ran his fingertips over the nest of hair at the juncture of her legs. Wiry, yet soft. "Beautiful. And perfect."

"Oh, wow," she breathed. "Your *dynzla* has *ridges*?"

Gods, just when he did not think he could get any harder.

Flora stared down at Fander's engorged penis. If she hadn't seen the dark green lines running the length of it actually rise she would've thought they were just skin pigmentation. But, they were *ridges*. Honest-to-God ridges.

"Doesn't every male have them?" He asked.

"No. Terrian men don't, at least." She raised her gaze to his and grinned. "I have a feeling this is a good thing for me."

Fander tipped back his head and laughed. Then he wrapped his arms around her middle, lifted her, and carried her backward onto the bed. A half-squeak half-laugh bubbled out as she sank back-first into the fluffy bedcover.

Fander fell half on top of her, grinning. "Before I show you mine, you're going to show me yours."

"Really?" *His* was pressed against her thigh, out of sight but definitely not out of mind.

"Yes, really." He circled a fingertip around one of her areolas, raising little puckers in the pale pink skin. "What does this do?"

"Makes me all fuzzy inside."

"I see. What about this?" He dipped his head, closed his lips over her nipple and sucked it into his mouth.

A bolt of pleasure rocketed straight between her legs. She inhaled in a sharp breath and arched her back. "Oh, God."

He released her with a small wet sound to hover over the other breast. "Where did you feel it, Flora?"

"Between…my legs." All over. Outside. Inside.

He went still, his gaze locking with hers. "Have you…." He stopped, and his Adam's apple bobbed. "Have you ever…touched yourself?"

God, yes, she had. She gave her head a small nod as heat bloomed over her chest and crept up her neck.

"I have too," he whispered. "I pretended it was you even though you weren't there."

She blinked against the sudden sting of tears. "Me too."

"Don't cry, Flora." He pressed his lips to the corner of her eye and smoothed his hands over the hair on top of her head. "We don't have to pretend anymore. Show me where the imaginary me made you feel the best."

A watery chuckle escaped her. "Everywhere?"

He raised his eyebrows but didn't move.

Well, darn. She'd have to be more specific. "Kiss me first." That was something only the real Fander could do.

He didn't hesitate, and she parted her lips and snaked her arms around his neck. The kiss was hard and heated, and so unlike the sweet kisses they'd shared so far. His tongue swept over hers, a teasing duel before retreating. It was only natural that she pursue it. She bent her knee, running the side of her foot along his leg. The movement left space for him to slip between her legs. His tip nudged against her and he dug his fingers into her hair.

A little mewling sound came from her throat. She *mewled*. Who would've guessed that was possible? She wiggled her hips from side to side, locking him in closer.

Fander broke the kiss, panting. "Gods, Flora, please tell me you're ready because I need to feel you around me, love. Please, let me."

Every raw emotion in him showed in his eyes. His arms trembled as he braced himself. This meant everything to him, and to her. She reached up and stroked her palm over his smooth face. "Now, Fander."

He lowered himself, until only his face filled her vision. "I'll go slow. Tell me if it hurts."

She wouldn't, but she nodded anyway.

He pushed forward, entering her, stretching her, filling her.

"Oh, God." She panted at the wonder of this moment and the way her body softened to receive him.

But, he stopped. "Am I hurting you?"

"No. No you're not. Don't stop." She lifted her hips, taking him deeper. "Yessss."

"Flora." He groaned her name like a benediction—his salvation—as he drove forward until he was all the way inside. He touched his forehead to hers and released a shaky breath. "At last."

She warbled a soft laugh. "At long last."

He wet his lips with his tongue. "I have loved you since the day we met, Flora."

"I have loved you since then too, Fander. It just took me a while to figure it out." She gave her hips another suggestive wiggle. "Move. Please."

He pulled out almost as slowly as he'd entered, and pushed back in. Someone moaned, or maybe both of them did. It didn't matter. Her whole universe had narrowed down to the man moving inside her, his hard ridges stroking the bundle of nerves as a sweet ache built and built.

Instinctively, she wrapped her legs around his hips and...*God all mighty*. The ridges *rippled*, and wave after wave of soul-shaking pleasure exploded through her. He covered her mouth with his and claimed her cry as he pumped into her faster, harder, then stiffened. She took his roar as his release jetted into her.

Time had no meaning for a while. Just floating in the bliss-zone with Fander's weight covering her was all she needed.

Finally, she stirred and opened her eyes and smiled at the ceiling. "That was *so* much better than pretending."

Fander's body vibrated with a low chuckle. "Definitely." He moved, sliding out of her and to one side so he wasn't pressing her into the mattress. "And, we were not caug—."

A sharp rap on the door cut him off. "When you are finished in there, my prince, it would be well for us to discuss future protocol for these situations."

Nor's voice was muted through the door, but the meaning was clear. He—and probably K'rona—had found them.

She met Fander's startled gaze. A silly boyish grin lit his face. "I stand corrected. We are royally busted."

Royally was right.

Fander turned toward the door. "Go away, Nor. We are busy."

Had she really just heard K'rona giggle?

"Now." Fander spanned her waist easily with his hands and pulled her body against his. "Since *they* know we are safe, we are unlikely to be interrupted again until last meal is served. This leaves us with plenty of time for you to show me those places you used to touch while thinking of me."

K'rona flopped onto the couch in Flora's sitting area and lay her forearm over her eyes. It was an un-captain-like flop, but it did not matter. The man she reported to was in the next room experiencing the joy of new discoveries with the woman she was charged to protect with her life. Under the circumstances, she deserved a flop, especially after the momentary panic of discovering both of them missing.

It was well that the faint musky scent of sex had invaded her olfactory senses as she had run toward the bedroom door. Bearing witness to her future *ymero* copulating with his *tangol* was not an image she wanted burned into her memory. Besides, Terrians in general were protective of their privacy, and Flora was no exception. K'rona would respect and guard the privacy of her *fyhen*.

The cushion next to her sank under the weight of the only other being in the room with her. Nor Danol. He was a good man, loyal to her prince, and dependable as a fellow warrior. And exceedingly handsome with his icy blue eyes and dark hair.

Not that she had noticed, of course.

"I believe they will be a while longer." Nor's baritone voice sent a shiver through her.

She raised her arm far enough to view his profile. He sat near the edge of the cushioned bench seat, his forearms resting on his long, muscular thighs and hands clasped between his knees. The direction of her thoughts and the increase of her heart rate set her on edge. Such feelings were dishonorable to Mendiko's memory, even though most days she could barely recall his face.

The feelings her lost love had generated in her sixteen years ago still lingered. Even the discovery of her *tangol*, Storo Z'bel, while exiled on Matir had not taken her thoughts in the intimate direction she now experienced with Nor. Storo was not a love match as she had once hoped her *tangol* would be; even he had agreed. He was more like a brother. And a very protective brother, at that.

Especially the first time he had caught her gaze lingering on Nor longer than it should have. And every time since.

"I believe you are correct, Kapit Danol." She pushed herself upright. Slouching was unprofessional and she was on duty. "I, for one, am relieved they have finally bonded."

His mouth pulled into a tight grimace, and he turned his head far enough to meet her gaze. The color of his eyes was unusual for their kind. Rarer than a night without any of Anferthia's five moons overhead. At one time, it was believed such eyes could see into another's soul. Now she understood why.

"My name is Nor." His voice was so low it was almost a whisper. Seductive.

No, she had no right or reason to think that way. He'd been nothing but kind to her since they had met. A friend and fellow warrior. It was wrong to presume he felt anything more for her than that.

She wet her lips with her tongue and his gaze riveted on her mouth. "We are on duty, Kapit Danol."

His gaze flicked back up to hers. "My name...is...Nor." He turned to face her fully, cupping her cheek with his warm palm. "Please call me such, at least when we are alone."

Great creators, he *did* have feelings for her. It would be so easy to allow herself to accept him in this way. To press against his palm and acknowledge her own attraction. But, it would not be the honorable thing to do.

She pulled away but he followed, not allowing the space between them. "There was another."

His lips compressed into a flat, hard line. "Storo."

"No. Not Storo. He is my *tangol*, but that is all."

Confusion clouded his eyes. "I do not understand. Wait, you said *was*. This was someone you lost, then?"

It was too much to continue looking at him. Too much pain and regret buried inside that he did not need to see. She lowered her gaze to her hands, twisting together on her lap. "Yes."

Silence filled the space. The only sounds were the barely perceptible whoosh of the ventilation system and the soft hum of the ship's engines. And her heartbeat. He would withdraw his hand now. No one wanted to compete with a ghost.

Except, he did not move. He did not even tremble or flinch.

"How long has it been?"

"Mendiko was executed by my uncle the day the Terrians reclaimed their planet."

This time he did flinch, but still his hand remained upon her cheek. "You have grieved this long, K'rona." He used her given name, and the tone of his voice conveyed compassion. "I do not seek to replace him—Mendiko—in your heart, but I do hope there is enough space in there for me to share."

Did he speak true? She met his gaze again. There was nothing but open honesty there. He meant his words.

And perhaps, just perhaps, there was a little space for him.

Twenty-Eight

Flora pressed her nose to the glass portal of the transport. Excitement welled in her chest. Below, lush jungle land raced by as they approached the K'nil family estate. This was it. Anferthia. She'd finally arrived, and not in the way she'd imagined—alone, or as part of a delegation with people she barely knew. Instead, she had Fander at her back, his arms around her middle and his chin resting on top of her head. Once again, reality had turned out so much better than imagination.

She nestled her back up closer against his chest. "Why am I not surprised Anferthia is as green as you?"

The soft rumble of Fander's chuckle vibrated against her back. "Not all of it is. Grandfather's family home happens to be located in the Wydea Forest. Just far enough from the urban population centers to keep me isolated from the public, and near enough to trot me out for special occasions."

Yeah, the Arruch sure wouldn't want the heir to put ideas of rebellion into the heads of the people they were trying to control by having him out where everyone could see him all the time. "What are we going to do, Fander?"

"Bury Grandfather."

"I mean after that."

He nuzzled his cheek against her hair. "I want to be alone with you, Flora. I need to be, before we confront Isel T'orr and his followers."

Before they started something there would be no coming back

from. They would either win freedom for their people or die. "Do you think enough people will step forward?"

"Even on your planet, some revolutions have been won by the minority."

True. But, in most cases the minority got trampled. He probably had that one figured out already, so saying it was pointless.

Below, several low buildings came into view, then a large, rambling house. She leaned closer to the window again. "Is that it?"

"I told you it was small."

"It's larger than the *entire* town of New Damon Beach. I'd visualized more buildings like the Matiran cubes we've lived in for so long. Or the climate-controlled sky scrapers of Old Earth." The old stone buildings below were homey and comforting, and silently begging to be explored.

"The charm of the old with the convenience of the new." Fander tightened his arms around her, then relaxed. "We love our old buildings, but we also love the efficiency of climate control. Now that you're here, it will feel more like home."

"True." Fander's mother stepped up next to them. "We have anticipated your arrival for far too long, Flora. It is well for my heart to have you here finally."

"Thank you, Mother—"

"*A nat*," Fander swore. He stepped around her to get closer to the portal, one arm still around her waist. "Supreme Warden Tusayn's skimmer is here."

The Supreme Warden Tusayn? T'orr's second in command? The jerk that'd tried to pin Grandfather's murder on her less than an hour after it'd happened? "What do you think he wants?"

"Whatever it is, I'm sure we won't like it. K'rona." He turned around, moving her with him.

K'rona startled and jerked away from Nor as if they'd been caught doing something other than standing shoulder to shoulder. "My prince."

"Tusayn will likely attempt to send a guard detail aboard to escort my grandfather's body, so keep the dissenters out of sight. Comtat Cynto can cover your position as Flora's guard. Nor, inform the UDF transports we have company, and to take peaceful measures to conceal the dissenters traveling with them. I do not wish to stir the Arruch's suspicions more than necessary."

As if bringing the daughter of Isel T'orr's public enemy number one home with him wasn't the least bit suspicious.

"As you command." K'rona thumped her fist to her chest, then exchanged a heated look with Nor and strode from the room.

Storo curled his upper lip at Nor before he too strode away.

Well, okay then.

Something weird was going on between the three of them, and it'd started the day before yesterday, after Nor and K'rona had busted her and Fander in bed.

The gentle brush of Fander's palm against hers drew her attention away from speculations that weren't any of her business anyway. He threaded his fingers between hers. "Time to…face the music."

A giggle slipped out at the Terrianism. "Cute."

A few minutes later she stood at the hatch with Fander, their fingers still laced together, ready to exit in a show of unity. This time both his and her guards had arrayed themselves in front of them. If Tusayn had assassination on his mind, at least the two of them might have a chance of surviving. Unless the Supreme Warden just blew up the transport. That'd be a perfect cover.

In general, Anferthians frowned on assassination, which had to be another reason why Fander and his mother had been kept alive. Easier to explain away one death than three. But, in this case, the official cause could be blamed on a faulty engine. No one would question it, and the Arruch wouldn't bother opening an investigation.

The hull creaked and the hatch slid open. The muggy scent of recent rain pushed away the stale recycled air. Flora inhaled, filling her lungs with its freshness. The guards moved forward into the bright Anferthian sunlight. Nor glanced over his shoulder and exchanged a look with Fander, then he and Cynto also moved out.

"Be ready," Fander murmured next to her ear. "Things could change in an instant."

They descended the ramp together. The Supreme Warden was frowning so deeply it'd be a miracle if his face didn't freeze that way. "My greetings, Fander K'nil."

"My greetings, Supreme Warden. The pleasure is mine to introduce Flora Bock, designated junior ambassador of Terr."

The hum of two more surface-to-ship transports drew Tusayn's attention to the sky above. "Unusual that the Unified Defense Fleet would bring such large ships to a Well of Peace ceremony."

"Standard operating procedure when visiting another planet." Flora gave her shoulders a casual shrug. "Travel to impress. Everything and everyone on Anferthia are large, so the Terrian and Matiran representatives will bring appropriately outfitted ships."

Not bad for making it up on the fly. Anything to ensure he didn't suspect the illegal transport of dissenters happening right under his bulbous nose.

"Why have you brought *her*?" The Supreme Warden made "her" sound like something disgusting he'd found in his armpit.

Why, oh, why did everyone feel the need to discuss her with others when she was standing right in front of them? "To answer your question, I am here to complete my Anferthian education, Supreme Warden. As I am sure you understand…because I *am* fluent in Anferthian…the K'nil family is honor-bound to oversee what Ambassador K'nil began. Now, since we seem to have gotten off on the wrong foot, I am willing to give introductions another chance." She extended her hands, palms up. "I am Flora Bock of Terr. Great is my pleasure to meet you, Supreme Warden Tusayn."

Tusayn's eyes had grown wider and wider with each sentence she spoke, in Anferthian, no less. But she couldn't stop herself. The need to make a point had kept her mouth running. In about thirty seconds, she'd probably forget exactly what she just said, but he wouldn't.

The towering Anferthian scowled down his nose at her. So not a good sign. He lifted his huge hands and settled them palm-to-palm over hers. Now, that was a promising turn of events. Tusayn wrapped his fingers around her hands and squeezed until her bones crushed together and pain shot up her forearms. A small, wordless cry squeaked out of her and tears blurred the vision of his face.

She blinked rapidly to clear them. The points of two *luz-bas*, Anferthian spear-like long blades, pointed at Tusayn's neck, and the business end of Fander's *fusil* was inches from the man's nose. "Release her, now, Supreme Warden."

"You dare threaten me?" The son-of-a-bitch squeezed harder, and she could swear she heard popping sounds. With each one came a fresh wave of pain, and black dots danced at the edge of her vision.

"It is not set to stun."

"You will not do it."

Kick him. The message wasn't getting to her useless legs. They slowly folded instead.

Fander pressed the weapon's muzzle against the Supreme Warden's nose. "I have little to lose. The Arruch has seen to that."

The crushing pressure around her hands disappeared, and the sting of blood rushing back amplified the agony of broken bones as the blackness rushed in.

"Flora." Fander's voice came from the other end of a very long tunnel. "Come on, love. Come back to me."

She forced her eyes open. Dampness from the ground seeped through the shins of her *wysgog* leggings from knee to ankle. Fander had her tucked against his side, holding her against him with one arm, his *fusil* still pointed in the general direction of Tusayn.

"Keep your hands still, love," Fander murmured.

No problem there, with the pain throbbing with every beat of her pulse, which seemed uncharacteristically rapid. Sweat beaded on her upper lip. "When I get my hands back, I'm going to fuck up his face." Using English this time seemed the best way to avoid more trouble.

One corner of Fander's mouth twitched. "I'll hold him down for you."

"You're a good man, Fander."

Tusayn crossed his arms over his chest and frowned down at her good man. "It is the will of the Divine Warden that Ambassador K'nil's Service of Internment be held at the old palace in Sala D'eu."

Fander look up. "The service will be here at my grandfather's beloved home the day after tomorrow. Isel T'orr is invited to attend and pay his respects. You, however, are not."

"You defy the wishes of Anferthia's chosen leader?" Tusayn sounded incredulous.

Fander shifted, moving her into another set of arms. Then he stood. "Supreme Warden, you forget, *I* am Anferthia."

"Can you move if you must, Flora?" Fani whispered next to her ear. Flora forced her head to move up and down. "It is well."

Tusayn's face was flushed with fury. "*Treason.*"

"I am weary of hearing that word, especially since I am not the one who committed that egregious crime. I will, however, be the one bringing justice upon those who did. Leave now, Supreme Warden, before I begin with you."

Tusayn fisted his hands so hard his knuckles turned pale and they trembled at his side. Then he turned away, his long strides making short work of the distance between him and his surface skimmer, his guards following in his wake.

The last two guards cast longing glances at Fander, then one touched his palm to his chest. "They have our families, my prince." He spoke the words so softly she strained to hear them over the rustle of soft breeze in the nearby trees.

Fander nodded. "When the time comes, I will fight for your *fyhen*."

Relief lit their eyes. "We stand with you."

As soon as they were out of hearing range, Fander was kneeling back on the ground at her side. "Flora, can you feel your hands at all?"

"Hurts. Throbbing." And useless. She lowered her gaze to where they rested in her lap. They shouldn't be all bent and misshapen, with crooked fingers. "That's not normal." Her voice cracked on the last word and hot tears flooded her eyes.

He tapped his comm. "Get one of the healers out here immediately. No, I do not care which one…the first one you come across. And carry them if you must." He switched positions with his mother, pulled her to him and rocked her back and forth. "Help will be here soon, love."

Twenty-Nine

Fander dabbed a cloth over Flora's upper lip. "Would you please reconsider allowing your uncle to put you in the healing sleep, love?"

She looked so helpless laying in the recliner, her broken hands propped on a tray. What that creeping sewage worm, Tusayn, had done to her was just the latest crime he would answer for.

"No. Staying awake." Flora's bloodless lips barely moved.

Stubborn, more so than he. "No one will fault you for it, I swear to you."

"Can't take the chance. Have a reputation to uphold. Ahhh…."

Nick Bock looked up at her from where he perched on a stool to work on her hands. "You're annoying me, Red. Listen to Fander. I've barely started repairs, and things are going to get worse before they get better."

"Don't care."

The afternoon sun poured through the solar's windows, igniting her hair with a burnished glow. She looked how he had always imagined a Terrian angel would.

Nick snorted. "More like a devil in disguise. But, whatever, man."

He must have said that aloud.

Nor stepped into the room. "Ambassador Olivarius's shuttle is landing. Healer Yamata will be here soon."

At one time it had made sense to put the healers in separate landing groups. Nick had come with the first wave, while his wife was held back in case something went wrong. She would be able to escape with their children. It was astonishing how quickly Sakura Yamata's absence had become a detriment.

He moved to wipe her brow. "What are the chances she'll just pass out?"

"Excellent." Nick refocused on Flora's pale slender deformed hands. "Especially once Saku gets here. She's going to be pissed about this. You know that, right, Flora?"

Flora did not reply, but she did swallow hard and run her tongue over her lips. On some level, her petite aunt must intimidate her. Probably not to the same degree Graig Roble intimidated him, but close.

The thump of running footsteps came from the hall outside the solar, and K'rona rushed into the room carrying something. No, someone.

"I'm here." Healer Yamata's voice bobbled as K'rona set her on her feet. The Terrian female propped her fists on her hips. "Why is Flora still awake?"

Nick shrugged. "She refused dormio."

"I see." She pressed her mouth into a disapproving line, then strode to her husband's side.

For a long moment, both healers studied Flora's hands, then her aunt pointed to the back of her left hand. "That one there should do it."

"I agree." Nick sat up straight, rolled his shoulders back, and traced his forefinger over Flora's skin.

Flora's scream of agony shattered the air.

Fander reached out and twisted the neck of Nick's shirt in his grip and yanked the man up until his toes barely touched the ground. "What the hell are you doing?"

"Making a point. You can put me down now." The healer seemed completely unperturbed that his life was about to end.

The fleeting touch of a much smaller hand fluttered over his elbow, and he gave his attention to Sakura.

"It's okay, Fander. Flora's fine, she's just stubborn as a rock. Let Nick go."

He glanced at Flora. Other than her rapid breathing pattern and clenched teeth, she did seem as fine as she could be, given the circumstances. He released her uncle and stepped back to her side.

"All right, Flora," Sakura said. "Still want to stay wake for the rest of this?"

Flora rocked her head from side to side against the recliner. "Not really, no."

"Wise choice." Sakura tapped her finger against Flora's forehead. "Dormio."

The result was instantaneous. Flora's entire body relaxed, pain lines smoothed away from her face, and her breathing slowed. She was comfortable, pain free, and safe.

Fander released his breath. "I apologize for my reaction, Healer Bock."

"No sweat, kid. I'm used to it." Nick's grin was easygoing as he moved back into position next to his wife. In the next breath, his professional healer persona took over. "It's not nearly as bad as Dennis Gilbert's foot, so healing should only take a few days."

"I agree,' Sakura replied.

Fander frowned at Nick and gave his head a shake. "I don't know this person. Who is Dennis Gilbert?"

"A friend. He was incarcerated with us after the invasion. Healer Dacian and my sister tried to fix his crushed foot, but Vyn Kotas killed him anyway."

Fander's stomach churned, as it did with each life he discovered lost to this new branch of his family. His Terrian family. Odd how he barely noticed the physical differences now. Their skin color, stature, planet of their birth, no longer defined them in his mind. Family did. *Fyhen.* They were his, and they had suffered enough. Too much.

Once, years ago in the naivete of his youth, he had envisioned a bloodless restoration. He had been so wrong. Isel T'orr and those who served his agenda must be destroyed.

What a difference a day makes.

Flora half-smiled to herself as she strolled along the path through the garden surrounding the K'nil family manor, Fander at her side keeping his pace short so she wouldn't jar her hands while trying to keep up with him. Spring was in full bloom. The air was warm and heavily scented with flowers. All of them were huge, just like Fander had told her when they were kids. And, of course, they all did smell really good. Some even bordered on edible-delicious. Who could blame her for sticking her nose into every single one of them?

She stared down at her bandaged hands. At some point she would pick a bouquet of them to put in her room, but not until her hands were healed. Uncle Nick and Aunt Saku were adamant that they remain immobile until the bones had knitted back together. That meant two more frustrating days to complete the process, which further meant that she'd be helpless at grandfather's funeral tomorrow.

Fander slipped his arm around her shoulders and drew her against his side. "It'll be okay, Flora."

She smiled up at him. "I know. And thanks for using English when we're alone. It makes me feel more, I don't know, comfortable, I guess."

"I remember what a transition it was for me when I first arrived on Terr. There are a lot of differences between our planets and our cultures. The only thing I can promise is that it'll get easier as you adjust." He bent and kissed the top of her head. "We'll visit your family on Terr as often as possible once things settle down here. And, they are always welcome here."

"Thanks, Fander." She leaned her head against his shoulder and allowed the beauty of his home to seep into the lonely, I-miss-my-family hollow spot in her heart. "Once I can contribute to the household, it'll be better."

Everyone had jobs to do, outside of their primary responsibilities, to keep the household running. And those chores would shift from time to time...because who wanted to clean the bathrooms every day for the rest of their lives? They operated as an extended family in that regard, and because of it they were close-knit. K'rona hadn't been kidding when she said *ymeres* didn't lounge around all day and thank God for that. Living a pampered life would drive her crazy.

Speaking of K'rona.... "Do you think there's something going on between K'rona and Nor? They've been acting...I don't know. Strange."

"I told Nor you'd figure it out."

"What? You knew?"

"How could I not? He carries her scent on his clothing."

Of course, that'd be dead giveaway for Anferthians. There was no way her Terrian nose would ever catch a whiff of Nor on K'rona's clothing. "Are you okay with it...their relationship, I mean?"

"Pfft. Of course, I am. The better they know each other, the better they will be able to work together to keep us safe."

"But, what if they break up?"

"What if they don't?"

Good point. "I hope they do."

She gazed up into the towering trees and the variety of birds flitting in and out of the branches. Anferthia sure had its share of birds, and one in particular caught her eye. It was at least two feet tall and looked like a brilliant rainbow-feathered duster with a beak and inky blue eyes.

"As do I." Fander waved in the direction of the colorful bird. "That's Juja. He's a *musae'n*, a song bird. Which means he does more than flit from branch to branch tweeting. He appeared here about five years ago and has been in residence ever since. He's quite a show off."

"He reminds me of a parrot on steroids."

"*Musae'n* are similar to parrots, but they have the voices of nightingales and the egos of peacocks." Fander shook his head. "Don't be fooled."

A laugh bubbled out of her, and Juja cocked his head and regarded her from his perch.

Fander nudged her. "Sing something."

"What, seriously?"

"Yeah. He'll pick up the tune and start singing with you. Like a Terrian mockingbird, but better."

She gave him an unladylike snort. "If this is a trick, I'll get even, you know."

"You'll get ahead, is what you mean. That's why I'm not lying. I value my life."

Scary how well he knew her. "Okay, fine. Let's see what an Anferthian mockingbird can do."

She rolled her shoulders. Something simple to start with. Then, if the bird actually came through, she'd try something more complicated. "Row, Row, Row Your Boat" would work.

Halfway through the verse, Juja warbled a dozen notes, then stopped and turned his back to her. Fander doubled over, his laughter filling the shady space beneath the trees.

"What? Why's he doing that?" She fixed a glare at Fander. "You *did* trick me."

"No. No, no, no." He backed away from her a couple of steps. Not that he had to worry. She couldn't very well beat him without setting back her recovery by several more days. "No tricks, I swear to you. He thinks the song is beneath him."

Oh. Well, then. "Pretty sure I've never met a bird who was such a snob."

"I told you he's full of himself. Try something different."

"Okay." She took a cleansing breath and ran through a few scales. "My mom used to sing this one when I was really young, but it was Uncle Nick who taught me the words. We used to sing together a lot, before he moved away."

The words of Amazing Grace were peace harmonized, flowing through her like a mountain stream flowed over stones. On the word "sound", Juja turned his head to peer at her from one deep blue eye. On "found", he hopped around on his branch to face her, and by "see" he swayed his head side-to-side keeping time. Maybe Fander was right.

As she launched into the second verse, the bird opened his beak and the most beautiful sound emerged. He was singing along with her, sweet and clear like an aria, but without actual words. She couldn't stop now; it was like magical fairy dust had been sprinkled over them and everything in the garden stilled, as though afraid to shatter the spell.

A moment later, as the last word seemed to shimmer in the air, she glanced at Fander and nearly choked on her own breath. The look of mesmerized wonder on his face touched that special place in her heart that was all for him.

He blinked and swallowed. "I...that...I always loved to hear you sing that one."

She gave him a perplexed look. "When did you ever hear me sing that song?"

"Well." He grinned, looked at his feet, then back at her. "I used to sit under your window at night, sometimes, just to listen to you sing."

"Geez, you're such a stalker."

He grinned and shrugged. "I will not apologize." He stepped closer and brushed a stray wisp of her hair off her forehead with his fingers. "You have the most beautiful voice I've ever heard. Is that the song you're going to sing at our *maitz'a*?"

"Nope."

"Good. I have another small favor to ask."

"If you want to kiss me, you don't have to ask."

He chuckled. "I'd like that too, but that's not what I want to ask. What do I need to do to convince you to sing that song at the end of Grandfather's service tomorrow?"

"Hmm, well." She moved in close enough to rest her hands on his chest. "I'm sure I can think of something."

"Can you?"

Juja warbled the opening notes from Amazing Grace, and Fander shot the bird an annoyed look. "Let's go somewhere private before he starts flirting with you. He's shameless."

Fander offered his arm, and together they crossed the expanse of green grass toward the house.

THIRTY

Fander stood between Flora and his mother as the officiant chanted the Service of Internment to the Well of Rest. No breeze stirred the morning air. All was still as though the planet itself honored Grandfather and prepared to accept his body once the Well of Rest was filled in.

The Well was not a grave in the way Terrian's knew it. No coffin was lowered into the hole, only the body, dressed in a white *wysgog* made from organic fibers. When the service was complete, the officiant would hand him and his mother the fire spheres. Once they dropped the flammable ignitors into the Well, cremation would begin. The flames would quickly consume the body, then naturally extinguish. Grandfather's ashes would then be covered with soil. He would forever become one with the world he had loved in life. The world he had died to protect. It was fitting. Grandfather may have spent more than a decade living on Terr, but his heart had always belonged to Anferthia.

From the far side of the estate came the sweet notes of Flora's Earth hymn. Juja must really like the song, as he had sung the tune at least three times an hour since yesterday. And he would likely sing it again with Flora as Grandfather's well was covered.

Fander allowed his gaze to touch on the front row of attendees here for the service. They were fanned out to his left and right in the semi-circle around the Well of Rest. Terrian vice-ambassador to Matir, Kapoor; Ambassador Olivarius from Matir; Terrian ambassador to Anferthia, Malakar; several coalition members and high-ranking Arruch representatives. But, no Tusayn, and no Isel T'orr. Should he be relieved by this, or worried?

So far, no one seemed to have noticed the large number of dissenters scattered throughout the crowd. Someone would soon enough, though. K'rona may be older than the official image the Arruch had on file, but she was still recognizable. And none too inconspicuous either, standing directly behind Flora. Nor had given her a kapit's helmet, but it was only a matter of time before someone took a second, closer look.

The officiant came to stand in front of him, one small glass sphere in each of his upturned palms. "The fire spheres."

"My thanks." Fander accepted one of the palm-size ignitors.

Its smooth surface was warm with the contained energy inside, waiting for release. He met Flora's gaze and gave her an understanding smile. As she was not an official member of his family yet, she could not participate. Sure, he could issue an edict of exception for her, but over-stepping her bounds by inserting her alien self into a time-honored tradition was not the best way to earn her place with the Anferthian people.

He stepped forward, his mother right with him, and closed the distance to the well. Then he stood at its edge and peered down. This was the last time he would see the face of his grandfather in this life.

Be at peace, Grandfather.

He raised his arm and dropped the fire sphere, his mother's following just a split second behind. The moment the spheres came in contact with the fibers of Grandfather's garment, the outer glass-like shells disintegrated, the air mixing with the contents and igniting it, sending low flames dancing across the body.

It was done. Soon grey smoke would billow from the well. He turned, extended his hand toward his mother palm up and she placed her hand atop his. For so long it had been the three of them, Grandfather, Mother, and himself. Now they walked away from Grandfather, but they were also walking toward Flora. One soul lost and another gained. Bitter, yet sweet. Hope filled him. Somehow, they would triumph over the Arruch Union and displace Isel T'orr, the self-proclaimed *Divine* Warden.

A faint whistle of air being sliced cut through the respectful silence.

Thump.

The force of something sharp stung the back of his knee. Pain blossomed up and down the back of his leg. He stumbled forward and caught himself, his hands skidding along the slick grass until his chest impacted with the ground.

"Fander?" Concern radiated from his mother as she kneeled next to him. Then she was over him, shielding him with her body. "Gods of mercy, there is a dart in your leg. Stay down."

Cool dampness seeped through the front of his mourning *wysgog* and the scent of the soil of Anferthia filled him. "It is drugged. I cannot feel my leg."

"Rauc, Nor, to us!" Suppressed fear strained her shouted words.

Fander raised his head. Nor was coming, running with Rauc. K'rona already had Flora on the ground and covered. His *tangol* was safe, for the moment. The numbness was spreading fast, up his back, and a metallic tang coated the back of his throat.

Plink.

His gaze riveted on a small metallic device as it bounced twice on the grass near his head. A shock grenade. "Mother, go." *Get to safety.*

The device popped, and it was as if his senses were sucked out of him. No sight, no scents, no hearing. The world around him ceased to exist, even though common sense dictated it was still there. Cold sweat prickled his upper lip and between his shoulder blades. He was truly helpless now, at the mercy of whoever had shot him with the drugged dart.

Move. Fight back.

Still no response to the order from his muscles. Whoever had him grasped the back of his *wysgog*, yanked him up off the ground, and draped him over their shoulder. If he could feel that, then the effects of the grenade must be wearing off already. A wave of nauseating dizziness churned through him, and the distant clash of metal striking metal rang in his ears. And there was the distinct whine of a *fusil* being discharged. Was that his mother screaming?

"Nooo, Fander!"

Flora.

Gods, keep her safe, because there was nothing he could do to help her.

"Sleep well, little prince," an unfamiliar woman's voice said, uncomfortably close to his ear.

Stars exploded behind his eyelids, and black nothingness took him.

Flora sat in a chair in the middle of the great hall, a calm center to the chaos that swirled around her. A calm, stunned center, actually. Still shaking off the effects of the shock grenade.

Fander was gone. Taken. Right in front of everyone. It'd all gone down so fast. There'd been no way to stop the armed Anferthians who'd come out of the trees, leaped through the thickening grey-white smoke from Grandfather's grave like the apocalypse, and carried off Fander's limp body.

Damn, her heart had nearly choked her when he'd first stumbled and fell. Then the shock grenade tossed just far enough away to make her dizzy and stupid, but not blind. No, she'd seen every terrifying moment, even after K'rona had knocked her to the ground. Thank God her friend and body guard had controlled the fall so they'd both landed on their sides, K'rona taking the brunt of the impact before rolling to shield her. The maneuver had saved her hands from further damage. Even so, they still throbbed from the jostling.

She shook herself from her reverie and turned her attention to the groups and individuals congregated in the massive room that resembled a modern version of a medieval banquet hall. Someone should be organizing a search party or something, shouldn't they? Yet, no one seemed to be doing anything except shooting furtive looks in her direction. Or Fani's direction, more likely. The K'nil matriarch sat in the chair next to hers, an expectant air hovering around her.

Flora leaned in Fani's direction. "Why isn't anyone doing anything? Shouldn't we go after Fander?"

"They are waiting for you to recover and take his place, daughter."

"*Me*? Why me? You're his mother, and I am not an..." *Anferthian*.

That was a cop-out. It wasn't enough anymore to dress in *wysgog*, or speak their language, or comprehend several aspects of their culture. *Tangol* meant something. She was Fander's bond mate, second hand, and his soul, if he needed her to be.

His soul mate.

Realization flooded her, and she wiggled upright in the chair. He was *her* soul mate, too. The one she'd dreamed of having as a little girl. The one who'd stand by her against the evil that had changed not only their lives, but the lives of trillions on three planets.

And that evil now had her soul mate.

"Will they...will they really follow me?"

Fani smiled. "Need you really ask?"

Flora raised her hands and studied the gauzy white bandages holding her bones in place. "Where are my aunt and uncle?"

"You know that rushing the job could lead to irreversible damage, right, Red?"

"I don't care." Flora plopped down on the dispensary stool and placed her wrapped hands on the worktable. "And, there's no choice. I'm going after Fander, with or without healed hands. I'd rather go with them fixed, but I *am* going. So, the ball's in your court, Uncle. You gonna play, or punt?"

Uncle Nick exchanged a dubious look with Aunt Saku and sighed. "We'll play."

Game on.

Flora strode into the main hall like a princess. Or, at least as she imagined a princess would enter, head high, shoulders back, chin up. Easy to do with nine feet of furious future mother-in-law sweeping along in her wake. And the woman's thirteen-foot-tall body guard.

Then, again, there was an equal chance she just looked like an arrogant ass.

She curled and stretched her fingers at her sides to speed circulation, as Aunt Saku recommended. Even though her grip was still weaker than normal, her hands should be fully functional by the time she needed them. When she caught up with the Arruch bastards who'd kidnapped Fander.

And speaking of Arruch bastards, one seemed to have decided to stay around even though all his counterparts had left. She narrowed her glare at the man standing in the middle of hall as if he had every right to be there.

"Member Bylug," Fani murmured, distain evident in her tone.

Flora gave her head a slight nod and approached the Arruch representative. "Greetings, Member Bylug. What—"

Bylug looked pointedly at Fani. "I will speak to you *only*, Lady K'nil."

Well, lovely.

"I defer to my son's *tangol*." Fander's mother stopped a deferential step behind her.

"That is impossible. She's...she's," his disgust filled gaze raked her. "*Terrian*."

Flora folded her arms in front of her. "You say that like it is something filthy."

"It is."

"Hurry up, Member Bylug, I have things to do and my prince to rescue. Talk now or shut up and leave while you still can."

Bylug's face darkened and he raised his hand. The tip of K'rona's *luz-ba* appeared between them. It didn't seem possible, but his face got darker. "K'rona Zurkku."

"It has been too long, Member Bylug." There was an edge to K'rona's words, as though this wasn't the first time they'd been at odds.

"Why is there a *dissenter* here?"

The rustle of several people moving closer whispered through the hall. "Kapit Zurkku is not the only dissenter, Bylug."

The coalition representative stiffened even more at Storo's words and turned his attention back to Fander's mother. "You harbor Terrians and traitors. I knew we should not have spared the lives of you and your son."

A green blur shot passed Flora's head, and Bylug clawed at the humongous hand now clamped around his throat. Flora twisted her neck far enough to look up at the Anferthian guard leaning over her shoulder. "Rauc, would you like to assist our guest to his new quarters?"

"The pleasure is mine, my princess." His voice was rough, as usual. Whether it was natural or from lack of use was anyone's guess.

"Do it." Flora waved her hand in his grandness's direction. "Just make sure he is chained to something permanently attached to the building. Storo, accompany him. You are in charge of keeping him alive. Fander may want to talk to him once he's back."

Bylug wheezed. "You cannot do this. You have no power."

"Yes, I can. Yes, I do. But, you can think about that while I am off trying to fix the mess I am sure you had a hand in making." Damn, it felt good to put someone in their place for a change. She tipped her head at Rauc and he grinned. In a blink, he flipped Bylug around, grabbed him by the scruff, and half carried, half dragged the loser toward the nearest doorway.

The same doorway Nor had just appeared in, grim and determined. Rauc murmured something to Fander's kapit and glanced back at Fani. Nor nodded and strode across the hall toward them.

Six feet away, he went down on one knee and pressed his hand to his chest. "My princess."

Yep, still awkward. Would she ever get used to it? "Did you find out anything, Kapit Danol?"

"The dissenters tracked the perpetrators to the edge of K'nil territory. Their paths diverge in three directions just beyond that point. The groups are reportedly evenly split. My feeling is that they will either continue to three different destinations or converge again at a predetermined point. Whether that point is their final destination or not is open to speculation. We also do not know which group has our prince."

"I never thought I would be so thankful that Administrator Corvus relocated the dissenters to the southern hemisphere of Matir." If it weren't for the need to hunt food on Matir, there wouldn't have been a need for the exiled Anferthians to learn to track prey. Some of them were damn good at it. "K'rona, do we have enough dissenters ready to track all three groups?"

"We do. I can assign three to each group. I advise we be cautious in our strategies, though, my princess. Sending a full war party will leave the K'nil estate virtually unprotected. Small groups have the advantage of speed and stealth, yet they would not have the numbers they would need if they are attacked."

It was so tempting to send a massive, ass-kicking army after the kidnappers just to scare the crap out of them. But, K'rona had a valid point. "So, maybe a double patrol to track each group?" Six warriors didn't seem like enough if there was a confrontation.

"This is what I would recommend." A vertical line appeared between K'rona's brows. "We do have enough for a triple, but again, such a number may attract too much attention."

"I agree," Nor said.

"That works for me." Flora jerked her thumb in the direction Rauc and Storo had just gone with Bylug. "What about our prisoner? Any chance he knows where they are headed?"

K'rona twisted her mouth into a grimace. "Miracles are always possible, but I doubt this one will capitulate. Yet, my belief is that there are many present here who would appreciate the opportunity to try."

Grumbles of assent and the pop of knuckles traveled through the hall.

"The prisoner is secure." Rauc strode toward Flora. "I claim first right to interrogate him."

She tipped her head a fraction to the right. "Why?"

He came to a stop next to Fani and crossed his tree-limb arms over his massive chest. "My lady K'nil's life was threatened by them. Her son is now missing, a pain like no other for a mother. That must not happen again, and Member Bylug will know the consequence."

Loyalty was strong in this one, and she almost felt sorry for Bylug. Almost. "All right, then. Lady Fani, will you come with us?"

"I do not like the idea of staying behind, but I can best serve this hunt by being a distraction to cover your absence."

Good point. "It is well. K'rona, how long will it take until everyone is ready to go?"

"Until the next hour, my princess." K'rona flicked her thumb against her long-bladed *luz-ba*.

"Great. Rauc, report back to me five minutes before then with whatever you find out from Member Bylug. Go."

They went, scattering to prepare. The only one who remained was Fander's mother. Fani placed a hand on her shoulder. "There is grave danger in you going on the hunt, my daughter."

"Not half as much danger as *they* face. I plan to live up to their preconceived notion that I am their worst nightmare."

"Of that I have no doubt. Have care, though, and always remember that when one opportunity fails, another will arise. I want both of you home safe."

Thirty-One

The jungle-like forest hid secrets, especially at night. Flora crouched under a tall frond that resembled a banana leaf but grew like a fern. All the chirps, clicks, and croaks of insects and critters filling the humid darkness didn't sound so different from the ones on Terr. Even the scents of fragrant night-blooming flowers and the faint but ever-present earthy dampness seemed familiar.

She cast a glance at the K'rona-shaped shadow squatting next to her, waiting and listening for Nor's return. For the news he would bring. With any luck, it'd be the news Flora hoped to hear; that Fander was with the Arruch they'd shadowed for nearly two days. And that he was alive. If he was, then they'd head back to the clearing and the *coid'n* tree where the others hid. Then they'd plan their next move.

The cacophony of the nocturnal orchestra dipped, and K'rona raised her head. Something had just changed. Could be Nor or could be a predator. A towering shadow glided out of the darkness on silent feet. Or, it could be one of their enemies. Her body tensed, ready to fight if need be.

Remain still.

As long as K'rona wasn't alarmed, there wasn't a reason to worry. Much. The shadow crossed the clearing toward them, taking on the familiar form of Nor Danol. A sense of relief bloomed in her chest. Soon she'd know.

Nor slanted two fingers across his lips in the Anferthian signal for silence, then he turned in the direction of the *coid'n* tree. The message was clear: Follow, but don't speak. He was making her wait to hear what he'd found out. She ground her teeth together and rose, moving though the shadows behind him.

Nor paused at the base of the *coid'n* tree, then took five measured steps backward and rushed toward it. In a blink, he was up the pale bark trunk of the scalloped-leafed evergreen tree that easily dwarfed any redwood on Terr. Unlike the redwoods, the branches began lower; easily accessible if you were an Anferthian.

It was also the most untraditional place for a camp, but *que sera sera*. She raised her gaze to the thick shadowy branches. Not even the light from two of Anferthia's five moons gave hint of the two Anferthians and Uncle Nick roosting on those branches. Completely invisible to anyone below. All in all, the perfect place to catch a few hours of sleep.

A large hand appeared in the air just above her head.

Here goes nothing.

She reached up and grasped Nor's hand. One firm tug from him and her body rocketed upward, and suddenly her butt was parked on a branch next to him. He made a shooing motion indicating she needed to move up the branch. K'rona would need a space too. She gripped the next branch and hefted herself up, repeating the process until she was safely past the point that any conversation could be heard below. K'rona perched next to her as Nor straddled the next branch over and flashed a wide grin.

Flora leaned forward. Even though they should be able to talk without being heard, she wasn't taking any chances. "Is he there?"

"Blindfolded, bound, and alive," he whispered back. "They have settled in for the night. If they continue in the same direction tomorrow morning, they will pass through this clearing. We are safely ahead of them now. It is well."

Those three little words seemed to unstop an invisible plug inside, and all her stress drained away. Fander was as safe as he could be while in enemy hands.

K'rona shifted, leaning forward. "Rest now. Nor, Ita, and I will take turns with watch this night."

"I don't think I can sleep."

K'rona made a soft chirping sound and Uncle Nick moved across the branches like a spider, or a monkey. Spider monkey. She swallowed back her laugh at that image.

"You okay, Red?" He whispered.

"Fine."

"She says she cannot sleep," K'rona explained.

"I can take care of that. Lay down on your stomach, Red."

"And I will make sure you do not fall, little one."

She would've rolled her eyes, but the effort would be wasted in the darkness. Besides, they were right, and there was no point in arguing against both of them. "Fine. Four hours, Uncle Nick."

"Sure. Eight hours sounds about right."

"I hate you." She lay flat on her stomach and K'rona secured her to the branch so she could sleep without fear that she might fall.

Uncle Nick brushed his fingertips over her hair. "*Dormio.*"

The soft darkness of sleep wrapped around her and she sank into her dreams.

At first, there wasn't anything strange about her dreams. Just the normal, random, Terrian dream pattern of nonsensical scenes and memories linked together like a confused necklace of plastic beads, pearls, and stones. But then they turned oddly realistic. *Rywoud* real, which shouldn't be possible because it wasn't her birthday. But, why else would she be in her old bedroom at her parents' cube watching Mama curled in the fetal position on her bed? Bloodshot eyes, wet, clumping eyelashes, damp cheeks…she'd obviously been crying pretty hard. But now she just stared straight ahead at the window as if she'd used up all her tears.

"Mama?" No response. Maybe she hadn't heard. Flora reached out her hand, then froze. The tip of a pinkish grey bunny ear rested against Mama's neck. "I left McRawr behind."

How had she done that? The toy was her last connection to all of her parents.

The door opened and Poppy stepped in. "Alexandra…*animi.*" My soul. It was Poppy's special name for Mama.

"She's out there somewhere, Gryf." Mama swallowed hard.

Poppy stretched out on the bed behind Mama and drew her against him. "If anyone can find Fander and get both of them back, it's Flora."

"I know." Mama closed her eyes as Poppy stroked his hand over her hair. "That doesn't mean I'm not…"

Collision

The room faded and humid darkness enveloped her along, with the song of the Anferthian common forest birds. But, she wasn't lying on the *coid'n* branch. There was soft, damp ground under her butt, and legs. They were stretched out and bound at the ankles. Even though she couldn't see through the soft blindfold wrapped over her eyes, she was most definitely back in the forest. Light seeped under her blindfold, steady, not flickering like a campfire. Daylight, maybe? Good thing she'd figured out she was in the dreaming or she'd flip the freak out. For now, she'd let it lead her to where she needed to go and show her what she needed to see.

"Don't worry, my prince." The feminine voice spoke Anferthian next to her ear. Every muscle in Flora's shoulders tensed. "Once the Terrian has been eliminated, you will be free of her spell. Then you will see that Anferthia should only be ruled by Anferthians." There was a pause, and then the mysterious woman whispered, "With an *Anferthian* female by your side. Maybe I will be chosen to fill that role, as I have served loyally. If you fail to grasp this reality, perhaps the Divine One will care for your new heir as one of his own."

Warm lips pressed against Flora's and her mouth was forcefully invaded by the woman's tongue. She jerked her head to one side, breaking the connection. A sultry laugh filled the air. Nearby, a man chuckled deep but not loud. She tightened her jaw and ground her teeth.

"Flora?" Fander's voice whispered in her mind.

The dream fog closed around her.

"So, this is how it ends." Haesi Velo crouched on the ground at the base of towering grey boulder. The wind swirled, creating little eddies of dirt and dried leaves and raising loose strands of her blue hair. "It is either you or me, but only one of us will leave this desolate wasteland. I intend it to be me."

The assassin rose in a fluid motion, her arm swung forward. A silver and aquamarine object flashed in the sunlight on a direct line to Flora's heart.

No....

She jerked awake, catapulting out of the dream and into reality. A reality where she was pinned under a heavy weight, with a large hand firmly over her mouth. What the hell?

"All is well, little one." K'rona's whispered words parted the curtain of panic rising inside. "You appeared to be receiving *rywoud* and we feared you might cry out."

The tension across her shoulders eased. That had been a smart move on K'rona's part. Flora gave her head a nod. K'rona removed her hand and levered herself away to sit on an adjoining branch next to Nor. Thigh to thigh.

Flora pushed herself upright and perched cross-legged on her wide wooden bed. The *coid'n* tree was bathed in the dim pearly greyness of predawn.

"Tell me," K'rona murmured.

There would be no escaping it. No matter if she was ready to talk or not, her friend would probe until she was satisfied and the dream had been analyzed. "It makes no sense, K'rona."

"*Rywoud* seldom does make sense at first."

"No, not what happened in the dream. My birthday was months ago. I shouldn't be having *rywoud*."

"For that, I have no explanation." K'rona frowned as though the lack bothered her. "It should not happen except on the eve of your birthday. But..."

"Yeah, I know. I'm Terrian." Always the exception to the rule here. She made a dismissive waving gesture with one hand.

K'rona's expression turned bemused. "Can you say what was revealed to you?"

"Hold on. Give me a minute to sort it out." She took a few deep breaths, in, out, in, out. Calm creeped over her with infuriating slowness. What had happened first? Mama crying. Poppy holding her. That was self-explanatory: her parents had found out...or would soon find out...she'd gone after Fander. Then, Fander blindfolded at the camp. "Crap. K'rona, a woman may have threatened Fander, and not in a nice way. It sounded like if he didn't cooperate, T'orr would use him to create a new B'aq heir that *he* could raise." Without Fani or Grandfather's influence.

All the bemusement turned to fierce determination. "This must not happen."

"No, it must not." It would've helped if she'd seen the other woman's face. Would a voice be enough to identify her? "The parts of him I share with our people have limits."

Now that was damn possessive of her, wasn't it? But, it was true. Fander might be Anferthia, but he was also Fander. Hers. In the same way she was his. And the gleam of approval in K'rona's eyes confirmed this.

"Ick. I'm trying to scrub *that* visual from my mind." Uncle Nick dropped from one branch to the next above.

"You're a *healer*."

"*You're* my niece." He landed on her branch, then lay on his stomach and shimmied over the side feet-first to the one below.

"That didn't seem to bother you when you gave me my shot. Where are you going?"

He flashed a grin up at her and hopped down another branch. "To pee."

The word alone was enough to trigger that urgency in her own bladder. "Wait. I'm coming too."

Thirty-Two

As soon as Flora was finished with her business in the bushes, she returned to the clearing and trotted over to where Nor stood at the base of the tree.

"So, what's our next step?"

Nor glanced up at the branches. "Ita has returned from observing the Arruch encampment. She reports that they already prepare to depart. Now it is time to return to roost as we await their coming."

"Good idea. Give me a boost?"

"Of course, my princess."

That title still made her feel like she should be wearing fluffy pink dresses, not Anferthian camo. "Nor— *Eep.*"

He didn't even let her finish asking him *nicely* not to call her that. With an almost effortless heave from him, she was airborne, sailing upward toward the lowest branch, her arms and legs splayed. K'rona grabbed her by her wrists and hauled her onto the branch. Good lord, they made tossing a person twenty feet into the air look so easy.

"Well." She smoothed her hands over her clothing. "That was…interesting. Are we all accounted for?"

"We are." K'rona made a shooing gesture. "Nor is the last one up. We must progress to the higher branches to make room for him."

Now came the hard part. Waiting. Even though the Arruch were only a few miles away, thirty minutes dragged by before Ita gave a curt hand signal. Flora held her breath and cocked her head to one side. A moment later, the first enemy scout crept into the clearing. He was good, really good. And thorough too, by the way he scanned the ground. The Arruch scout hefted his *luz-ba* in one fist and stabbed it into the underbrush near where he'd entered the clearing. Then he moved around, repeating the motion. Hopefully he wouldn't go too far off the trail and discover where she'd relieved herself.

He tipped his head back and studied the branches of a nearby tree. Time to retreat. She drew back before he got to their tree. Even with her hair tucked up under the close-fitting green mottled cap, and her face striped with green and black smudge paint, she couldn't possibly blend in as well as the others. She raised her gaze to the branch where Uncle Nick sat stone still. At least she wasn't the only one with this problem.

A quick, sharp whistle came from below, and a moment later more of the party entered the grove. Flora counted to fifty, then scooted to the edge of her branch and peeked over. Six Anferthians dressed in their version of Anferthian camo. A double patrol. All but two had brown, black, or green *tiriks*. Two, a man and a woman, wore dark brown caps. Wisps of blonde hair escaped the woman's cap as she crouched down next to a cross-legged figure sitting at the base of the next tree over. A figure in a dirty, stained, used-to-be-white mourning *wysgog*.

Fander.

He *looked* all right, but from where she sat it was difficult to tell if he had any injuries. The blindfold over his eyes and the cord binding his hands together in his lap were pretty obvious, though. The blonde woman yanked the gag down and raised a Bota bag-shaped cask to his mouth. A thin stream of water trickled down his chin and dripped onto his folded hands. Thank God he wasn't playing the martyr by refusing to drink. Even better, the Arruch must intend to get him to their destination alive. Otherwise, they wouldn't bother taking care of him.

The woman lowered the bag and gently wiped the excess water from his chin with her fingers, then leaned indecently close to his ear. Every muscle in Flora's body went rigid. What the hell? The full green lips moved, forming unheard words.

But, Flora didn't need to hear the words. She already had. It was *her*. The unseen woman from *rywoud*. Blondie snuggled in close to Fander, her breasts against his chest. She covered his mouth with hers. He jerked his head to one side with a snarl of disgust. Blondie and a nearby male, with a thick scar running from his cheek to the corner of his mouth, laughed. Red mist dropped over Flora's vision like a sheer curtain, and she clutched her hand around her reliquary under her clothing.

Destroy her.

The violence of the word burned in her chest. A yelp came from below, and the woman pushed away from Fander, her expression one of complete surprise.

"Leave him be now, Ponira." The order came from Scarface.

Ponira touched her fingertips to her chest for two full heartbeats, then she moved so fast the word knife barely registered in Flora's mind before the tip of the woman's *labu-ba* had slit the front of Fander's *wysgog* from neck to sternum.

"*Ponira.*" Scarface growled the name low, like thunder.

"*A nat.*" K'rona's whispered curse didn't bode well.

Ponira sliced the cord of Fander's reliquary and yanked it from his neck. She stared at it, then lifted her gaze to search the trees.

"What are you doing?" Scarface clomped toward the woman.

Ponira's gaze locked with Flora's. "The Terrian is *there*." She pointed.

"Move higher, princess. Stay with Nick." K'rona didn't give her a chance to answer before she stood and bellowed a battle cry in her Anferthian "big voice." The others joined in and swung down the branches to engage the enemy.

This was all wrong. She should be in there with them, sharing in the battle.

Uncle Nick grabbed her by the arm, his grip firm and no-nonsense. "Their job is to get you to Fander, alive. *Then*, it's your turn."

"But—"

"Flora." Dammit, he'd actually used her name instead of Red. He never did that unless he meant business.

"Fine." She jerked her arm free and redirected her attention to the skirmish below.

It was a battle of *luz-bas*, the conditions too close, too risky for shooting *fusils*. Death by friendly fire was something no one wanted. Nor worked over his target while K'rona spun and ducked her opponent's long blade. The others were similarly engaged.

Collision

Flora frowned and drew her brows together. Where were Ponira and Scarface? Her gaze flew to Fander still under the tree, slumped to one side.

Scarface bent and hefted his limp form up and over his shoulder. Fander's arms swung loose, and...his *tirik* was *gone*.

"*No*." The bastards had cut the braid off, an action that indicted shame in Anferthian society.

Both Arruch warriors looked up at her and grinned. Ponira raised her *fusil*.

"Shit."

Phapt.

Flora scrambled back on her branch.

Crack.

Splinters of bark exploded from the branch right where she'd been peeking over. Close one. Too close. Uncle Nick gaped at her all wide-eyed and pale.

"I'm okay."

"I'm not. Jesus, Flora, you took five years off my life. Don't do that again."

He had to know she couldn't make that promise. She creeped back to the edge of the branch. Scarface and Ponira jogged into the jungle with Fander bouncing on Scarface's shoulder. "They've got Fander."

"Mother fudge," Uncle Nick swore. Sort of. She opened her mouth to ask, but he cut her off. "Keep it to yourself, Red. I'll remind you of this once you have kids."

Okay, then.

"We gotta stop them, Uncle." But climbing down the tree would put them smack in the middle of the fighting. "Is there another way down?"

"Ita used a different tree. Come on."

She scrambled after Uncle Nick, moving through the branches faster than was safe, but this wasn't the time to be careful.

Less than a minute later, her feet were on the ground in the exact spot Fander had been sitting in. She took off at a dead run in the direction his abductors had gone.

"*Princess.*" K'rona's warning shout was lost to the call of a wild beast from beyond the trees.

Flora froze in place. The sound was somewhere between a trumpeting elephant and a bugling elk. And whatever made it had to be humongous because it sounded like it was knocking down small trees as it came closer. Small trees by Anferthian standards, that is. A flash of white caught her gaze and a creature almost twice the size of a Clydesdale burst out of the underbrush into the clearing near Nor.

But, it wasn't a Clydesdale. "That's a…that's…what the hell is a unicorn doing here?"

The unicorn snorted, its breath steaming in the early morning air through its fist-size nostrils. It moved its head from side to side as though sizing up the competition with its caramel brown eyes. In no way did this beast fit the stereotypical gentle, dainty-hooved, magical creatures of Terrian mythology.

Uncle Nick stopped next to her. "Not a unicorn. That's a razor-horned hellion."

Say what? "You're so shitting me."

"I'm so not."

The hellion tossed its head, its bellow setting the air and her teeth vibrating. She slammed her hands over her ears. It sounded pissed, and that wasn't likely to work out in their favor. The beast dipped its head, its serrated purple horn flashed in a beam of sunlight that had somehow penetrated the leafy canopy, and charged toward Nor and the Arruch he fought. The two Anferthians broke apart in recognition of the greater enemy bearing down on them, but the Arruch didn't stand a chance. His protective leathers were no match for the hellion's horn. Burgundy blood spurted and a roar of agony filled the clearing.

Flora drew in a sharp breath. It was one thing to defeat an enemy in a fair match, but this….

"To roost. Go to roost!" Nor's "big voiced" words penetrated the morbid stupor that had gripped her.

The trees were the only safe place to be now. But the killing creature was between her and their tree. "Back the way we came, Uncle."

Together, they raced for the tree, feet pounding the soft ground.

"Up you go." K'rona had caught up with them. Flora's feet left the ground and she was airborne for a disconcerting second before her belly connected with the lowest branch and all the air in her lungs rushed out.

"Oof." Uncle Nick landed next to her. "Climb," he wheezed.

She did, as if her life depended upon it. Which it did, and so did K'rona's. The scraping sounds below her had to be K'rona climbing. She peered down at her friend now squatting on the first branch. On the ground below, the decapitated body of another Arruch lay at the base of the tree. K'rona's handiwork, for sure.

But, what'd happened to the last two Arruch? And had Nor and the others made it to roost? The blood-thirsty unicorn from hell bellowed its fury at the sudden lack of targets, then set to spearing and tossing the two Arruch bodies until they became unrecognizable as having ever been Anferthians. Or anything else, really.

Something twisted like a knife in her heart. Enemy or not, they had family somewhere who cared for them. Loved them. "We need to find out who they were."

Uncle Nick snorted. "Seriously?"

"Their families will want to know where they are."

"Good point."

K'rona looked up at her. "It will be done, little one."

Thirty-Three

"But...a *unicorn*?" Flora reached up and yanked the cap from her head. Her braid swung down with a thump between her shoulder blades.

The vicious beast had stomped around through the grisly mess it'd made for about five minutes before bugling and charging off in the direction it'd come, which was thankfully not the same direction Scarface and Ponira had gone with Fander. Hopefully it hadn't scented the other two patrols either. Nor and K'rona were playing it safe by enforcing a one hour stop, giving the hellion plenty of time to be distracted by other things farther away from them. Unfortunately, the wait also put more distance between them and Fander.

"Forgive me, my princess, but I understand not what this is, u-nee-corn." Ita worried her lower lip between her teeth.

Uncle Nick unfolded the cloth keep-fresh wrapper from a protein bar. "A magical animal from ancient Terrian mythology. No idea how our ancestors got the notion of a one-horned horse stuck in their heads, nor how that exact animal just happens to exist on Anferthia."

A blood-thirsty version of that exact animal. "You told me hellions were like bad-tempered rhinos."

"That was when you were seventeen. Storo set me straight a couple of years ago."

"Well, thanks for sharing." She blew a strand of hair off her forehead. "Nor, what happened to the other two Arruchs?"

Collision

"One of them ran into the forest, and the other found safety in the trees. I saw her following the branches going east."

The same direction Fander had been taken in. "What's to the east?"

"The Pog Po mountain range."

"Could they be hiding there?"

"It is possible."

K'rona lowered her water flask. "There were villages in the mountains before I left. But, it has been so long."

"The Arruch were not merciful on them, as most revolted after the Profeta denounced the invasion." Nor shook his head. "While it was a refreshing event to see them aggravate the Arruch, what happened to them was…tragic."

Ita shifted, leaning forward. "I can track those who took our prince, do not fear."

Flora gave her a grateful smile. "I never doubted that, not even for a moment. Shouldn't we get going, though? It's been at least an hour."

"We could continue through the canopy for a time, as the Arruch female did." K'rona reattached her flask to her pack. "At least until we are certain we are beyond the razor-horn's territory."

Nor nodded. "Our rate of travel will be slowed by our packs, but it should not—"

Ita sat up straight and placed two fingers to her lips. "Others approach."

Friendly others, or more Arruch? Flora peeked over the branch at the blood-soaked ground below. A minute later, two Anferthians loped into the clearing and came to a dead stop. The female pulled her *fusil* from its holster while the male reached behind him and placed his hand protectively over the small person attached to his back in a sling.

The small person peered over his shoulder. "*Eh? Nani ga okitano?*"

Uncle Nick grinned widely and leaned forward to peek over the edge of his branch. "Saku?"

The three turned to peer up at them. Aunt Sakura waggled one fine-boned hand in the general direct of the gore. "Nick. What have you done? Who were they?"

"Arruch, and they were annoying me, so…." He spread his hands in an encompassing shrug.

"Are you all well?" The female dissenter squinted as if trying to count all of them.

Eight more figures, all Anferthians, moved into the clearing. It looked like both the other patrols had hooked up. Or, most of them had, at least. They seemed to be one short of a quad-patrol. The missing one had probably been sent back to report to Fani.

Flora gave them a wave of her hand. "We are well, Kapit F'dol. We are coming down."

Minutes later, she was meeting with the patrol captains for their reports.

"Once we confirmed our prince was not among their numbers, we eliminated the enemy patrol we followed, as ordered." Kapit F'dol stated this with a straight face, but pride shone in her eyes. "As we tracked you, we encountered Kapit Olyt's patrol, who had done the same."

"I regret to report that we had one causality." Olyt bowed his head.

"I am sorry, Kapit. Anferthia grieves with you."

Olyt seemed to shake himself and met her gaze. "Thank you, my princess. We obtained information about their destination. There is a small village northeast of this place, about two-day's distance by foot. This is their camp. We can get there ahead of them if we go off trail."

"That is fantastic news, kapit. It is your honor to send a patrol back to Lady K'nil for reinforcements." Flora turned to K'rona and Nor. "The rest of us will continue on. I am not leaving Fander at their mercy any longer than I have to."

"I recommend splitting us into two groups of seven," K'rona said. "We will approach the village from different sides."

Flora nodded. "And one healer in each group, just in case. You okay with that Uncle Nick, Aunt Saku?"

"Saku and I knew what we were signing up for when we chose to stay with the dissenters. We're good to go."

Icy fingers of cold wracked through Fander from his head to his toes. Not so much as a blanket between his back and the frigid, hard floor of his prison. At least, he assumed he was in a prison of some sort. It was hard to tell since no one had bothered to remove the blindfold or untie his hands. The aching numbness humming at the back of his head, his shoulders and hips told him he had been here for some time. The situation was intolerable, really.

A minuscule snort escaped him. What a pompous thought. He would gladly endure far worse to put an end to the tyranny that had ruled his world and destroyed many others—including that of his *tangol*—for almost his entire life.

Flora's image rose in his mind's eye. How many times had he relived the moment when she had made the all-too brief connection between their reliquaries? She had been so close, but the connection had been lost when Ponira yanked his reliquary away. Somehow the heinous woman had known his rescuers were close at hand. The explosion of stars from a bash against the side of his head was the last thing he remembered before waking up here, empty and bereft of Flora's presence. She must be alive. If she had died, he would know. He would feel the emptiness of her loss in his soul. But, where was she now?

Silence was his only answer, heavy and pressing against his eardrums. Similar to the silence induced at higher elevations. Could he be in the mountains? The closest range to the estate was the Pog Po Mountains. Had they come that far? Would Flora be able to track him to this place?

If only he could dream like a Terrian, then all his dreams would be of her. Her smile, her laugh, the way her lips thinned when she was angry, her face in passion as they made love.

A floor board cracked like a branch splitting away from its tree, breaking the silence as it rebounded through his body. He opened his eyes to the blindfold's blackness. It could just be the building settling, a typical night noise. But that did not explain the faint hint of light glowing at the bottom edge of his blindfold. Someone was nearby. Had Flora found him? Hope flared in his soul and he took a long, slow whiff through his nose, searching for her sweet scent. Another's less welcome aroma invaded his nostrils. Ponira.

"So sorry to wake you, my prince." She chuckled in that throaty way of hers. "It is time to discover your fate."

She tugged his blindfold up and over his head and he squinted up at his present enemy. An odd glimmer of an inexplicable emotion danced in her blue eyes as she studied him in return. The hollows of her sharp-boned cheeks were cast in shadow by the solar lantern. Her pale-blonde *tirik* rested on her shoulder and breast. She appeared every bit as creepy as he had imagined.

"Ah, you are adorable, little prince." She squatted, grabbed his arm, and jabbed a needle through the thin material of his mourning *wysgog*.

He jerked away at the sting, but her fingers dug into his arm with bruising pressure. A moment later, she released him and sat back on her heels. A chill of foreboding creeped like ice through his veins.

"What was that?" His words were garbled by the gag, but her smirk was all he needed to see to know she understood.

"That is the antidote to your *atolce*." She flicked her wrist and the syringe clattered against the wall before rolling into the corner. "In a few hours you will be as fertile as me."

No. Please, no. There was a chance she used the threat to coerce him into cooperating with T'orr. But, there was an equal chance T'orr would give him to her anyway. Either way, he was as good as dead.

"Maybe you can scent my readiness?" She ran her fingertips over her crotch.

He gave his head a vehement shake of denial. Even if he did, he would never admit it.

"Too bad. I was hoping—"

The abrupt rattle and creak of a door opening stopped her mid-sentence.

"Is he awake?" T'orr's voice filled the small prison with the presence of self-confidence and merciless power.

Ponira stuck her lower lip out in a dramatic pout, then she leered. "We will talk more later, little prince."

She snaked out her hands, grabbing wads of the sliced edges of his shirt and tugging him up off the floor. A disconcerting and dizzying moment later, he was on his feet.

Isel T'orr watched from over Ponira's shoulder, his gaze full of contempt. "I do not tolerate betrayal. But you already know that, of course, do you not, Fander K'nil?"

THIRTY-FOUR

Flora perched in a frog squat, her bare toes curled against the tree branch as she eyed the shadowy outline of the small stone building. Hut was a better description. A rather primitive hut compared to the other buildings in the village.

"That is the prison of my prince," the nine-year-old Anferthian boy at her side whispered.

She gave him a curt nod. "Thank you, Sef."

Nor had detained the boy as they'd passed through a valley of bones earlier in the day. The gruesome burial place of the villagers from when the Arruch had come in and squelched their uprising years ago. She suppressed a shudder. Hundreds of voices silenced and their bodies cast onto the grey stones of the barren chasm. Adults, children, infants—all of them denied an honorable burial because they'd been branded traitors.

"They put him in there yesterday morning." Sef met her gaze. All the fear from being discovered had been replaced by hope. So young, even though he was nearly as tall as her adult brother.

"Anferthia thanks you for your help, Sef. Our healers will go with you now to tend your own. Will you deliver my message to your elders?"

Sef nodded. He'd been reluctant to divulge the whereabouts of his family, his *fyhen*, which was completely understandable. But, offering to send her aunt and uncle to help anyone in need seemed to be an acceptable compromise. Apparently, two small Terrians seemed a whole lot less threatening than even one full-sized

Anferthian warrior. And they were healers, and that more than anything would ease the villager's worries while keeping her aunt and uncle safe.

"Are you really Prince Fander's *tangol*?"

"I am."

A glimmer of satisfaction flashed in his young eyes. "Seer Gwela was right, and my sister T'rya will wish she came with me to visit our grandparents today."

"I look forward to meeting your sister."

"Come, young one." Ita leaped to the ground, and Sef followed. Both disappeared into the darkness between the long-abandoned remains of the outer buildings of the village.

Flora worried her lower lip between her teeth. "The villagers may not come, even in Fander's name."

"Then we will do this on our own." K'rona sounded so sure that this whole situation would work out. If only she felt so certain.

Nor made a low rumble sound in his throat. "I do not like that there is no guard at the door."

That bothered Flora too. Hopefully, it didn't mean Fander had been moved somewhere else. Or, worse, that he was…. She squashed the thought. He was fine. He had to be. And, if he'd been moved, well, she'd have to come up with a Plan B.

She allowed herself the luxury of a self-indulgent sigh. "All right, let's go."

Flora reached out for Nor's hands and he lowered her until her bare toes touched the cool gravel. First K'rona, then Nor, dropped to the ground to flank her as she moved forward a step at a time. Carefully, because damn, some of those stones had sharp edges.

At the door, she paused to allow Nor to go first. He pushed the door open and peered inside. "Empty."

She sidled past him and into the one-room hut. Dammit to hell, it was empty, except for a blob of knotted material on the floor. She bent to pick it up. "It is a blindfold. He was here."

K'rona kneeled and poked at something on the floor. Then she held it up. A long nasty-looking needle and syringe.

Flora's heart went into gallop mode. "Can you tell what was in it?"

"I cannot." K'rona ran the cylinder under her nose. "The scent is not unlike the fish young William burned the first time he helped his mother cook dinner."

"So, it could be anything." Including poison.

"I fear so, my princess."

That meant they needed a new plan. Fast.

"This plan, I do not like."

Flora gave her head a nod. "I heard you the first three times, K'rona. But, I am going in alone. T'orr is less likely to have me shot on sight, but you would be instantly expendable." She made direct eye contact with her friend. "I cannot lose you, *fyhen*, and if you come with me now, that is exactly what will happen."

The tick of K'rona's jaw proclaimed her continued unhappiness. "Fine."

"I hate it when you throw my words back in my face."

"I would throw you in the hut if I could, if only to keep you safe."

"I understand." She really did, but that wouldn't dissuade her. She turned to Nor. "Okay, time to light it up, my friend."

"As you command, my princess." The flash of fierce pride in his eyes was just the shot of courage she needed.

Three minutes later, flames licked up the sides of the hut, lighting the pre-dawn with a warm glow. It took a couple more minutes before the first cry went up. By then, the hut was engulfed. Flora reached up, pulled the hood of her *wysgog* over her head, and slipped around the far side of the next building.

Ready or not, I'm coming for you, Isel T'orr.

No one paid any attention to her. They probably thought she was a child, but eventually someone would stop her, because how many children walked through an Arruch-occupied town fully armed?

Apparently enough children that she could get almost to the center of the village just by slinking from tree to building to tree. The place reminded her a lot of the dissenters' villages on Matir. Built to harmonize with nature, not dominate it.

"Where do you go, *trelltyn*?" The voice was male and gruff. And the name he used loosely translated into child-whore. "Show me your wares. I may be interested."

Was *nothing* sacred to the Arruch? The guard's gaze moved to her hands as she grasped the edges of her hood and drew it back. "I am Flora of Terr. Take me to Isel T'orr."

The Anferthian warrior gaped at her for several heartbeats, then leaned back and laughed deep, long, and loud to the sky. A mocking sound that set her teeth on edge.

This was not quite how she'd imagined things would go.

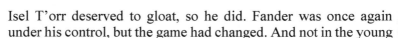

Isel T'orr deserved to gloat, so he did. Fander was once again under his control, but the game had changed. And not in the young prince's favor.

"The execution cuffs suit you, Fander." He ran his palm over the hand-width black and burgundy striped bands wrapped around the young man's upper arms. "Quite appropriate, considering the depth of your betrayal of me."

"We both know which of us truly deserves to wear these, T'orr."

"Do *we*?" Isel gave him a speculative look. "I had held such high hopes for you, treated you like a son, and you repaid me with ungratefulness. My heart almost bleeds that I must lose you."

Almost.

Ponira shifted from foot to foot but did not move from her position near the wall alongside the scar-faced Trosol. He would have to deal with her soon enough.

"I am sure you will not lose any sleep over this," Fander said.

True. He probably would not. "Too bad about your little Terrian. If you prized her so highly, then you should have left her on Terr instead of bringing her here to her death."

"If you had really killed her, I would know."

"Yes, yes." Isel turned away, giving a one-handed wave of dismissal. "She being your *tangol*, of course. That is impossible, though. Yet another thing we both know."

"Do *we*?"

He chuckled. "Very original." The boy could be amusing at times.

"I learned both originality and betrayal by your tutelage."

That was not so amusing. Isel gave him a narrow-eyed glare. "Do not fear, *son*, once I find your...*tangol*...I will dispatch her quickly to join you, and your father." He stepped toward the wall of *luz-bas*.

"I am not your son."

"Ach." He clutched his fist over his heart. "This, even after I spared your young life all those years ago? You wound me with your words."

Should he stab or behead the ungrateful child? Behead. Swift and final, with no chance of a healer swooping in and saving him. Now, which would serve his purposes the best? *Ah*. He reached for a *luz-ba* with a particularly wickedly-curved blade.

"Terr will not react well if you kill the daughter of the *Profetae*."

"That is the intent." Isel lifted the curved long-blade from its rack and hefted it a couple of times to test its weight. Yes, this would serve his purpose. "Are you ready?"

"You say that as though I have a choice."

Isel flicked the pad of his thumb across the blade and fixed his icy stare on Fander. "You do not."

"Divine One." At last, Ponira spoke up.

"What is it, *bawgoro*?"

The female flinched at the slur. "I am prepared to give you the next heir to solidify your position as Anferthia's true leader."

"You would copulate with this traitor for me?"

She licked her lips, glanced at Fander, and nodded. "It is what I have prepared for, shunning all who came to me to ensure there would be no question of legitimacy. I would do anything for you, Divine Warden. You are Anferthia."

"Ah, my devoted child." He raised his hand and traced her smooth jaw with the backs of his fingers. "Very well. Go, wait in my room. Trosol will bring him to you shortly."

Her green eyes lit with greedy anticipation, and she grabbed and kissed his hand. "I live to serve you, Divine One."

Of course she did, as long as serving him served her own sneaky agenda. She turned away. The time was now. He lifted the *luz-ba* and swung. The blade sliced through her graceful neck as easily as it had the air, and her head hit the floor with a hollow thunk.

Fander drew in a sharp breath as her blood sprayed him, but no words came from his mouth. Ponira's body tottered and fell to the side.

Isel huffed a snort. Pathetic. "Do not fret, my loyal one. I will bind Fander's body to yours and bury the two of you on the rocks in the chasm so you may sleep in his embrace for all eternity. A just reward for your loyalty." He gave Trosol a sharp look.

"Retrieve the B'aq reliquary from her. I will need it later."

A grin split Trosol's ugly scarred face. "As you command, Divine One."

He moved to the far side of Ponira's decapitated body, out of reach of the *luz-ba*. Wise choice.

A growl emitted from Fander. "You never intended to—"

Anger surged like a tidal wave crashing over him. "I do not *need* another heir, you pathetic little boy. Once you are gone, there will be no one to challenge my rule."

"Isel. *T'orr*." The unfamiliar woman's voice came from outside.

"Now what?" He spun and stalked toward the front window.

"Sounds like your rule is being challenged."

"Shut your mouth." The little muckrat would not be so smug for much longer.

He peered out the window. There was a sizable crowd in the common square outside his residence, and they all seemed to be focused on the small woman standing by the fountain in the center. A *Terrian* woman. Her fire-orange hair was mostly hidden under a plain brown cap, but she was without a doubt Fander's Terrian. And she was not in a good mood. Even his warriors gave her—and her *luz-ba*—wide berth.

"Terr has come to free Anferthia, Isel T'orr," she shouted.

A slow grin curved his mouth. "So she has. This will be all too easy." He gave Fander a triumphant over-the-shoulder smirk. "Let us not keep her waiting."

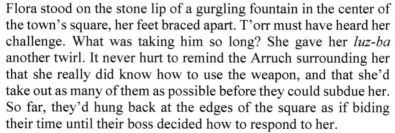

Flora stood on the stone lip of a gurgling fountain in the center of the town's square, her feet braced apart. T'orr must have heard her challenge. What was taking him so long? She gave her *luz-ba* another twirl. It never hurt to remind the Arruch surrounding her that she really did know how to use the weapon, and that she'd take out as many of them as possible before they could subdue her. So far, they'd hung back at the edges of the square as if biding their time until their boss decided how to respond to her.

The fine hairs at the base of her neck tickled. Someone was watching her, but from where? So far, no one had appeared in the windows of T'orr's lavish residence, which wasn't in the center of the village for maximum protection. Who would've guessed the

Collision

murdering tyrant's hideout was a building carved into the cliffside protecting one side of the village?

It was kinda brilliant, in a way. He probably had escape routes through the mountain as well. It'd really suck if he was beating a hasty retreat in that direction now.

"Make way," a voice boomed from the doorway.

The crowd melted farther back to the edges of the square. The bellower stepped into the pinkish light of dawn before moving to one side and bowing to the man now filling the doorway. She squinted. That must be Isel T'orr. He was tall, of course, close to twelve feet. Black hair touched with grey at the temples, eggplant purple eyes, and a strong, square jaw. He stepped forward, shoulders back and head held high, as though he really did carry divinity.

"Terr was not invited to this planet, dear child."

So, this was going to be one of *those* conversations. She raised her chin. "Call it an invasion, then."

T'orr's eyes widened briefly. "I see." He murmured something else too low for her to hear, then stepped from the protection of the doorway into the tree-filtered sunlight, not stopping until he was less than a dozen feet from her.

Brazen. He must have the upmost confidence in is abilities to overpower one little Terrian female. Either that or he counted on his sheer size to intimidate and cow her. If that were the case, how divinely arrogant of him. In reality, it was the condition of who followed behind him that concerned her. Fander, being shoved along by, of all people, Scarface.

Her heart stuttered. Was that his own blood splattered over his shirt and in his hair? Or what remained of his shirt. There were no marks on him that she could see, but he was filthy from his unplanned travels.

She met his love-filled gaze and warmth blossomed through her. They might be in the viper's nest with no way out, but at least they were together.

"As you see, *Terr*," T'orr smirked, "you have mistaken young Fander here for Anferthia, when all along it has been me. By Divine Will, I am to lead Anferthia into its glorious future."

"There is no future for a floundering regime. Your grip on our people is not what it once was, is it?"

T'orr's mouth twisted into a snarl. He flicked his fingers at

Scarface and the burly behemoth tapped the back of Fander's knees with the side of his foot. Fander's legs folded under the force and he went down, faster than she could blink. It was like a macabre slow-motion dance as T'orr raised his *luz-ba* and swung it down, its trajectory aimed for Fander's neck.

No!

Instinct kicked in and Flora surged forward, raising her own long-knife with both hands to intercept T'orr's. The clang of metal impacting metal echoed through the square. A jolt of pain spiked through her newly healed hands, up her arms, and rattled her teeth. T'orr pushed forward, his weight just enough to topple her into Fander. But, Fander met her partway or, his shoulder did. Like he'd expected T'orr's maneuver. His support gave her just enough counter balance that she kept her feet under her. He had her back in the most literal sense.

Rage rose from the depths of her soul and she swung her weapon from left to right. T'orr, the miserable bastard, dodged back several steps, his *luz-ba* at the ready position for combat. It was time. She stood straight, inhaled deep, filling her lungs to capacity as if preparing to sing, and then let loose with her battle cry.

"*An-fer-thiaaaaa!*"

Her voice echoed off the buildings, and her cry was taken up from all directions, even from the cliffs above. A fearsome fury that would not be ignored. Not anymore.

Scarface grunted and collapsed to the ground next to her, a long, lethal dart protruding from the base of his skull. Then a quiet presence radiated warmth against her back. Fander was on his feet. "Anferthia is speaking, T'orr. Can you hear?"

Hell, yeah. Judging by the dark expression, he'd heard all right. And he wasn't too happy about the message. But there was no time to think anymore. Like demons from hell, the shrieking dissenters, the Anferthian royal guard, and a whole bunch of raggedly-dressed villagers dropped out of trees and rooftops.

"Cut my bonds, Flora." Fander's terse words cut through her wonderment at the unfolding scene around her.

What…oh, right. She yanked her *labu-ba* from its sheath and sliced through the cord around his wrists, then spun around just in time to deflect T'orr's blow. Dodge under, two steps in, stab. Her blade tip sank into T'orr's side. Not a fatal blow, but it earned her

Collision

a death-glare.

She gave her weapon a tug and it slipped free. "That was for my parents." Lunge, stab. "That's for Mama and Poppy." Retreat, sweep. A line of blood appeared across the thighs of his *wysgog*. "For Fander."

"*Enough*," T'orr roared. "This is for *you*."

He raised his *luz-ba* like a spear. This would hurt to block, but she wasn't finished with him yet. Not by a longshot. She lunged for his unprotected middle.

Fizzzzthwump.

Something long, narrow, and aquamarine zinged by her ear as her short blade sank fully into his stomach. T'orr's eyes went wide as he stared stupidly at the turquoise-handled knife buried to the hilt in his heart, directly above her *labu-ba*. His lips moved, but no words came out, only bubbles of blood. Flora gave her blade a yank and it slid free. She jumped to one side as T'orr crashed to his knees and pitched forward, the impact with the ground driving the sharp tip of the blade out his back.

The thing must be the size of a small sword. How had someone thrown that? "Aqua...." Oh, shit.

Bam!

Fander hit her hard with his tackle, carrying her to the ground, his body covering hers. "Nightshade on the rooftop!"

His bellow drowned out most of the commotion going on around her. "It's Haesi, Fander. It's Hae—*oof*."

"Stay low, both of you." Nor's order came from above her somewhere.

Why was she always at the bottom of these dog-piles? She twisted in the dirt until she could see over her shoulder. There she was, the hooded figure half-running, half-loping along the spine of a pitched roof.

"Is that your *uncle*?" Fander's incredulous tone drew her attention away from Haesi.

Fear clutched her heart and the sound of the battle around her receded. "Where?"

A man dropped out of a tree onto the roof, crouching low and not moving, like he didn't want Haesi to notice his arrival. "I don't think so. He's a lot bulkier than Uncle Nick."

"No, I mean your scary uncle."

"Uncle Graig? What would he be doing here?"

"I might have had something to do with that," Nor's mumble was so low she barely caught it.

"How?"

Silence, then, "Remember the wager?"

"Yeah."

Fander groaned. "Oh, merciful creators, Nor. You snuck him aboard one of the ambassador's ships?"

Uncle Graig inched forward, flattening himself to the peak of the roof. Flora shifted her attention back to Haesi. The Matiran woman held a spherical object about the size of a tennis ball in her hand. The steady thump, thump, thump of running feet somewhere nearby kept time with her rapid heartbeat. Haesi pulled back her arm and launched the ball like a major league pitcher. It was metallic, the ball was, and the early morning sun flashed of its smooth surface as it sailed toward her.

"Flamer incoming." And it would bring instant fiery death when it detonated. Haesi really must want her dead. Normally, Nightshade assassins could take out only their targets. Unless Fander happened to be one of her targets too, which was always possible. But Nor? That wasn't so likely.

K'rona's shout cut through her thoughts as her friend leaped between them and intercepted the device. A flash backlit K'rona's body, then flames erupted, encompassing her like a hideous nightmare. Someone screamed. Her? Or K'rona? It didn't matter. Her friend writhed in a death dance with the flames.

Suddenly, Nor was up, sprinting toward K'rona. He grabbed her, lifted her burning body and threw her into fountain, then plunged in after her to extinguish the flames with his bare hands.

Flora tore her gaze away from them to check on Haesi. Both the assassin and Uncle Graig had disappeared.

THIRTY-FIVE

Flora curled into the cradle of Fander's cross-legged lap and pressed her cheek against his chest. He stank of blood and sweat, but at least he was alive. *They* were alive, and together. And T'orr wasn't a threat to them or their people, or even the galaxy, any longer. All the Arruch in the village had either surrendered or run like the cowards they were. They wouldn't be able to run forever, though. Fander had already sent hunting patrols after them.

A situation she'd only imaged and hoped for less than three hours ago was now a reality.

Fander stroked his hand along her *tirik*. "Would you like me to rebraid it for you?"

"Maybe later." She reached up and brushed the loose strands of his hair back from his face. "I like what you've done with your hair."

He snorted. "Thanks. It feels weird without the weight."

It would take a while before he had enough hair for his own *tirik*. "I think it's kind of sexy."

"Do you?" He lowered his head, his lips so close she could almost taste them.

"Yeah. I do."

Ita cleared her throat, loudly. A not-so-subtle reminder that there were others around. Well, at the very least a quick peck should be acceptable. Flora leaned in and brushed her lips over Fander's, then backed off. "So, what did your mom say about Sala D'eu."

Fani had taken the remainder of the K'nil troops and dissenters into the capital city to clean house, so to speak.

"She found no resistance and a welcoming committee."

"The Arruch hierarchy ran?"

"They were arrested by time she got there. And, Tusayn was already…dealt with."

"That's code for dead, right?"

"It is."

Good. "I guess we're off to Sala D'eu next?" Taking back a planet seemed to involve a lot of long hours and travel. And this was just the beginning.

"Not before your aunt and uncle have a prognosis on K'rona. And," he pressed his lips to her forehead, "after we stop at the estate for a long hot bath and clean clothing."

That sounded like a solid plan. She cast a glance at the firmly shut door to the makeshift healer's station. Poor Nor had paced back and forth in front of it for hours, and still no report from her aunt or uncle about K'rona's condition.

The wait to hear hadn't seemed so daunting right after the fighting ended. Fander had been needed, everywhere, by everyone. Which wasn't surprising, of course. But what had been surprising were the number of Anferthians who needed *her*. To see her, to touch her, to pledge fealty to her. After they had done so to Fander, of course.

Including young Sef, their young hero, who had brought in the cavalry in the form of the displaced, Arruch-hating villagers.

The village elder—who couldn't be more than thirty-five—had requested a boon from her. To take the boy with her to train as a warrior, and perhaps even to be part of her personal guard someday. Not all of these mountain people had accepted her with such ease. She was an alien after all. But, they'd opened their hearts to Fander so maybe she'd grow on them too.

Fander sighed. "I am about ready to knock down the door and demand answers."

"You will not." Ita didn't even look up. Her gaze had been on her folded hands on her lap since she'd sat down. "It was enough that Kapit Danol threatened the Healer Bock with bodily harm if he did not save K'rona. It is up to K'rona if she wishes to remain, or not."

Good lord, that'd been a tense situation, up until Fander had threatened to lock Nor into the building being used to house the Arruch prisoners. With the mood Nor had been in, he could've whipped all their slimy asses, then kicked the walls down. But, he'd declined the offer and taken up his relentless pacing.

At least the burns he'd suffered from throwing K'rona into the fountain hadn't been deep. Uncle Nick had taken care of them quickly despite Nor's insistence that he should be working with Aunt Sakura to heal K'rona.

"You are right, Ita." As always, Fander knew when to concede.

Flora leaned close and brushed her lips over his smooth cheek. He turned his head and claimed them. For a moment, nothing else mattered except the gentle way his mouth molded to hers, nipping and sucking until he pulled back. "Don't worry, love. K'rona is in the best hands right now. The healers will do everything in their power to help her, no matter the final outcome. She is their *fyhen*."

"I know." The other one she was really worried about was Uncle Graig. Where the hell had he disappeared to?

The door opened and Uncle Nick stepped out into a beam of afternoon sunshine filtering through the trees. It was as if all of them were suddenly in a race to see who could get to him first.

Nor won, of course. "Tell us, healer."

He towered over her uncle, but after nearly a decade of being towered over, Uncle Nick didn't seem the least bit intimidated. Probably because he knew Ita would wipe the floor with Nor's carcass if he tried anything.

"First, K'rona chose to fight. She chose to stay." It was the Anferthian way of saying she was alive and would survive. "Sakura and I fought for her, and she is now resting as comfortably as she can. But," Uncle Nick met Nor's gaze, "she asks that you not enter."

Hurt and anger warred in Nor's eyes. "Why not?"

"She says she frees you, and you would understand what that means."

"Uncle Nick." Flora waited until he turned to her. "Maybe you should tell us what her prognosis is first."

Her uncle sighed and nodded. "She will not be returning to her post, ever. Her battle leathers protected most of her body from the flames, but the burns on her hands, face, and head go too deep. Sakura and I did all we could but cannot reverse all of the damage. She will have partial vision in her right eye, but none in her left."

Silence descended. It was bad. Not being able to return to her post would be crushing. "What about the skin graft thing? Is there anyone who can do that anymore?"

"Absolutely. There are surgeons. Won't help her eyesight, but," he shrugged. "it is up to her."

"She will not see me?" Nor murmured.

"Here's the deal, big guy." Uncle Nick switched to English. "*I say she's lost and confused, and she will need you. So, be patient and allow Sakura and I to work our magic.*"

Nor nodded. "Two days, healer. I will be back." He strode away.

"Anferthians," Uncle Nick grumbled under his breath.

Fander stroked his hand over his chin. "We need to return home as soon as possible. When will Kapit Zurkku be able to travel?"

"Not for at least a week."

"I will leave a triple patrol for you."

Uncle Nick waved him off. "A single patrol and the villagers will be enough. We'll be back as soon as we can. I have no intention of missing my niece's wedding."

Wedding? How had she forgotten about that?

"And the coronation." Fander winked.

Eep!

THIRTY-SIX

Flora stood inside the front door of the main house and fluffed the ballet skirt of her dress. She'd barely finished sewing it yesterday afternoon, even with Maggie and Mama's help. The material reminded her of Terr. Blue and green, with wispy white cloud-like swirls.

"Ready?"

She gazed up at her husband.

Husband.

Husband, husband, husband.

Yeah, she loved the sound of that. Just as much as she loved her new last name: B'aq. Which sounded pretty much like Bock. "I'm ready."

Fander dipped his head, nuzzled her neck, and inhaled deeply. Okay, this was another thing she loved. The way he scented her was like a tonic that visibly relaxed him every time.

"You still smell delicious." His murmured words slid through her and hit her core with laser precision that turned her knees to water.

She glanced down and placed her hands over her chiffon covered lower abdomen. Damn, but the anti-*atolce* shot had worked fast. Uncle Nick'd said it could take a month or two for her cycle to go back to normal, not a week or two.

She turned her head, her mouth inches from his. "Just like last night, and the night before."

"And the night before that too, don't forget." His lips moved against hers as he spoke. Not a real kiss, but the effect on her senses was about the same.

Turn around was fair play. "How could I forget?"

With the way they'd been going at it, it wouldn't surprise her if she was already pregnant. If by some miracle she wasn't, she would be after tonight. Without *atolce*, the frenzy had a one-hundred percent fertility rate, and she was fine with that. A spike of joy shot through her heart. Creating a new life with Fander was such a natural next step in their relationship. A new challenge and adventure.

"I haven't forgotten." He ran the tip of his tongue along her lips, of all things. So damn tempting.

"Fander, there's like a thousand people standing in the garden outside this door, including my family and your mother. We have to do this thing."

"Doing *something* is exactly what I have in mind." He chuckled. "Maybe we can make the *maitz'a* shorter."

If he didn't stop, she was going after his ears now and to hell with the dance. "Don't change things on me now. I'm already scared I'll forget some of the steps."

He groaned in protest.

"*Fan*-der."

"All right, all right. I'm good to go."

Super. She reached for the door handle.

"Flora, wait. Look at me." How could she say no to that? She angled her head and met his gaze. "Don't worry, love, I'll get us to our room."

She smiled up at him. "I know you will."

A moment later, they strode into the humongous open space in the front of the main house. She inhaled and the clear evening air filled her lungs. Under her bare feet, the cool grass tickled her toes. A cheer went up from the "thousand" encircling the dance space. Or, maybe it was two thousand. Hard to tell, but either way, it was a larger wedding—bonding—than she'd imagined. But, she couldn't back out of doing this for Fander. No matter what he'd said inside, the tradition of *maitz'a* meant as much to him as having a small, Terrian white wedding ceremony with just her family had meant to her this morning.

But first, she had a little surprise for him.

She gave Mama and Poppy a little wave as she went past them

where they stood in the front row. Uncle Nick, Aunt Sakura, Will, and Tamiko were next. Juan, in his brand-spanking-new UDF ensign's uniform, stood between Maggie and Aunt Simone because that always made him feel taller. Her brother waggled his eyebrows, and she gave her eyeballs a deliberate roll.

Didn't see that one coming.

Still no sign of Uncle Graig, though. Her heart gave a little twinge. Aunt Simone hadn't seemed overly concerned about his disappearance, but still, it would've been nice if he was here to share this special day.

Farther down, K'rona stood in the circle of Nor's embrace, Storo at her side. A much less suspicious Storo, once he'd heard how Nor had saved the life of his *tangol*. It was because of Storo that K'rona had finally relented and allowed Nor back into her life. It was good to see true love win against adversity.

Flora stopped in front of the trio and gave K'rona a nod. Not even the pink scar tissue stopped her friend from smiling as she drew her *labu-ba*. Now the trick was to get the buy-in of the rest of the Anferthians. She turned to face Fander and K'rona moved behind her.

Fander's expression was one of confused concern. "What is this about, Flora?"

And he wasn't the only one wondering, judging by the deep hush that had fallen over their guests. A gentle tug was followed by the shush of K'rona's short blade slicing through her hair. The whisper of gasps flowed through the crowd as K'rona handed her the severed *tirik*.

Normally the taking of the ritual braid was a dishonor, but not this time. Tonight, it was a proclamation, a pledge. And all the dissenters were in on it. *And* her powerhouse mother-in-law, Fani K'nil.

She draped her *tirik* over her hands and lowered herself to her knees. "Fander of Anferthia, I present you with my *tirik* as a symbol of a new beginning for our people. A statement of my commitment to grow—and *re*grow—with you."

"*Cymere!*" The word of agreement was roared by the dissenters as they raised their own newly-cut *tiriks*.

Fander gaped in awe as more and more of the guests got out their *labu-bas* and hacked off their braids.

Then he met her gaze and kneeled, facing her. He opened his

mouth, but no words came out. But he kept trying. "I…this is…." He swallowed hard. "It is my honor to grow with you as we begin anew. *Cymere*."

The guests echoed his shout again as he pulled her close against him. "You honor me, love. Thank you."

There was no way to stop the tears of joy from overflowing her eyes. The only thing to do was let it happen. She was Terrian, after all. "I love you, Fander."

"I love you too, Flora." He wiped the ends of his flowing *wysgog* sleeves over her cheeks. "Let's get on with the *maitz'a*."

A watery chuckle bubbled up. "Yeah. Let's do this thing."

She passed her *tirik* to K'rona and allowed Fander to help her up and guide her to the center of the cleared area. The heat from the fire set in a pit to the right of the center of the space caressed her skin. She tipped her head back and absorbed the wonder of the crystal-clear points of light in the black night sky. One of those stars was the sun of her birth home, and her heart was happy that she could still see it from her new home.

Fander stood behind her, the comforting weight of his hands resting light on her hips. She raised her arms toward the stars and sang, a cappella, the same Irish blessing of deep peace she'd sung for Mama and Poppy at their wedding over sixteen years ago. The song her birth mother used to sing to her every night at bedtime. Somewhere in the trees, Juja picked up the tune and sang with her.

As the final note wavered out of existence, she counted two beats, then a single massive drum beat vibrated through the air. She flipped herself around to face Fander, the gauzy blue and green material of her skirt billowing around her. She leaned her head back and arms out to her sides and fell away from him—and almost laughed with joy as his large hands closed around her waist. He'd never missed catching her every time they'd practiced the move that represented the Anferthian invasion of Earth. The pivotal moment in time that had set their lives on a collision course.

Four beats later, the drums began in earnest. Fander pulled her upright, and she placed her hands on his chest and pushed away from him. This was the most fun part of the dance, spinning away, orbiting, and coming back together as though irresistibly drawn to each other. The story of their childhood, wild and joyful, filled her with an almost drunken jubilation that couldn't possibly be from

Collision

the tiny sip of *ryma* she'd had during the ceremony.

The final come together would be their "first kiss." She stepped toward him, and Fander cupped her face between his hands. "May I?"

That wasn't the way they'd practiced, but it was what he'd said to her all those years ago. A laugh bubbled out. "Make my toes curl again, my prince."

He brushed his mouth over hers once, twice, reclaiming the innocence of that perfect, beautiful moment.

Cheers from their guests echoed in her ears. There was much consuming of *ryma* going on around them, no doubt.

Fander released her, his fingertips sliding along hers as he turned away. She mirrored his steps in reverse, dragging her toes through the cool blades of grass as though reluctant to put distance between them. Nine steps, one for each year, then she sank to her knees and reached toward the stars. Grandfather K'nil would never know how they honored him today, but every Anferthian in the crowd would.

She got to her feet and twirled her way to the fire pit to face Fander across the low flames. As her dress settled around her, Fander stepped over the stones ringing the pit. A gasp escaped her. He was supposed to circle the outside of the pit. The turd was going off script, *again*.

But, she couldn't stay annoyed, not the way he was looking at her like she was the reason for his existence. Another cheer went up from the crowd.

Ah, geez, don't encourage him.

But, his action held strong symbolism for the Anferthian people. To walk through a fire for someone was just about the most noble and pure thing one person could do for another in their culture. It could also put the kibosh on the rest of the evening while he got his feet healed.

She scanned the crowd for Uncle Nick and found him with his arm around Aunt Saku. He made a calming motion with his free hand. Fine. It was too late to stop Fander anyway, he was almost all the way across. She moved back two steps to give him space as he stepped over the stones for a second time.

He held up his open palms, and she pressed hers against them, threading their fingers together loosely. Then they raised their hands over their heads; she stretched as far as she could reach, which was nowhere near how far he could reach. He trailed the backs of his fingertips down her arms and sides until he reached her hips, then kneeled at her feet. He leaned close and placed a kiss on her lower abdomen to honor the children they hoped to create. Maybe as soon as tonight.

Her heart thumped harder in her chest. Babies. A family. Good thing Uncle Nick and Aunt Sakura had agreed to stay with them for a while.

Fander sat back on his heels. It was time. She closed her hands into fists, gave a wordless shout to the sky, then bent forward until the tip of her nose almost touched his.

"You scared the crap out of me with that fire-walking stunt, you know. Maybe I should do some improvising too."

He grinned, the dare glittered in his eyes. "Go for the points."

"Oh, I will." She brushed his hair off his left ear, leaned forward, and delved her tongue into each fan-point. All four of them.

A shudder wracking his body confirmed each direct hit. She drew back, their faces inches apart.

He breathed shallow breaths through his clenched teeth, tracking her with his hooded gaze as he held the frenzy at bay. "Flora, I love you."

"Forever." She whispered the word, because it was only his to hear.

As she moved toward his other ear his eyes closed. She ran the tip of her tongue along the curved shell of his ear and into the first point.

The vibration of his growl through his body was all the warning she got before he leaned back and roared to the sky. Her feet left the ground with unexpected force, and a small squeak popped out of her as she bounced on his shoulder. The firepit dwindled in size faster than it seemed possible. Fander really was determined to get her inside and to their room before he became completely unglued.

A shout of joy ballooned inside and she levered herself up against his back with her hands, sucked in a deep breath, and thrust her fist in the air. "*Anferthia!*"

The crowd exploded, repeating her cry with raised fists. Fander also punched the air and roared with them.

And now, she belonged…to all of them.

Thirty-Seven

"Whoop." Flora giggled as Fander took the stairs two at a time. "Faster, Fander. Hurry."

It was tempting to spank his firm ass, but who knew if that would be too much of a distraction? Getting to their room was a priority; any naughtiness could wait until they were behind closed doors.

Fander kicked the door and it shut with a bang. Then she was airborne for a full two seconds before her back sank into their sofa mattress. Woo! She flipped her short loose strands of hair back and gazed up at him. Fander yanked his shirt over his head, the pop of seams accompanying his action. No wonder Anferthian wedding garments were onetime-only outfits. As much as she loved the dress she'd made, it wasn't going to last.

And she wasn't going to last long either, judging by the wetness on her thighs. *Maitz'a* might translate into "bonding dance", but in her personal dictionary it meant "sexy foreplay."

"Flora." Fander's eyes blazed with hunger, raking over her body with an intensity she'd never seen in him. An internal struggle seemed to be happening.

She extended her arms toward him and he climbed onto the bed, covering her with his long body. His hands trembled as he stroked her hair. Almost tender compared to the tightly leashed energy simmering just under the surface. "It's about you…too. Your pleasure…enhances mine. If I do this right."

She took his face between her hands. "Stop fighting it and

show me."

"Afraid...I'll hurt you."

"You won't." Fine time for him to voice that concern. She ran her fingertips up his hips and sides and his body shivered in response. "You can't. Let it go, *tangol*."

Recognition flashed in his beautiful eyes like a light went on somewhere inside him. He sat up, gripped the scooped neck of her dress, and pulled. The rough sound of tearing material filled the room and cool air caressed her body. Then, he was on her, moving, touching, his lips claimed hers, initiating an erotic dance with his tongue. He moved away, lower, closing his mouth over one breast while his fingers teased the other nipple into exquisite hardness. She dug her fingers into his hair and arched into his sweet attack.

"God, Fander, do it. I need you, now."

He raised his head, his gaze smoldering...and he growled. The low, primitive, possessive sound touched every nerve ending in her body. Oh, God, everything between her legs just melted. This was happening, total surrender, and she was along for the ride. Every wild and glorious second of it.

Fander hitched her leg over his shoulder and plunged into her, all raw male. Two strokes and her world exploded in cascading pleasure that went on and on until he stiffened and roared above her. She didn't have a chance to draw a breath before the bed disappeared from under her. The air rushed over her skin as the room spun, then the coolness of the wall pressed against her back.

Yes, yes, yes. They'd never done it against the wall before. She braced her hands against Fander's shoulders as he held her high and nipped and sucked at her breasts. Then she was sliding down, the head of his shaft rubbed over her entrance and he impaled her, his ridges teasing her nub.

"Flora, gods." His breath whispered over her skin where he buried his face against the side of her neck.

"Faster, Fander. Please."

He gripped her thighs harder and increased his tempo, each stroke building the pressure that would end in pleasure. She dug her fingernails into his shoulders and squeezed his hips between her thighs as a second wave washed over her. This time he came with her as he bit down on the curve between her neck and shoulder.

A slick sheen of sweat coated her and it seemed like she'd

Collision

never be able to catch her breath again. How much better could this get? He pulled out. A slightly disappointing turn of events, but that was only number two. One more to go. Fander moved her so her body was cradled in his arms, carried her back to the bed, and tossed her so she landed face down. Before she could roll over to see him, he grabbed her hips and tugged upward until her butt was in the air.

Okay, yeah, it just got better...God in heaven, was he kissing her tailbone? She arched her back like a cat in heat and Fander ran his hot, wet tongue slowly up her spine. His still-hard shaft bobbed between her thighs and pressed against her entrance. Then he dug his fingers into her hips and slammed into her. The gentle moment morphed into hardcore need. The touch of his fingers circling her clit amped up the tension as he pistoned into her. The only thing to hang onto was the comforter. She closed her fingers, twisting wads of material in her grip. So close, so close, so.... She pushed back against him, buried her face into the bedding, and screamed as her release cascaded over her. Behind her, Fander surged into her once more, roaring as his final release erupted deep inside her. Then he collapsed against her back, panting in time with her.

Fander pressed his lips to Flora's shoulder blade. His amazing Terrian wife who owned Anferthia. "Are you okay?"

It had taken at least five minutes to get enough of his voice back to ask that simple question.

She raised one finger and waved it from side to side. "Anferthia...yay."

An amused chuckle vibrated in his chest. "Earth...*whoa*."

She snorted a small laugh and turned her head so he could view her in profile. "We are *so* doing that again."

"Not immediately, I hope." If she could see the way he twisted his face in consternation, she would laugh harder.

"No, I think there's a mandatory recovery period."

"Did I hurt you?" She seemed well enough.

"Not a chance."

Relief spread through him and he nuzzled her neck. "Nice touch as we were leaving our guests. Anferthia is secure in the knowledge that their princess is truly theirs."

"I hope so, because they're stuck with me now."

Stuck was not the word he would use. Blessed, maybe. That sounded better. He shifted his weight and slid out of her.

"Aw. You don't have to go."

"I'm only moving my beloved wife and *tangol* farther onto the bed where I can hold her."

"Oh. Well, then, carry on. I can't move under my own power right now anyway."

He lifted her in his arms. "Could you at least reach down and pull back the bed covers?"

"Sure."

Once he got her under the covers, he climbed in next to her and pulled her against his body. After all the years of waiting, she was here, snuggled against him, finally. He stroked his hand over her hair and placed a gentle kiss on her forehead. "Sleep, love."

She responded with a soft snore.

Flora blinked, dead sleep falling away from her as her consciousness forced a takeover of her body. The room was dark, but something out of the norm had woken her up. A sound, low and melodic, like a.... Fander's voice reached her ears. She turned her head and the hair on the top of his head tickled her nose. His head rested in the hollow of her shoulder, his warm breath stirring over her bare breast as he sang softly. His reliquary rested on her lower belly, just above her pubic bone, his hand hovering over it.

"What are you doing?" She whispered because, well, it seemed like she was intruding on a special moment.

Fander kissed the top of her breast but kept singing. In Anferthian. She focused on the words. Love, protection, and family. Health and strength. Joy of a life and a mother and father. Her heart pattered a quick, irregular beat of excitement. Could it be?

She slid her hand down to cover Fander's, but he raised his hand in an action of invitation to place hers directly on his reliquary. She lowered her hand to the faintly glowing warm pendant, and Fander rested his on top. Gentle, yet protective. She lowered her eyelids, shutting out any visual distraction, and allowed her mind to drift until his reliquary tugged her consciousness in and revealed the cells newly implanted inside her. Tears of joy seeped from under her eye lids. She was pregnant; they were parents. Or would be, soon.

Turning her head, she rested her cheek against the top of her husband's head. Fander finished his song, and they lay unmoving as though reveling in the miracle taking place under their hands. Within her womb.

"Your scent changed." His murmured words stirred her out of her trance-like state. She opened her eyes to find him gazing down at her. "It woke me up. I thought I'd check without disturbing you."

"And that involved singing?"

"It's what we do for our unborn children. In the future, though, I'll try to relegate my singing to when you're awake. I didn't think you'd mind this once."

"I don't. And I won't. You can sing to our baby anytime."

Fander shifted, covering her body with his, bringing his face level with hers. "I want to hold you both as close as I can. I want to protect and cherish you both. I want the scent of you, of new life, to fill me."

"That is the most romantic thing I've ever heard." And such a turn-on to her highly sensitive body. She wrapped her arms and legs around him, opening herself to him. He slid inside, filling her the way he wanted to be filled, and she was home.

Epilogue

New Damon Beach, Terr.

Alexandra Bock gave the quilt a final critical eye. The thing was so large, the sides and one end touched the floor with about three feet to spare.

"Are you satisfied?"

She shot a lopsided grin at her husband. "Very. And, thank you. I couldn't have done this without your help. And Maggie's, and Simone's, and Dante's."

Who knew the Matiran men would jump on a quilting project with such enthusiasm, and be so damn good at sewing?

"It was a family activity." The pride in Gryf's voice was crystal clear. "In a way, our family is a patchwork quilt like this one."

"Oh? How so?"

"The shades and colors here represent each of us. The pales are you, Flora, Maggie, Nick, and Sakura. The tan, Juan." He hovered his hand over each color. "Brown for Simone, blue for Graig, Dante, Ora, and myself. And now, upon Flora and Fander's union, we have added green."

She stared at him with her mouth hanging open. "You are such a romantic, Gryf."

"But, I'm right."

"Yes, you are." She leaned into him and wrapped her arms around his waist. "I wish we could've had this ready three months ago for their wedding, but giving it as a coronation gift works,

Collision

too."

"I have a feeling Terrian patchwork quilts will be rather popular after this one is revealed."

"Wait until we finish the one for our future granddaughter." Cripes. She hadn't expected the title of grandma before she turned forty.

The beep of her personal data-device on the dresser interrupted the conversation. "And there's my alarm."

Gryf released her. "Are you sure you don't want me to go with you?"

"Graig's message said 'alone', so he must want to talk about something personal." In a secluded place in the Sierra-Nevada. Funny how some old names had stuck, but it was hard to imagine calling the mountain range anything else.

"He doesn't want to face me yet."

That was probably true. Graig had blown both of them off, and had had Kapit Danol smuggle him off the planet so he could chase down Haesi Velo.

"It's because I'm the nice one." She reached for her data-device, shoved it into her pants pocket, and gave her husband a grin. "Or, it *could* be about your birthday gift. I'll let you know when I'm on my way home."

Gryf dipped his head toward her and she met his kiss partway. Soft, gentle, full of love, and no possessive tongue action tempting her to stay home. After all these years, the man still knew how to say good-bye with promise.

He pulled back. "I love you, Alexandra."

"I love you, too, Gryf." She reached up to cradle his face between her hands. "Eternally."

"Eternally," he murmured back.

Thirty minutes later, Alex maneuvered the small surface skimmer down into a meadow between the tree line and a mountain river. She could walk the rest of the way to the coordinates Graig had sent. Stepping from the skimmer, she inhaled the crisp, mountain air.

It'd been way too long since she and Gryf had done any hiking. They were definitely overdue for a visit to the long-abandoned Camp One to reminisce, pay respects, and see how nature had reclaimed their former refugee site.

She set her data-device to transmit a beep every minute to alert bears of her presence, then set out toward the river. Spring pollen floated in the air, and Steller's Jays squawked in the pines behind her. There was something vaguely familiar about this place. She glanced at her device. Thirty more feet to the right along the river bank, very close to a huge boulder. Weird that Graig was so specific.

Weirder still that she recognized the boulder. "Oh, crap."

Not here. Not the boulder where, more than a decade and a half ago, she'd sat huddled, traumatized by her brief yet horrific imprisonment with Vyn Kotas and Haesi Velo. A chill crept down her spine like icy fingers. She'd only been twenty-two years old, but she'd felt ancient that day. Even after so long, the pain was still there. Buried, but there.

"Did you have any problems finding this place again?" Graig's words were just loud enough to be heard over the roar of the river.

Anger and hurt filled her heart and she turned to face him. "Why did you bring me back here?" *You knew I wanted to forget.*

"It was appropriate, *sorar*." Sister. He'd called her that for almost as long as they'd known each other and meant it with all his heart. Simone had explained this to her, and about the biological sister he'd lost as a child after they'd snuck out together for an "adventure." Iliana would've been her age had she survived the wild animal attack.

Alex spread her arms out in a brief, all-encompassing gesture. "Appropriate? For what?"

"I have something for you." He closed the distance between them until less than a step separated them. "Hold out your hands."

She raised her chin. It would serve him right if she didn't cooperate.

"Please."

How could one gently spoken word be so full of compassion and understanding? She huffed a sigh and raised her hands to receive whatever it was he had to give her in this of all places.

He brought his hands out from behind his back and balanced the ends of a foot-long knife with his fingertips. Then, he lowered it into her hands as if it was a treasure. The weapon was exquisite, with its thin silver blade and carved aquamarine hilt.

And vile. More hated memories rose to the surface. Bile roiled in her belly and a tremor in her hands nearly cost her her grip.

Graig supported her hands with his own. "As promised, I gave her *our* regards."

Alex blinked back the blur of tears and met his gaze. "Haesi is dead." There was no question about it. Graig always, always fulfilled his promises.

"She will never hurt you, or Simone, or Flora, or any of our loved ones again."

"Including you." A hot, wet tear escaped and rolled down her cheek. Graig had never told her exactly what Haesi had done to him, but after what the Psycho Queen had done to her, she could imagine. "One question…no, never mind."

"It was a fair fight, sorar."

"I know." It would've been. Anything less wasn't Graig's style. She lowered her gaze back to the knife. "What am I going to do with this thing?"

Graig shrugged his wide shoulders. "Take it home. Sell it. Throw it in the ocean. Your choice. Nothing you do will offend me. I've laid my ghosts to rest, as you Terrians say. Now it's your turn."

She pursed her lips together and nodded. "I want to bury it. Here. Far away from everyone I love, in the place where you gave voice to my pain and freed me of my fear."

Because, until today, this moment, she'd watched over her shoulder for any sign of Haesi Velo coming after her children. There would always be some sort of threat for them, especially for Flora, but that one was gone for good.

"I also want Gryf with me." She tapped one finger against the side of her head.

Graig nodded. "Contact him, then we'll find a place to bury the past forever."

It took ten minutes, but she found a place just inside the tree line that was agreeable to all three of them. Graig helped her dig a deep enough hole, and Gryf wrapped her in his calming presence through their telepathic link.

After covering it with dirt, Graig rolled a large rock over the site, then stepped back, brushing his hands together. "How do you feel, sorar?"

It was good. No one would find it now. "Lighter. Free. Happy."

He nodded and a small smile curved his mouth. "I understand."

Of course he did. Better than anyone else would, except Gryf. Because of her soul link with her husband, he'd shared her experience after the fact.

Graig brushed his hands against his pants. "I don't suppose I could catch a ride back to town with you, could I?"

"Make him walk."

She made a small cough to cover her laughter at Gryf's telepathic comment. "What, did you walk all the way out here?"

He raised his eye brows in a you-have-to-ask gesture. She should've seen that one coming. "All right. Come on."

"You really are *the nice one,"* Gryf grumbled.

"Hush."

She moved in the direction of the skimmer. "I have a feeling Simone doesn't know you're back yet and she'd throttle me for keeping you here longer than necessary. Especially when we're all about ready to head to Anferthia for the coronation."

"Simone will not be going to the coronation."

"Oh, you think not, huh?"

"Cut me some slack, Alex. I haven't seen my wife in *months*. When I get home, I'm barricading the doors and keeping her to myself for at least a week."

After the selfless gift he'd just given her, it was hard to call him out as a misogynist caveman asshole. "A week? Then you two will still have just enough time to get to Anferthia."

"You're impossible."

"I know." She pressed her palm to the skimmer's palm reader and flashed a grin at him. "Let's get you home."

About the Author

USA Today Best-selling Author Lea Kirk loves to transport her readers to other worlds with her romances of science fiction (and one vampire paranormal!) Her Prophecy series began with a day-dream in high-school. It's taken thirty-five years to complete the story arc, and now she's looking forward to exploring (tormenting) some of her other series characters.

Ms. Kirk lives in California with her wonderful hubby of twenty-eight years, their five kids (aka, the nerd herd), and a spoiled Dobie-mix.

Stay in touch with Lea Kirk through social media:
Facebook: @AuthorLeaKirk
Twitter: @LeaKirkWrites
Bookbub: @Lea-Kirk
Amazon Author Page
Goodreads Author Page

To keep up with Lea's latest book news visit her website and signup for her newsletter

www.LeaKirk.com

To My Dear Readers:

I hope you enjoyed *Collision*. This is the final installment of the Prophecy series arc, but there *will* be more stories set in this universe, I promise! In fact, my next project is a Christmas story featuring Alex and Gryf as new parents to Flora, Juan, and Maggie. I hope like crazy that I can get it out in time for the 2018 holiday season, but if not, then watch for it in 2019.

Other Prophecy related projects currently on the horizon are (in no particular order): Juan's story (this story is crazy in an epic sort of way as it spans most of Juan's adulthood until he's an old man. Definitely not your typical Romance trope); Dante's Story (yes, you'll get to find out what happened to Dante's wife); Maggie's story (if you thought an Anferthian hero was shocking, just wait until you find out who *she* falls in love with!)

Keep in eye on my website for updates. Or, for early cover reveals, sneak peeks, and exclusive quarterly giveaways, subscribe to my newsletter.

Writing may be a solitary occupation, but no writer can do much without their "support team". Thank you from the bottom of my heart to my team:

- My family for supporting me as I strive to make writing a viable career.
- My critique partners, De, Di, Ti (names have been abbreviated to protect their secret identities.)
- My beta-readers. Holly, Anne, Beth, Rosalie, Amanda, Teresa, Andrea, Mary, and Suzy.
- My cover artist, Dani, who got her man-chest this time. (Yes, I caved, people.)
- My editors, Sue and Laurel, and their lovely red pens! Any errors in this book are completely my fault.

- My formatter, Nina, who even as I'm typing this, is patiently waiting for my ms.
- My Japanese language team, Taron and Yoshino.
- My kids' pediatrician, Anne, who set me straight on the medical stuff—including the stuff I *should* have known. (At least we can laugh about it now, huh?)
- My "sisters & brothers" in the SFA-RWA, SFR Brigade, CLAW, and the Goal Getters' Café, because you're always excited for me, and that means a lot.
- My favorite blurb peeps, including Blurb Babes (Beth & Therese), and all my Lucky Stars, who seem to be hanging around online 24/7!
- My readers! I do what I do for you. If you are happy when you finish one of my stories, then I'm doing my job right.

As always, I live in dread fear that I forgot to thank somebody, but that does not mean I don't value and appreciate you! THANK YOU!

Don't ever give up on your dreams!

~Lea Kirk

The Prophecy Series

PROPHECY
Book One

ALL OF ME
A Prophecy Series Short Story

SALVATION
Book Two

COLLISION
Book Three

Who was Tommy?

Often times I wonder about author dedications at the beginning of their books. Who is/was the person to the author? So far, I think mine have been pretty straight-forward and self-explanatory. But this time it's clearly not. So, who was "Tommy" to me?

I only had two first cousins, and Tommy was one of them. He was the first-born of my grandparents' four grandchildren. As my sister and I were part of an often-moving military family, we didn't spend a lot of time with our boy cousins on that side of the family. But, Tommy always held a special place in my heart. He was like a big brother to me. I always looked forward to seeing him.

Today, as I type this, I am the same age he was when he was diagnosed with ALS (Lou Gehrig's disease). If you don't know anything about this disease, it's about as horrific as they come. Think of it as the polar opposite Alzheimer's...the body rapidly deteriorates until the patient cannot walk, talk, and eventually breathe. The mind becomes trapped even though it stays as sharp as ever. The average lifespan after diagnosis is one to five years.

Tommy survived three years.

That was five years ago. And there's still no cure.

It's still difficult to talk, or write, about losing him, so I'm not going to dwell on that. I do want you all to know that I am quite an advocate for the ALS Association. This organization helps patients and their families, and they are the leaders in research for a cure for ALS. Every year I participate in the Napa Valley Ride to Defeat ALS (either virtually, or by actually riding my bike through the lovely Napa Valley...and sometimes both!) If you'd like to know more about what I'm doing, or how you can support the ALSA, please go to my website and click the blue "Support ALS" button in the right sidebar.

Made in the USA
Columbia, SC
21 November 2021

49230064R00169